The Tyack & Frayne Mysteries

Books IV-VI:
Kitto
Guardians Of The Haunted Moor
Third Solstice

Harper Fox

FoxTales

FoxTales Publications
www.harperfox.net

The Tyack & Frayne Mysteries—Books IV-VI
Copyright © 2014 by Harper Fox
ISBN 978-1910224571

Cover art by Harper Fox
Cover image licensed through Shutterstock

Book IV

Kitto

Harper Fox

A FoxTales Publication

Dedication

Dedicated to Jane,
a true partner in all my endeavours,
and to the memory of my wonderful Uncle Gordon,
who taught me to seize the day

Chapter One

Rain hit the glass overhead, a vibrant midsummer drum. Noise pitched and ebbed as crowds of tourists milled around the covered space, their chatter echoing in its weird acoustic. The arcade was Boscarney's only indoor attraction and sole refuge from the downpour. Soon its narrow gallery of shops was full, a chaos of bright waterproofs, laughter, and complaints in half a dozen languages about the Cornish weather.

Lee Tyack, normally painfully aware of every soul around him, was oblivious. His whole attention was fixed on the bright-lit interior of one jewellery store. Boscarney was a reconstructed tin mine. Fine Cornish silver and gold were still brought out of its ancient treasure caves, and a team of artisan jewellers worked to create from it the most beautiful of Celtic designs. Here and here only would Lee so much as consider carrying out his mission today.

"And even here might not be good enough."

Ezekiel Frayne turned to frown at the group of little crewcut brats taking advantage of the crowd to harvest unguarded wallets. A couple had jostled up to Lee, who could have been robbed blind and picked to the bone at that moment and not cared. "Sorry?"

"The things here. The... The rings. Do you think they're nice enough?"

Ezekiel sighed. Boscarney was a small place, but Lee had given him a very long afternoon. This was what the Methodist minister got for accompanying his gay brother's boyfriend to pick out a wedding ring, a situation he could no more have imagined eight months ago than he could have flown and perched naked atop the Truro cathedral spire. "It hasn't been my habit in life," he said dryly, "to observe such trivia. I'm certain the baubles in here are very well—as good, at least, as any in the dozen other shops you've ransacked and found wanting."

"Wow." Lee surfaced from his abstraction. He tilted his head and looked at his companion, eyes catching silver from the glittering lights in the store. "Are your feet hurting you, Zeke?"

Ezekiel glowered. "My discomfort isn't relevant. You're allowing yourself to be distracted by the material side of what should be a deeply spiritual event."

"Yes. Probably. But I want a nice ring for him, and you're his brother. Can't you help me choose?"

The atmosphere in the little mall intensified. Lights flickered, briefly plunging the shop into underground darkness, then the glitter returned, accompanied by a huge boom of thunder. A few screams and reactive giggles rang out in the crowd. "Gideon and I weren't close," Ezekiel said, more severely than he'd intended. "We weren't brought up in such a way that I know his preference for rose gold over platinum or whether he'd like a jewelled or a plain band."

Lee placed one hand on the glass. He withdrew it immediately, leaving a damp print. "Sorry. I'm actually sweating with nerves here. But you go on home, okay? I've taken up enough of your day."

Ezekiel had witnessed Lee wrestle demons of his own, and on the behalf of strangers, without turning a hair. He'd seen him run after a rifle-toting nutcase on a cliff. He could scrape barnacles off the hull of a boat or, in his bartender role, subdue a rowdy pub crowd with equal calm strength. Everyone had their limits, Ezekiel supposed. "I may not have had the opportunity to observe... much detail about Gideon," he said, glaring so fiercely at a marauding child that it let out a yelp and shot back into the crowd. "However, I know his broad brushstrokes. The very fact that you have been out and chosen this will mean more to him than any richness of design or craftsmanship. Besides, if it's any consolation, he's gone to buy yours today too. I should think he's in a worse state than you are right now."

***

Gideon walked into the Mandel jewellery shop in Bodmin. He only had half an hour before he had to be back at his desk, but that didn't matter. He knew exactly what he wanted. Jake Mandel's son greeted him with a brilliant smile from behind the counter. He'd taken on the business wholesale, and he ran a tighter ship than his dad. The blood had come out of the carpet. Life went on.

"Afternoon, Sergeant. The time has come, has it?"

"That it has, Ronald."

"The platinum band with the green-agate inlay, wasn't it? A very good choice, if I might say so. Matches Mr Tyack's eyes."

Gideon resisted the urge to roll his own. Mandel senior would never have ventured a personal remark. But Ronald was a good lad, more in keeping with the times, and in his hands the store might actually survive. He was right about the agates, too. Gideon had made his choice on his first trip past the shop after meeting Lee. Or entertained the fantasy, at least, that if by some miracle such a man were to stay in his life, only that ring could possibly grace his hand. It would cost a month's salary and Gideon would have paid ten. Even then. He was in uniform, and so had to repress a jubilant air-punch while Ronald found a pale-green velvet box and tucked the ring inside.

The radio on the shelf behind the counter ceased its burble of Cornish gossip and hits from the eighties. Gideon glanced at his watch, afraid that he'd lost some time in the pleasure of this errand. Local news came at the top of the hour. It was only quarter to. He repressed a smile: only Radio Kernow would still say *we interrupt this broadcast*, as if the nation were at war and Spitfires about to soar out over the Channel. The card-reader beeped its acceptance of his PIN and began to rattle out a printed receipt. Ronald paused, the box and a small plastic bag in his hands. "Bloody hell," he observed. "That don't sound good, do it, Sergeant Frayne?"

Gideon hadn't heard over the whir of the machine. In the following silence, he listened, blindly tucking away his card. The news anchor repeated his message. Before he'd reached the end, Gideon's own radio unit was crackling. He heard a place name, a time. Leaving the ring behind him, he tore out of the shop into the deadly summer rain.

***

"There. That wasn't so difficult, was it?"

Lee and Ezekiel left the shop and joined the surging crowd. Lee was clutching a small wrapped box. "Are you sure it's the right one?"

"It's a plain band of Cornish gold, mined and made right here. Gideon takes an almost heathen pride in his heritage. He'll love it."

Lee smiled. He said, a bit unsteadily, as if he'd just remembered it was his and Gideon's duty to bait Zeke whenever possible, "Ah, right. *Cornish born, Cornish bred, strong of arm and good in—*"

"Locryn Tyack! Have you no shame?" If Lee and Gid now freely called the starchy minister Zeke, he in his turn sometimes invoked Lee's proper Revivalist name to bring him into line. This time the Methodist thunder was no match for the heavenly kind. A peal of it split the air, sending a vibrant reverb through the arcade, rattling the glass in its panes. Hard on its heels came a machinegun roar of hail. Ezekiel glanced up at the glazed roof, where marble-sized lumps were sliding down among the streaks of rain. "That doesn't sound too good, does it... Lee, are you all right?"

"Yes, fine. Why?"

"You're very pale. The hard part's over now. In fact..." He put out a hand and took the box. "I believe it's my job to look after this from this point on."

"Oh. You'll do it, then? You'll be my best man?"

"Since your insane uncle Jago insists on being Gideon's, somebody there had better be sound of mind. I suppose I should be grateful the pair of you didn't ask me to conduct the service." Ezekiel took Lee's arm to steady him against the jostling crowd. "Come and sit down. You really do look awful. I'll buy you a coffee to help you recover from your horrible ordeal."

"Just wait till it's your turn with Eleanor, my friend. Just wait."

There was one table left in the arcade café. Ezekiel deposited Lee there and went to join the queue at the counter. Left to himself, Lee began his automatic shutdowns. He drew a transparent shield around himself, so he wouldn't have to know the hidden delights, fears and hates of every random soul who had come to drink coffee and take shelter from the rain today. He closed down every link except the friendly wire that bound him to Ezekiel—and the deeper one, deeper now than his own marrow and blood, the permanent carrier signal to Gid. He glanced through the advertising flyers on the table to aid his distraction. Cornwall was set to explode in Midsummer madness in a few days' time. The Golowan festival, the dances and theatrics, the sinister old Penglas, a hobby-horse figure with a horse's skull for a head. The ancient drama of the meeting of the oak king and holly king, a reminder that the height of summer meant the turning of the wheel, that from now on the days would grow shorter—yes, even now, at the full-blown blazing peak of the sun's power...

"Lee? Do you want a biscuit with that?"

Lee flinched. He looked at the coffee Ezekiel had placed in front of him. "No, ta. I feel a bit sick, actually."

"You have gone green." Ezekiel sat down opposite him. He folded his big bony hands on the table. He put his head on one side and began, cautiously, as if it hurt him more than his listener to broach the subject these days, "You know, if you are experiencing physical symptoms of illness when you undertake tasks associated with your—"

"Zeke, shut up."

"I'm sorry?"

"No—*I'm* sorry. I want to be your friend, and I know how good you are. But I will not..." Lee paused, drew a breath, then banged his palm down so hard on the table that the coffee and the leaflets jumped. "I will *not* listen to some oblique bloody diatribe about same-sex marriage. Do you understand?"

Ezekiel stared. "In fact, I was just about to... Oh, wait. You're going to have one, aren't you? One of your visions."

"No." Lee rubbed his brow, where the pounding of the rain had merged with a rhythmic pulsation from the deepest coils of his brain. "Maybe. Yeah, I think am."

"Shit. What do I do?"

Lee gave a soft snort of laughter. Every time he or Gid had been about to give Zeke up as a hopeless religious bigot, he said or did something that revealed the sweet, entirely human soul beneath. "I'm not going into labour. You don't have to run for hot water and towels."

"Gideon knows what to do, doesn't he? I'll call him."

"Don't. He's at work."

"Can I help? Do you need me to unmask a monster?"

"No. It's not happening like that any more, not since..." Lee shut himself up in time. He and Gideon had talked, and come to the conclusion that the fewer people who knew about Jago and the Cornish Panther, the simpler the world would be. "I just get... insights. They can hurt a bit. Don't worry, okay?"

"Well, it seems to me a dreadful thing, when a mortal man claims powers that only the Lord most high should ever—"

But Lee was gone. Ezekiel sat for a moment, gazing across at the empty chair. He'd moved so fast that one downward glance had been enough for Ezekiel to lose him. Bewildered, he turned and looked around.

Lee was a blur in the crowd. Before Ezekiel could draw breath to call his name, he'd reached the far side of the arcade. He came to a halt by the wall. The faintest sound of breaking glass reached Ezekiel through the background noise, and then the fire alarm set up a wail.

Lee darted back into the café. People were starting to look up, to make disorganised grabs for their coats and their kids, but nothing was happening fast enough. Skidding to a halt by the table, Lee grabbed the nearest child out of its high chair, causing its mother to leap upright with a shriek that cut through the alarm. "Get out of here," Lee told her, compounding his errors by grabbing the hand of a second, older child and pulling that one to its feet. "I'll carry these. Just get out."

"What are you doing, you freak? Let my kids go!"

"You have to get out. There's a... Oh, to hell with it." Lee dropped the older girl's hand and scrambled onto a chair, not relinquishing the baby. "Hoi!" he bellowed, his voice carrying clear and strong. "Get to the exits, everyone. Get out now. There's a bomb!"

He might as well have thrown one himself. It was the right word for all the wrong reasons, and people began to run. "It's not enough," he told Ezekiel, jumping down. "Help me tell them. They've got to get to high ground."

***

High on the moors above Boscarney, three hours of torrential rain caused the Clarence river to burst its banks and join with its neighbouring stream. The conjoined waters ripped out a chunk of the hillside and sent a roiling, mud-laden flood straight down the valley towards the old mine. The only warning was a clatter of startled jackdaws lifting off the trees that crashed down in the path of the surge, and, in the valley—a tale to tell the grandchildren—a low-down, dreadful rumble, swiftly rising to a roar.

The couple of hundred souls who had chosen that day to visit the Boscarney shops were already outside when the flood cannoned into the mall. The fire alarms and threat of a bomb—absurd in rural Cornwall, but nowhere was safe these days—had sent them running for the exits. Once out, they'd found themselves being herded upslope by a frantic group of mine-safety workers who had just dodged the torrents upstream. The strong ones carried the weak. Kids were passed freely from hand to hand.

Lee and Ezekiel stopped yelling once their message had gone home and saved their breath for helping their share of old ladies and toddlers the crucial few yards up the hill.

Lee crashed to his backside in the wet grass. He was close enough to the snarling water's surface that his boots were getting soaked, and Ezekiel went to haul him a few inches further up the bank. He was still clutching the child he'd seized from the high chair, and he was laughing between ragged gasps. Ezekiel flopped down beside him. "Are you all right?"

"Fine. Have you still got the ring?"

Ezekiel checked his pocket. "I can't believe that concerns you right now, but yes."

"What were you about to say to me back there, Zeke? That gay marriage is causing climate change? Because..." He hefted the squalling infant in his arms. "I'm beginning to think you might have a point."

"As a matter of fact," Ezekiel said grimly, "I was about to ask if you're taking on too much too soon. You and my brother have only known each other for eight months." His voice altered, and he surveyed the brown torrent now filling the valley, bearing a small raft of cars from the car park in its stream, including his own hearse-like Volvo. "You... predicted this, Lee. You saw the future."

"No. I just felt a vibration or something, like a sewer rat before a flood. As for Gideon and me..." He stopped. He inhaled once deeply, and gave Ezekiel a brilliant smile. "He's here."

Sirens had begun to weave their song through the roar of the water. The valley road had been swamped but the route over the moor was still open. Blue lights were casting strange wings through the rain. As Ezekiel watched, the crowd on the slope above them started to shift and part. Five seconds later his brother emerged from it. He was in his sergeant's uniform, as solid and strong as ever. He had aged twenty years beneath his smart peaked cap.

At last his gaze fell on Lee. The years dropped away. He strode downhill, pausing only to steady a woman who'd detached herself from the group and begun to run beside him. "That's him!" she shrieked. "That's him. That's the one!"

"Uh-oh," Lee said, gratefully accepting Ezekiel's help to stand upright. "Looks like I'm in trouble now." He held out the child like a propitiatory offering and the woman shot forward to seize it. Then he walked into his lover's arms.

Gideon held him. He tugged off his cap and clamped it onto Lee's head as if that would somehow shield him better still, then hauled him close and tight enough to break a rib. "I thought you were in there," he said against Lee's ear. "Down there in the bloody shops."

"Well, I was. But I'm out now."

"Yes. Thank holy Jesus fucking Christ." Gideon looked up. "Oh, sorry, Zeke." There was his brother, less of the lonely crow now that he had Eleanor—his own source of terror and joy—in his life, but still the stiff outsider at times like these. He put out an arm. "Come here. I thought I'd lost you too."

Awkwardly Ezekiel joined them. He accepted and even returned Gideon's embrace, then stepped back, straightening his shirt. "You haven't lost either. As you can see."

Gideon retrieved his cap. "Well done, everyone. Embarrassing group hug over. Now I'd better get back to work."

"How are you out from behind your desk?" Lee asked happily, gazing at him as if the world began and ended with his smile. "Oh, wait—did you get the results of your physical?"

A shadow brushed Gideon's face. It was faint, evanescent amidst so much light. "Not yet. They let me come because I had a vested interest, and..." He paused, looking upwards as a thump of helicopter rotors began. "It's all hands on deck now."

"Right. Be off with you, then. How can we help?"

"You and Zeke go on up to the doctor's surgery at the top of Westover Hill. They're trying to sort out some kind of emergency centre in there. Do what you can, and someone will take you home in one of the squad cars later." He made a mournful face at his brother. "I see the hearse has gone the journey."

"That car was our father's, and it's hardly respectful—"

"That's him. It was him."

Gideon turned. The distraught lady who'd followed him downslope was still standing close by, clutching her child to her chest. Her eyes were wide, the forefinger of her free hand pointing unsteadily at Lee. "Yes, ma'am," Gideon said soothingly. "But he only took your baby because he was trying to save it. Come on with me, now. You've had a shock."

"No. It was him. He knew the flood was coming." Gideon frowned and took a shielding step in front of Lee as the woman stumbled forward, but she was holding out her kid like a bewildered bouquet. "He saved us. He saved Charlie."

Lee took back the child. His hands were callused from the yacht refit he'd just finished down at the Falmouth marina, but Gideon knew he would never refuse any small, helpless thing that came into them. He handled the little limbs tenderly, setting the child on his hip. "What's this?" Gideon asked, unable to keep a smile from his voice. "Have we got a baby now, then?"

Lee contrived to look shocked. He glanced up at Gideon, his pupils dilated, and Gideon decided he would get that squad car for him sooner rather than later. "Please, sergeant. Not before marriage."

Chapter Two

"Do you think there's any chance your ma would sit next to Jago for breakfast?"

Gideon wiped his hands on a tea towel and came to have a look at Lee's strategy board. Apricot light was filling the living room. The day's storms had rolled off over the Channel, leaving behind them a serene June evening, the sun still high and gold above Minions Hill. Lee seemed to have let his afternoon's trials go south with the clouds. He'd eaten a good dinner and returned his attention to his foolproof seating plan, the one that would keep all their wedding guests happy and socially integrated.

His latest inspiration had been to set out chess pieces on the coffee table to represent the guests. Taking a seat beside him on the sofa, Gideon surveyed the battle lines. Old Mrs Frayne was regally represented by the white marble queen. Beside her was Jago, a barely tamed knight errant. "Not so sure about that," Gideon mused. "Two wrongs might not make a right." He picked up a stately bishop. "Is this one meant to be Ezekiel?"

"Yes. Have I got him in the wrong place?"

"No, but don't you think..." He reached into the box. The chess set was an imaginative interpretation by a local sculptor, and he'd taken the concept of the rooks quite literally. Gideon lowered one hunch-shouldered carrion bird into the place of the bishop. "There. Much better."

Lee snorted. "Don't you be mean about Zeke. He ran about shouting *bomb* like a good 'un this afternoon, once he'd got the idea."

"So I gather. I had to persuade Inspector Cole to drop charges against the two of you for falsely reporting an explosive device."

"Shit. Really?"

"Yeah. He cooled off when he realised why you'd done it. How many lives you'd saved."

Lee looked down. He began to shuffle their sample set of invitations like a pack of cards. "Makes a change from having him assume I was responsible. There isn't really an alibi big enough for that, is there? *No, officer—I was off the planet when the irreversible climate change occurred, honest.*"

"Well, it might've been you up there loosening the topsoil. I tell you what—I'm sure I've got a set of toy soldiers packed up in the spare room somewhere. Would you rather have those?"

Just for a second Lee took him seriously. His eyes widened. "We're not having that many guests, are we? I've still got loads of chesspieces left. I haven't even started on the pawns."

"I thought the soldiers might be more appropriate. Why is it becoming a warzone, love?"

Lee gave a reluctant laugh. "I'm making a fuss, aren't I? I just want everything to be right."

"It will be." Gideon put out an arm. His heart lurched painfully as Lee pushed the chesspieces aside and curled up on the sofa beside him, hiding his face against his shoulder. This was where hostilities had broken out a few weeks ago, in front of the TV after a *Panorama* show on marriage equality. Newlywed same-sex couples stumbling out of registry offices and churches, sobbing with joy, tears and confetti flying everywhere... Absurd and divine, and Gideon couldn't even remember which of them had spoken first. *I'd like to marry you.*

Well, I'd like to be married.

As simple as that. Gideon wasn't sure why Lee had grabbed the idea and run with it so far, why the registration office had become the Falmouth town hall and then the Victorian gardens at Trebah. Gideon didn't mind. He was charmed by all the plots and plans, and he'd done as good a job as a big Cornish copper could of helping hatch them. He'd never have figured Lee for the Bridezilla type, but people were full of surprises, and no matter how the gig went down, at some point Gideon would get to sign his name in the registrar's book next to that of Locryn Tyack. "Why do I get the feeling," he said, stroking Lee's hair, "that there's a huge amount of displacement activity going on here?"

"What?"

It was barely a grunt from his shoulder. Gideon smiled. "You know. Like when the dog scratches her ears because she's got a tick on her arse."

"Oh, charming." Lee shifted, planted a kiss under Gideon's ear. "I don't have a tick. Would you like to check?"

"In a minute. Once you've told me what happened this afternoon. Because you see a hell of a lot of things, sweetheart, but so far the future hasn't been one of them."

Lee lay very still. His breath stirred warmly against Gideon's neck, the rhythm of it taut and too quick. "That's what your brother said."

"Zeke? What was his brilliant take on the situation?"

"He said, *you predicted this. You saw the future.*"

"Then he chucked holy water on you? Snapped out his handy portable stake?"

"No. He seemed... a bit thrown, actually."

"And so are you."

"Well, I..." Lee put out a hand and felt along the edge of the sofa. "Where is she, by the way? That dog I used to have?"

"With Lorna again. Sarah says she and the kid are inseparable. Do you miss her?"

"Yeah, but a kid should have a dog. And once we're married we can get another one. And a cat, and a goldfish, and a baby I haven't had to steal out of a high chair in a café."

"Yes. All right, the whole menagerie. Now talk."

Lee looked up. He gently cupped Gideon's jaw in one hand, his expression peculiar. "You know, any normal guy would be running screaming for the hills right now."

"I've got my taxi booked."

"It's not the first time I've seen the future, no. It happened once before, when I saw the St Piran's flag in my dream and sent you running off to get stabbed."

Gideon sighed. This was a sore that would take longer to heal than the hole in his thigh, nicely scarred over as that was now and almost—almost—fit for active duty. "I don't care how often we have to go through this. You had a dream. The rest of it was up to me. I was furious about poor old Jake Mandel, and I went off half-cocked." Christ, he'd left Lee's ring at the shop today, hadn't he? It didn't matter. Ronald would look after it. His mind had been a blank of fear until he'd crested the hill at Boscarney and seen Lee amongst the crowd. "You saved hundreds of people today."

"If you think that—if you want to give me credit... Don't you see, Gid, you have to give me responsibility for anything bad that happens as well?"

"Nope." Gideon shook his head stubbornly. "Not one bloody bit of it. What happened to me was down to my interpretation of what you said. Predicting a flood, though—there's not much room for doubt, is there? It's just a good thing. You ask Charlie."

"Bloody hell. I can't believe I did that. I thought missus was gonna have my eyes out." He rubbed his brow against Gideon's shoulder. "I liked Charlie. Were you serious, about the full menagerie?"

"Well, I guess I'd thought of it as a ten-year plan, but we can do it sooner if you want. Think carefully, though. A goldfish is a very big responsibility."

Lee broke into laughter. As ever, the sound of it infected Gideon, and he tried and failed not to join in. But he was getting to know his lover, and this was Lee's MO—if he didn't want to talk, nine times out of ten he'd try for a diversion rather than a block. Babies were a pretty good tactic. Gideon let it ride for a minute, watching the curtains shift in the breeze from the open window. Then he sat up far enough to look into Lee's face. "So, what's the problem? With being a local hero and saving all the kiddies and grans?"

"I'm not a hero. I seem to have got away with it quietly for once—I don't think most of them had any idea why they got out of there when they did. But whether that kind of vision's a good thing or a bad one, I don't want it. You know how the Cyclops traded one eye to be able to see the future?"

"Is that how that happened?"

"Yep. And all they could foretell after that was the day of their own death."

A chill touched Gideon's bones. Lee was thirty one years old, healthy and bright as a star. "*You* don't know that, do you?"

"No, but why not? Why shouldn't I start to see everything? There's a reason we're made the way we are, Gid. We'd be paralysed—we wouldn't get out of bed in the morning—if we could see some of the shit coming down the pike toward us. As it is we just deal with it bit by bit as it arrives, and that's how I want my future too."

Gideon stroked his brow. Time had already laid premature marks there, traces of other people's pain. Bad enough to have that to deal with moment by moment, let alone in advance. "Do you feel as if you could do that—start to see everything, I mean?"

"I don't know. Getting rid of Morris Hawke from my head left a lot of space in there. I feel like something else might be expanding to fit. But at the moment I'd have to think about something in particular, really reach out and focus on it, and..." He paused, swallowed roughly. "And I'm not about to do that. Obviously."

"Good. Because you know I think you're the only true clairvoyant I've ever met, and I'd put good money on anything you say, right?"

Lee nodded. "You've let me lead you up the garden path half a dozen times. It's very endearing."

"But as for prophecies, there must have been half a dozen St Piran's flags I could've seen that day in Bodmin. I fixed on the one I wanted. And... you're a Cornishman to the bone, love. You know this land. You knew it had been raining for a week, and you know those valleys up near Boscarney are prone to flash floods. Maybe you heard something—a rumble, a vibration—and you threw it all together just in time."

"You think that's all it might have been?"

"You know me. I'm a copper—I tend to look for the obvious first. But I think there's a good chance that's what happened."

"Yeah, you're a copper," Lee said, his voice rich with affection. He laid a hand to Gideon's thigh, pressing his thumb to the place where the blood beat strongly in his femoral artery and the denim hid a wound that had almost denied them any kind of future at all. "Why's it taking so long to get the news about these fitness tests, then?"

Gideon sighed, this time allowing the distraction. Lee deserved his honesty, God knew, having stuck by him through his near-death experience and put up with the forty types of bastard he'd turned into while he was healing. Just yesterday he'd driven Gideon to the Truro admin centre and sat in the car park while Gideon had run, jumped and swum, then paced for half an hour tied up to electrodes on a treadmill. "The police physio has to pass all my results on to Trelowarren hospital so they can be analysed by the docs. It might take a few days."

"But you were fine after you finished. Not even out of breath."

"You didn't see me gasping my last in the locker room. I dunno, sweetheart. We might not be out of the woods yet."

"How many times do I have to tell you?" Lee shifted round on the sofa and pounced, sending his chesspieces flying. "I like the woods." He bore Gideon down hard enough to squeeze the breath from him. "I don't care if you're deskbound or chasing the bad guys round Bodmin in a squad car. I don't care if you want to pack it all in and come and help me varnish boats down the marina. As long as you're happy, my..." He stretched out luxuriantly on top of Gideon, carefully keeping his weight off the injured thigh. "My beautiful heart-of-oak lover. I'll roam the forests with you. We'll live on acorns."

"That's not a sensible attitude. Not if we're gonna keep goldfish."

"Ah, we made a killing with Anna's *Spirits of Cornwall* show. Hordes of sceptics are still trying to prove that footage from the fogou is a hoax. And maybe we don't have to buy the tank just yet."

"Oh, okay." Gideon closed a comfortable grasp around Lee's backside and rocked him. "Not *right* now, eh?"

"Not just at this very moment, no."

***

Gideon pounded steadily down the flank of Rough Tor. He loved this route for his morning jog and had only recently been able to reclaim it. He was strong again now. In a way it didn't matter if he made the stretch between the Cheesewring rocks and the magical rings of the Hurlers stone circles in under ten minutes—his die was cast, his physical over and done with, and either he'd be passed fit for full active duty or he wouldn't. But he wanted to be on top form for roaming the forests with Lee, or for settling down and raising goldfish. He wanted to be a good husband.

Christ, he was getting married. Delight and panic seized him and he powered up to a sprint, letting the overflow burn off. It bothered him that Lee was losing his pleasure to the stress of seating plans and invitations. Gideon decided to find out why and fix it. He stamped his resolution into the turf and ran on. It bothered him that the fogou video had gone viral, that any aspect of Lee's gift had to be commercialised, let alone that most intimate of spiritual encounters. Still, that was up to Lee, who somehow retained a cool business head about his own talents, and used them along with his income from the pub and the marina to help pay the rent. Gideon's miracle was Lee's daily bread. So Gideon put that worry back where it belonged, threw it into the stone stile ahead of him and cleared it in an easy vault.

He was doing well with his projection therapies. He'd laughed when the Truro police psychologist had suggested them, convinced that all he had to do was recover physically for everything else to drop back into place. But the fact was that his injury had knocked him for six. He'd always been able to rely on his strength. Anxiety had rushed in through the gaps the knife had punched in his confidence. He'd started having nightmares, endless scenarios where Lee was hurt or needed him and Gideon couldn't get there because his leg wouldn't work, or he couldn't leave the house until he'd found his damn crutches. The shrink had suggested that, given who he was, rather than attempting complex analysis, he should just try chucking the things he feared outside himself, where he could jump over them, stamp on them or run them down.

Whether he passed the physical or not, Gideon had to be strong. He didn't know why it seemed so crucial. And it wasn't about remaining on the force, much as he loved that life. It was to do with Lee.

Deliberately Gideon steadied his breathing. The air was still cool, but a hot day promised in the sunlit haze on the horizon. He had to be strong for Lee, and that meant pacing himself. He didn't understand his compulsion. Lee sometimes needed the tough fibres of Gideon's nature to hang on to, but physically he was as solid a customer as Cornwall made, equally at home in a pub fight or on the deck of a boat. Why was Gideon so afraid for him?

It didn't matter. If strength was required, Gideon would provide it. Up ahead of him, the first of the stone circles lay brooding, enclosing its endless sphere of time and ancient light. He let his fear pitch and hurled it outwards into the granite blocks—let the stones take it all and sweep it round him in their boundary, taming it, taking it down into the earth.

Gideon ran to the centre of the circle and stopped. He checked his stopwatch: nine minutes and fifty seconds. Not at all bad. He leaned over, rested his hands on his knees and caught his breath. He listened to the various messages his body was giving him, the aches and pains and pleasures. His blood was running bright and strong. The scar tissue in his thigh said it was doing its job of healing and holding him together, but had taken enough of a pounding for now. Straightening up, he bid a silent farewell to the stones, and set off for home at a measured jog.

He liked this part of his run too. Every step of it reminded him of his first days with Lee. There in the lane was the old Frayne parsonage, where they had made their stand against the Bodmin Beast. The house was for sale now, likely to be bought by an enthusiastic young couple who loved its gloom and had been heard to speak of its damp as *heritage moisture*. Here was the corner where Isolde had slipped her leash and gone running after Lee. Here on the main street was old Mrs Bradley, precision-timing her shopping so that Gideon could grab her bags and jog them to her front door. He deposited them carefully and backed off smiling. Then his route led him down Sarah Kemp's terrace. Isolde heard his approach and came bounding out to meet him, weaving three circles around him before abandoning him in favour of food and affection indoors. She was fatter than ever but beaming with contentment. In spite of its name, all was sunny and well in the village of Dark.

When Gideon had left home that morning, only a handful of vehicles had been parked in his own street. It was Saturday, most of his neighbours at home for the weekend. From lifelong copper's habit, he knew the makes and models of their cars. He didn't recognise any of the dozen or so pulled up by the kerb now. He didn't know why there was a crowd of strangers around his front door.

Lee was on the steps. He looked fine—a lovely morning sight in jeans and T-shirt—but his arms were folded over his chest. Gideon picked up his pace. A couple of the vans were marked with the logo of the local TV news. It was hard to be swamped by the press on Bodmin Moor, but it looked as though Lee had managed it. Gideon was almost disappointed to think that his unease, his gut feel that strength would soon be needed, might boil down to nothing more than knocking a couple of reporters' heads together.

So be it, though. He could move quietly as well as fast. Once he was within a few yards of the group, he dropped to a walk and silently took his place on the perimeter. Lee caught his eye. Gideon read the small movement of his hand which meant he was okay for now, that Gideon should hold fire. He was patiently explaining, for the West Cornwall Herald mic being poked perilously close to his face, that the incident at Boscarney yesterday had had nothing to do with psychic powers. That he knew the area well and had seen the weather forecast. He'd heard the flood coming down the valley, that was all.

It was the same explanation Gideon had offered, and it wasn't convincing at all. The Herald guy pushed the mic closer, causing a small competitive ripple among the others in the front line, and Lee retreated up one step towards the door. He was very good with journos and press on the whole, accepting that people were curious, that he needed a certain amount of publicity for his work. "I'm not sure what else to say to you, guys. I am a clairvoyant, yes. I don't tell futures, though, and even if I did, yesterday wasn't about that. I'm just glad Mrs Cooper and her kids were okay."

So that was it. Charlie's mum had talked. Lee's hand continued to signal that he had the situation covered, so Gideon just bunched his fists, propped them on his hips and waited. "Nobody else heard it coming," the reporter said. "Mrs Cooper told us you raised the alarm at least five minutes before it hit. There's no way everyone could have got out otherwise." He grinned. "What's the matter, Mr Tyack? Don't you want to be a hero?"

"No, I want to go inside and have my breakfast. Mrs Waite's café down the road is very nice, gentlemen, if you haven't had yours."

He edged towards the door. Another reporter—not the Herald guy, whom Gideon recognised and who therefore knew better—tried to block his route. Gideon supposed there was competition these days even between the Turnip Channel and Clotted Cream FM. And now at last Lee's distress signal did flash, beyond the need for gesture, glance or word. Gideon drew a deep breath. "Police!"

He was just one policeman in a sweaty tracksuit, but he knew he sounded like ten. He suspected it was one of the reasons Inspector Cole had kept him on at sergeant's rank. He was a bargain. Every one of the gathered newshounds flinched or jumped. They swung to face him. The little creep trying to crash the door had the grace to squawk and fall down the steps: Lee grabbed his elbow, as naturally and unstoppably as he'd taken Charlie the day before. He looked up ruefully at Gideon. "Morning, Sergeant Frayne."

Well, they might as well play it out full pantomime. Gideon rocked a little on his heels. "What's all this, then, Mr Tyack? Are these gentlemen bothering you?"

"Not exactly. I just wish they'd take my word for it that I don't have anything to say."

"Sounds reasonable." Gideon surveyed the faces. "Sounds reasonable, lads, don't you think?"

"We've got a perfect right to be here," the creep ventured. "We're not doing anything wrong."

"For the sake of accuracy, the gentlemen to this side of the garden wall aren't doing anything wrong. The rest, including yourself, are on Mr Tyack's property—and mine—without permission. So, what's it to be, everyone? Breakfast at Mrs Waite's caff or a morning wasted down the station on trespass charges?" He grinned. "Seems like a no-brainer to me."

The reporters dispersed. Gideon nodded to the lads he knew, keeping it friendly as far as he could. This wasn't London, where the fourth estate formed up into a pack of faceless jackals, pursuing their prey to the death. He stayed on guard until the cars and vans were pulling away down the street, then strode up the steps to join Lee. "Bloody hell. You've gone and done it this time, haven't you?"

"Looks like it. Catch *me* saving little Charlie next time."

"Next time you'll leave all the buggers to drown."

"Damn right."

They went hand-in-hand into the hall, where Lee pulled him to a halt, shoving the door closed behind him with one foot. "Mm," he said, reeling Gideon in, grunting in pleasure when his lover took the hint and slammed him up against the wall. "Hot sweaty copper. My favourite."

Gideon kissed the willing mouth turned up to him. He was startled by his own hunger. Night had come down and every sofa-cushion cover had been in need of a wash by the time they'd got finished last night. Seeing Lee surrounded and in danger sparked deep vibes in him, he supposed. "Are you all right? You're shivering."

"Fine. I wasn't expecting that lot, that's all."

"Why not just give them their story? I know you're freaked out about it, but there's nothing wrong with what you did at Boscarney."

"Shut up, Gid." The order came soft and fierce against Gideon's neck. "I'll tell you when you can start talking again."

A slithering thud from the study broke their silence. Gideon froze, his hand on Lee's zip. "Can I speak?"

"I think you'd better."

"I met your dog in the village. Did she come into the house?"

"No. Back door's shut."

"I suppose there's no chance you'd stay here and let me go take a look?"

"No chance at all."

But neither of them had to go anywhere. The study door swung wide. A skinny, dishevelled young man stumbled into the hall. A journalist's camera was slung round his neck and he was shamelessly clutching a sheaf of Lee's script notes for *Spirits of Cornwall*. "I know I'm in your house," he rasped. "I know your boyfriend's a policeman. I had to get in, though."

This time it was Lee's turn to step in front. He did it with quiet authority, untucked shirt and ruffled hair notwithstanding. Blindly he put out one hand and held Gideon back. "Okay. You got in. Do you want to tell me why?"

"I was with the guy who stopped you in the doorway. I sneaked in behind him. We're not from a paper or anything. We just... I just had to find out."

"Find out what?"

"If it's real. If you can do it. See into the future, I mean."

"Do those notes help?"

"No. I was going through your stuff to see if there was anything to prove you cheat, but... No."

Lee held out a hand. "Give them back to me, then, please."

The young man obeyed. Then he sank down onto the little seat by the phone. He curled up and laced his fingers at the back of his skull. "My ma's getting chemo. It's fifty-fifty chances, and she's all I've got. Nobody can tell, you see. Nobody knows. I've got to fucking *know*." He began to weep.

Lee went to crouch in front of him. He put a hand on the boy's knee, and his face went still in a way Gideon had learned to recognise. This was part of Lee's job, his reason for being. It still made Gideon want to seize him, snatch him away from the fire, pick up this poor little bastard who had crawled to him for help and sling him back into the street.

After a moment Lee blinked and raised his head. "I don't see anything about your mum, mate. All I'm getting is your pain." He shifted a bit and looked at Gideon. His eyes were lifeless and hollow. "This is why I can't just give them their story, Gid. This is what's wrong with what I did. Can you go and put the kettle on?"

***

Next day in the supermarket, Lee was accosted by two old ladies concerned about their savings bonds, and a huge drunken rugby player absolutely determined to have the mid-week lottery prize. Lee chatted to the pensioners until they'd forgotten why they'd cornered him by the dairy fridge in the first place, and he settled up with the drunk in the car park. Back at home, he showed Gideon his grazed knuckles and the Sunday copy of the Herald. *Local Psychic Saves Hundreds* was the banner headline on the front page. Beneath it: *Cornwall's own Colin Fry predicts the future.* There was a nice picture of Lee in the doorway of his very identifiable house, and a lurid account of the Boscarney flood. Gideon propped his elbows on the kitchen table. "I don't bloody believe this."

"Me neither. They actually spelled *psychic* right."

"They've mentioned Dark. They've practically given your address."

"Look, there was a bit of a flap after we found Lorna Kemp too. It'll all blow over in a few days."

Lee didn't sound optimistic. He was pale and tense, and Gideon had come off shift to find him sitting in the kitchen with his still-packed shopping bags all around him. "Here," Gideon said gruffly. "Let me see that hand."

Lee held it out, and sat passively while Gideon dabbed antiseptic onto the knuckles. "Ta. But it's nothing."

"The guy assaulted you. You should've called the police."

"Ah, they'd only have sent you. And I was seeing you at tea-time anyway." He smiled wanly. "Besides, how often do I get to be violent?"

That was true. Lee's gentle nature had fire at its core, but even under dire provocation he normally held back: nine times out of ten, his opponent's pain would backlash out at him, making the endeavour too uncomfortable. "I gather this guy was comfortably numb?"

"From the neck up and the chin down. I didn't feel a thing."

"God bless White Ace cider." Gideon repressed a jump as the doorbell rang. "Hang on a second."

"I'll get this one."

"Oh, no. You've had enough fun for one day. Stay there."

The lads on the doorstep this time were mates of Darren Prowse, a long-time bête noire of Gideon's, a devil he'd grown to know so well that the boy and his villainous parents were on Lee's wedding list. He sent them off with the usual dire warnings about Aylesbury youth prison, throwing a brief wave at Darren himself, who'd actually hung back across the street, looking a bit shamefaced. There was hope for the little thug yet. Shaking his head, Gideon went back in. "Just the Prowse gang. Will you believe the little buggers wanted—"

"Belladonna's Ball for the three-thirty, and Radjel for the four o'clock."

"Jesus, Lee."

"It's all about money, isn't it? Money and greed."

"Not for that poor sod who was in here crying about his mum."

"But I can't control it." Lee pushed to his feet. "It's expanding. Why would I know something as fucking trivial as who's gonna win at Wadebridge this afternoon? What happens if I miss something in the middle of all this crap, someone who really needs me? Why can't I see the important stuff, like..."

His voice broke. Horrified, Gideon strode over to grab him. Lee cried at the end of his tether, and it took a lot to put him there. "Don't you get yourself upset over this," Gideon whispered. "You'll be all right." Lee let go his rigid stance and hugged him roughly in return. "I tell you what. Can you get next week off?"

"From scrubbing decks and predicting the horses? Probably."

"I'm due some leave too. I'll see if I can swing it, and if I can..." He planted a noisy kiss to Lee's brow. "I've got just the place for you."

"Where? Broadmoor?"

"Don't spoil the surprise." Gideon waited for a moment, then observed thoughtfully, "So, Belladonna's thirty-to-one. Do you fancy a flutter?"

Lee shook with painful laughter. He spared a hand for long enough to give Gideon a slap on the rump. "No, you idiot. No!"

Chapter Three

Even a Cornishman born could still be surprised by his county. Cornwall was a rich mosaic of little kingdoms, and passage between them could feel like shifting the veil between worlds. The gale-swept cliffs of the north coast existed in a different sphere to the moors where the megaliths dreamed, and the merry clatter of a fishing town like Padstow seemed a thousand miles away from the starlit hush that could fall over Bodmin on a still night. Deep in the south, in a sheltered curve of the coast between Falmouth and St Keverne, a hundred little rivers carved the sedimentary rock into ria country, a network of inlets, creeks and pitching valleys, all of them steeped in rich woodland this close to summer's height.

Yes, even a native could get lost here. Lee switched off the satnav, which had locked into a cycle of despairing recalculation, and after a moment tossed their map book into the back seat. "All right," he said. "I've no idea. And I don't get it, because according to the map Falmouth's only ten miles away."

"Ten miles of single-lane labyrinth," Gideon replied in satisfaction, steering the Vauxhall to a forty-five degree angle on the grass to avoid a head-on with a truck. The windows were open and a rich scent of crushed greenery filled the car, blending briefly with exhaust. Then there was only silence, and the nod and sway of wildflowers through the passenger window. "Do you feel piskey-led?"

"I don't have a clue where I am, if that's what you mean, you clown. Do you?"

"Just about. Can you see down into the crossroads there?"

"Not really. You've parked me in a hedge, but..." Lee leaned forward, pushing his sunglasses up. "Oh, wait. There's a stone cross there, just about buried in the long grass. I think I can see some standing stones too, and a huge rock—a megalith, maybe—down on its side on the verge. Anna and Jack would love this."

Gideon started the engine. "Feel free to tell them about it," he said tranquilly, "if you can get a signal on your phone."

"Not a squeak. Where are you taking me?"

"It's called Kelyndar. The tourists say *Calendar*, but it means..."

"The place of the holly and oaks." Lee grinned. "Hollyoaks. Are you serious?"

"Yep. We're almost there. Look out for the statues."

"The what?"

"You'll know them when you see 'em."

The narrow road began a plunge between tree-tangled hillsides. Soon it became a green tunnel, sunlight filtering through young oak leaves and beech. Brambles from the stone-built Cornish hedges flicked the screen. Soon a scatter of houses appeared, granite-brick or half-timbered, shingled with slate, all of them set deeply into lush gardens. At the foot of the hill, a solitary cottage stood in a jungle of camellias. Its glass porch protruded almost into the road. Lee put a hand on Gideon's thigh and leaned across him to take a look as they drove slowly past. Two marble statues—larger than life-size, a man and a woman, each of them caught in a moment of graceful dance—stared back. "Wow," Lee said softly. "They're painted."

"Mind my gearstick, love. What do you think—outrage or beauty?"

"Both. A beautiful outrage. Who did that?"

"There's a story that a Victorian lady who lived there brought them back from Italy. She got bored with all that pale marble, so she painted their togas, their hair and their eyes in bright colours to cheer herself up."

"In carnival colours. They're just surreal."

"They're a good local landmark. There's half a dozen tiny creek villages east and west of here, and if you drive past that porch, you know you've come to the right one."

"Is this where we're staying?"

"Oh, no. This is way too bustling a metropolis." Gideon changed down into second and cautiously guided the Vauxhall past a handful of parked cars, all with their wing mirrors tucked in. Here the road appeared to run out, and Lee caught his breath as they carried on to the very water's edge. The tide was high in the creek, concealing a boat ramp and the start of a grass-and-mud track that ran along the river's edge. "Hang on. It gets a bit bumpy."

There were a few houses here as well, no two of them remotely similar. A couple were architect's dreams, huge glass-and-timber constructions rising up from riverside to hillcrest. The rest were vernacular, ancient, using any trick they could to clamber up the slope and hang on through the centuries intact. Narrow stone staircases twisted up and away into nowhere. Dusky arches gaped among the trees. Lee was wide-eyed and silent, as always when he was encountering somewhere new—absorbing it helplessly, a wide-open receptor struggling to process new information. Sometimes Gideon wished the poor lad could have the restful experience of just being bored. "Do you like it?"

"It's like diving slowly down through cool water. The statues and this little street... It's like a cross between a Roger Vadim film and *The Wicker Man*. I love it."

"Good, because this is it." Gideon rounded a bend in the track and the wide Helford estuary opened out in front of them. He pulled up on the harbour's edge and stopped. "Got a mobile signal yet?"

"I've never actually *seen* this symbol on it before. The aerial sign's disappeared."

"Well, Ray says nobody down here can get TV via their freeview kit. It's some kind of reception black spot." Gideon drummed his fingers on the arch of the wheel and gave Lee an assessing glance. "And I know it's a dumb analogy, but I did wonder if your signals might have trouble getting through too."

"Gideon," Lee said with dignity. "I am *not* a digibox." He leaned his elbow on the window frame and took a couple of deep breaths of the rich, moist air. He rubbed his brow. "Now you come to mention it, though... it is a bit quieter in here at the minute."

"At the very least, I reckon we're out of reach of the Cornish Herald and all your new fans. It'll be a nine-days' wonder, you know, this business about Boscarney. Everything will be all right."

Lee relaxed visibly, as if he'd taken a conscious decision to believe it. "You're a good man, Gid. I don't know where you've brought me, but thanks. Who on earth is Ray?"

"You'll know *him* when you see him, too. Come on."

There was a shop by the harbour. Like the waterside houses, it was built into the cliff behind it, hard to see until you were directly outside. A covered wooden balcony further hid the shady interior. Fruit and veg were set out in the crates along with the day's newspapers, but there all resemblance to a village general dealer's ceased. The balcony posts had been carved into spirals. Mermaids and dragons peered out through their coils. Above the door was an eye-popping fractal, blazing in every colour under the sun, and in the centre of this wondrous design a name had been picked out in glittering fragments of mirror—*Cosmic Ray's*. Gideon went to stand beside Lee, who had scrambled out of the car and was gazing at the sign in wonder, his hands tucked into the back pockets of his jeans. "You probably see what he did there."

Lee took off his sunglasses, gave a low whistle and put them back on. "I see it, yeah. And you were right—I'm pretty sure I see Cosmic Ray."

"Gideon! *Fatla genes?*"

"I'm fine, thank you, Ray. *Fatla genes, ha ty?*"

"Thriving. Blossoming." The man who'd appeared in the doorway did look like an exotic bloom, something the Victorians had imported from the jungle and left forgotten to thrive in Cornish soil. He was barely five feet tall and almost as broad, his thickset frame resplendent in surfing shorts and a T-shirt that matched the sign over the door. He trotted down the steps, making the whole porch jounce, and ran across the car park, beaming. "Ah, you look grand, Gid. Proper 'andsome!"

He threw both arms around Gideon's waist. Gideon rocked under the impact and returned the hug, grateful he had a reason to break into laughter: Ray's approach had been so like Isolde's when she came barrelling up to greet him, and the dog's build so resembled that of the man, that Lee would surely have made the connection too. Ray's jet-black dreadlocks barely came up to Gideon's chin. He stepped back, still laughing. "It's good to see you too."

"And this must be..." Ray gave Lee a onceover that was pretty lively for a man with a missus and three kids. "Oh, dude! Your boyfriend?"

"Fiancé," Gideon gently corrected as Lee stepped forward to shake hands. It still took Gideon a small effort of courage, but the difference was important, and finding and employing the right words all part of being gay in a small county with a large UKIP contingent. As soon as it was accurate, Gideon would say *husband*. He would say it proudly, every time. "Lee Tyack. Lee, this is Ray Tregear, a good friend of mine."

"Lee, it's a pleasure. It's Gideon who's the good friend, though. Got me off a drugs charge, he did."

Lee shot Gideon a small, astounded look. "Really?"

"I did *not*. You've got to stop telling people that. There was insufficient evidence, and I believed your intention to reform."

"Which was more than my own bloody lawyer or social worker did. See, he put a good word in for me, Lee, and it made all the difference. You just ask my kids."

"Maisie, Rafe and Jim, isn't it?" Gideon pulled out his rucksack and Lee's from the boot of the car. "They must all be past five now, right?"

"Right. Come on, hand me those bags. Come into the shop and I'll sort you out with your keys."

Gideon hoped to God he'd been wise to give the cautious character reference that had sealed him forever into Ray's good opinion. At the time it had felt right—Ray, newly married with the first of his brood on the way, had got mixed up with Bill Prowse, the very black sheep of Dark village, and through Bill with Ross Jones, whose shameless arse Gideon had been patiently busting for years over his living-room cannabis crop. Bill had brought good men down before, and Ray had been in mourning for someone, a relative or friend he couldn't even name without breaking down into tears. Gideon had helped persuade the judge that a new business on the far side of Cornwall from Dark would be better for the Tregear family's future than a jail term, and here

Ray was, cheerfully ushering Lee ahead of him into what looked like the archetypal hippie hash den. Long embroidered curtains drifted in the breeze. New Age music blended with the ripple of wind chimes. Every brand of incense anyone could require was for sale alongside silver statues of Ganesha and scarves bearing peace symbols and pentacles, and one wall was lined with a range of bagged-up herbs unequivocally labelled *Cosmic Ray's Finest Herbal Highs.*

Gideon closed his eyes. "Oh, no way, mate. I'm on leave. Please don't be showing me this."

"Ah, I know what you're thinking!" Ray squeezed his bulk behind the tiny counter and set down their bags. "But I learned something from you, Gid. You made me see that I could have a second chance *and* use my, er... knowledge of the recreational industry. These aren't your so-called legal highs full of chemical crap that kills teenage kiddies in nightclubs, no." He grabbed a green bag with its bright fractal logo and tossed it at Gideon, who caught it on reflex. "These are teas, my friend. Organically grown and sourced right here in Cornwall—analysed and approved safe by the BMA. All my certificates are right here, if you want to take a look."

Gideon made a placating gesture. "No, I don't need to look."

Just at present he was too busy watching his fiancé. Child of the far-west Celtic Revivalists, Lee was turning slowly round to survey the little treasure cave, clearly enjoying it as the Methodist minister's son had failed to do. He glanced at Gideon. "This place is pretty cool."

"You're marrying a man of taste and flair, Gid." Ray unhooked two sets of keys from a surfboard rack nailed to the wall. He leaned his elbows on the counter. "See," he went on seriously, "it might all look like feckless hippie junk, but I'm really doing all right here, thanks to you. Cosmic Ray's is becoming a brand. The name, the fractal..." He reached into a box. "The T-shirt! This one looks about your size, Lee. I bet it'll suit you. Now, the cabin's all ready. There's milk and all the basics in the fridge, and if you want to pop down later and give me a list, the grocery store up in Helston will deliver whatever you want."

"Thanks," Gideon said. He couldn't take his eyes off Lee, who was following the movements of a shoal of rainbow fish cast from a crystal prism, his face rapt. "Hoi, you," Gideon said gently. "Would you like a Cosmic Ray's T-shirt?"

Lee smiled. "You know, I believe I would."

"Okay. And would you like..." He hesitated, sighed. Ray was nodding enthusiastically. "Would you like a legal herbal high?"

"God, no. You know what I'm like when I'm drunk?"

"Sadly, yes."

"Imagine that on hyperdrive."

"Jesus. I guess we'd better pass."

"No problem," Ray declared, pushing the keys across to Gideon. "No harm, no foul. Know thyself and know the cosmos, eh? Off you go, gents. Through the shop and out the back. It's right at the top of the steps. Great views, clean air, peace and privacy, and anyone wanting to see you..." He patted his broad chest, right on the heart of the fractal. "They'll have to get through me." As Gideon was turning away, he took the little bag of herbs and held it out. "Here!" he whispered, subtle as a Cornish gale through pine. "Keep it. On the house. That's one of the lightweight ones—the worst he'll get from that is a good night's sleep."

***

"Wow, Gid, he did look like—"

They weren't quite out of earshot of the shop. "Stop it!"

Too late. The image of Isolde flashed between them, and they stumbled up the first flight of stone steps, racked with hopeless laughter. "He's amazing. Where did you find him?"

"In a getaway car with Bill Prowse, unfortunately. I never did get him off any drugs charge, you know. He just thinks I did, and ever since then I've had a standing invitation to his cabin in the woods."

"Ah, I see. Police corruption at its finest."

Gideon shouldered his rucksack and took a swipe at Lee's backside. "I'll show you police corruption in a minute, you—"

"I'm not complaining. I benefit from it, don't I?" Lee reached back to steady Gideon up a steep twist in the granite-boulder stairs. The track clung to a near-sheer flank of the valley. There must have been a stately garden here a century or so ago: the tumbledown steps led through sunlight-filled arches, and ivy clung to marble balustrades. "I love this place. More than anything I love that you brought me here to try and help me. I must be a liability sometimes, I know."

"Never. And tell me you love it once you've hauled arse up a couple of hundred more of these steps."

"I'll be fine. How's your leg holding up, though?"

"Surprisingly well. Of course another advantage of a phone-free wilderness is that I won't get my fitness results until I'm good and ready."

"You don't have to worry about those."

Gideon glanced up, caught by the calm assurance in Lee's voice. He'd never asked him to use his gifts on his behalf. Sometimes he hadn't been able to stop him—but to *ask* for those insights, to join with the mass of needy souls whose demands could rip Lee apart—no, that had never been part of their dynamic. This was being held out to him on a plate, though, and

Gideon couldn't deny that he would love an answer. "Is that... Is that something you just know?"

"Yes, of course. You pass with flying colours. Inspector Cole's so pleased with your last case that he recommends you for CID, if you want to lose that sexy sergeant's kit and go plainclothes."

Gideon gave a startled laugh. "You're dreaming, love. My last active case was that royal fuckup in Bodmin."

"No, I mean your *next* last. I... I guess I just mean your next." Lee stopped. He leaned his shoulder against a tree. He turned to Gideon with the despair of a man who could forget the difference between past and future and lose himself in the abyss."Shit. Looks like I'm getting signals again."

"You'll be okay." That was Gideon's own attempt at a prophecy. It was all he had, but it was strong—hope, love, faith in his own power to act as a shield. "Come on with me. It's a long climb, but..." He stood close behind Lee and ran a hand down his chest and belly, not stopping short of a quick caress further south: "I'll make it worth your while."

"Will you, now, Sergeant?" Lee chuckled and pushed upright. Then he froze, sobering. "Stop. We have to wait here for a second. We have to wait."

They stood together in the sunlight. There was no sound but the splash of water in the estuary below and the song of a thrush in the oak leaves, cooler and more liquid still. After almost a minute, Gideon said, "I don't want to ask stupid questions, but... any idea what we're waiting for?"

"No. None." Lee shook himself. "Don't mind me—I'm just going bloody bonkers, looks like."

They carried on up the track. The afternoon was hot. Distractedly Gideon noted the point at which his lover's sweet deep scent overrode his morning shower and his cologne, the changes making Gideon's spine tingle and a powerful yearning begin along the insides of his hipbones. He tried to resist the prickling warmth of an erection: it was a long walk still, in close-fitting jeans, and...

Something rustled and creaked on the high crags behind them. They turned in time to see a huge boulder detach from the edge of the cliff. It began its fall in a kind of majestic slow-mo, then picked up speed and crashed with deadly force down through the rhododendrons and across the track.

Gideon watched Lee working out timing and trajectories. "I don't think that one can have had our name on it. We'd have had to set out sooner to avoid that, not later. Hey, though," he added, brightening, when Lee didn't respond. "Imagine if it *did* have our names on it... Make a hell of a wedding-table centrepiece, wouldn't it?"

"Gideon..."

"And, you know, you still haven't told me if we're gonna be Frayne-Tyack or Tyack-Frayne." It seemed a good ploy of distraction: Lee had spent at least half an hour the night before trying to decide which of the good old Cornish names sounded better in front of the other. "Shall I go look at the rock, just in case—"

"Pack it in. I know what you're doing, but... I checked up on those horses. Belladonna romped home, but the other one kicked off his jockey in the paddock and never made a start. Whatever this is, it's coming in scrambled for some reason, spectacularly wrong or just... backwards, like that rock. And then there's the..." His voice caught in his throat and he swallowed audibly. "The *gaps*. What if I'm wrong about your fitness tests too?"

Gideon sighed. He checked the crags directly above them, just in case the cosmos felt like rectifying Lee's mistake, then looked directly at him. "Listen. Even if I end up in a wheelchair and they bust me back to constable, that wouldn't be your fault. You do understand that, right? Whatever you see or you don't see—none of it's your *fault*." He paused, unable to resist. "Besides, I could be Ironside."

Unwillingly Lee snorted. "You're such a moron."

"But you do get that, don't you?"

"I don't know. Seems to me that if I open my mouth and tell people what I see, in a way that does make me responsible. They're gonna act differently because of me."

"That's up to them. If I'd gone and made a bet on Radjel, that would've been my choice." He considered. "Then again, if I'd put down a tenner on the other one... Oh, my God. Why didn't you make me? This really *is* all your fault."

"You're not funny."

"I know that. But do you take my point?"

"I'm trying really hard to take it, yes."

"That'll do for now, then. Come on."

Chapter Four

There were dragons and mermaids here too. The holiday cabin Ray let out to guests was beautifully sited on a headland over the creek, and the open porch had been carved by the same craftsman who'd made the pillars for the shop. Gideon ran his fingertips over the sunwarmed veranda rail. A rich tang of cedar rose up to him. "*An Kelyow*," he said, reading the rough-cut slate sign by the door. "You'll have to teach me Cornish properly sometime. What does it mean?"

Lee set his rucksack down. He looked around appreciatively at the gardens with their tumble of moss-covered rocks and deep, magnolia-scented shade. "The hideout. I'll teach you Cornish, don't worry. When we're old married men sitting roasting our nuts by the fire."

"I'll look forward to it. Are you going to let us in?"

"Give me a second. I'm absorbing. Wow, this is lovely. There's an oak sapling here by one side of the steps, and on the other... Is that a holly? There's no spines."

"I think they only grow spines when there's animals around that might, er... eat them." Gideon flushed. What was wrong with him, that an innocent botanical explanation had left his lips so suggestively? Lee, never slow to catch such nuance, was looking at him in amusement. "Sorry. Apparently it's a very sexy bush."

"Apparently." Smiling, Lee allowed his gaze to focus on Gideon's groin, where the erection he'd managed to quell on his way up the slope was coming back full force. "You know what I like best about *An Kelyow*?"

"The lovely view? The gardens?"

"The total lack of neighbours."

He was right. There had only been one track, and this house was at the end of it. The nearest pair of human ears belonged to Cosmic Ray, and he was half a mile away, wrapped in his own sonic landscape of windchimes and prog rock. The flat in Bodmin had thick walls, but still was part of a shared building. Out of courtesy, Lee and Gideon had kept a volume cap on their lovemaking.

That wouldn't be necessary here. And that was what they were talking about. Lee too was blushing, a delicious colour spreading underneath his tan. "I mean," he went on, hooking his thumbs into the pockets of his jeans, "we wouldn't even have to go indoors. Not if we didn't want to."

"You want to do it outside, Bear Grylls?"

"Can we?"

No point in mincing words. "Sweetheart, I could put you over that balcony rail right now."

Lee made a sound between a sob and a groan. There was so much urgency and hunger in it that Gideon dropped his rucksack on the spot: strode up the wooden steps and grabbed him. "Lubricant," he said, hustling Lee forward to lean on the rail. "My pack or yours?"

"Mine. I think I brought it."

"You better have. I'm not going caveman to that extent."

"Try the front pocket."

Gideon found it right away, to his shuddery relief. He wasn't sure what he'd have done without, but he'd have had to find a way. No sane man could let a technicality deprive him of the glories being offered to him now—Lee Tyack giving everything up for him, flexing that tough, compact frame of his over the rail without the faintest shyness or restraint. He gripped the top bar with both hands. "Come on, lover. You're so good at this. I want you in me."

He was hard inside his jeans. Gideon took a teasing moment over undoing them, pretending the zip had stuck. He loved the push of Lee's cock against the denim, all that vigour and heat. He took up a strong, steady position behind him. For long weeks after his injury he'd been so afraid that he'd given his last stand-up fuck, and he'd known that Lee would find ways round it, work like a devious angel to keep them both satisfied, but oh, he was glad it hadn't turned out that way. "Are you sure you want this?"

Lee shivered. "Yes. Why the hell would I not?"

"Because that rail looks strong. And I feel like trying to break it."

"Christ. Fuck me head-first into the rhododendrons if you want. All the way back down to Cosmic Ray's shop."

Gideon undressed them both far enough: Lee's jeans and briefs down around his thighs and then his own. Next time they did this he would rip every stitch off them. They wouldn't be sweaty and tired from the climb, and the sunlight drifting through the tree canopy could caress every inch of them. This was an emergency. Gideon sensed that, not knowing why or what he had to fix or patch up here. He just knew he could do it. He pushed up Lee's T-shirt and kissed his shoulder blades.

Lee writhed and arched at the touch. "Come on," he whispered. "Please."

He was tight, for all his eagerness. He flinched when Gideon pressed one lube-slicked finger into his body. Quickly Gideon withdrew, ignoring his rasped-out apology. He squeezed more KY into his palm, dipped down to caress Lee's balls and the silk-velvet patch of skin behind them, the place where a gentle, firm thumb pressure could make him writhe and melt. "You're okay," Gideon told him, finding the good spot and pushing. "You're just all wound up."

"You'll fix me."

"You know it." Gideon tried again. This time Lee's muscle ring pulsed at the touch, clamping and squeezing round the first and second joint of Gideon's finger. "All right?"

"Mm. Deeper, Gid. All the way."

There was his prostate. Gideon had felt like a newborn god the first time he'd found that target, and almost died of joy when Lee had touched the corresponding place inside of him. One day when he was drunk—very, very drunk—he would have to ask Ezekiel how he thought anal sex could be wrong, when some benign, divine creator being had provided each man on earth with that jewelled cluster of nerve endings, ecstasy to be had at such a little cost of learning, lust and love. He put an arm around Lee's waist. "There you are. There."

"Such good hands. Do that to me harder, love. Open me up."

Gideon drew a sharp breath. His cock was pressed to the muscular curve of Lee's arse. Soft-voiced commands from Lee in the sack could make Gideon come on the spot if he didn't take care, and he mastered himself now. He pushed his index finger into the hot, cramping space. Lee grunted, shifting to accommodate the pressure. "Too much?" Gideon asked, but Lee shook his head fiercely.

"No. Not enough. I want more."

They might be good hands, but they were big to match the rest of him. "I'll hurt you."

"I don't care."

Gideon frowned. That didn't sound like Lee, who always brought a fiery self-respect into bed with him, a proud passion that burned on Gideon's behalf too. When they broke one another, indulged tender humiliations, it was all the more bloody memorable: Gideon would keep his brown silk boot-lace ribbons till the day he died. "That means I've got to take care for both of us."

"No. Stop caring. Do it, Gid—you've no idea how much I need it. Don't make me beg."

He was opening up. Gideon had done this much to him before a fuck. Cautiously he pressed his third finger in, and Lee gave an uninhibited yell that sent the woodpigeons clattering up from the trees. "Wow," Gideon said breathlessly. "This no-neighbour thing is good, right?"

"Fuck, yeah. More."

"No." But it was token refusal only. Lee spread his legs as far as he could in the tangle of his jeans and pushed his arse back onto Gideon's hand. He cried out again, a great raw shout of surrender. Then he lowered his head until his brow was almost touching the rail and began to thrust back in a hard rhythm.

"Lee, take it easy!"

"Nn-nn. Fuck me. Christ!"

Gideon would end up fisting him if they followed this road to the end. He'd slid a fourth finger inside him almost without meaning to. Lee's cries were turning him on so hard that he was fighting not to shoot against his heaving, trembling flank, and Gideon would have loved this—would have folded his thumb close and flat and let him have it—if he hadn't felt Lee's fever, the edge of desperation, an off-kilter pitch that would send their act spinning wildly out of control. "Easy," he whispered again, dropping his free hand to seize Lee's cock. "Give it over for me now."

Lee froze, and Gideon thought he was coming. He was staring off over the garden. Gideon had been wrong—the track did go on further, leading up to a carved wooden bridge he hadn't noticed before. Lee's attention was fixed there, a wide vacant gaze. But whatever had distracted him had come too late: he groaned, shuddered his way an inch further onto his impalement, and climaxed with a deep sobbing wail.

Too much for Gideon. He buried his face against Lee's shoulder and cried out as wave after wave of pleasure tore through him. It made him want to shove deeper into the convulsing flesh around his hand: he caught the impulse and instead drew back, just a little, far enough to wring them both to the far side of this spending without doing poor Lee a mischief or letting him down. Twenty seconds later they were clinging to each other and the rail, sweatsoaked and trembling. "Jesus," Gideon grated. "What the... bloody hell was that?"

Lee didn't answer. He was hanging on to Gideon's arm, but his eyes were still fixed on that point between the trees where the bridge began its arc. Orgasmic fog clearing, Gideon could see that it led across a deep gap in the headland, a fragile link from rock to rock.

And there was someone standing there. A slender male figure was poised midway across the bridge. From his attitude, he'd neither just arrived nor was in any hurry to depart. The bastard must have watched.

"Oh, that's just fucking great," Gideon snarled. He didn't give a toss about voyeurs for his own sake, but he couldn't bear that anyone should have stood there and witnessed Lee's stripped-down vulnerability in the act they'd just shared. "So much for no bloody neighbours." He scooped Lee off the rail, held him ferociously for a moment, then helped him struggle back into his jeans. He barely waited long enough to fasten his own before turning and running down the steps. "Let yourself into the house," he called over his shoulder. "And just wait there, okay?"

***

Of course Lee disobeyed him on both counts. The man who went indoors and locked himself up might have been easier to deal with, but Gideon couldn't have loved him so well as the one running across the garden now, ready to help slay his dragons in any shape or form. "What did I tell you?" Gideon demanded, striding to catch him. "You're whiter than Ezekiel's conscience. What's the matter?"

"Did you see him?"

"Zeke?" Gideon clapped a hand to his brow: a foot-chase after a climax that size had been a really bad idea. The blood hadn't stood a chance of making its way back to his brain. "Sorry. Yeah, but the guy was gone before I got near him." He stroked Lee's pallid face. "Just as well—I'd have skinned him. He really freaked you out."

"I'm okay. You did see him?"

"Yeah, I... Oh, hang on. This one was real, love. He had an iPod. I could see the little headphones."

Lee stood swaying. He was breathless, a sheen of sweat over his brow. "An iPod? What the bloody hell difference does that make?"

"Well..." Gideon tried to give it thought. "If he was a visitation from the other world, shouldn't it have been a... harp or something?"

"Or the organ from Truro cathedral?"

"Exactly." They both began to laugh. Gideon cupped a protective hand around the back of Lee's skull, checking over his shoulder for further invasions of their turf. He should have kept a better watch. "I'm sorry he saw that. I'm sorry." Then another reason for Lee's distress hit him, and he swallowed sudden nausea. "Lee, are you hurt?"

"What?"

"From what we did. Did I tear you, or—"

"God, no." Lee made a palpable effort to pull himself together. "My gentle sex god... You'd never hurt me. It was just overwhelming, and then I saw that guy on the bridge." He found a smile. "He might've just been some poor lost walker, you know. And if he was listening to his iPod..."

"He might not have heard the beasts caterwauling in the woods." Gideon chuckled. "Well, I'm damn sure I wouldn't have known whether to carry on or run away either. I tell you what, though—if you're gonna look like this after a fuck, you're going to get your next one covered in rose petals on a chaise longue. With a medic to hand just in case."

"Stop it, Gid. I'm fine."

"I'm sure you are. But..." Gideon took an assessing look at the distance back to the cabin. "I'd like to try an experiment."

"No way. My medic isn't here yet."

"Not that kind. I was just wondering if I could still..."

Lee gave a truncated squawk. "Don't you dare."

"I've got to practise, haven't I?"

"For... For what?"

"For the day I cart you over the threshold of Frayne Manor. I know we talked about doing it the other way round, but I'm scared you'll put your back out."

Lee stopped fighting. His abdication of control was total, and filled with sorrow, and was something to do with their wedding. A cold fear touched Gideon. He leaned down, got an uncompromising hold and hoisted him up off the ground. "Hoi, you. Everything will be all right."

Lee didn't answer. Normally Gideon could expect an elbow in the ribs for this kind of liberty. But Lee put both arms round his neck and hung on, closing his eyes.

Gideon carried him back across the mossy lawn. He'd been kidding about the threshold: he and Lee had borne one another back and forth across it in so many ways now that the physical act would be irrelevant, or at least just the icing on a cake already handsomely made. It would have been a joke, a nod to traditions from which they'd freed themselves and now could honour on their own terms, just as their wedding plans had started off light-hearted, an excuse for a party and a chance to give Ezekiel a few more grey hairs.

Everything felt deadly serious now. Muscles ached in his thigh and he straightened up, forbidding himself the pain. He was glad that Lee had got as far as tossing their bags indoors. The cabin door was on the catch. He shouldered it open, relieved to see that Cosmic Ray had limited his psychedelic tastes to the carvings on the porch: inside, the cabin was plain, full of sunlight but cool. On the far side of the living room a door stood open. Beyond it was a broad double bed, already made up with white linen. That would do.

He dumped Lee carefully onto the quilt and knelt over him. "Tell me what's the matter. Talk."

"You don't want to know."

"Maybe not, but I'm asking. Something to do with us."

Lee stared up at him, bitter dismay turning the sunshine to ice in his eyes. "No."

"Yes. You're the last man in the world to sit up all night fretting over wedding invitations. And..." Oh, this was hard:

Gideon was so much better at doing sex than talking about it. "I loved what we did out there. You weren't ready for it, though, and neither was I."

"Please don't push this, Gid."

"That's just it. I feel like *you* are—pushing something, that is. Forcing things on when maybe they're not ready to happen yet." Gideon swallowed. His throat was sore. "What I'm trying to say is, if we've taken on too much too soon by getting married now, you can tell me. It's all right."

The wrong thing to say. The last of the colour left Lee's face and he twisted out from between Gideon's thighs, rolling over to stare blindly out through the window. "It's not all right."

Gideon tended to agree. He'd had to open the door, but doing it had made him realise just how much he'd come to want his half hour in the registrar's office—or field, Victorian gardens or stone circle—with Lee. "Why not?" he asked roughly. "I love every part of our life together as it is. What difference does a ceremony make?"

"None, if I could only... Look, I can tell when a flood's coming. I can tell you that a jay's about to fly into that tree outside and scare the crap out of a squirrel." He waited, drew a breath, and promptly came the flap of wings and outraged chittering skirr. It was almost funny, like a rimshot after a joke, but fear had dried up all the laughter in Gideon's soul. "When I try to see our wedding, though... there's nothing, all right? Just a blank. I can't see it happening at all."

Gideon got off the bed. He went round to the far side of it and knelt beside Lee, who now had no choice but to look at him instead of whatever future wastelands lay beyond the glass. "Bloody hell. Is that all?"

Lee frowned and rubbed a hand across his eyes, as if clearing cobwebs. He pushed up onto one elbow. "What do you mean, all?"

"You had me scared shitless. I thought you'd changed your mind, or..." Now the laughter was coming back, irrepressible green shoots after rain. Gideon fought to stay serious. "Listen to me. You are the most talented, amazing guy I've ever come across, and some of the things you can do make my hair stand on end. But you get stuff wrong. Anything can throw you off, stress most of all. And you've said it yourself—sometimes you see things arse-backwards, like that horse at Wadebridge."

"Yeah, but—"

"Hush up. This is the one time when I'm telling you to let all your feelings and visions go and trust in my reality."

Lee focussed properly on him. His eyes were still bleak with doubt but hope was dawning there too. "That's so sure and solid, isn't it—your grasp on what's real?"

"Solid enough for both of us. You can hang on to it too."

Lee reached out. Shivering with relief, Gideon launched onto the bed to meet him, rolled him until he was squashed, shielded, safe. "My God, that's what all the fuss and the planning was about. Wasn't it?"

"Mm. I feel like such an idiot now. I couldn't see the wedding, so I was trying to construct it. Every detail, you know? Then it would have to happen."

"Makes a warped kind of sense. And... the menagerie? The goldfish?"

"I still want those. You'll be such a perfect father, Gid."

"So will you. We'll adopt 'em, have surrogates, grow them in the veggie patch. Okay?"

"Yes. But not all at once—your ten-year plan sounds good. I was trying to make that future happen straight away too."

"And... the growling beasts on the veranda?"

"Yes, that was part of it." Lee made a rueful face. "Ugh. Moments of insight suck. I guess I thought if we were pushing the boundaries of what we were doing sexually..."

"Oh, my God. Like there wasn't enough going on there already." Gideon kissed the hollow of Lee's throat, where a flush of embarrassment was turning into something else. He was absurdly happy in the wake of his fear. "So, are we still on for the canapés? The napkins folded into swans?"

"Absolutely. Why can't I bloody see it, though? Why?"

"You're trying too hard. Forget it all. And as regards the sex—how about the dirty, sweaty, come-soaked sort we're already really good at?"

Lee gave a bitten-off moan. "We *are* really good at that, aren't we?"

"We could give lessons. Speaking of which..." Gideon reached out and tugged at the cord of the blind. The wooden slats unfolded in a rush, throwing the room into sun-striped, glimmering shade. "I'd rather not give any more to our mate on the bridge."

"Oh, man. I could die."

"He got quite a show, didn't he?"

"Shut *up*, Gid."

"But it's just the two of us now. Just us."

Chapter Five

Just us. Gideon wondered if it ever really would be. He'd slept for hours, wrung out from their lovemaking, and woken to the murmur of Lee's voice.

He sounded quite different when he was talking to the dead. Still ordinary, nicely modulated, everything Gideon loved, but with an overlay of desperate intensity. When Gideon had overheard his conversations with the monster Morris Hawke, that had been the difference. As if every word had to be pushed through the veil between worlds.

At least this time he didn't sound frightened. Gideon sat up, running his hands over his hair. The voice was coming from the living room, not loud enough for him to make out anything more than a vibration. Gideon pulled off his creased shirt—Lee had divested him of everything else during the long delicious tumble that had finally sent him off to sleep—and shrugged into a cotton dressing gown from his rucksack. He needed a shower. But first he had to go and see that Lee was coping with this encounter. Stupid of him to think that, after Hawke, there might not have been any more, that Lee might have regained that much peace.

He opened the connecting door silently. And the young man sitting opposite Lee at the table looked directly at him and smiled.

Gideon almost burst out laughing. He didn't know the sound of Lee's spiritual conversations after all. There was a whole lifetime's worth of things he still had to discover about his lover, and that was bloody wonderful. Stupid of him to presume, and such a relief to be proved wrong. At last it struck him that he was standing in front of Lee's guest in a short, unfastened robe. "Oh, shit," he said, quickly covering up. "Sorry. I didn't know anyone else was here."

Lee jerked round to face him. He and the young man were sharing the small table in the cabin's kitchenette. He shoved back his chair with a scrape and got to his feet, his motion jerky, almost a recoil. He glanced between Gideon and the newcomer. "Gid, what are you doing?"

"I just woke up. I heard you talking, and I came to see you were all right. Is this a friend of yours?"

"No. No. It's..."

"Oh, hang on." Gideon forgot his state of undress. Post-coital fog and sun-dazzle had clouded his last view, but he was a copper. He didn't forget a face. "This is the guy who stood on the bridge and bloody well—"

"Watched you. I didn't mean to." The young man stood up. "I came to apologise. I was here, and I couldn't help homing in on Lee. He shines like a beacon."

"Lee, do you know this guy?" Gideon waited for Lee's brief headshake. "Right. In that case it's *Mr Tyack* to you, son, and you can just step outside with me while you explain what you mean by that."

"You're a policeman. That's good. He needs someone like you." The boy stepped obediently forward, and Gideon reached for his arm.

"No!" Lee shot forward. He got between Gideon and the boy. "Don't try to touch him."

"I'm not about to hurt him." Gideon shook himself: Lee knew that. "Look, what's going on? Are you happy to have him in here, because..."

"Yes. I... I'm happy, yeah. Will you listen to what he has to say?"

"If you want me to, of course." Gideon eyed the boy sternly. "It had better be good. What's your name?"

"Kitto. I'm Ray Tregear's stepbrother. My first name's an old Kernowek one, hard to pronounce. So I use my own dad's surname. Kitto."

"Lee's bilingual Cornish. I'm sure he could pronounce it. And, like you say, I'm a copper, so I'll remember it. Why did you stand and watch us on the bridge?"

"I couldn't help it. I found myself up on the old track through the woods. I used to love it up there, so I suppose... Anyway, I felt Lee's—Mr Tyack's—light, and I followed it, and there you were. You were both so perfect. You'd have stood and stared too, Gideon, if it had been you."

Sergeant Frayne. Somehow the growled correction died on Gideon's lips, and he watched in silence while the boy sat back down. The trouble with Kitto was that he was damn near perfect too. Gideon had never seen such an absurdly handsome young man. Thick blond hair tumbled in curls around his shoulders. His eyes were summer-sea blue, and his long legs were tanned from his worn leather sandals to the fray on his cut-off jeans. Gideon had used to joke with Lee about the godlike brood of surf instructors who appeared around this time of year at Porth Bay and the western beaches, that they looked as if they ate nothing but sunbeams and bathed in liquid moonlight, such a regime being the only possible explanation for their beauty. This lad looked as if he could be...

"Yes. I teach surf down at Porth." The boy was beaming and nodding, as if Gideon had done something right. "Oh, don't worry—you don't have to say stuff aloud for me to know. I'm like Mr Tyack, you see. That's why I could find him. We're the same."

"We're not," Lee whispered. He let go his defensive stance by the cupboards and came to sit down. "We're not the same, Kitto. But... go on talking to Gid."

"Okay. I'd just as soon you didn't mention to Ray that you'd seen me, if that's all right with both of you. I love him, but he thinks I've gone away, and he'll just get upset if he hears I'm around."

Deciding he'd better join what he clearly couldn't beat, Gideon drew a third chair up to the table. "Why would that upset him?"

"Ray's a good big step-brother. He always wanted me to get away from our crappy family and their nonsense. So I did. And I'm only back for a very short time, so it's not worth disturbing him. Is that okay?"

"Yeah, sure, if you can give me a good reason why you're disturbing *us*. We're on holiday here." Gideon was finding it hard to stay angry. Kitto's smile was broad and genuine, and after all the alfresco sex had been his Gideon's own idea. Probably the track to the bridge was a public footpath. "Would you like a cup of tea, since you're here?"

Lee's hands clenched on the table. "Don't. You can't."

"Don't you want me to? Lee, are you sure you want to talk to this guy?"

"It's not that." Leaning forward, Lee rubbed his eyes. "Oh, Christ, okay. Make the tea."

Gideon took mugs out of the cupboard and set the kettle to boil. He had wondered if Lee would pick up where he'd left off, but only an intense silence radiated out from the table behind him.

Belatedly it hit him that perhaps Lee could only talk to the boy when the two of them were alone. A restless ache stirred in Gideon's chest: stupid of him to assume that he was either useful or wanted. He put one of the three mugs back in the cupboard. "Milk and sugar, Kitto?"

"Both, please. And please stop worrying. Lee's a clairvoyant and so am I. That's all. I know how hard things can be, and I thought I could help."

"Well..." Gideon brought the mugs over and set them down. "If Lee thinks so too, you're welcome, I guess. I'll get dressed and nip down to see Ray and put in an order for groceries. Do you fancy some scallops from the oyster farm for dinner, love?"

"You don't have to go," Lee said. But he wasn't looking at Gideon—seemed instead transfixed by the homely sight of their visitor raising the mug and taking a sip of his tea. "Although... Yeah. Actually, would you mind? The scallops would be great."

***

Kitto was sitting on the cabin steps when Gideon returned. He looked very much in his element between the carved columns of mermaids. If Gideon had been ten years younger and as lonely as he'd been at that time, this boy would have melted his knees from under him. "Why are you out here?" he demanded, stern in proportion with the unwanted thought. "Is Lee all right?"

"He was tired, so I came away. I didn't want to leave until you came back." He gave Gideon a sapphire look. "Thanks for not mentioning me to Ray."

I don't think I can cope with two mindreaders. Gideon set down the bag containing his polystyrene icebox of scallops and leaned on the banister. "I said I wouldn't unless you gave me reason to.

Look, either my skull is made of glass or you really can do some of the same things Lee does."

"Well, you're not hard to figure out. But yes, I can."

"You said you could help him. What did you mean by that?"

"When my talents started unfolding, I was terrified. There was no-one I could turn to." His shapely mouth quirked into a sad smile. "It's all right for people like *you* having glass skulls. Not everybody's full of love and virtue in there."

Gideon ignored the compliment. "I'm a policeman. I know."

"So I wasn't very popular in some quarters."

"At home?"

"Yeah. That's why I... why I left. And it was lonely. I wouldn't want anyone else with those kinds of gifts to be alone."

Lee's not alone. Gideon found he couldn't say it. For all he'd shared with Lee, there were times when the multiple worlds his lover inhabited had to be out of bounds to him. "But Lee's not... just a kid starting out. He's been dealing with this stuff for years."

"Yes, since long before you met him. Think how it's expanded since you've known him, though. He's gone from telling old ladies where to find their purses to rescuing hundreds from a flood."

"And you reckon..." Gideon hesitated. He wasn't sure he wanted an answer, and he hated that his voice was unsteady when he asked. "Is that something to do with me?"

"Hell, yes. He's got a rock to hold onto, a wall he can put his back against. No wonder he's started to fly. But he's dead right— seeing the future isn't good, not for him or anyone. Our brains are evolved to flow with the stream of time. So when he called me up, I came to see if I could help."

"Wait. He called you?"

"Oh, not like that. Not on the phone." The boy got up, dusting moss from the seat of his shorts. "He didn't mean to."

"I don't have the least idea what you're on about, Kitto. *Can* you help him?"

"I tried. But I don't think he'll let me come back."

Alarm prickled Gideon's nape. He picked up the bag and headed for the cabin door. "Why? What happened?"

"*You* did. He'll have to explain that to you himself." Kitto paused at the foot of the steps. He stretched out his hands so that he was holding one branch of the oak sapling and one of the glossy-leaved holly. "It's funny how the world gives us signs. Are you coming to the Golowan?"

"No. We came up here to get away from crowds of nutcases."

"Not the Penzance one. We have our own festival down in the village on Midsummer's Eve. It's tomorrow. You should come." Kitto looked wistfully at the cabin, the trees, and finally at Gideon, as if he would have liked with all his heart to stay. "I might see you again there. Yes, you really should come."

***

Lee was curled up on the sofa. He'd made a kind of tent for himself with a rug and didn't move when Gideon came to sit beside him. His voice was muffled by the wool. "Did you see him again?"

"Yes. He was waiting outside when I got back. He said he was worried about you. He seems a nice kid, but if he's done or said anything to hurt you, it's not too late for me to kill the little fucker."

Something about this struck Lee as funny. His laugh was a raw, pained rasp. "You do pick your words, Gid. You saw him. You had a whole conversation with him while I wasn't even bloody *there*."

"Yes, I did. I don't understand. Is there something wrong with that?"

"You have no idea. I can't do this to you. I can't."

"He said you needed to explain something to me." Cautiously Gideon lifted a corner of the blanket near Lee's face and peered in. "This might be the time."

"Oh, God. He said having you near me was making my clairvoyance grow, but..."

"He said the same to me. And I'm getting scared that's not a good thing."

"It's nothing. Don't you get how being near to me's changed *you*?"

"In a billion ways." Gideon tried to meet the green eyes shining eerily in the blanket's shadows, but Lee was looking past him, far, far away. "I had nothing. Now I have everything. Lee, *please* tell me what's wrong."

"You told me to hang on to your reality, and I tried. But you can't hang on to it yourself. You think it's just me who sees spirits."

"When did I say that? I saw Morris Hawke, and..." Gideon hesitated: this was still such a tender patch for Lee. "And your father."

"Yes, with me, in a dream. What about all on your own? In broad daylight?"

Involuntarily Gideon glanced at the table where Kitto had been sitting. There was his mug, leaving a ring on the woodwork. The chair cushion was still wore the indent of his neat backside. He wanted to laugh, but sensed it would be the worst possible time. "You're kidding. We've been through this. That lad's as real as you and me."

"What else did he say to you?"

"He said you didn't want him to come back. And that's fair enough—we're meant to be on holiday, not looking after stray pups. He's just a kid, though. I don't think he means any harm."

"Gid, are you not listening?"

"Yes. You're telling me I'm seeing a ghost, all on my own without you there to help me. A ghost who drinks tea and... Look. Leaves his iPod behind him."

"He wants to come back."

"He's very welcome. He can pick that up and go away." Gideon pushed back the blanket from Lee's face. "Sweetheart, you are so tired. I even had a text from Zeke to say he's worried about you. Yes, I've seen and heard all kinds of mind-spinning things when I've been with you, but Kitto's not one of them."

"You don't believe me."

Gideon sat back a little. The sting of pain in Lee's voice touched him like a whiplash too. "That's not what I said."

"What else, then? I don't have proofs, Gid. I never do. You've been the only man who's taken what I say on trust, even back when we first met and you thought I was some kind of table-rapping charlatan."

"I do believe you. I believe you're convinced that—"

"Oh God, don't do that!" Lee scrambled off the sofa, clutching the blanket. He stood with it wrapped tight round his shoulders, a desolate Roman emperor surveying a city in flames. "Don't do the *I believe you believe*. It's one step off humouring me, and you've never—"

"*Humouring* you?" Now it was Gideon's turn to jump to his feet. From a great distance out he registered the absurd drama of his movement—of their confrontation, here in the teeth of their first fight. Then grief swept him. They were *fighting*. It felt nightmarish, impossible. "Is that what it means when I see how worn out you are, how much all this is getting to you, and I'm trying to be kind?"

"But you do think Kitto's real."

"Of course I do, you nut job! He invited us both to the village Golowan tomorrow."

"And you'd put that reality over everything I've tried to tell you?"

"No, but if it's a choice between the two—"

"It *is* a choice! Not for me, but you can still decide whether to take my visions—the futures I've started to see—and accept them, or you can relegate them to the twilight. Dreams. Echoes. Things Lee's *convinced* himself about."

"Jesus. I'd never have... Does choosing your version mean I have to believe that lad's a ghost? Why are you putting my back to the wall like this?"

"Because I want to know what you'll say. How you think when your back's to the wall."

"All right," Gideon said hopelessly. "I'd choose what's real, okay? What I can see and touch."

"And the rest of it? Everything I see?"

"I can't buy into it. Not if it means I have to buy into all your fears too, into... prophecies that tell me some dark nebulous thing is gonna stop our wedding." He was starting to shout. There was never any call to raise his voice to Lee, who heard everything—especially the unspoken—all too well.

Who was watching him now with a kind of feverish despair. "Look," Gideon went on more quietly. "I don't know how to explain. I had a mate once, a lad I knew at school. And he got his palm read one night when he was drunk at the Padstow fair, and the old girl who read it said he had a very short life line. I don't think she meant to scare him, but he took it right to heart. And for ages after that, if he was out with his mates he would drink like a fish, eat whatever crap he wanted, and he'd say it didn't matter because he was gonna die young anyway." Gideon ran a hand into his short-cropped hair, wishing he had more to tug: he wasn't exactly sure where he was going with this story, but he supposed he had to finish it now. "And he did. He had a stroke when he was twenty eight, brought on by—"

"Drink and bad diet. The self-fulfilling prophecy. Right." Lee swallowed with a dry effort. "And that's what you think I'm doing. You think I'd be irresponsible enough—destructive enough—to say or do anything to risk our marriage."

"Fuck. No. Not at all." But Gideon could see how Lee would grab that meaning from the stupid tale he'd just been told. "We make our own reality, love. Our own futures. *Please* believe that. I... I thought you already did."

Lee turned away. He collided with the chair where Kitto had been sitting, hard enough to hurt himself, and jerked out from under Gideon's concerned grasp. "Leave me be," he said hoarsely: stumbled through into the bedroom and closed the door.

Chapter Six

Gideon sat for a long time at the table, unmoving. The light in the room began to change, the tireless June sun at last beginning to let go its dominion of the day. Tomorrow would be midsummer, and even this far south, the glow would barely leave the sky all night long.

He put the flat of his palms to his eyes and hid in the self-created dark. He wished it was midwinter solstice instead; wished he was standing with Lee in a frosty street in Falmouth, watching the first flakes of snow, knowing that he'd helped his lover fight off a demon that had tried to take his soul. Because that was what Gideon did. He loved and protected Lee Tyack.

He found himself thinking, for the first time in months, about his previous boyfriend, James. They'd done their share of fighting, when poor James had realised he'd never be able to persuade Gideon to acknowledge him in public, but it had never felt like this, not as if someone had torn out Gideon's guts and laid them along the veranda for the crows to pick at. His parents had never fought at all. He'd come across the view that a conflict-free relationship meant a passionless one, and also that true lovers shouldn't ever need to quarrel.

Probably every couple under the sun had a different take on it. He couldn't reach outside himself for help. He only knew that it was desperately wrong for him and Lee. He went and tapped softly on the bedroom door.

Nothing. Not even the subtle shift in the air that told him Lee was waiting. Gideon had learned to pick up that signal without realising. How much more had Lee brought out in him? Was it absolutely beyond the realms of possibility that Gideon had learned to see a ghost?

Maybe he had. But not Kitto. Gideon glanced at the mugs on the table. They were both empty. No ghost drank his tea and left the faintest lip-mark smudge at the rim. Well, if he couldn't meet with Lee on this, he could at least not throw his weight about and make the poor sod miserable. He had to find a way.

He decided to start with the basics. He found a frying pan in the cupboard along with some sunflower oil. The oyster farm had sold him some garlic and a lime, and he knew from experience that the delicate combined aroma of these ingredients frying would usually bring down his hungry bird from the tree. He took out the scallops from their ice box and went to work.

Still nothing. This was a bad case. Repressing the urge to sit down and cry, Gideon boiled a kettle. Nothing Lee liked better than a good pot of tea with his fish. Damn, though, he'd used up the last of the tea bags when making a round for their visiting ghost. They wouldn't get their groceries till tomorrow, and it was too long a walk to the village...

There was Ray's baggie on the counter where Gideon had left it, small and green and looking like an arrestable offence. Well, Ray had said it was harmless, and Gideon had an odd trust in him. It smelled good when he opened it, too—PG Tips with a mystical kick. He spooned some into a pot.

He set out the scallops in one big bowl—for sharing, he prayed to God—and the tea cups on a tray. Cosmic Ray had kindly left a nice cob loaf for them too, and he sliced up half of it, buttering generously. He'd become good at such things. With James, and later on his own, he'd used food for survival. Neither he nor Lee had been much of a hand at cooking when they'd met, but in an expanding, brightening world, a world where a meal could be offered as a daily gift, they'd learned.

This time he didn't knock at the door. He couldn't have borne a third silence. Lee sat up with a jolt on the bed. He was still tangled in his rug, and his eyes were red, a sob half-choking him as he tried to swallow it. "Oh, fuck," Gideon said, setting the tray down on the bedside table. "Don't do that, sweetheart. Don't."

"I didn't mean to. Cry, I mean."

"I know, hard-arse." Gideon peeled the blanket off him, replacing its dubious comforts with his own warm hold. "But it's okay."

"It's not," Lee contradicted him, muffled against his shoulder. "I wasn't exactly brought up to think it was wrong, just... that it was better to *deal* with things. And I didn't. I came in here and started..." Sitting back a bit, he indicated the tearstained mess of his face, the single bit of tissue he'd found and destroyed. "And I couldn't stop."

"Because of me. Because of what I said."

"No—because of us having a bloody row. *Us.* No way." He reached for the tissue again, but that was a really bad idea, and Gideon offered him the kitchen roll he'd brought in with their supper instead. "Gid, I feel like we can't. I feel like we just can't fight."

"I've reached the same conclusion myself."

"Why can't we? Is it because..."

"We're linked? We feel too much about each other?"

Lee blew his nose. A pleasure and relief like wintry sunlight crossed his face. "You believe that?"

"What, that we have that bond? I wasn't throwing out everything you ever taught me about other worlds, spiritual realities, all the truth you've shown me. I just have to make up my own mind about Kitto."

That was still tough for Lee to swallow. He nodded staunchly, though. "Of course."

"So what I thought of doing was, I'll go down into the village tomorrow morning and ask around. Just very subtly, like a good copper, and if people back off crossing themselves, I'll take that as a strong hint. But if I get the feedback that this lad's alive and well..."

"If you do, I'll accept it. I'd like nothing better. Do me a favour, though—don't talk to Ray yet. Not until you're sure."

"Okay." Gideon tore off another sheet of kitchen roll and made a few gentle dabs at the bits Lee had missed. "What a mess. Are you in any fit state to eat?"

"There's food?"

"Garlic-fried scallops. I was trying to lure you out with the smell."

"Oh, wow." Lee smiled weakly as Gideon lifted the tray onto the bed. They sat cross-legged with the meal between them, their world slowly righting itself on its axis again. "I couldn't smell anything. I was too snotty."

"Charming. And now?"

"Much better. You're not obliged to cook for any sour-faced little gits, though."

Gideon picked up a scallop on his fork and held it out. "Well, if I come across 'em, I promise I won't."

***

"I'm never gonna let the sun go down on it, you know."

Lee looked up. Gideon was kneeling across his lap. Over the treeline on the far side of the creek, the sky was trembling with silver-bronze light. "I know," Lee said. He shifted to sit a little more upright, propping himself on one arm. His fingers drove into the mattress with the effort of control. "Why did I?"

A bright rim crested the oaks."I bet you'd never have let the moon rise on it, anyway."

Lee pressed his brow to Gideon's chest. His voice shook. "You kill me with your faith in me. We *are* like the sun and the bloody moon, aren't we?" He grasped Gideon's backside with his free hand. "I don't want it to be that way. I want to be warm and constant to you like you are to me."

"Look, don't make me say *you are my sunshine*, or I'll have to kill us both." Gideon kissed his brow. "But you are, love. You are."

Lee closed his eyes. He thrust up a little, settling Gideon harder onto his cock, and Gideon grunted at the deeper engagement. They'd used up nearly all the lube already and were having to move carefully, but what was left had got them this far. They'd gone at it urgently after the food. Lee was still fully dressed. Gideon had pulled his jeans off, but his briefs were still hooked round one ankle. The beauty and indignity of doing it like this was a turn-on in itself, a spiralling feedback of arousal. The dressing-table mirror reflected their awkward perfection, and that was hot as hell too. No-one could be blamed for wanting to watch.

No-one. Gideon was almost sure that the pale oval patch among the burnished leaves was only a happenstance pattern of camellias. He grabbed Lee's shoulders and began to grind down on him. This was their third round of the day and they could make it a good long one, the desperate steam blown off. Gideon's thigh was aching but he wasn't about to let that stop him.

He increased the pace. Lee gasped and tried to slow him, but Gideon liked the friction, the slight inner scrape the lack of lube was causing. Lee's normal policy was *too much is almost enough.* Gideon loved getting fucked, though, and he could see a day when he would like to bend over a rail somewhere and have Lee do to him what they'd tried on the balcony. Could see a day when he did it again for Lee and got it right. "Oh, God."

"Yeah, handsome. Go easy, though."

"You okay?"

Lee raised a sweat-damped face. "Take it slow. We won't get to do this again."

Gideon froze. If anything could have stopped the blood in his veins at that moment and made his hard-on wilt... "That had better not be one of your fucking prophecies, mate."

Christ, was that mischief in the dilated silver-green eyes? Gideon would never fathom him, not if he married the little sod and lived with him for fifty years on Bodmin Moor. "No," Lee said softly, squeezing a hand between their bodies to shield and stroke Gideon's cock, as if he'd read the imminent collapse. "It's just that we won't have *this* any more, will we? The make-up sex. Not if we're never gonna fight."

Laughter sent a weird, hot surge through Gideon's whole body, mixing itself with arousal, tightening his sphincter around Lee's shaft. Sex with James had been so serious. A lover who would crack an awful gag like that on the brink of orgasm... He shook his head. "I'll pick a scrap with you from time to time, okay?"

"Because make-up sex is good, right?"

"So good. So good." *Not good enough to fight with you for,* Gideon wanted to add, but everything was blurring out for him, turning to liquid heat. He tipped his head back, groaning, as Lee seized his arse and dragged him in, down and in, for the final deep stroke that would finish him. They shuddered together in climax, and the night and the camellias and the new-risen moon looked on.

***

Midsummer's day dawned warm and was rising to hot by the time Gideon crawled out of bed. He looked in amusement at the mess they'd made of Cosmic Ray's nice sheets. Gideon would bundle up the linen for a run to the laundry in Helston, if his crashed-out lover ever woke up. They had stripped one another of most of their remaining clothes but otherwise Lee was lying where wrung-out passion had dropped him, flat on his stomach, one arm trailing the floor.

Gently Gideon turned him over and tucked a pillow under his head. He got a beatific smile for his trouble but the long-lashed eyes stayed shut, and he grinned and went to take a badly needed shower.

He was searching for instant coffee in the kitchen when warm arms closed around his waist. "Hi, sleeping beauty," he said. "Didn't expect to see you for a while."

"You haven't. I'm not really here." Lee yawned against his shoulder. "God, what's wrong with me? I know you're the grand shag-master of the universe and all, but I feel like somebody drugged me."

Gideon glanced at the counter top where he'd made the tea last night. The little bag lay open, looking potent and somehow pleased with itself. "Uh-oh. I think it might have been me."

"That's unusual of you, sergeant."

"Well, I'm off duty. I made us a pot of Ray's special brew when I couldn't find the teabags last night."

"And is that what I had with my scallops?"

"Afraid so."

"You had loads of it too."

"Maybe it only works on zoned-out psychic hippies." Gideon checked him over. He looked better than he had the night before, rosy with warmth and whisker-burn, but exhaustion still shadowed him. "And people who really need it. Why don't you go back to bed?"

"Aren't we off on our investigative mission today?"

Like there was ever any chance I was taking you with me for that. "Let me do it. It's gonna be nothing, okay? Just a few subtle questions here and there. Maybe better if I'm not walking around with a ridiculously handsome guy on my arm to distract people."

"You are a shameless bloody flatterer," Lee told him past another giant yawn. "Oh, my God. I really can't stay on my feet."

"Go and put 'em up, then. I'll bring you your coffee and some toast, and then you can kip for as long as you want." Gideon watched him walk away. He'd pulled on his Cosmic Ray's T-shirt. It wasn't long enough to hide the tantalising curves of his backside, and Gideon considered throwing aside all concerns about Kitto's reality or lack of it and following on where that beautiful sight suggested.

But he needed to know. Or rather, since he knew already, he needed to reassure Lee. That the boy was a slightly odd, flesh-and-blood drifter, not a lost soul in need of salvation. "Sweetheart," he said quietly, and Lee turned in the doorway, his eyes already full of oncoming dreams. "Do me a big favour. Just get your rest today, and don't answer the door—not even to our new friend."

"Okay. I probably wouldn't hear if he knocked."

"And if he walks through the wall, tell him to keep walking. I'll take his iPod with me. I bet you by the time the sun sets tonight I'll have found him and given it back to him."

Chapter Seven

The day's heat increased as Gideon made his way down the track. The leaf canopy closed over him. The air would be heavy and silent in the creekside village: no bad thing for Lee to be out of it, catching up on his sleep. Briefly Gideon worried about leaving him alone. He dismissed the fear. Lee had looked set to crash for a good long while, and Gideon only intended to be gone for a couple of hours.

He didn't think he could cope with more. Maybe it was the weather or the rising midsummer sap in the verdant world all around him, but he was distracted and racked with desire, his mind awash with images of what they'd done, eagerly reaching for their next encounter. Hunger building up in him hard on the heels of satiation...

He missed a step on the rocky track and just barely caught himself, jarring his leg and his spine. With an effort he got his mind out from under the duvet. This was ridiculous, and he'd hurt himself, too. Just as well his tests were over. He hadn't checked to see if there were any messages from the hospital or his boss, and he didn't intend to. He was on leave, and Lee could take the driver's seat for their next few rounds, in bed or out of it. Gideon adored to be bossed by him. He hadn't brought the ribbons but he was sure they could improvise. The bed in the cabin had a good solid headboard with slats.

Oh, for Christ's sake. Gideon heard music drifting up from the trees, a shimmer of Pink Floyd. Cosmic Ray was up and active, then, and Gideon was here on police business of a sort, to find out what had become of his little stepbrother. If anything had become of him at all, and the fey blue-eyed creature wasn't already watching him from the trees, finding all this fuss and effort hilarious. Grateful for the pain which had come in time to quell an erection, Gideon emerged onto the harbour.

For once the place was busy. Kids were dashing about, helping and hindering a group of lads setting up the fixings for a huge bonfire. A dozen little market stalls had appeared around the harbour's perimeter, bright with local artwork—the lovely if inevitable Cornish sapphire and gold—and a grand array of glittering shawls, gleaming jars of honey, all the hallmarks of a summer feast.

Of course. It was Golowan day. This would make it easy, then: Gideon would be just another visitor, inconspicuous in the crowds. Already the little harbour road was getting parked up, curious holidaymakers emerging from their cars and VW buses, fanning themselves in the heat. An old lady had just finished laying out a rare old collection of home-knitted babywear on a trestle and was clearly hoping for her first customer, or at least a bit of company and a chat. An ideal first target—Gideon gave her a smile and strolled over to look at her wares.

***

He was very good at this part of his job—talking and listening, the quiet aspect of being a village policeman. The running around and reining in villains was great, of course, but he sometimes wondered if this wasn't the best of it. Just hearing people, winnowing their words, waiting for the grains of trouble and truth to fall. He had years of experience in putting ordinary souls at their ease. He was ordinary himself. Being with Lee sometimes made him forget that, but it was a useful trait. His old lady trusted him without a second glance, told him her life story and sold him a tiny crocheted hat. He went off with that in his pocket as well as her thoughts and opinions on Gwylim Uchdryd Kitto.

It was a hell of a name. But that wasn't why the lad had insisted on avoiding the first two parts. Gideon chatted to a greengrocer, three more old ladies sunning themselves on their doorsteps, and the local eccentric millionaire out on the deck of his yacht. From all of them he got the same story. Kitto was a wild child, a sweet but ungrateful little rebel who'd been offered everything and thrown it away. There wasn't much sympathy for that down in cash-strapped rural Cornwall. All Gideon had needed to do was pull a mildly reproving face, and the stories had come forth. Such a lovely family, the Tregears, Ray and his dad. Old man Tregear was a widower who'd decided to marry again, and hadn't been afraid to take on Dilys Kitto with her teenage boy. Tregear was kindly and well off, a good resting place for Dilys's pretty but clueless feet, and she'd landed squarely on them, in the opinion of Kelyndar.

The story was the same across the board. Inconsistencies would have troubled Gideon, but everyone said the same. Kitto had resented his new dad so fiercely that he'd thrown everything back in his face, including the family name. No-one was allowed to call him Gwylim any more: it had to be *Kitto*, like the dad who'd left home before the boy could understand what a good father was. Too late for him to learn, apparently. He'd run off to Porth to teach surfing two years ago, and never come home. His clothes had been found on the beach one morning after a storm. He'd surfed in all weathers, like the feckless brat he was, and after costing the lifeboat service and air-sea rescue a fortune in searching for him, he'd been declared lost, presumed dead.

Two years. Gideon made his way slowly back to the harbour, pulling his sticky T-shirt away from his stomach to let the air touch his skin, not that there was much point now in the heavy midday warmth. It had been two years more or less since he'd offered extenuating circumstances and helped keep Ray Tregear out of jail. Instinct had told Gideon that Ray was a good man who'd hit bad times and deserved another chance. And he'd been so cut up about a recent loss in his family...

It was odd for a boy who'd so hated his mother's new marriage to love his step-brother the way Kitto seemed to care for Ray. Second-marriage kids tended to surrender completely or reject the whole deal. It would be hard for anyone to take a serious dislike to that kind of big brother—a laidback hippie bear in permanent state of adolescence—but still...

His route had brought him back to the shop. The fractal over the door seemed to shift and revolve in the heat. He understood perfectly why Lee wanted him to keep quiet, but Ray was the only source of good information here. Gideon had drawn a tentative conclusion from his afternoon of idle gossip, and it was simple enough: Kitto had come home. However much trouble he was in, it wouldn't matter to Ray, who probably knew all about his return and was giving him shelter.

If so, fair enough. Dark Village and Bodmin were Gideon's turf, not Kelyndar. And he'd let the dead stay buried at Drift farm. He just wanted to reassure Lee. Before he could make up his mind to move on, Ray appeared beneath the fractal, resplendent in one of his own T-shirts. Gideon would have to be careful not to go down with heatstroke today: already the two sets of patterns appeared to be rotating in opposite directions. "Gideon!" Ray greeted him, beaming in delight. "How are you, mate? Everything okay at the cabin?"

"Fine. It's a great place."

"Cool, cool. Not on duty, are you?"

"Far from it."

"Come in out of this swelter and have a beer, then. I've got a couple of cold ones in the fridge—three, if your other half's around."

"No, I'm on my own. Thanks—I don't mind if I do."

For a moment Gideon couldn't see a thing in the sandalwood darkness of the shop. Then his eyes adjusted and he found himself staring into the sockets of a vast horse's skull laid out on the counter. "Christ," he said, backing up a step. "I thought these things were made out of... papier maché or something."

"Not the Kelyndar one," Ray told him cheerfully, emerging from a corner with two bottles in his hand. "That's our Old Penglas come to dance in the Golowan parade. They don't have nothing like him down in Penzance, now, do they?"

"I should think not. I doubt they could lift him."

"Oh, no. The only man here who can do that is my dad." Ray uncapped the bottles with a shop-branded shark's-head opener. He handed a beer to Gideon, then stroked the skull fondly. "Yeah, my dad's Old Penglas around here. Has been since we first came."

The thing was hypnotic. Gideon stared dubiously at its terrible, yellow-toothed rictus, the nose-bone worn satiny with touch. People would grab it for luck during the festival. It made him want to run a mile. "It looks ancient. Where did your father find it?"

"That's the weird thing. Tucked away in my grandmother's house—you know, the one with the statues in the porch. We stayed there for a bit when we first came back here. She said my granda used to carry it in his day too. I bring it down to the shop every year to fit it up with its pole and its new clothes."

A hereditary Penglas. Gideon missed Lee with a sudden sharp pang. He'd love to hear of a legend surviving like that. "And what about you? Will you get to carry old Greyhead one day?"

"Oh, I don't know about that." Ray made a comical survey of his own barrel-shaped belly and chest. "I could lift 'im, I reckon, but you see I'm the first one in my family to be born without much height. You can't have a short-arsed Penglas."

Gideon chuckled. Then timing and instinct and years of good police work came together in his head and he asked, casually, not shifting out of his relaxed pose by the counter, "How about your brother, then? Kitto's a nice tall lad."

Ray Tregear was the last man who should ever have gone near drugs. Two gulps of beer had made his pupils dilate and laid him open like a book. If he'd been shielding a fugitive, down in the cellar or somewhere off behind the beaded curtains, Gideon would have had it from him right there and then in response to the shock of the question.

All he did was gape. Then tears came to his eyes. "Kitto's gone," he said faintly. "He disappeared. The police say he's dead, but I've never believed..." He set his beer bottle down on the counter, missing the first time and having to make a second unsteady attempt. "Oh, hang on. I'd never have asked, because I know you brought him here to get away from everything, but... your boy Lee. I've been to one of his shows up in Falmouth, and I know he can... Why were you talking about Kitto like that—like one of you had *seen* him?"

"Hold up, Ray. I didn't mean—"

"He used to love it up there. That path through the woods and the bridge by your cabin. He always used to come and go that way, and your Lee, he can see people who've... who've *passed*, can't he?" The tears spilled. "Oh no, Gideon. Don't say Lee's seen my poor Gwylim's ghost."

Enough was enough. Gideon had the ghost's iPod in his pocket, together with Mrs Brown's godawful baby hat, which no human child could ever deserve to have placed on its innocent head. "No, of course not," he growled. "Listen to me. Your brother's—"

A shadow filled the doorway. The stifling heat in the shop seemed to drop through ten degrees. On reflex Gideon turned, adrenaline spiking, muscles tensing ready for a fight. He had no idea why. It wasn't likely that Ray's little hippie shop would ever fall victim to a stick-up, unless someone had got the wrong idea about his herbal highs. And after a moment the vast shape blocking the sun took a few steps forward and became a man— one of the biggest Gideon had ever seen, but smiling benignly and a spitting older image of his son. "Dad," Ray said weakly. "This is my mate Gideon Frayne, who's up in the cabin this week. Gideon, this is my father, John Tregear. Old Penglas."

Tregear put out a hand. Gideon took it. He wasn't often confronted with a grip that could more than match his own, and he fought off a primitive reaction: Tregear's eyes were as mild as Ray's, and it wasn't his fault that he was built like a brick garage. "Good to meet you, Gideon. I hope Ray's got everything comfortable for you up in the house?"

More than Ray's life was worth for Gideon to say otherwise. He picked that up easily. Ray was surreptitiously wiping his eyes, coming to a stance as near to attention as his squat frame would allow. "Perfect," Gideon said. "I've never stayed in such a nice clean place."

"Good. My Ray's a good boy, but he sometimes forgets that even surfers and hippies like clean sheets." He sized Gideon up, his expression still genial. "Not that you look like either, if you don't mind my saying so."

"Not at all. I'm a policeman." Gideon threw that piece of information onto the counter along with the horse's skull, as casually as his gambit about Kitto. He was looking for reactions, although he could hardly have said which ones. Tregear just nodded. It was poor Ray who was wincing, staring at the ground. Gideon guessed that Old Penglas didn't know about the drugs bust. The talk about Kitto had to stop as well, to judge by Ray's pallor. "I'm on leave, though. Just here to see the Golowan."

"You'll enjoy it. People come from all the villages around. We have a serpent dance and choose an oak and a holly king, and I take this great thing around the streets to frighten the kiddies." He laughed, a booming vibration that shook Ray's little buddhas on their shelves. "That's what they say down here in Kelyndar, isn't it? *Be good, or Old Penglas will get you.* I'm only joking—they love it. And that reminds me, Ray. The big room's ready up at my house for Maisie and the boys. You should get them settled in there before things get rowdy tonight."

Time for Gideon to go, unfinished beer and business or not. Ray had started blushing miserably at the mention of his kids. Gideon gave him a nod, and edging past Tregear, made his way outside.

He was halfway across the harbour when the crowd behind him began to exclaim and jump aside. He turned in time to see Ray cannoning through them, scattering children and dogs right and left. "Easy," he said, guiding Ray's torpedo rush into a gap between the stalls and stopping him by main force. "What's the matter?"

"He's in the back checking stock."

"Who is?"

"My dad. I've only got a second." Ray gripped Gideon's arms. "You said Lee hadn't seen Gwylim's ghost. That means... Oh, God. He saw him *really*?"

"Hang on. I can't talk to you about this here, but—"

"Ray!"

It was a casual roar. The tourists looked around but none of the stallholders reacted with surprise, and Gideon guessed the locals were pretty used to hearing bellowed orders from the shop. "Shit," Ray whispered. "He's already done. I've got to go."

"Because he shouts at you? Is he a problem for you, mate?"

"No, not at all. He just..." Ray backed away. He hesitated, sunlight catching on fresh tears. "You don't understand. This stupid little shop of mine, it don't make any money. My wife got sick of it and left me last year. Dad's bailed me out a hundred times. He's a good man. I can't even keep a roof over my kids' heads any more. That's why he's taking them in. I'm nothing but a fuck-up, Gid. The only one who ever thought different was Gwylim. My Kitto."

***

Gideon made his way through the crowd and along the shady creekside lane that led out of the village. It was time he was getting back to Lee, but he needed to think. His head was aching and spinning a bit, and his thoughts were ugly in direct contrast to the overflowing gardens on either side of him, the foxgloves springing from their walls and the long-stemmed irises shimmering in the heat like a vision of Van Gogh's. Probably he should have stopped and eaten somewhere. His stomach was tight with unease, though, and once he was clear of the clatter and buzz of the harbour, he could admit to himself that he wasn't yet ready to make the climb back to the cabin.

A deep disappointment seized him. He'd let himself believe that being well again meant he would be the same man as before his injury, capable of all the same things. At the top of the road he'd seen a footpath which seemed to lead back through the clifftop woods, a longer but flatter route which would probably bring him back to the cabin via Kitto's bridge.

The only one who ever thought different was my Kitto. Gideon was sorry as hell for having raised this spectre in Ray's mind. If Lee was right, that had been a terrible thing to do. Gideon recalled his lover's warning with a sinking in his guts. He could easily put himself inside Lee's head now, see his way of thinking. Here was this great slab of a man, John Tregear. Superficially civil, capable of scaring a husky lad like Ray so much that he ran like a frightened dog to do his bidding. Hated so much by his stepson that the boy wouldn't even take his name. And now, at this weird, hot time of year, when Lee would have said the veil between the worlds was thin, bringing in his grandkids underneath his roof, without a mother to guard them.

Yes, ugly thoughts. There weren't enough foxgloves and irises in the world to take away the stench, and Gideon sat down heavily on the top of someone's garden wall. If Kitto was a spirit who had loved his brother Ray, what better time to come back and offer a warning?

Spirit or flesh, Gideon could help with that too. He was high enough up the hill to catch a drifting signal on his mobile, and he dialled the Truro station—not the main line but a desk number, fairly sure that Constable Spargo was on duty today.

She picked up with businesslike flatness, but brightened up right away. "Sergeant Frayne! How are you? I heard you were down the centre the other day to do your tests."

"Yeah, I was." Gideon strove to sound cheerful about it. He could hardly growl at the woman who'd broken his fall onto the

Bodmin cobbles and staunched his wound with her jacket until the ambulance arrived. "No results just yet. I tell you what, Jenny—I'm meant to be on holiday, and I couldn't half use a favour. Can you do me a background check on a guy called John Tregear, resident of Kelyndar village?"

"No bother. Hold on the line if you like. There's only about thirty permanent residents there, so..." Gideon waited, listening to the tapping of keys, the familiar background buzz of a busy squad room. "Yep. Here we go. John Tregear, no priors, but... Hang on. Have you seen this guy?"

"Yep. Talked to him no more than half an hour ago."

"He's got a bloody nerve, then. Did you tell him you were a copper?"

"It came up. He didn't react much. What's he done, Jenny?"

"Nothing as far as we know, but his stepson went missing a couple of years back, and Tregear sidestepped every stage of the inquiry. Failed to turn up to court dates, and by the time the inquest happened, he'd blown out of the country completely, and it looks as if we lost track. I can't believe he's come back to Kelyndar and calmly settled down."

"Want me to unsettle him?"

"I'd better pass this on to DI Cole. I'll get him to ring you—"

The line went dead. It didn't really matter. Gideon knew what Cole would say. *Don't scare him off. He's flighty, and he already knows you're a copper.* Cole would send CID officers down, plainclothes men who could merge into and out of the Golowan crowd.

Very possibly he wouldn't do it in a hurry. Tregear was wanted for questioning, but the Kitto case was an old one, starting to cool off. And Ray was moving his kids in with Tregear today.

If Lee was right about Kitto, what fate had the poor lad met? Gideon had dealt with a couple of child-abuse cases since his promotion. Both of them had made him wish himself busted back to constable in Dark, where everyone knew him so well that they'd ask his permission before so much as docking their children's pocket money. A shudder went through him, ice-cold under the heat-fretted surface of his skin. *Shit, Lee—have I been so wrong?*

If there was even a chance of that, he had to start putting it right. Tempting though it was to go and throw a harness onto Old Penglas right now, he knew he needed backup before tackling the arrest. The point was to give Ray the heads-up, get him to keep the kids at home. He'd think about the complexities of that on his walk back into the village, and he might have plenty of time: to his dismay, his thigh was as stiff and sore as during the first days out of hospital.

His route had brought him up past the house with the statues in the porch. He'd sat down almost opposite to it. This was Tregear's old place, wasn't it? He must have set up home somewhere else. This house looked derelict and dark behind the painted statues.

The old lady must have acquired a third one. Gideon had never noticed before. This one was harder to see, tucked back in the archway to the hall, and she hadn't got around to painting it. A marble youth in his late teens, elegantly posed with one arm over his head, a mass of beautifully rendered curls obscuring his profile...

The odd thing was that he was wearing jeans. Gideon sprang up from the wall, relief and fury exploding. "Kitto!"

Chapter Eight

The statue doubled up laughing. It detached itself from the shadows and made its way out through the porch, tangling en route with the ivy that had grown in through a broken pane. With every step it became more solid and real, picking up colours from the sunshine, until it was standing in the road in front of Gideon, still laughing. A study in bronzed skin and gold. "You little sod," Gideon said. The old village gossips had been right. Kitto was a feckless runaway, and old man Tregear had probably faced so much heat and suspicion that he'd shipped out till it died down. "Do you have any idea how much trouble and heartache you've caused?"

"I'm sorry." Kitto almost sounded it, even if he was still wiping away tears of merriment from his eyes. "Did you really think I was a statue? One of the cold marble dead?"

"You don't want to know what I think you are at the moment, son." Gideon rubbed his brow, where relief had not yet eased a thumping headache. "Right. I know you had some trouble at home, and your step-dad's not the easiest of guys. But I can help you with all that. I can get social services to work with you and find you somewhere safe to live. In the meantime, I want you to put on your damn shirt and come back to the village with me, and show poor Ray Tregear you're alive. You've just about killed him."

Kitto listened. He'd put his head on one side and caught his lower lip in his teeth. "Ray is the only one," he said distantly. "The only one I can come back for."

"Okay. Well, whatever it takes. He's down at the shop now, and he's not mad with you or anything else you might be worried about. Just come with me. I'll deal with your stepfather."

"Would you be more comfortable, Gideon?"

"What?"

"If I put on my damn shirt. You're looking at me."

Gideon fell back a step from him. Had he been, other than eyes up and front? God, he supposed it was possible. Vertigo was tugging at him, colours from Cosmic Ray's fractals dancing round the edges of his mind. He felt a wash of excruciating shame, that anyone but Lee could draw his attention in that way. Was that why Lee had been struggling to foresee their wedding—because Gideon couldn't stop himself from scoping out the teenage talent in a hothouse little village on the edge of the world?

It *was* a hothouse. There was something strange here, something wrong. Cool Bodmin air filled Gideon's lungs, restoring a bright clarity. His natural moor-bred commonsense asserted itself. He was a man. Getting engaged hadn't castrated him any more than it had done Lee, who still cheerfully pointed out the handsome lads who strutted their stuff in Falmouth of a Saturday night. And Kitto, unfortunately for himself, would raise a hard-on in a corpse. "You're an attractive young man," Gideon said quietly. "If you're gay, I can tell you that won't be easy down here for you either, but there's ways I can help you with that too. And I'll tell you one thing right now. Take all that hot seductive stuff, pack it away and keep it for your boyfriend. I'm sure he'll be overjoyed, and..." He shrugged, took the sting out with a wry smile. "It's *definitely* not for me."

"I'll get my shirt." There were tears in Kitto's eyes again, and not of laughter now. "I'll try, anyway. Sometimes I can't, not near here. I think it depends on what I was wearing the last time I was at a place."

"I don't have the least idea what you're on about, but go ahead. Hurry."

"Did you bring me my iPod?"

"Yeah." Gideon dug into his pocket. "As a matter of fact, I did."

"I knew you would. You're such a good man, aren't you? You listen to people. Listen, Gideon. Please—please listen."

Gideon sighed. He wanted to be home with Lee. He didn't need a teenage nutcase on his hands right in the middle of what was meant to be a holiday, but he had to try. Kitto was clearly disturbed. He had taken the iPod from Gideon with careful dexterity, a fingertip touch that avoided direct contact. "All right. I'll listen to anything you need to say. Talk to me."

"No. Listen to this." Kitto had switched on the iPod. As Gideon watched, he unravelled the little ear-bud headphones and extended them, one in each hand. Gideon could hear a tinny beat, some summery generic dance tune from a couple of years back when there'd been a rash of such music in the charts. "Please listen to it."

"Kitto, I think you need help."

"I do. Oh, God, help me. Please listen."

Gideon reached out. Before he could take the headphones from Kitto's grasp—whatever good that would do—his eye was caught by sudden movement in the harbour square below. There was just a wide enough gap in the trees for him to see it clearly, though in weird crystalline miniature, like a toytown scene set out to entertain him or give him a puzzle to solve—Ray Tregear, exiting the shop at high speed. Pausing long enough to lock it up behind him and then setting off at a flat, frantic run for the steps that led up to the cabin. "Oh, hell," Gideon said. "Kitto, come with me or I'm gonna have to leave you. Your brother's heading off to find Lee, and..."

He was talking to empty summer air. He blinked. There was no way the boy could have vanished in that time. The gardens on either side of the lane were hushed and vacant, not a leaf or petal stirring. In the tunnel formed by the overarching trees, there was only drifting light.

Kitto must have gone back to the house. Gideon climbed the cracked steps to the porch. They were thick with moss underfoot, and when he reached the door, he could barely see through the glass for dust and cobwebs. The handle resisted his grasp. The statues stared at him from their eerie painted eyes, and a vast air of undisturbed silence descended upon him, together with a few flakes of plaster from the lintel overhead. There wasn't so much as a glint of sunlight on sea-bleached hair to hint at the boy's existence.

***

Gideon should have been able to catch up with Ray, even on the steep path up the cliff. He could feel the way he once would have done it—vaulting the garden walls to cut the corner, then the long bounding strides he would have taken, devouring ground between himself and his quarry. Ray was fast on the flat by force of sheer momentum, but a steep haul up a hillside ought to slow him to a crawl.

If Gideon could imagine this so clearly, he could bring it about. That was another thing the counsellor had taught him. Of

course back then his goals had been more modest. *Just* envisage
yourself getting to the toilet on your own, Sergeant Frayne. Visualisations,
externalisations. Gideon took a deep breath and projected all his
fear and weakness out onto the pitiful broken-down wall coming
up on his left. It was ugly, useless. Nobody would want such a
thing protecting their garden. He cleared it awkwardly and
mentally demolished it in his wake. He just missed landing in
someone's potato patch. A huge Doberman sprang out of the
shadows, growling in protest. "Good dog," Gideon said sincerely,
the beast's curled lips and exposed fangs motivating his leap over
the next wall and out onto the track.

Perhaps he'd got too good at projecting. Maybe, the universe
being what it was, he'd begun to set up ricochets, equal and
opposite reactions. If he'd hated that wall, with its crumbling
mortar and failure to protect, it seemed to have taken a healthy
dislike to him in its turn, and it was his own structure—bones, not
stones—that was being knocked down piece by piece.

Still he ran on. From time to time he thought he heard Ray up
ahead of him, crashing in the undergrowth like a reintroduced
wild boar, and his hopes lifted. Maybe he should start yelling his
message through the trees. *Your brother's alive. Everything's okay.*

But Gideon didn't have the breath, and he was far from sure.
Some of the blocks being knocked out were foundation stones.
He had just spoken to Kitto. He could still feel the boy's warm
breath on his cheek. And still he wasn't certain that he could look
Ray Tregear in the eye and tell him...

Whatever he would have said, it was too late. He burst into
the clearing. The cabin was in front of him, its timbers shining
serenely in the shade. Lee was sitting with Ray on the front steps.
Ray's face was buried against Lee's thigh. Lee had an arm around
him, and Ray's whole bulk was shaking under the force of his
sobs.

Gideon crashed to a halt in front of them. He propped his hands on his knees. He couldn't get enough breath to speak, and nausea was crawling through him. Sweat chilled in clammy stripes down his belly and spine.

Lee looked up. For the first time since the spirit of old man Fisher had assailed him, his expression was unreadable to Gideon, his eyes cold. "I asked you not to do this."

"Things changed. I had to."

"It took me a lifetime to work out what I could and couldn't say to people. When I thought I knew about their missing person."

"Looks like you worked it out pretty fast this time."

"He came here asking me about his living brother, and all I had to give him was a—" He stopped short at Ray's anguished moan. "I'm sorry, okay, mate? I'd have done anything rather than have to say that to you."

Gideon looked grimly at the grief-stricken man. "I'm sorry too. Because I think you've jumped the gun here, Lee, and—"

"Please don't mess with what you don't understand! I don't get how you've been seeing... the things you've seen, but if it was the other way round—if I'd started turning into a policeman for some unknowable fucking reason—I wouldn't walk into your squad room and ignore everything you told me about how to do it."

Gideon tried to follow this through. Then he got it. Lee was the qualified sergeant here, Gideon the rookie who'd shattered the rules. The analogy only worked so far, though, and Gideon was past his limits. "Point taken," he rasped. "But it isn't that way. I'm a cop, and I think someone's been harmed here at the very least. I need to question Ray and his father, and—"

"Christ, not now!" Lee tightened his arm around Ray. "You've done enough damage. Get out of here. I mean it, Gideon—fuck off."

He might as well have hit Gideon in the face with a pan. Biting back a cry, he turned away.

***

He had to take the downhill route. Gravity was just about his only ally now, and he used it to retrace his steps out of the clearing and onto the track.

He was paid out. He believed what he'd just told Lee, though, and he wasn't about to abandon his duty to the helpless young, even in a village that wasn't his own. He either had to find Kitto again and drag him to Ray's feet, or he had to do something about Old Penglas.

He stumbled over a rock, jarred his damn thigh again, and started to retch dryly with the pain. Or with sunstroke, or with sheer cold shock at Lee's words, but whatever it was, he had to hide. He stumbled as far as he could into the ferny undergrowth and leaned against a tree.

Great. He hadn't eaten since breakfast. That didn't deter his guts from trying to reject everything he'd put in them since last Sunday, and he doubled over, almost scared at the power of the expulsive spasms. Did his overwrought system think it could get rid of memory this way? By the time he was done, he knew that he'd lost enough water to be in a state of dangerous dehydration. *Fucking great.* Add to that the injured leg and his sudden and total exhaustion, and he was in brilliant shape.

A stream was whispering nearby. Once Gideon's ears had stopped popping, the sound of it was sweet to him, a music beyond resistance. He made his way unsteadily a little further into the woods. There it was, thank God, a ribbon of bright water unwinding from the top of the crag. He knelt on a rock by the side of the pool it had formed. First he drank until his throat stopped burning, then he stuck his head under the waterfall. That felt bloody marvellous, so he stripped off his T-shirt, soaked it in the shade-chilled water and pulled it on again. The blessed coldness wrapped around his labouring lungs and his heart, and he fell back onto the rock, stretching out.

There was so much that he had to do—so many broken things to mend. Water trickled out of his hair and touched his brow like gentle fingertips. Above him on the crag, a silver-leafed holly—one of the rare kind that hadn't grown prickles because it never came under attack—cast a deep and soothing shade. Sleep was a good cure for sunstroke. He would just rest here for a short while.

***

Kitto came and tended him. Gideon didn't want him, alive or dead, so he closed his eyes and turned his head away while the boy swore with surprising range and intensity and began to work around him. Something soft had been tucked behind his skull. It smelled so familiar that he wanted to weep. Cupped palms brought water to his mouth. Kitto pleaded with him to drink a little, then ordered him to, adding that he was a stubborn git. The water splashed into his face instead. Another cold dash came straight after, then a none-too-gentle slap—the blow in its turn followed up by an apology, and the passage of a work-roughened palm down his cheek.

Gideon risked a look through his eyelashes. He was fairly sure that Kitto had no calluses from hauling ropes down at Falmouth marina. The light through the holly leaves shifted, and Kitto disappeared like the heat-born apparition he had been. There was only Lee Tyack, kneeling beside him, brow rucked in concern. Gideon opened his eyes. "Lee."

"Jesus, Gid. You wouldn't wake up."

Gideon heard the dark notes. He'd emerged from a five-day coma to find just this anxious face above him, harrowed with sleeplessness and fear. "I'm fine. Where's Ray?"

"I took him back down to the shop. He was still upset, but he had a load of customers waiting, and he said he'd be better off at work."

"What about his dad? Did you see someone who looked like him, only about twice the size?"

"No. Ray's keeping the kids at home tonight, though. He's gonna tell Tregear they're ill. That's what you wanted, isn't it?"

Slowly Gideon sat up. The soft thing under his head turned out to be Lee's cotton hoodie. He'd used his Cosmic Ray's T-shirt as a sponge to wipe Gideon's face, and was naked from the waist up. "How the hell did you know about those kids?"

"Is there any point in telling you?" Lee slapped his mobile phone off his palm. "Screw this godforsaken place anyway. I couldn't get a signal to call help for you."

"I don't need it. Yes, there's a point telling me." Gideon frowned. "What do you even mean by that?"

"I mean, will it get chucked onto the pile of stuff you can conveniently ignore if it doesn't fit with your opinion as a copper?"

"For fuck's sake. I am so bloody sorry for what I said to Ray. But am I in the..." Gideon had to pause and steady his voice before he went on. "In the habit of ignoring you?"

Their eyes met. The contact was burning, painful, the restoration of blood to a cramped limb. "No," Lee said angrily. "You never have."

Which is why it hurts so much now. That didn't need to be said: Gideon nodded in acknowledgment. "The kids. Please."

"Ray wouldn't accept it, about Kitto. So he did what people often do—he got out a photograph of him. Photos and video are cruel. Our brains aren't set up to understand how something that looks so alive can be gone."

"And you got a read off the picture?"

"Not that one. But he had a photo of his children in the same wallet. And... I think I'm going nuts. I had a full-on flash right there and then of a room in a house with three beds in it, all fitted out for kids with soft toys, murals on the walls, and... in the dark doorway, a man with a bloody great horse's skull for a head."

"You're not going nuts," Gideon said grimly. "You told Ray what you'd seen?"

"Yep. And from that point he was terrified of me. But he said he wouldn't let it happen—that he'd keep the children at home. So I gather *he* knows what I was talking about, even if I didn't know myself, and... I guess you know too."

"Ray's wife left him. His business is on the rocks. Old man Tregear's been helping him out. I overheard him tell Ray in the shop that he'd got the room ready for the kids—he's taking them in."

"Shit."

"Yeah. So I had Truro run a background check on Tregear, and it turns out he skipped town when Kitto first went missing. And the reason you saw your skull-headed man is that Tregear is Old Penglas—he takes the horse round the village at Golowan."

Lee picked up his soaked T-shirt. He took it to the stream and wrung it out as if he'd have liked to squeeze the fractal into an alternate universe. "Damn you anyway."

He was so beautiful. His olive skin was unflawed. His frame was such a mix of delicacy and toughness that Gideon still lost a breath each time he saw him naked. He was the source of all the pain and joy in Gideon's world. He coughed to clear his throat, but his voice still came out raw. "What am I being damned for now?"

"For being so... honourable. So logical. For doing what you have to do, no matter..."

"How many people I have to run down in the process? I'm always going to do that, Lee—if I think it's a police matter and there's someone alive to protect. Just like you're always gonna do what *you* think is right. We're both going to have to get used to it."

"Great." Lee snapped the T-shirt out, then folded it and came to kneel at Gideon's side. He began to dry him off with it, not much more gently than a bear with a well grown cub. "I couldn't find you. After I'd left Ray, I came back up here and searched and searched."

"I'm sorry. I didn't feel well."

"Why? What was wrong?"

"Touch of sunstroke, that's all." If Lee wanted to forget the termination of their meeting outside the cabin, that was fine with Gideon, who never wanted to think about it again either. Sunstroke would do as a reason. "I threw up like a dog, then came here and drank like a rabid one. Then I just fell asleep. Look, I hardly dare say this to you, but I saw Kitto again. I gave him back his iPod just the way I said I would, and he... made a kind of inept teenage pass at me."

Lee's eyebrows went up. "He did?"

"Yeah. He's just a kid, full of hormones, and I think he does it to disarm people. Which worries me in itself—about his stepfather, I mean, and what might have happened there."

"He physically took the iPod from you?"

"He did. Just the way he physically had his cup of tea up at the cabin and left the mug on the table."

"The mug that wasn't there when I got up, even though mine was where I'd left it."

"Okay. To be fair, he never touched me when I handed the gadget back to him. And he vanished between one blink and the next, far faster than he could have done, and I couldn't find him again. So... I don't know what to think any more." He shook out Lee's hoodie and handed it to him. "But I've got to do something about Old Penglas. Come on."

"You're not well enough."

"I told you, I'm fine. I lost my phone signal to Truro, but I reckon they'll send CID guys down to round up Tregear senior. I want to get down there, make sure he doesn't make another run for it before they arrive."

"Big tough cop," Lee growled. "Not indestructible, though. That *has* sunk in with you, right?"

"I thought I could be again." Out of habit Gideon tried to stop Lee from hoisting him onto his feet, or at least to take enough of his own weight that the effort wouldn't wrench muscles. But Lee was strong. He could cope. "I thought I could be just the same."

"If you mean the same bloody good cop, that's exactly what you are. We got to the same place by different routes, about those kids. And you *didn't* have the psychic flash to help you out. So, come on—how are we gonna lasso Old Penglas?"

"You'll help me?"

"Jesus Christ, Gideon—what else would I do?"

"Okay, okay. He might have gone already. But if not, we just join in with the Golowan crowds and keep him close."

"We'd better get you some dinner first. You must be starved."

Gideon looked them both over. His own T-shirt had dried on him, and Lee had laid his out on a rock and was more or less presentable in his hoodie. That would have to do. "You can buy me a pasty. Come on."

Chapter Nine

In the village, a borderline had been crossed between day and night. The sky over the creek was still saturated with light, but all along the waterfront tar-filled barrels were blazing, casting all the world behind them into orange-stained dusk. Young men and women moved about among the barrels. They were dressed in close-fitting black, carrying long wooden torches. Every now and then one of them would dip an unlit torch-head into the burning tar and raise the brand with a shout. The air was vivid with the scent of pitch.

Gideon and Lee made their way through the crowd beginning to gather on the harbour. They kept near the outside edges, just a couple of tourists come to see the festival. Gideon strove to take an interest, to watch for any sign of John Tregear, but it was tough—his attention was fixed on the man beside him. Lee was like fire and ice. He was either not concealing what happened to him in a crowd or no longer trying to stop it. Gideon felt the weird radar sweep of his perceptions in a pressure like static on his skin. "Does it hurt?"

It was the first time either of them had spoken since they'd left the stream. Lee shivered at the soft-voiced question. "Lady over there in the white jacket has lost her cat, a big black tom called... I can see green carnations, so it's probably Oscar. The guy behind the hot-dog stand is crazy happy—he's off backpacking to Thailand tomorrow. Those are the strongest pulses just here. The lady hurts me, the hot-dog guy not. I wish to hell it would all stop."

Gideon wanted to reach for him. He looked through Lee's eyes at the cat lady, who had a layer of fur on her nice jacket and marks of recent tears on her face, and then at the hot-dog vendor, who was layering mustard with generous last-minute glee. "Will you tell her about the cat?"

"No need. She'll go home tonight and find him waiting on the doorstep."

"Good."

"But it's a future thing, a layer of things that happen next. I'm already drowning in the layer of *now*. I can't shield myself tonight."

They had stopped by the harbour rail. Gideon put out a hand to grasp it, wanting an anchor before he met Lee's gaze. "Why not?"

"You've become so important to me. I have some kind of wavelength link to you. When it's working, I can tap into it even in a crowd like this, and all the noise and static just... fades out."

Gideon didn't need to ask if it was working now. He looked into Lee's face, pain welling up in him. "Let me take you home, then. At least I can get you out of here." *At least I can still do that.*

"No. We need to stay. He's coming, Gid—the horse-headed man in the doorway. Old Penglas."

All Gideon could see were tourists and torch-bearers. The latter were forming up into a column along the narrow street. They had begun to sway and stamp to a music that had entered Gideon's bones before he'd become aware of it—a pulsating drumbeat that came from everywhere and nowhere at once, that seemed to vibrate out of the air. Two thumps then one, two and one. It was the riff to *We Will Rock You* and a million other blood-stirring chants, ancient as the human urge to dance. Here it was ominous and joyful at once, filled with threats and promises. Gideon put an arm around Lee's waist, not caring—insisting to himself that he didn't care—when he met stiff resistance. "It's all about to kick off here. I really think we should... Oh, wait. The CID lads have arrived."

"The ones buying pasties from the Philps' stand, right?"

"Right. Is that because they're really lousy undercover, or..."

"They're fine undercover." Lee squeezed his eyes shut, briefly pressed his palms against his brow. "This is getting worse. Old Penglas is coming. He's here."

The door to Cosmic Ray's flew open. The dancers let out a great roar, and the crowd picked it up as a figure appeared beneath the glittering fractal. John Tregear emerged from the shop, grinning enormously, clutching the skull. He was fantastically dressed in long, billowing skirts, draped over a hoop round his waist. The Kelyndar villagers began to cheer in welcome.

Ray appeared at John's side. He was still pale but he lit up when he saw the crowd. He stepped to the front of the porch, punched the air three times and broke into laughter. "Welcome! Welcome, welcome! Call hail to the Old Penglas, the life and the death of the village!"

The crowd bellowed back in response. Gideon drew Lee closer to the harbour rail. "Ray looks too happy. He did believe you, didn't he? About what you saw, and the kids?"

"Yeah, but..." Lee shook his head as if trying to clear it. "He couldn't hold onto it. He loves his dad, and Tregear never laid a hand on *him.*"

"Only Kitto."

"That's right. And Ray loved Kitto too. He never had a little brother and when John married again, he just adored Dilys's kid. So Ray can't think about this stuff. He knows, but then he makes himself forget, by..." Lee swayed. Alien laughter rattled out of him, and Gideon caught his shoulders and held fast. "Oh, great. He's fallen off his wagon. High as a bloody kite."

"Not on his own herbal remedies, I'd guess."

"Oh, no. Something much better than that."

"And you can feel it?"

"Cheap date, aren't I? You could probably get pissed on my behalf if I was in the right mood."

"And what about his kids? Has he made himself forget about them too?"

"Yes, like so much dust. Or a handful of sand. Or sparks on the wind, blowing out over the creek, or..."

"Lee!"

"Yes, he's forgotten them. Nothing matters any more."

"Right." Gideon straightened up. The CID boys from Truro were too busy cracking beers and looking authentic to notice any signal he might give. "I want you to stay right here. Keep out of people's heads if you can, and don't piggyback off anyone else's buzz. Okay?"

"Spoilsport. Cosmic Ray's head is lovely at the moment. Where are you going?"

"I've got to stop all this. Right now."

Another huge roar went up. Tregear had raised the horse's skull high above his head. He held it there for a long moment, and then with Ray's help, slowly lowered it to conceal his face. The transformation was complete. He took up position at the top of the wooden steps, slowly turning the terrible Penglas visage from side to side. The empty eye sockets swept the villagers, visitors and dancers as if looking for a victim. Then he leapt into the crowd.

The tourists scattered, shrieking and laughing. The impact spread outward in concentric rings until the people near the harbour's edge began to back up. Gideon reached to steady Lee and found himself being propped and shielded instead, Lee a fierce-eyed barricade between him and the jostling bodies. "I really am okay, love."

"No, you're not. Your leg's hurting worse than it did when you first left hospital, and you're scared if you run any more you'll tear your scar tissue and cripple yourself for good."

"When I told you to stay out of people's heads—"

"You meant yours too. But I can't any more, not out of anybody's." Lee spun suddenly to face him. "How can you still call me that?"

Something in his head or something aloud? Gideon couldn't keep track. "What did I call you?"

"Your love. Like I hadn't behaved like a total dick to you up at the cabin. Told you to fuck off, and made you feel like I'd... Oh, God. Hit you in the face with a pan. So bad you went off and threw up."

"I was asking for it. I had a hell of a nerve, telling Ray that Kitto was alive."

"Well, maybe I had a nerve to tell him he was dead. It's so hard sometimes—seeing people light up with hope. Maybe it was just easier for me to snuff it out."

Their eyes locked. The music of the Golowan was rising all around them, the dancers in the crowd beginning to swirl. They were here at the heart of the mystically ordered chaos of Ray's fractal, and the olive branches they had tried to hold out to one another felt like swords. "So much for not fighting," Gideon said hoarsely. "But I still call you *love* because I mean it, and I always will. Now let me go—I've got to try and get to Tregear, or at least tell the Truro lads over there who they're meant to be chasing."

Lee nodded, abruptly businesslike. "Come round the back of the stalls here. There's a bit of a gap, and we'd better move before the harbour rail gives or someone sets themselves on fire. No wonder they banned it for so bloody long in Penzance."

The serpent dance had begun. Old Penglas was at the head of it, in the centre of the harbour square. He was clutching Ray by both wrists, and as Gideon paused on the edge of the crowd to look back, he saw Penglas hoist Ray's hands into the air so that their arms formed an arch. Ray was swaying, his eyes closed. The black-clad torchbearers were forming up into a column, two by two, throwing their brands at the people surging around them, who could catch them or be burned. A few shrieks of genuine fear went up. Then the maelstrom of voices cohered into a chant, deep and demanding: "*An eye! An eye! An eye!*"

Ray and his father were the eye. Lee had told Gideon all kinds of folklorists' theories for this ancient moment of the dance—that *an eye* was a corruption of a Kernowek call to a sun god, that the archway was the womb of the life-and-death goddess through which the crowd would dance into the unknown. The couple at the head of the column plunged through to a triumphant roar from the rest, as if they'd passed an ordeal, and the others began to follow. One after another they threaded the eye, dancing onwards on the far side. Once everyone was through, it would be the turn of the pair at the front to stop and create a new arch.

It was beautiful, and could go on for hours. Gideon slowed up as the crowd bottlenecked ahead of him, wondering why he was in such a hurry: he could hardly lose a giant in a horse's skull, and Tregear clearly had no thoughts of escape, swaying to the beat of the dance, the lord of his domain. And as long as he was there, no harm would come to Ray's children. All Gideon had to do was cross the thirty yards or so that divided him from the group of CID officers and hand over this whole mess to them. Lee was just ahead of him, a sturdy human snowplough. He would get there, and once he was done he would take Lee back to the cabin and...

"Gideon, wait." Lee halted, shielding his eyes from the firelight. "There's something... I don't know what there is. But this is it. He's gonna try to get away."

The serpent dance had stretched from the centre of the square to its perimeter. There was nowhere for it to go but out, and the leaders wound their way into the narrow cliffside track that ran behind Cosmic Ray's. They emerged on the other side, laughing, and the rest followed on, having to drop into single file to get through. Tregear was now at the tail of the serpent, still the most visible target in the world. He went through the passage as quickly as everyone else, and Lee shook his head as he appeared again, still dancing. "No. I must've been wrong."

Gideon seized his arm. "Wait up. That's a hell of a short-arsed Old Penglas they've got there all of a sudden, isn't it?"

The horse's skull came lurching back into the square, borne a lot less steadily than before. The hoop and flowing skirts were missing too, not that anyone seemed to have noticed. When Penglas stumbled and dropped to his knees, the throng around him hoisted him upright and shoved him on his way with a roar of laughter. Again the chant began for the front-runners to stop and make the arch: *an eye! An eye! An eye!* "Bloody hell," Lee said. "They've done a swap."

"Not a very good one, but enough for this mob, I guess. Tregear must have legged it off up the cliff. You stay here."

"No. *You* stay."

"This is police business. Just go tell the CID guys over there, and—"

But Lee had fastened an iron-hard grip on his shoulders, a stark reminder of which of the two of them was best equipped to go running and jumping up rocks. "There's no time. I'll get him back." Lee's eyes blazed. "I'll do anything for you, Gid, up to and including death. Let me make things right."

Chapter Ten

And after that—Lee's passionate declaration, and Gideon's helpless acceptance—the night delivered a perfect anticlimax. Lee darted away, and Gideon, who of course couldn't allow him to undertake a foot-chase on behalf of the Cornwall police force, started off through the crowd to alert the Truro boys himself.

Before he could get even halfway there, they had set down their beers and pulled out hidden radios. Two of them made a dash for the trees behind Cosmic Ray's, and the third ducked back into the car. Gideon tangled with a howling teenage girl whose floaty chiffon top had caught one spark too many and was beginning to catch fire, and by the time he'd patted her back into safety and serenity, everything was over. Lee must have cut off old Tregear's retreat. Still half-tangled in his skirts, Tregear came floundering out of the woods and straight into the arms of officers Pascoe and Bell.

Gideon stopped watching. His work was done now with regard to Old Penglas, and he had only one concern. He stood stock-still in the shifting, heaving crowd until Lee appeared on the slope behind the shop.

They met on the wooden steps, between the monsters and mermaids carved into the pillars. Both sat down wearily. Lee was laughing, out of breath. "Fantastic," he said. "I was gonna be such a hero. But he took one look at me up on the path and turned tail and ran for his life. He's three times my size."

"Yeah, but Ray might have told him what you can do. I don't want you to be a hero. I just want you to..." But Gideon wasn't sure what he was about to ask of him. The world was still in mirror-glass pieces around them, weird and bright as the firelight reflections spinning from the fractal over Ray's door. There was so much they didn't know about each other, so many conflicting necessities. "Just stay with me, all right?"

"Sure you don't want me to try and bring short-arsed Penglas back to his stable?"

"Not much point." In the midst of the crowd, Ray was staggering beneath the weight of his inherited burden. "Even if he and Tregear planned this together—which I doubt—he's winding down. Still, I'd better go and see he's okay."

Ray might have been on his last legs, but the dance went on, the serpent beginning to coil itself round in a tightening spiral. The tempo of the music had changed, resolving from a rock beat to slow, solemn drums. At last Gideon could see the musicians. They emerged from their hiding places around the square, almost hidden behind the discs of their great crowdy-crawn drums. At this signal, the dancers looked around, their shouts cohering into a new chant. Part of it sounded like the name of the village, but the rest was pure old Cornish, and he turned to Lee for a translation. "Any ideas?"

"They're saying *Kelyndar*. No, it's two separate words, the holly and... They want to choose the oak and holly kings."

"Oh, okay. Do I even want to know how they do that?"

The porch creaked behind him. Before he could react, a dark cloth dropped over his eyes. His surging response came too late: his arms had been seized and pinned, and what felt like half a dozen pairs of hands closed on him, gentle but firm, hoisting him upright. "I have 'im!" a triumphant voice rang out by his ear. "I have 'im! Was ever an oak king so fine?"

Not a rhetorical question, apparently. Gideon waited, breathing shallowly, until the answering bellows of *no, never, no* had died down. His heart was jolting painfully up under his throat, and it was only by force of will that he was holding back from knocking his captors off him like flies. "That's nice," he said through gritted teeth, when he thought he would be heard. "But I should tell you right now, I'm *really* not in the mood."

The voice changed—became human and contrite. "Oh, I'm sorry, dude. But you really are perfect. Nobody'll hurt you, and we'll only be a minute with you, I swear."

"Never mind me. If you've laid a hand on my mate—"

"You don't have to worry about him."

Gideon *was* worried. Lee's normal response to a development like this would be unrestrained violence. For a gentle lad, he had zero tolerance where threats to Gideon were concerned. "Lee? Are you all right?"

"I have 'im! I have 'im!" That was a different voice, female and a few yards off. "Was ever a holly king so fine?"

"Oh, no," Gideon said. "You *didn't*."

"I tell you, you don't have to worry about it! Just come along with us now. We'll guide you. We won't let you come to any harm. Here, Jenna, give me that... Look now, all, look now. I crown 'im! I crown 'im!"

Something leafy and soft descended on Gideon's skull, smelling richly of tannin and sap. He drew a breath to demand what the fuck these lunatics were playing at now, but then had all his work cut out to stay balanced as they half-lifted, half-marched him down the steps.

He could have broken free, but only with a huge unseemly struggle. And what would be the point? The oak crown was painless, the brush of the leaves quite pleasant. As long as Lee was safe, he had no serious objections. The blindfold was made out of some kind of velvet. He was being drawn into the crowd, a mass of expectant electricity and warmth, and other than his lack of choice, he was being handled like the royalty he'd suddenly become. Cries of approval shot up like fireworks. *Oh, he's a fine one! So 'andsome—a proper big oak king this year. Not like poor Will'm last time—that were a dandelion king.* Laughter came in waves. Gideon gave up. The less fuss he made, the sooner this would be over.

He was brought to a halt in what he sensed was the centre of the square. That meant the serpent was coiled all around him, all those waiting dancers. The drumming softened to a heartbeat and stopped. Gentle fingers worked at the back of his skull and the blindfold was whisked away.

Lee was standing opposite him. He too had just been unmasked and was blinking in the torchlight. And he also bore a crown.

Gideon jerked forward. He was only being held lightly now and almost crashed to his knees before he caught himself. The holly crown had torn one side of Lee's face open. "Christ!" Gideon gasped—then the shifting light changed, and the blood was only ruby flames. The crown had been made of the leaves without thorns: all except one, which had traced the tiniest scratch on his brow. "Are you all right?"

"Fine," Lee said, smiling uncertainly. "Well done for not killing anyone."

"The night is still young, Your Majesty. Any clues about what's going on?"

"It's summer solstice. The nights get longer after this—in a way it's the start of the winter. I think I might have to slay you."

"Oh, great."

"Well, like you said, the night is still young."

The tight-gathered circle around them shifted and broke apart. Gideon denied himself a shudder of genuine fear. Ray might not have his father's height and presence, but the slow emergence into firelight of the vast horse's skull was a solemn and terrifying vision. Ray was walking carefully, the heavy mask well balanced now, as if he'd become used to it. His arms were held out at his sides. He was clutching two long wooden poles, one of them wrapped round with oak leaves, the other sprigged with holly at each end. "This is the rite of midsummer," he said. For the first time in Gideon's experience of him he sounded clear, perfectly calm and certain. "The people of Kelyndar chose well. Will you take your weapons, O duly sanctified majesties?"

Gideon stepped back. "You have to be kidding."

A ripple of laughter ran through the crowd. Lee too smiled— a bit wanly, Gideon thought, and he'd gone very pale. "It's okay, Gid. It's only ceremonial."

"Terrific—but I still don't know what to do."

"You will. Just listen to Old Penglas."

So Gideon took the oak-covered staff, and watched while Lee accepted and hefted the other. Ray lifted his empty hands, and the last restless mutter from the crowd died away. *"The oak stretches upward and reaches full height,"* he declared, his voice made potent and sonorous by the mask, *"to catch in his branches the start of the night."*

All right. Gideon could guess what he was meant to do for this part. Besides, all the people gathered across from him were showing him, either from pity or as part of the ritual. Obediently he took the staff, laid it across his palms and held it as high as he could. He wished he was a bit less sweat-stained—that his T-shirt hadn't shrunk to expose his midriff—but nobody seemed to mind. A murmur of satisfaction arose, and somebody ventured a wolf-whistle.

He felt like an idiot, and then all of a sudden he didn't. The sky was rich with sapphire light through the leaves of the oak. It was lovely, but the earth was hot and tired, growing impatient for the change. As if he had been waiting for Gideon's realisation, Penglas dipped his great skull and went on, *"But here in our village the dark will not come—we must have release from the rule of the sun."*

He wanted Gideon to lower the staff. The people were showing him, but now he understood. He kept it balanced across his palms, and held it out towards Lee. It was the holly king's part now.

Lee took two strides towards him. They were face to face, and nothing could be hidden any more. Lee met his eyes, and their bond—worn to cobwebs by the world and their own expectations—leapt between them, crackling, renewed and hot as blood. Lee drew a half-drowned breath. Penglas and the crowd were signalling again, and Lee raised the holly staff as they were bidding him, not as the oak king had done but straight up, as a weapon. "Sweetheart," he said to Gideon, softly so that no-one else would hear. "I think we have to get this part just right."

Gideon had no doubts or fears left at all. "We will."

"The holly descends on his brother the oak," Ray cried, his voice for the first time unsteady, *"and hews down his might at one merciful stroke!"*

Lee took the cue without hesitation. His eyes never left Gideon's, and Gideon grasped the oak staff just hard enough to meet and resist him, just lightly enough that when the blow fell he would break cleanly, and in the right place, and survive. He nodded. "Yes. Now."

Lee cracked the holly staff down. The gesture might have been ceremonial but the force of it wasn't: Gideon grunted and braced, and the oak stave snapped at an exact centre point between his hands. A howl of joy leapt skyward from the onlookers. Gideon dropped the broken halves, useless to him now, and put out his hand to receive the holly staff Lee was holding out to him. "Come here. Come here."

Lee strode to meet him. Gideon didn't know if this fitted in with the rite and didn't care: seized him with all his strength and held on, knocking the holly crown off his head. Old Penglas seemed delighted. Someone had handed him the broken halves of the oak and he was gesturing skywards with them, bellowing over the racket of the crowd. *"We welcome with joy the dark half of the year! From Litha to Yuletide, let our path be clear!"*

It was over. The whirling forces left the circle as suddenly as they'd arrived. Penglas and the kings had done their job and were no longer the focus of the night. People began to turn away, shuffling to a new dance beat. Old Penglas, nothing but a worn-out beast, turned his heavy head from side to side in confusion, then dropped to his knees. "Shit," he croaked. "Get this thing off me. I can't breathe."

Gideon and Lee disentangled. Even to help a dying man, Gideon couldn't have released his lover willingly, and Lee grabbed a last hungry kiss as he eased back. Then they ran to Ray's side. Lee eased him forward and pushed his head down. "It fastens up the back here," he said, grabbing the end of a lace. "Hold still, Ray. Gid, can you steady the skull while I just... There you go."

Gently Gideon drew the mask away. As soon as it was clear of his face, Ray sat down hard on the tarmac, gasping for breath. "Oh, thank God," he said. "My dad said... He said he were going to hand Penglas over to me tonight. I didn't know he'd do it like that. He jammed it on my head behind the shop and told me to keep dancing."

Gideon exchanged a glance with Lee. There was scarcely any need. He knew without looking that whatever he had to do or say,

Lee would back him. He crouched beside Ray and put a hand on his shoulder. "Is that all he said to you—about what he meant to do tonight?"

"Yes." Ray rubbed sweat off his face. "But I knew he meant to try and get away. And I didn't try to stop him. I didn't know how. And... I wanted him gone, Gideon! Did he go?"

"Not very far. He was arrested."

"Shit!"

"I know. I'm sorry. But he really needs to tell the police what he knows about your brother, and... you'll need to talk to them too."

Lee brushed his fingertips over Gideon's skull, then lifted off the crown he'd forgotten he was wearing. "Not tonight, though, eh?"

The deal worked two ways. It would never be easy. Gideon might want to pick up the whole of Kelyndar village, turn it upside down and shake it until Kitto or the truth about him dropped out of its pockets, but he could only reach individuals, and Lee could warn him better than anyone which ones were likely to break under his hands. "No, not tonight. What have you done to yourself, Ray? Because I've got to tell you, falling off that wagon will lose you your children even faster than if your old man was a threat to them."

"I know!" Ray jolted forward, hiding his face in his hands. "I know. I just couldn't stand to think about any of it. Give me the mask, will you, Gideon? Give me old Penglas back. I could hide inside of him, and I knew just what to say."

"Never mind that. You need to go home and sleep this off. Where are your kids tonight?"

"Home and safe, like I promised to Lee. I don't want to lose them. I can't. Please give me the mask."

He was reaching out blindly. Lee picked up the skull and set it carefully over his lap. "There you go. Does it help you to talk to us?"

"Yes, but..." Ray stroked the grim old nose bone, tucked his fingers into the empty sockets. "But not about me. Penglas has something to say to both of you. About why he chose you for the oak and holly kings. Your light and your darkness is all bound up in one another, you see. You can't escape it, and nor should you so desire. But the pains of love are the pains of life, and a lifelong love it will be." He cut off abruptly, dropping back into his ordinary skin, coughing. "Oh, my head hurts. What was I on about?"

"I've no idea," Lee said, flickering a smile at Gideon. "Looks like Kelyndar might have a pretty good new Old Penglas, though."

"I can't. I'm too short. He always said that I would never do."

"I really don't think size matters, as long as you can carry the skull. And stay out of jail, like Gideon says. Come on. We'll help you home."

***

They dropped Ray off outside a tiny terraced cottage by the creek. Gideon didn't know how Ray had managed to squeeze his own bulk in there, let alone accommodate three children, and didn't wonder that old man Tregear's house with the beautiful nursery room had looked good. The neighbour who'd been minding the kids came out to meet them, her expression wry, as if this was far from the first time she'd seen Ray half-carried home by his mates. Reverently Gideon set down Old Penglas on the kitchen table, and then he and Lee retreated, trying not to bang heads and elbows on the door's narrow frame.

They walked slowly up the lane that led out of the village. Gideon was certain that he wouldn't make it up the steep crag path again today, and they could find the easier clifftop route from here.

The racket of the Golowan died away behind them. Lee had brought down a deep, sweet night in his guise of holly king, but summer lingered in the glow of white clematis on a trellis and the scent of arum lilies, intense as a song, as if their trumpet throats had found a voice. They walked for a while side by side. Then their hands fumbled for their familiar clasp, and that was good enough for a while, until Gideon tugged his grip free and wrapped his arm round Lee's waist. Lee reciprocated fiercely, and that made walking awkward, so they came to a halt just beyond the derelict Tregear house. The painted statues were alone tonight, the shadows in the archway behind them just shadows. "I'm beginning to wonder," Lee said, kissing the side of Gideon's neck, "if that's why I've been having trouble seeing our wedding. I mean, I still want the fuss, and the stupid little place-cards that people ignore when they go to sit down, but I almost feel as if..."

"Like Cosmic Ray just did it for us?"

Lee chuckled, a delicious vibration against Gideon's mouth as they kissed. "Yeah. Handfasted by a lunatic on Kelyndar harbour. Oh, Gid, forgive me for the bad things I said to you."

"Forgiven hours ago. Forgive *me* for not listening. For rushing in."

"Yes. Yes. We *are* gonna fight, though, love, aren't we?"

"Yes. That wasn't a great rule to try and have. Too much strain on any relationship. What are we gonna do, though? It kills both of us."

"Well..." Lee cupped his hand around Gideon's nape, scratching at the short hair in the spine-melting rhythm he loved. "We'll have to find a way of doing it so that it doesn't. A kind way. We could just try... talking to each other, I suppose. Even about the bad stuff."

Gideon nodded. They'd had little practice at that. Their enemies had lain outside of them, their time together so intense that few internal conflicts had seen light of day. "Sounds pretty radical, but okay. Of course the good part about waiving the no-fight rule..."

"We get the make-up sex back. Don't think I hadn't factored that in."

"Good lad. Considering how bad a fight we had, I reckon we owe each other a pretty big one."

"Right here?"

Gideon gave it serious thought. Not exactly here, of course—he could see a nice old couple making their supper in a kitchen over the way, and if they looked out they'd be able to see him—but like Robert Frost's, the woods were lovely, dark and deep behind the old Tregear house. "I could lean you up against a tree," he said slowly, speculatively, and Lee's eyes kindled. "I could take you off into the woods, unzip that hoodie, peel you out of your jeans, and—"

"Gideon, listen."

He fell silent. All he could hear was the rustle of breeze-stirred leaves and the song of a distant thrush. "What's wrong?"

"Listen. Oh God, please listen."

Their route had brought Gideon back to the place where he'd last stood with Kitto. To the exact spot, and those had been Kitto's last words to him. *Listen. Please listen.* "What are you hearing, Lee?"

"I don't know." Lee raised his hands to shield his ears. "Everything. I can hear everything. Every thought of everybody in this place. It blocks signals from the outside, but down here it amplifies them." He broke out of Gideon's embrace and staggered back. "No. No. I want it to stop. Gideon... Oh God, please listen!"

His nose was bleeding. A fear seized Gideon more sharply than any manifestation from the spirit world. Lee was supposed to get checkups every six months, to eliminate a brain tumour from the list of reasons why he might hear voices and see the unseen. "Sweetheart, did you go for your last scan?"

"I forgot. I was making wedding plans." He doubled over, and a sob tore from him. "I can't do this any more. Gideon, help!"

Gideon caught him. "I will," he vowed—meaning it absolutely, whether help entailed a dash to Trelowarren ICU or a fistfight. He'd shouted out a challenge to Lee's monsters before. On instinct he wanted to do it again: to roar at them *fuck off and leave him alone*, drown them out with his own strength and power.

But Kitto had begged him to listen, not to speak. He drew Lee's head down onto his shoulder, wrapped a protective arm around it to try and block out the noise. He rocked him in silence, and Lee's fractured breathing eased, his hands clamping tight in Gideon's shirt. Even the birdsong stopped.

And there it was at last. The sound that had been tugging at the edges of his perception ever since their arrival outside the strange old house—tinny and small, a mechanical beat and a wisp of a melody from two summers ago. Something about the beautiful boys, and sunshine, and how at the end of the season they would all be blown away like autumn leaves, forever gone. There at the side of the road lay Kitto's iPod, the little in-ear headphones crying out their plaintive song. "Lee," Gideon said. "Kitto's in there. We have to get into that house."

Chapter Eleven

The porch door was still locked. Lee had darted up the steps to try it. He stepped aside. "Break it down, Gid. Please."

To wrap a cloth round his fist and smash a pane would be a better option. Best of all would be to wait, to find a fellow officer—somebody who *was* on duty, and weirdly for this world's-edge place the air was full of distant sirens—and do this by the book. A discarded iPod was hardly probable cause.

But there was no time. Gideon didn't need Lee to tell him that, although the message was stark in his lover's bloodstained face and wide, blank eyes. So he did what nature and his training had prepared him for so well—took a big step back, got his balance and aimed one powerful kick at the door.

He hit the lock square on and the door flew wide with a minimum of noise, and not so much as a crack to its dusty stained-glass panes. The action ripped out one more brick from the slow-built foundation of his healing, but that didn't matter now. He could rest when Kitto was found, and Gideon was certain that he would be, that he was here in this house, hiding out or playing some kind of enigmatic game. Terrified, maybe, by hearing the door kicked in. Gideon followed Lee past the painted statues and under the arch. "Kitto," he called. "It's all right, mate. It's Gideon and Lee from up at the cabin. Are you in here?"

He couldn't be. The house wasn't just derelict. It was gutted, as if a restoration project had been started on it and abandoned. The ground floor was one huge space, the dividing walls knocked away. Gideon could see through to the old kitchen windows in the back, and there was nowhere to hide. Even the staircase had been taken out, the upper floor a gaping hole above them. He turned to Lee. "I don't get this. I was sure. So were you."

"Still am," Lee informed him brusquely, dabbing the sleeve of his hoodie at his nose. "Still am. He's in the shadow lands, the place between. That's why we've both been seeing him."

"The place between?" Automatically Gideon began trying to interpret. "Is that a... Do you think there's a hidden floor, some kind of space between the walls?"

"Between life and death. He's trapped and hanging on. He's too bright and strong to die, but he doesn't know he's living any more—he's too far gone. He sends his spirit out through the tunnel."

"The tunnel?" Gideon thought frantically. Lee knew folklore, the deep ancient reasons why people did what they did in the old Cornish towns, but Gideon knew their streets. Their back roads and crack dens, bricks and mortar, ancient traditions of a practical sort. The creek towns had always been a useful back door. He took Lee's shoulders. "This tunnel. The one with the angels and the light at the end of it, or..."

"No. Granite."

"Okay. Ten to one this was a smugglers' house. I thought we were on solid rock here, but there must be a basement."

"Where? There's no access. And I can't see the start of the tunnel, where it exits out, even if we did have time..." He swallowed and coughed, his breath rasping. "I'm losing him."

"Right. Well, I'm not bloody well losing *you*. I want you to put him aside, okay? Forget him."

"What? I can't."

"You can. Because I need the deckhand right now, not the psychic. I need you to help me lift floorboards."

Lee gaped at him. There was a touch of outrage in his expression, and just for a second, Gideon wanted to laugh. Then Lee twisted out of his grasp, scanning the room. "The edge of one of them's up a bit over there. Come on."

The tough new boards were just an overlay. The ones beneath them hadn't been removed, as if someone had suddenly needed to make the floor secure, innocuous to any passing glance from outside. Lee grabbed hold of the upraised edge and prised it higher, pulling till his fingertips bled, just far enough for Gideon to get a grip. "Shift," Gideon commanded, crouching over the board and bracing. He jerked upward and the whole length of pine tore free, splinters flying. "That's it. Now the next one. He's barely bothered to nail 'em down."

One board and the next. A cold and dreadful scent began to drift up from the old wood below. Gideon knew it. Not decomposition, not quite. What happened to human bodies left alive to rot, the smell of an old lady's house he'd once had to break into when the neighbours had finally noticed the junk mail sticking out of her letterbox. She hadn't survived. He swore sharply and took out the next board with a furious effort, Lee diving in immediately to start work on the next.

And the old wood gave way. Lee had rested his knee on one exposed rafter. It was rotten as the rest and shattered with a sickly crack beneath him. He was there by Gideon's side at one instant, and then in a flicker of darkness—sudden and absolute as Kitto's disappearance from the lane—he was gone. A body thudded onto hard-packed earth, and there was silence.

Love and instinct almost took Gideon down too. He almost threw out every future chance for both of them right there, almost took his leap into the dark and buried them both alive in a cellar with no mobile signal, in a house no-one but the death's-head horse had entered for years. His hands clenched in spasm on the broken rafter, and he clawed his way back. Love and instinct were all very well. He had to use his bloody brain too. "Lee! Lee, can you hear me?"

Nothing. He checked his mobile on the remotest off-chance, but all was shut down and silent in midsummer Kelyndar...

Except for those sirens. They were getting closer. Maybe someone had set the village ablaze with an overturned tar barrel. So much the better—police, fire and ambulance would suit Gideon just fine right now. "Hang on, love," he shouted. "If you're hurt, just lie still. I'm going to get help for you."

"Hadn't you better ask me about that, Sergeant Frayne?"

He whipped round. The archway into the porch contained a strange shape. Until that moment Gideon had barely noticed the slow loss of light: the sky's glow and the rising quarter moon had been sufficient to let him see. Now true night had come, and Old Penglas was at the door.

For an instant Gideon thought he had made a dreadful mistake, the worst of his career, worse than his belief in Joe Kemp's innocence. Then the figure mounted the two steps that had been making it look small and became not Ray but old man Tregear. He wasn't wearing the skull. That had been a product of the shadows. His unmasked face was more dreadful still, fixed in the genial grin that had greeted Gideon in the shop. His eyes were empty. His shirt was daubed in glistening patches of black, the moonlight's rendition of scarlet.

Gideon's shock dropped away. He rose onto the balls of his feet, knucklebones clicking as his fists clenched. There were wounded men below him, and somewhere off in the lanes of this godforsaken village... "What have you done to my colleagues, Tregear?"

The huge shoulders shook in silent laughter. "It's a sign of age, isn't it, when the coppers start looking young? Those three broke like kindergarten babes. Easier than Kitto."

"John Tregear, my duty means I've got to give you one chance. I'm arresting you on suspicion of abducting your stepson. You can give yourself up to me now, or—"

Tregear roared. He put his head down, squared his shoulders and unleashed the sound like a bull impaled on a spike. In Gideon's experience the noisy ones fell hardest.

Not this time. This was the last-second prelude to a charge. He leapt aside, barely missing the gaping hole in the floor. Tregear missed it too. He was limber and fast as well as strong, and he spun round on Gideon with murder in his eyes. "Nobody touches my home, copper! I do what I like with what's mine."

He collided with Gideon hard. The impact knocked them back against the wall, shaking down plaster dust. Gideon blocked the disabling blow to his gut, the arm Tregear was trying to slam across his windpipe. Just for a second Gideon held off. But for once his opponent was not only taller and half his weight again: from somewhere the bastard had learned unarmed combat, and there was no reason on God's earth why Gideon shouldn't hit him like a six-ton truck.

He had his work cut out. His injured leg gave under him and he shoved off on it anyway, pain ripping through him unnoticed. He returned Tregear's blow to the stomach, careful to pull it, avoid liver and spleen and just knock the wind from him. Tregear doubled up with more drama than the punch had deserved. Gideon read him a fraction too late—reached to jerk his arm up his back and instead left the ground in a neat shoulder throw.

He landed on the floorboards with a thump. Something like laughter rattled him. Tregear was good. In another world—a world where Lee wasn't buried in darkness below him, in terrible ongoing silence—Gideon would have enjoyed this. He surged to his feet. His blood was up now, and if he'd finally done for his leg, the rest of him was in great working order. "Come on then, you bastard," he growled, beckoning. "Come and get me."

Tregear dived. This time Gideon intercepted the move and used it, dropping him like a dislodged granite monolith. They rolled together, Tregear knocking Gideon's skull a good one off the boards, Gideon returning the favour with a flying roundhouse punch that finally wiped the grin off that savage mouth. He followed up his advantage and scrambled on top, pinning Tregear flat on his face beneath him. "Is Kitto down there?" he roared, getting the arm-lock he'd been looking for. "Is he still alive?"

"He shouldn't be, the little..." Tregear spat blood. "The little shit. Little runt, with his hair and his blue eyes. Not a proper lad at all. Not like my Ray."

"Christ, man—what did you do?"

"I never laid a hand on Ray." With a huge effort that must have torn muscles in the arm Gideon was holding, Tregear flipped over onto his back. Gideon got ready to thump him into submission, but Tregear grabbed his wrist. "Listen," he said. "He was begging for it, that brat of Dilys's. Hugging me and stroking me, batting his eyelashes like a girl. He had it coming."

Gideon ripped his hand free. A shimmering blue light was rising in the room, blue and then flickering red, but he couldn't take it in through the fog of rage in his head. He seized Tregear's shoulders: thumped them down. "I don't care if he... came into your bedroom and danced naked in the moonlight, you fucker!" Another thump. "He was a minor child. Kids practise these things on adults, and kids who feel threatened do it to placate 'em, to save their poor little lives." He grabbed the front of Tregear's shirt, hauled him up until they were nose to nose. Tregear's last mask dissolved into wild-eyed terror. "And what do the adults do? They *let* them. They don't bloody take it as an invitation to the waltz." Gideon shook him like a rat. "They keep... hands... *off!*"

"Gideon!"

Suddenly there were hands on him. They were gentle but strong, and Gideon recognised their grip from a moment of bloodstained dissolution on the Bodmin cobbles five months ago. He jerked his head up. There was PC Jenny Spargo, clutching his shoulders to haul him back. Beyond her were other faces he recognised. The room was full of radio crackle and sweeping torch beams, and outside in the lane, every emergency vehicle Gideon could have prayed for was grinding to a halt. "Jenny! What happened to the lads from CID?"

"This bastard assaulted them. Left one of 'em for dead. The others are okay—they got a call through and chased Tregear here. Brought the paramedics and the rest of us after them."

That was why Gideon now had resources. He let Tregear go, losing interest in him as soon as he saw Jenny and two burly colleagues snapping out handcuffs and immobilising him. "I need a ladder!" he yelled. "Lee's down in the basement—Gwylim Kitto too. I need a torch, and..." He stumbled to the edge of John Tregear's black abyss. He knelt beside the paramedic who was already shining a torch beam down into the hole. What the light picked out made him want to curl up and howl. Lee lay motionless on the cellar floor. The side of his face Gideon could see was covered in blood. He must have crawled a few feet and collapsed. He was clutching the outflung hand of a skeletal boy: nothing but a collection of bones and blond curls. Naked but for a pair of cut-off denim shorts...

As Gideon watched, the skeleton's chest rose and fell in a shallow inhalation. Gideon couldn't see that Lee was breathing at all. "I need a ladder," he repeated brokenly. "And someone... go to the village, the last house by the creek. Someone go and fetch Cosmic Ray."

***

The ambulance crew had hung up powerful portable lanterns in the cellar of the old Tregear house, and its confines looked harmless. Just a space now, not the maw of the beast. The lights and movement made it almost festive despite its slime-damped granite walls and merciless old flags. The sole mark of its purpose was the door: narrow, closely fitted, made of heavy black wood and lacking any means of opening from the inside. Gideon imagined the boy waking up in the dark. The surge of his heart in hope when he found the door's edges, and the drop back into lonely despair as his palms skimmed the featureless wood.

Gideon was five miles out. It was easier to float here dreaming of other people's terror than to face his own. There was plenty to keep him going. Cosmic Ray was terrified. The medics had hitched up the skeletal boy to drips and wires and every benign thing that would coax the flicker of life in him, and then they had lifted him carefully into Ray's arms. Ray was rocking him, tears streaming down his face. And yet Ray's terror had an ending. Kitto's eyes were open. Whenever they focussed on his brother, a smile would light his wasted face. He had looked at Gideon once, without recognition, but he was responding.

"Mr Tyack? Mr Tyack, can you hear me?"

Gideon hadn't been allowed to lift or hold Lee. He hadn't asked: he knew better. Lee had a gaping head wound, bleeding so profusely that one of the paramedics was taking time out to stitch it up. She hadn't bothered with a local anaesthetic. Lee hadn't flinched or flickered an eyelid when the needle drove into his skin. The other medic was kneeling behind his head, holding an oxygen mask into place. From time to time he patted Lee's cheek with one gloved hand. "Mr Tyack? Come on, now. We need you to wake up."

A head injury could mean anything. The bleeding was the tip of the iceberg. Gideon knelt very still, barely breathing. The medics wouldn't even attempt to move Lee until they knew more, although a stretcher was being lowered from the floor above for Kitto. "Sergeant Frayne?" the female paramedic asked, tying off her needlework. "You're his friend, aren't you?"

Friend. Boyfriend. Lover, fiancé, husband. All the things that Lee had been to Gideon, everything he might have been, rattled through Gideon's head. He had learned so conscientiously to use the right words. Now he couldn't speak at all. He nodded.

Perhaps the paramedic understood all the significance of the word *friend.* Maybe that was what everything boiled down to anyway. "Then you need to speak to him," she said. "It's all right. You can take his hand."

"I was afraid to."

"We can't find any broken bones. His pupils are responsive. He just won't come round for us."

Oh, Lee. Please do it for me. Gideon swallowed a hot metallic pain in his throat. Just yesterday that would have been enough— the thought, the silent plea. He didn't know how or when, but slowly over the months his mind had touched Lee's, invisible tendrils meshing between them. Gideon, without a psychic bone in his body, had learned to speak wordlessly into his lover's mind. Never anything coherent or spectacular. Random things sometimes, just Lee turning round from the kitchen counter at home, one eyebrow on the rise, reaching for the teabags instead of the coffee he'd been about to make. A smile of conspiracy at a boring party when it was time to go home.

All gone now. The link was destroyed, and so Gideon leaned over him, picked up his chilly hand and held it tight. "Lee, my love. For God's sake wake up."

Lee twitched hard, a whole-body spasm that made both paramedics grab him in readiness to deal with a seizure. But he only drew a deep, long breath and let it go. A smile touched his mouth, sweeter to Gideon even than Kitto's to the brother who had come down to lift him out of hell, and he opened his eyes. "Gideon?"

"Right here."

"I can't see."

There were strengths inside Gideon he never knew he possessed until events threw him back on them. The cry of panic never even made it out of his lungs. Instead he said, with perfect calm, "Now, you just listen. You've banged your head. These things can be temporary, or..." He looked to the medic, who was nodding, shining a light into the wide green and silver. "Or psychosomatic. Don't be scared."

Realisation dawned in Lee's face. His grasp tightened round Gideon's, and he sat up, too fast for the medics to restrain him. "Not like that!" He threw his arms around Gideon's neck. "Not like that. It's okay."

Now Gideon could let the panic have sway. He buried his face against Lee's neck. "Thank God."

"I just mean... I can't see anything but you. All the visions, all the shadows, the reflections... All the stuff I see around everyone everywhere—it's gone."

"It'll come back. You'll be okay."

Lee eased back a little. Not far: he kept his grip on Gideon's shoulders. "You don't understand." Nor did the paramedics. In a minute Gideon was going to have to explain that this kind of talk was normal for their patient, not signs of an imminent stroke. "You don't understand at all. I feel like I did... when I was six years old, before Morris Hawke ever came near me." He smiled, a sudden brilliant flash. "I feel so *quiet.*"

"It's a good thing?" Gideon hardly needed to ask, not with that bright gaze on him, taking him in hungrily, as if seeing him without interference for the first time. "You're okay?"

"I'm bloody beautiful. Gid, don't you get it—this is why I couldn't see our wedding. There was nothing in my head—no visions of the future, nothing—beyond this point at all."

Gideon kissed him. He tasted of antiseptic and blood. Gingerly Gideon turned his face to examine the stitches running from his temple to halfway down his cheek. "Well," he said. "This will look bloody lovely in our photos, won't it?"

Chapter Twelve

Gideon and Lee tied their knot in mid-July, barely three weeks after the Kelyndar Golowan night. Their rush to the Falmouth registration office was partly sheer joy in knocking aside every obstacle and getting the job done, and partly practicality: Lee had been hired to help refit a millionaire's yacht and wouldn't have an hour to call his own from August to the end of the summer, and as for Gideon...

Gideon was being transferred, to his absolute astonishment, from his uniformed sergeant's role to the Truro CID. Old Penglas had used an alias while he'd been on the run, and if John Tregear had no record, the creature he'd turned into during his months of anonymity and freedom had ensured he wouldn't see the outside of a prison for over a decade. He'd been a spectacular catch for Gideon, who'd not only found the Kitto boy but brought his target down singlehanded, after Tregear had put three officers into hospital. Inspector Cole had been well pleased. The results of Gideon's fitness test had been waiting on his return to the flat— he'd passed, and in fact all had turned out as Lee had predicted, except that Gideon's last dance with Old Penglas had undone months of physio and healing, and probably he would always have a weakness there.

He hadn't minded as much as he once would have. The first weeks of his CID induction would be classroom-based anyway, and he'd barely begun to get his head around the excitement and honour of plainclothes investigative work. It meant a chance to nip growing monsters like Joe Kemp, like Morris Hawke and John Tregear in their bud, not just clear up in their wake. And in practical terms, the salary bump meant that Lee had been able to ditch his stage and TV work without sinking their financial ship.

The induction course was set to begin in two weeks' time, and that, together with the millionaire yacht-owner's schedule, had sent all Lee's plans flying out the window in a whirlwind of personalised napkins and seating plans. They'd simply notified Falmouth of their intentions, and hired the nice pub next door for a catered wedding breakfast, and here they were on the brightest of seaside mornings, a cool breeze making the trees around the car park dance.

They'd had to drive up the hill to find a space: it looked as though they'd had full turn-out on their last-minute barrage of invitations, and the registration-office car park was packed. Everyone was early, too, in hopes of a ringside seat. Well, they could wait. Certain traditions should be observed, and with no bride involved, the grooms could be a bit late if they chose. The little back-street car park was shady, and as an ex-beat copper, Gideon knew it had no CCTV. "I'm glad," Lee said softly, unbuttoning Gideon's beautiful pale-grey shirt, "we decided against the vintage hire car now. I'd have worried about the upholstery."

No need for concerns about that in Gideon's old Vauxhall. The cancellation of the fancy car and driver had been a mutual decision, a compulsion they'd both felt to get here under their own steam after all that they'd been through. "Me too. Might've been a bit more room in the back seat, though."

"Yeah, but imagine having to..." Lee paused and shivered as Gideon lifted his jacket off his shoulders and reverently folded it onto the parcel shelf. "Imagine having to skid a Rolls Royce down Bodmin high street because you'd forgotten my ring and left it in the bloody shop."

"Well, forgive *me* for being a bit distracted. I only thought you'd drowned in a flash-flood, that's all." Gideon gave his own jacket—also neatly peeled off and folded—a nervous pat to make sure the box was there. "I was so sure you'd love it. Now I'm scared you won't. Do you want to have a look?"

"Isn't it bad luck for me to see the ring before the wedding?"

"I don't know. If anything, I think you're not meant to see *me*."

Lee surveyed Gideon, half undressed, cock rising irrepressibly in the open front of his trousers. "Oops."

They opened the box between them, brow to brow in the Vauxhall's cramped seat. Scents of hot vinyl rose up around them, blending with special-occasion aftershave and sex. Lee prised up the little velvet lid. He stopped laughing: caught his breath. "Oh my *God*, Gideon."

Gideon was glad he'd seen it for the first time in sunlight. The platinum blazed, the inset agates shining like a moon-fretted sea. Maybe it conveyed some shadow of Gideon's feelings to Lee, some fraction of his perception of his beauty. "Is it okay?"

Silence. Then a raw gulp and inhalation. "Uh-oh," Gideon said, his own voice unsteady. "Time for the extra man-size Kleenex already?"

"Afraid so. Take it back, quick. I want to put it on forever right now. Yours is in Zeke's safe hands. I wasn't sure you'd like it, but now... now I am. It's solid and made of pure gold. You serious about those tissues?"

"Mm-hm," Gideon said happily, snatching a kiss. "Shoved a packet under the seat in case of emergencies today. I hope your uncle Jago won't be freaking out that I've still got the jewellery."

"With Jago, we'll be really, really lucky if he's remembered to turn up at all, let alone what he's meant to be doing. Slip it to him thirty seconds before he needs it. And get that tissue-box open, fast."

"Are you okay?"

"Yes, but I'm so bloody horny I'm going to die if you don't sort me out right here. And these pristine dove-grey trousers you insisted on us wearing are gonna show every mark."

Gideon pushed him back against the door. Their sex-life had gone onto a kind of shocked hold on their return from Kelyndar, as the dust settled and they both had tried to adjust to the new way things were. Gideon had missed their exchanges, but he'd also learned the sweetness and poignancy of long entangled nights, the arts of intimacy and waiting. The trail of a fingertip down Lee's scarred cheek, the brush of lip to lip... Oh, he'd have waited forever, but if Lee was back in the game, that was absolutely fine with him. "Let me have you, then."

He jerked him off strongly, short straightforward strokes wrapped round a handful of the tissues. Lee clung to him, bucking up to meet his touch. His breath came shallow and fast against Gideon's neck. He was fighting to keep it quiet, even though the Vauxhall must have been bouncing on her springs. "It's all right," Gideon gasped as his muffled sounds became frantic. "Everything's gonna be okay. I promise, I promise." The words tore from him fiercely, a vow more intense than any he was about to make in the Falmouth ceremony room. Lee's belief shot out to meet it. He let go one unstoppable cry, thrust up wildly and came, a pent-up flash that soaked the tissues through, challenging

Gideon's deftest efforts to mop him up in time. "Oh, Gid, I love you. What do you do to me? Just with your beautiful hand..."

"Looks like you can do for me with less than that. Just listening to you—"

He didn't get any further. Lee, more flexible, built on a smaller scale and uninjured, had ideas of his own for containing bodily fluids. He writhed out of Gideon's embrace, bore him back and dived down. His mouth closed hot and tight around Gideon's shaft. Gideon threw back his head, banging it off the window— glad of the pain, which let him hold off and enjoy Lee's assault— the powerful grip on his thigh, the deep-throating dip of that silver-starred skull—for a grand total of twenty seconds. No more. He seized the collar of Lee's shirt and climaxed, red pulses bursting behind his eyes at the desperate rush and release of it. Yes, it had been a long three weeks: Lee swallowed and swallowed again, burst out laughing and grabbed another handful of the man-size. "Bloody hell, handsome," he commented, dazedly sitting up. "We both needed that, didn't we?"

***

They tidied one another as best they could, standing outside the car in the sunny salt breeze. It was quarter to eleven—time to go, even allowing for their bridal prerogative. They'd settled for plain grey suits, their shirts and waistcoats in a lighter shade, a touch of colour in blue-green silk ties. Gideon clumsily fastened Lee's, then stood still while Lee returned the favour. "I should've thought about... What are they called? Corsages?"

"That's what our imaginary brides would wear. We should have... Oh, God, I nearly forgot."

Lee dived back into the car. To Gideon's astonishment he produced from the glove compartment two perfect roses, just beginning to open, their creamy petals tinged with pink. "You old romantic!"

"Not really. They're just from our garden in Bodmin."

"Well, you can't beat a Bodmin rose."

Lee looked him over in satisfaction. "No, you certainly can't. Here, yours goes through this buttonhole—I even remembered the silver foil and damp cotton wool to keep them fresh—and you pop mine through here. Gideon, I need to talk to you."

Gideon waited in apprehension and relief. There wasn't time, but their guests and the Falmouth registrar would have to be patient. Talking was something Lee hadn't done over the last three weeks, not in his old, frank way. Gideon knew without being told that he'd been dealing with the newfound silence in his head. He'd been like a kid with a new toy, or maybe a kid without one, deprived of internet and iPad and knocked back to a seventies childhood, left to go and play in the fields. He'd been living on the surface, watching TV football, dragging Gideon down to Falmouth marina to check out the new boats. He'd cancelled a week of stage shows he'd been booked to do in Launceston, asked Jack and Anna to postpone their next run of *Spirits of Cornwall*. Gideon had been happy to play into all that, to let him rest and settle into whatever he was going to be. Carefully Gideon tucked the rose into place. "Talk."

"I was so upset that you could see Kitto. I know I made that... abundantly clear at the time, but I want you to understand why. We've been through some stuff together, you and me—you heard things in my flat and at Rachel's house, and down at Drift in the fogou, but you were with me for all those times. I thought I was somehow channelling things to you. The idea that you'd seen and spoken to a ghost—in broad daylight, all on your own..."

"But Kitto wasn't a ghost."

"Even so. Think about it. You were able to pick up and interact with the spiritual projection of a dying boy. Just you."

This was why they hadn't talked, not about this aspect of their day and night in Kelyndar. Lee had flushed up and was shaking. Gideon took hold of his hands. "Is it a bad thing, love?"

"I thought it was. Despite everything you'd seen, to me you were still so... I don't even know how to put this. Earthy. Solid. *Grounded*, I suppose, and I was afraid I was changing that, opening you up to all the stuff I could do. I value what I am—what I was, anyway—but the idea of inflicting it all on someone else... No, it hurts too much, and when I thought about you becoming prey to that kind of pain, I..."

"You went into shock. You panicked. I was there, remember?"

"Yes." Lee nodded gratefully. "And partly it was just selfish. I loved that you'd been my rock. I think in a way I loved the very fact that you *couldn't* see things, that you were... I don't even know how to put this without insulting you."

Gideon smiled. He took Lee's face between his hands. "My lovely man. This is too weird a vow for me to make to the registrar, so I'll say it now. If you need me to be your big impercipient lump of a copper for ever and ever amen, that's exactly what I'll be."

"But you can't choose, Gid! I think you've got massive latent gifts—like mine, only better. You weren't shocked or panicked once you knew what Kitto was. You just quietly got on and investigated Tregear. You can deal just fine with it, can't you—my spirit world?"

"I don't feel it the way you do." Gideon stroked Lee's cheek. "It doesn't hurt me. You know, when I met you last Halloween, you swore to me there *was* no spirit world. That we just hold on to and echo back aspects of the people we've loved."

"Christ, I never believed that. I'd seen things by the age of eight that proved that couldn't be true."

"The only way you could cope with it, though."

"Yes. Why do you see so much, Gid? Why do you see straight through me?"

Some tourists were scrambling out of a minibus across the car park: Gideon gave them a look which informed them how very little interest they should take in two smartly dressed men holding on to one another for dear life, crumpling their nice wedding jackets to ruins. "I don't see so much," Gideon told him hoarsely. "I've just always known there's more things in heaven and earth, you know? And weirdly that's because of that bloody awful Methodist upbringing of mine. It's strange how we learn. If I see inexplicable things, hear them, I can process them in that framework—they're never gonna rip me up the way they do you. So you don't have to be afraid." Certainty swept Gideon, a pure wave of conviction. "You don't ever have to be afraid. Now get your arse in gear, gorgeous, or we're gonna miss our slot."

The tourists had moved on. Lee took advantage of the car park's sun-filled vacancy to plant a passionate kiss on Gideon's mouth. "My God. It's you, isn't it? You're gonna be the psychic and the prophet, far better at it than I ever was. I've passed the torch."

"Well, I did hear the Bodmin Beast before I'd ever even met you. And it wasn't Joe Kemp who put those claw marks down my front door." Gideon smoothed Lee's ruffled hair, brushed tears off his cheeks with his thumbs. He gave him one last squeeze and let him go. "I think I'll leave all the clever stuff to you, though, provided..."

"Provided it ever comes back. Hell, we really are going to be late. Where's that poetry book we wanted Lorna Kemp to read from?"

"On the back seat somewhere. You know that kid, though—she'll have learned her lines by heart by now. Probably added an interpretive dance." Gideon took one last glance at himself in the wing mirror. He would do. Everything would do. He was going to have to stop smiling like a fool. Lee was leaning deep into the Vauxhall's untidy back seat, his backside in the nicely cut trousers a beautiful distraction. "What's the matter—is it not there?"

"Yeah, it's here." Lee emerged, the book in one hand, the other gingerly holding a small knitted cap. "But what the bloody hell is this?"

Gideon broke into laughter. "One of Mrs Brown's baby hats. I bought it from her stall in Kelyndar when I was pumping her for information."

"Shameless, you coppers are. Bribery, backhanders..." Lee gave the little object a thoughtful squeeze. "Did you start up a protection racket down there in the market? It's horrible, too. We'll want a much nicer one for our kid when she comes along. Which is going to be..." He went sheet white and fell back against the car. "Which is going to be soon. Oh, Gideon—no."

He didn't need to explain. Gideon had felt the kick and the spark, as if a huge engine had turned over and caught inside his own head. He went to lean beside him. "Back in business, Mystic Meg?"

"Yes. That was just too simple, wasn't it—one knock on the head to start it, another to switch it off."

"Seemed like a good solution to me. And you liked it."

"For a while. Yes. It was empty, but... it was easier. I'm not sure I want it back."

"I know. But what did I just tell you, about not being afraid?"

"You told me..." Lee swallowed, found a smile. "What every living soul on this planet would like to hear from the person they're about to marry."

"Yeah. And in return you tell me what would scare most sane blokes to death. Where's this baby, then?" Gideon glanced around nervously. "Has someone left one for us in the car park?"

"Oh, God knows. Probably a twinkle in some nice surrogate mum's eye ten years into the future. You've seen how this works, Gid. If it is coming back to me, it's probably even more scrambled than before."

"We'd better go and get married all the same—just in case."

Chapter Thirteen

Like Kelyndar, the seaward edge of Falmouth was built into pitching hillsides. Its bright-painted terraces were connected by flights of stone steps, and down the last of these Lee and Gideon ran, brushed by pollen from the elderflowers and valerian that sprang in summer abundance from the old granite walls.

They created a minor sensation. It wasn't intentional: Lee had grabbed Gideon's hand to steady him down the steps and hadn't let go. The town was full of tourists and natives, each with their own opinion on gay marriage. Gideon found that he didn't care about the smiles any more than the glances of scorn. He knew what he preferred, but approval wasn't necessary. He cared that his leg was holding up, that he would be able to walk, tall and strong, up to the registrar's desk. He cared that Lee's hand was wrapped tightly around his. And so they arrived at the foot of the steps across the road from their destination, just as the churches on the sea front began their eleven o'clock chime.

It was absolutely typical of their guests that not one of them had been able to wait where they'd been told. Zeke was making valiant attempts to shoo them back towards the ceremony room, but he might as well have tried to herd cats. Gideon's mother was the first to appear at the top of the steps, barging the glass doors open with her zimmer. Zeke's girlfriend—dressed in a surprisingly racy short frock—was hard on her heels, stopping her before she could take a nosedive. Zeke himself was perfectly beautiful in a suit to match Gideon's and Lee's. Jago, the other best man, had somehow made his outfit look as if he'd ploughed a field in it, and was taking advantage of the chaos to dash round the corner, unlit cigarette in hand.

And to top it all off, here came Sarah Kemp and Lorna with Isolde the collie romping between them. "I'm so sorry!" Sarah shouted, jogging down the steps. "I'm so sorry. I came down in the pickup truck, you see, and I could've sworn I'd left her locked up in the house, but when I looked in my rearview halfway down the A30, there she was in the back." She stumbled to a halt, smiling despite herself. "Oh, don't you two look lovely? I'm not surprised your dog invited herself. But the registrar's assistant's going spare. There's no dogs allowed."

Gideon scratched Isolde's ears. He pulled her away before she could slobber on Lee's jacket. "Crikey. Don't suppose we could pass her off as a guide dog, could we?" He glanced around. "Wait up. I've got an idea. Leave her to me, Sarah. Lee, will you go and see to Ma? She's dying to get her hands on you."

He watched while Lee ran up to greet Mrs Frayne. Gideon had his hands full, but still it was a moment he'd wondered about—the day when the old lady got to receive her third son. To his intense pleasure, that was what she called him—*my third boy*, so loudly that poor Zeke winced in his buttoned-up Methodist skin, then visibly got over himself and came to embrace Lee too.

All this might just work out, especially if Gideon could manage to deal with the dog. There was Darren Prowse, hiding in reception behind his mum and dad while he calculated which of the registrar's grand brass pen-holders to nick. Not the obvious choice of wedding guests, the Prowse clan, but in this case it had just seemed easier to invite Maleficent to the feast and have done. Gideon put his fingers to his lips and whistled sharply. Darren jumped with admirable guilt and shot out to do the village copper's bidding. "Morning, Darren," Gideon greeted him politely. "Fiver in it for you, if you'll take this dog for a nice walk while I get hitched." Darren's eyes gleamed, but Gideon knew his man, and dug in his pocket for two pound coins and a fifty. "You get the rest when you bring my dog back alive. Deal?"

"Deal," Darren growled, taking hold of Isolde's lead. "You drive a hard bargain, Constable."

"Sergeant, if you don't mind. Now bugger off."

Darren trotted away, the dog bouncing delightedly at his side. They would both enjoy the wedding more from the perspective of the seafront park, and if anyone could keep the boy out of mischief, it was Isolde. Maybe she *was* a guide dog of a kind. Despite her ordeal, Lorna Kemp still roamed fearlessly on Bodmin Moor.

Just for a second Gideon wished he had Isolde back, to guide him into the next great adventure of his life. Zeke had managed to cajole and threaten almost everyone back into reception. Two official-looking ladies were standing by the doors, and the steps suddenly seemed high, Gideon's sense of undeserving enormous. Jago came creeping back from round the corner, and Zeke collected him with a look, pointing at Gideon.

Jago approached hesitantly. He and Gideon had learned to get on well after their unpromising beginning, and Gideon could never feel anything but love for that Tyack face. "I think I'm supposed to bring you in," Jago said, tugging his jacket straight.

"I think you are."

"Bit nervous now, then?"

"Just a bit. Oh—I've got to give you this." Gideon took out the box containing Lee's ring, which Jago pocketed, frowning anxiously. "It's okay. You just hand it to the registrar when she asks."

"All right." Jago held out his arm with grave, old-fashioned courtesy. "You come along with me, then, and we'll see if we can't both get through this alive."

***

Something had jammed in the system. The official ladies had now taken up posts outside the ceremony-room doors, and were gesturing to everyone to wait. Various scenarios flashed across Gideon's mind. The previous bride—or maybe the groom—overcome by the sense of the occasion, having to be fanned and revived. Accidents, medical or biological, affecting the carpets or chair upholstery... Lee struggled to him through the crowd, putting an end to these speculations. "Look who came, Gid!"

The reception was lined with little sofas. Perched uncomfortably on one of these was Ray Tregear. He had his arm around the shoulders of a fragile, blond-haired boy.

Kitto clearly had no idea who Lee and Gideon were, or why he'd been brought to their wedding. He was watching everything around him with the same guarded interest and vague, sweet smile. He seemed more akin to Ray's three children, who clustered protectively around him as Lee and Gideon approached. Ray stood up, beaming. "I'm sorry. I had to bring the kids. It's school holidays, but they'll be good as gold."

Gideon shook his hand. "It's fine. We wanted you all to come. How have things been?"

"Better, much better. We've all moved into the flat above the shop. We're cramped, but we can make ends meet like that, and Kitto's helping me out. Does a bit of packing work down at the oyster farm now he's well enough."

"How's he been doing?"

"Not too bad. He's talking a bit now—aren't you, sunbeam?—to his counsellors and his doctor and people like that." Ray gave the blond curls an affectionate ruffle, then drew Gideon a step or two away. Lee had quietly taken up his vacated seat on the sofa by Kitto's side. "I never got to tell you properly what we owe to you and Lee, Gideon. He'd have rotted down there. The doctor said one more day, and he wouldn't have made it."

"He looks much better. He's filling out."

"My dad kept him down there for nearly a month. He was drinking the water that leaked in through the walls. I tell you, Gideon, he did it all for me. He ran off to the south of France to get away from the old man, and he was there for two years, almost. He was doing all right, just travelling round with some mates, picking fruit and working in factories. Then one of his friends from Kelyndar came back from a visit home and told him..." Ray paused, giving his dreadlock ponytail a savage twist. "Told him about all *my* problems, how I was struggling. Planning to move my kids in with my dad. So he travelled back to warn me."

His cheerful face had sagged with guilt and grief. "This wasn't your fault, Ray," Gideon said softly. He was watching Lee and Kitto, who were facing one another silently on the sofa now. "You couldn't have known."

"In so many ways it *was* my fault. I've got a counsellor now too, and she don't hesitate to tell me, if I hadn't been off my face half the time, I'd have seen what was going on from the very beginning. I'd have known what a brute the old man was, even if he never had hurt me. The trouble was... Kitto was like your Lee, you know? He could see things nobody else could. He could look into people's hearts. And my dad knew that, and there was no way he could risk my Kitto coming home. He caught him up in the woods—right on the bridge by your cabin—and he dragged him down through the old smuggling tunnel into the basement of the old house, and he locked him up there to die."

"Hush, Ray," Lee said softly. Gideon and Ray turned to look at him. Kitto had taken Lee's hand, and was sitting with his eyes closed, tears beginning to track down his cheeks. "Don't worry," Lee told Ray. "He's all right—just letting some of it come back to him. But he doesn't think it's proper conversation for a wedding."

The doors to the ceremony room flew open. The short corridor that led to it suddenly tripled in length to Gideon, who couldn't repress a gasp. Lee let go of Kitto's hand and came to stand beside him, close enough for Gideon to feel his warmth. "How are you doing, sergeant?"

"About to make a run for it. Say something to stop me."

Lee went on his toes and whispered. "I'll fuck you in your wedding suit the second I get you home."

That would do. Gideon grinned, aware that he'd blushed bright red and was probably clashing with his rose. Everyone around them—family, friends, the odd waif and stray they couldn't remember inviting—was on their feet, obeying the registrar's gesticulated orders that they get themselves into place right now. Jago and Zeke were already in position, one on each side of the flower-laden desk. "Bloody hell. The whole room's full of flowers. Who did that?"

"Your lovely mum. She said she never had flowers at her wedding, so she wanted to give them to us."

A lifetime of flowers deferred. Gideon's throat tightened. He grabbed Lee's hand, hard enough to make him grunt in pain and squeeze back harder. "This is it, isn't it?"

"This is it. The big one. Don't you dare start crying now."

They set off together down the corridor. The toilets were unromantically situated halfway along it. That was what you got for getting married in a cheap public office, and Gideon wouldn't have noticed—he wasn't really seeing anything now—if the door to the ladies' room hadn't suddenly edged open, revealing a tearstained female face. There was something devastatingly familiar about it, but before he could work out what, it disappeared again. The door slammed tight. Lee came to a halt. The registrar—behind her desk and waiting now—cleared her throat with an ominous crackle, but Lee had set like concrete. "Bloody hell, Gid. That was my sister!"

They turned as one. They apologised in unison to a startled woman on her way out of the ladies', and Gideon held the door for Lee to dodge inside. The room was empty apart from a slender dark-haired girl, huddled up and sobbing in a chair in the corner. Lee crouched in front of her. "Elowen! I thought you couldn't come."

"I didn't think I could." She heaved a choking breath, whipped Lee's beautifully folded handkerchief out of his breast pocket and copiously blew her nose. "But I couldn't miss my brother getting married. I jumped on a plane last night and... here I am."

"Here you are. And I'm so pleased to see you. But what on earth's the matter?"

"Oh, you know me! I always cry at weddings."

"Yeah, but this one hasn't started yet. What happened about your job? You were over in Spain for the interviews, weren't you?"

Elowen sank her face into her hands. Gideon pulled out his own handkerchief and passed it down. "Would you like me to get you a drink, Elowen?" he asked. "I saw they were putting out the champagne in reception. I can snag you a nice glass of that."

She sprang to her feet. Gideon gasped and laughed as she threw her arms around him. She smelled like Lee, only perfumed and with an indefinable hormonal tang that made his instincts flare. "Ah, he's been texting me for months about you," she sobbed. "About how good you are, and how handsome and kind and you always know what to do. But I can't have any champagne. And I'd have bloody loved one, too."

This seemed to finish her off. She let Gideon go and sank back into the pink velvet chair. Lee put his arms around her. "Elowen, sweetheart—for God's sake tell me what's wrong. Didn't you get the job?"

"I did! And I want it more than anything ever in my life. But... do you remember the guy I was seeing, the French archaeology prof? He's lovely. I love him, but I don't want to stay with him. And I couldn't face an abortion, Lee—I just couldn't do it, and anyway now it's too late. And I can't take up this job offer. Not with a baby on my hands. I just don't know what to do."

She lapsed into desolate silence. And Gideon met Lee's astonished gaze over the top of her bowed head.

Book V

Guardians
of the Haunted Moor

Harper Fox

A FoxTales Publication

Prologue—Winter Solstice, 2014

Gideon wouldn't have noticed the date, except that the Falmouth skies were already dark when he left the police building at four o'clock. Surely the days couldn't get any shorter. He'd driven down here this morning in the pitch-black too.

It was enough to depress a man who didn't have the world at his feet and a cherry on top. He glanced at his mobile. There was the date—21st December, the doorway, the depth of winter and the beginning of the return of the light—and there was the cherry, a text from Lee. He confined himself to one a day when Gideon was on duty, but it was always a good one, something he'd noticed about the places or people around him that would make Gideon laugh or shake his head in wonder. The clouds were heavy with sleet, not like this time last year when bright stars had shone over strange events in the quiet streets beyond the bay.

The wind moaned around the police station car park. Some joker had found flashing blue Christmas lights to hang above the doorway. Flecks of ice stung Gideon's neck, and he got into the Rover. Briefly he was distracted by the sight of the trainees and new constables spilling out of the building. What did it say about him, if the policemen were starting to look young to him? He chuckled, then pulled down the rearview to check that his gravitas and his sergeant's cap were in place. The shortest day had been a long one, teaching this latest crop, and he didn't want to lose his advantage over them now.

Yes, he had the world at his feet. As worlds went, it wasn't massive, but within its limits—from Bodmin to the far west coast, sunny days at Drift farmhouse and firelit evenings at home in Dark village—Gideon had everything. Six months of married life under his belt, only two weeks more of physio and teaching days like the one he'd just endured before he'd be passed fit for full active duty again, his recovery complete. He had a mother, a brother, a small but functional version of the family he'd missed out on as a child.

He had a baby on the way. Gideon opened his text hurriedly, suddenly afraid that his daily cherry might be news of Elowen, so pregnant now that she could barely waddle across the farmhouse kitchen to fetch her pickled gherkins from the fridge.

I'm at Roselands, visiting your mum, Lee's message read. *I know she's coming to us for Christmas, but I felt as if I should. Meet you there if you get out in time. I'll buy you dinner at Sam's.*

Sam's would be nice, though it was Gideon's turn to buy. They made a pilgrimage there every time business brought both of them to Falmouth, in memory of their first proper date. Doing so without incident was always a luxury. Gideon shivered, wondering if the restaurant's decorations this year would include the tinsel fish. A deeper unease touched him. Everyone who knew Lee well paid attention when he did something because he felt he should. The reasons would appear soon enough.

Gideon started the Rover and put her into gear. He'd only had about a year of feeling like a well-loved, loving son, but he didn't think he could bear to lose Ma Frayne, Methodist minister's wife and sudden, unexpected proponent of gay rights.

He set the fear aside. Lee would have spoken to him directly about any premonitions of that nature. Lee's gifts were in full play after his concussion and encounter with Gwylim Kitto, but they had come back under his control, and he was only your average incredibly talented local clairvoyant once more, running his stage shows and finishing up his popular TV series *Spirits in the Stones* so that he could concentrate on...

Gideon pulled his attention back to the present. It wouldn't look good for Sergeant Frayne to rear-end a citizen with the police truck. Whenever he thought too hard about the next few months, the change about to shake their lives to the foundation, the reason why his own job had become doubly important and Lee's was going on hold, he became barely competent to walk a straight line, let alone drive. He braked in time and pulled out of the junction into the rainy night.

***

The difference time and circumstance could make to the outsides of buildings! Last solstice, when Gideon had stood out here in the snow, Roselands had loomed above him like a cliff, its ordinary, pleasant Edwardian facade blocking the moonlight. His father had been immured here, imprisoned still more deeply in dementia, threatening to Gideon still as childhood's memories echoed. His mother had been almost a stranger to him. Since then Lee Tyack had overhauled his life, and the house was just a building, familiar now from countless visits, friendly because his mother was happy and well treated there.

He exchanged greetings with Mrs Harle the manager, and jogged down the corridor to the visitors' lounge. Manners dictated that he take off his cap, but the old lady liked to see him in full uniform, especially if her friends were about. Their children might have promising and responsible careers too, but none of them wore it on their sleeve like Gideon. She sat up, beaming, as he entered the room. "Here he is. Have you had a hard day, dear?"

"No, Ma. Just teaching the kiddies." He didn't like to disappoint her, and wondered if he should make up a burglary and a car chase or two. All that would be part of his routine again soon enough, though, and he settled for planting a kiss on her upturned face. "How's things?"

"Lovely. Your Lee's been making us a nice long visit."

Yes. There he was, in an upright chair by the table, clearly just as pleased with the uniform as Mrs Frayne, but for his own sweet reasons. Shadows of weariness dispersed as he stood up to accept Gideon's embrace, the unhidden exchange of a married couple. The residents of Roselands had got over it long ago, and Mrs Frayne soon brought any new ones up to speed by introducing Lee to them, loudly, as "my son's *husband*." There was nobody around to scandalise today, however, except...

Except the pastor. Gideon blinked, keeping hold of Lee's shoulders. "Hello, Dad," he said uncertainly. "It's, um.... It's nice to see you down here."

"He insisted on coming down. He wanted to see you and Lee."

Mrs Frayne was in the habit of speaking for him. In keeping with her nature, she often made him sound far more benevolent than he had ever been. Gideon looked to Lee for confirmation. His beautiful west-coast lad was all about the silver part of his spectrum today, a winter-beach pallor under his skin, his eyes full of strange lights. Lee nodded. "Yeah, he got his carer to help him downstairs. He's been here all afternoon."

No wonder Lee looked tired, more grey visible at his temples than usual. Pastor Frayne normally kept to his room. Ever since his mind had begun to vacate his body, his physical reality had become little more than a cipher, hard to notice. Today he was here. A presence, heavy and brooding, inhabited his gaunt frame, his stony, hawk-like face. It had a strange attraction, and Gideon went to stand in front of him. "Everything all right, Dad? Would you like me to fetch Ezekiel?"

He wondered how he'd have felt if his father had nodded, commanded him with all his old authority to summon the elder son. But the pastor had said his farewells a year ago, on a long dark night just like this one, and he remained silent, staring through Gideon and past the wall behind him. Gideon gave Lee a querying glance. "Wasn't it this time last year..."

"That he last spoke. Yes. I thought about Zeke too, but he's not answering his phone."

"Okay." Gideon took a seat at the table by Lee's side. He gave his ma a reassuring grin, and looked at the scatter of carrier bags around her chair. "Looks like my other half managed to do a bit of shopping as well as visiting the in-laws. Unless *you've* been ransacking the baby-clothes stores, Ma."

"Oh, no," she said comfortably, smoothing out a tiny T-shirt on her lap. "Lee's just been showing me all the lovely things he bought. All different colours, even though you know you're getting a girl. It's good that you're not..." She paused, and Gideon waited, not daring to meet Lee's sidelong glance. Her pronouncements were good as gold. "Not stereotyping her gender."

Gideon bit his lip. This kid was going to be Cornwall's new generation, for sure, with her two gay dads and a right-on zealot for a grandma. "We'll be sure not to do that."

"I can't keep saying *her*, though, Gideon. She's due any day now. Haven't you decided on a name?"

They had. They'd been planning on telling the old lady next time they saw her, so Gideon drew a breath. But Lee laid a silencing hand to his wrist. "Hang on a second, Gid. There's one more thing I was meaning to show Mrs Frayne. Saving the best for last, you know?"

Gideon was far from sure. Lee's other purchases came from the various boho-chic little businesses that dotted Falmouth's main street. The bag he was opening now was marked *Prowse Prints*, an outfit Gideon's local colleagues busted regularly for creating fake ID and passports. "Not sure you should be shopping there, mate. Supporting crime, and all that."

"You're a fine one to talk. They're only still open because you thought Daz Prowse would be better off working for his uncle than safecracking with the Bodmin burglary brigade."

"There is that. Did Jem Prowse say how he was doing?"

"Oh, yes. He nicked the cartridges out of the printers and sold them on eBay the first afternoon he was there. Jem had to fire him."

"Oh, dear."

"Still, he managed to get this little number run off for us. What do you think?"

Gideon spread out the romper suit Lee handed him and examined it critically. It was made out of a fabric that looked ready to catch light if you so much as looked at it, and would never, if he could help it, touch his daughter's skin. Then he got why this had been the final flourish in Lee's fashion parade, and nodded solemnly. "It's lovely. Tamsyn Elizabeth Tyack-Frayne—don't know how they managed to fit all that on such a little thing."

Mrs Frayne sat up sharply in her chair, almost upsetting her teacup. "Elizabeth? That's *my* name, Gideon."

"I know, Ma."

"You're giving your baby one of *my* names?"

"Don't mind, do you? A great big cumbersome Kernowek-English name, to go with her huge wardrobe and the five hundred books she already owns." Gideon went to sit on the arm of the old lady's chair. He passed her a handkerchief and patted her shoulder. Lee was beaming broadly. "I am right, aren't I?" Gideon asked him. "We are just expecting one baby—not the half dozen all this would seem to imply?"

"Just one. A very little one, too."

"You'd never think it to see the state of our flat, Ma. My library's gone. All the things I was going to do in there! Study for my inspectorate, write my memoirs..."

"All you've done in there so far is read old copies of *Auto Express.*"

"The cars I could've had, Ma! Now I have to drive Lee's clapped-out Escort forever, just because I have to keep Princess Tamsyn Elizabeth in bibs and nappies, and—"

"Shut up," Lee interrupted him amiably, lobbing the awful romper suit at him to catch. "Don't listen to him, Mrs Frayne. He wouldn't rest until we'd cleared every book of mine as well as his out of his so-called library, so he could strip it down and paint what he thinks look like ducklings and kittens all over it. Poor kid's gonna be traumatised for life, with those hawks and panthers glaring down at her."

"Oh, dear," the old lady gasped, caught between laughter and sobs, waving the handkerchief for mercy. "I think I'd better come and have a look at your arrangements, boys. I *have* done this before."

"We were hoping you might."

"How is Elowen? I saw her a fortnight ago when your uncle Jago brought her over for a visit, but things change so fast at this stage."

"She's fine. Ready to pop any minute, she thinks, though the docs are still saying New Year."

"Well, a woman knows best. My doctor thought you were twins, Gideon, you were so late and so big. But I knew it was just my fine, stalwart son on the way. And when you were born, you..."

"Please, Ma." Gideon waved her gently to silence. "Lee doesn't need to hear *all* my infant prodigies."

"What do you think we've been talking about this afternoon? Besides, you'll be doing the same thing to Tamsyn Elizabeth in a few years' time."

Gideon tried to imagine the years. It was difficult, with his little bird still in the bush, still an abstract baby despite all his efforts for her in the nursery and his visits to Elowen since she'd returned from France three months before. Glancing across, he saw Lee struggling with the concept too—not just the adoption, but the school days, the thousands of changes and shifting realities of bringing up Lee's niece as their own child. He went back to sit beside him, reaching out a hand. Lee took it, returning his grip fiercely. Between them they bridged the gap. "That's right," Lee said firmly. "I've got a special book I'm gonna write all her embarrassing anecdotes in, complete with photographic evidence." His mobile beeped. "Excuse me a second." He read the incoming text with just the slightest increase of his sea-bleached pallor, then looked up. "That's Michel. His plane got in on time. He reckons he'll be at Drift in an hour or so."

"Michel?" Mrs Frayne echoed nervously. "Why is he coming?"

Gideon called up a cheerful sergeant's smile. Both Lee and his mother looked as though they could use it. "Because he's a decent bloke, despite his propensity for knocking up his students. He feels responsible, and he wants to make sure that Elowen's okay."

"But if she's not due until New Year..."

"He's got some time off. He's just over on a visit." Other than his belief in Michel's decency, based on the handful of meetings they'd had since last June, Gideon didn't know what was tearing the French archaeologist away from his latest excavation. "He and Elowen are bound to have things to talk about. She's taking up her job on his team as soon as she can after the baby's born."

An odd silence descended on the room. The gas fire clicked and rustled in its imitation hearth. The residents' lift thumped in the distance, and then these sounds also seemed to suspend themselves. Lee raised his head suddenly. "What time is it, Gid?"

"The time? Er…" Gideon checked his watch. "Ten past five. Why? You getting hungry?"

"No. It isn't that." He drew in a deep, soft inhalation. "Mrs Frayne," he said distantly, "can you be brave?"

The old lady turned to him. She met his eyes, and her expression of bemusement firmed up into a resolution Gideon had only seen a few times in his life before, when her overbearing husband had pushed her gentle nature past its limits. "Very seldom," she said, "but yes, if I have to be. What do you need to tell me, dear?"

"It's the pastor. I'm afraid he's dead."

Gideon almost cracked into laughter. The pastor was sitting bolt upright in his chair in the corner, unmoved by talk of grandchildren or the arrival by night of decent, responsible biological fathers. Lee hadn't even looked in the old man's direction. His focus was on Mrs Frayne, his expression so gentle that Gideon could have died himself for love of him. Instead he went over and laid two fingertips to the artery at his father's wrinkled neck. "Fuck," he said, mercifully too softly for Mrs Frayne to catch.

All the rooms at Roselands were amply provided with emergency cords. They were large and obvious, their handles made of neon-bright plastic. It still took Gideon a nightmare ten seconds to locate one and pull it, the ice of shock slowing his limbs. He darted back to the pastor's side—loosened his collar, tipped his head back, made another, more searching check at his carotid. He was more concerned for his mother, whose frailty would scarcely withstand this loss, dropped like a thunderbolt into her tea-time peace...

He need not have worried. Lee had her. He was kneeling in front of her, holding her hands and all her attention. Gideon knew from experience how that grip could block out the world. Lee would offer no false comfort, deny nothing. He simply parted the waters, like the pier on a strong granite bridge, and protected the fragile human souls around him until they'd found their further shore. "It's all right," he said. "You'll be all right."

"Yes. It seems a dreadful thing, though, that he should just have... slipped away like that."

"He had no pain. It was time."

"You know that, don't you? You *know*."

The lounge door banged open. Mrs Harle appeared, flanked by two assistants, and allowed herself one brief shriek of dismay before snapping on her professional skin. "Oh, dear," she observed, running to dislodge Gideon from beside his father's chair. "Pastor Frayne... They all have to leave us sometime, but we thought he'd be with us for longer than this. Oh, Elizabeth, my love, what a dreadful shock..."

Gideon yielded the field to her. The doctor would be on his way, and he knew from his own years of experience that nothing more could be done. The old man had made his exit swiftly but absolutely. Gideon backed up, trying not to shudder at the slack mouth, the vacated features. He'd dealt with dozens of bodies. It shouldn't be worse just because it was flesh of his own. He was a copper, for God's sake...

"Yeah, right. Human, too."

He gasped in relief as Lee caught him. There would never be another grip like that, another warmth. "What?"

"Human first, copper a very close second. I've got you, sweetheart."

A death in the family, and my husband here to face it with me. Gideon was still getting his head around the differences between his old life and this new one. Half-heartedly he resisted. "Stop mind-reading me. Take care of Ma."

"Mrs Harle's checking her over. Come out of everyone's way and sit down."

Gideon did as he was told. His heart and lungs seemed to have drifted off towards the artexed ceiling and he fixed his gaze on Lee, a source of gravity he could borrow until the earth began to weigh him down again. "Sorry. We weren't even close."

"Take a deep breath with me. One, two..."

"For God's sake, you big New Age yoga freak—"

"Just do it. One, two, three..."

Helplessly Gideon inhaled, through his nose the way the freak had taught him, and after retaining the breath for five seconds, let it go through his mouth, watching Lee mirror and guide him. In, and hold, and out...

"That's the lad. Couple more and you'll be ready for anything. In again—one, two..."

Lee's smile of approval faded. His focus shifted from Gideon to a point at once far beyond Roseland's walls and deep inside. His mouth opened a little—a look of astonishment Gideon had seen when he'd bashed himself on the thumbnail with a hammer and not yet found the breath to start swearing. "Lee? What's up?"

"I don't know. I... absolutely do not know." He took hold of the edge of the table. "A pain of some kind, like an indigestion cramp but a billion times worse." He shook himself. "Sorry. Great timing, eh? Shouldn't've had that lunchtime pasty from Joe's."

"You all right now?"

"Yeah. It was only there for a second, then... Oh, *Christ!*"

He doubled up. Gideon forgot his own troubles and sprang to his feet. His mobile was ringing, and by some weird coincidence so was Lee's, but both would have to wait—Lee had flushed as bright a fever-pink as he'd been pale before, and he was clinging to the table for grim death. Gideon felt his damp brow. "Bloody hell. What's the matter, love? Food poisoning?"

"Must be. Never felt a pain like it."

"Stomach?"

"Not exactly. Lower, like..." He cut himself off with a grinding moan that made the care workers and Mrs Harle look up from their duties in alarm. "Oh, Gid, it feels like my guts are ripping out, or..." He caught his breath. His colour deepened as he noticed everyone's attention. "Sorry. Sorry. It's gone."

Gideon hadn't worked out yet how to set his new mobile handset so the ringtone wouldn't get louder and louder when ignored. He picked up distractedly, listened for twenty seconds to his elder brother's voice, distorted as it was almost beyond his recognition by excitement. Ezekiel—of late months *Zeke*, childhood's name and some childhood's affection restored— never got excited. Never let a phone line ring and ring. "Okay," Gideon said, when he found out why. "We'll be there."

Lee was staring at him. "What?"

Gideon's ma couldn't see him from this angle. He allowed the huge grin to blaze up, inappropriate as champagne and fireworks in this room of death. "Oh, mate. I know you pick up on people's feelings, but do yourself a favour and don't let it happen this time."

"Oh, my God. Elowen?"

"They just rushed her into Trelowarren maternity ward. She couldn't get hold of either of us, so she phoned Ezekiel."

"Seriously?" Lee straightened up, his smile answering Gideon's, releasing another burst of firecracker excitement across the hidden sky. "Poor Zeke—he'll be having a litter of his own."

"Just as long as *you* don't."

"What—you think that pain was..."

"A contraction, not a pasty? Only you can know for sure. But like I say, you might want to try and block it."

"You're not kidding." Lee gave a low whistle and laid a hand to his stomach. "How do they stand it?"

"They're stronger than we are." Gideon turned to his mother, who was pushing up out of her armchair, scenting new developments. "Aren't you, Ma?"

"Oh, yes," she said solemnly, evading her carer's grasp. "Very much stronger. We have to be. Why?"

"Elowen's gone into labour."

"Oh. Oh, my dear boys." She lit up like a Christmas tree, dead husband or no dead husband. "Gideon, is your car outside?"

"Yes, but—"

"Stop *fussing* over me, Jennifer! Fetch me my coat and scarf."

The doctor had arrived. He and Mrs Harle were unbuttoning enough of old Pastor Frayne's clothing to perform the last checks. Both looked up, equally scandalised. "Elizabeth," Mrs Harle said in horror. "You can't possibly go rushing off. You've had a great shock, and your husband—"

"My husband is dead," the old lady cut her off. "I did all I could all my life for him, but he's gone. Now my granddaughter is coming, and she has one of my names. Jennifer, please help me to the door."

Gideon paused by his father's chair. He didn't know how to take leave of him, how to do it respectfully, with this bustle of life in the room and his heart reaching out for the future. He wished he had the impulse of love to instruct him. But the pastor's policy of distancing his children had worked too well, at least on his younger son. "Sorry," he whispered, then decided his apologies were better addressed to the living. "Sorry, Mrs Harle. I know we're dropping you in it. I'll be at Trelowarren—you've got my number."

She tried for a reproving look but spoiled it with a grin. "Is this it, then? This baby I've heard so much about?"

"Yes. This is it."

"Well, go on with you, then. The undertaker's coming, and all your father's arrangements are in place. Is that all right with you, doctor?"

"Yes, yes." The Roselands GP tucked his stethoscope back into his bag. "Old chap's gone, all right. I'll note his time of death as ten past five."

There was a bottleneck in the corridor. Mrs Frayne's carer was muffling her in as many layers as she could carry, and some of her friends had emerged from their rooms at the sight of the doctor's car and were standing around in bewilderment, unsure whether to offer condolences or congratulations. Gideon thought about issuing a sergeant's bark—*move along! Nothing to see here!*—then heard the echo of the doctor's voice in his head. Ten past five. Not a precise time, but good enough for an unsuspicious death. Good enough as an answer to his patient other half, who'd been here making small talk with the in-laws for hours... "Lee," he said softly, drawing him aside. "Why did you come here today? Did you know?"

"No, but I think your father did."

"He died just after you asked me the time, didn't he?"

"Yes. Eleven minutes past five." Lee met his eyes across the narrow corridor. "It's okay, love. Whatever's scaring you, just ask."

Gideon could. From the day he'd met Lee Tyack, he'd told him his fears—sometimes without meaning to, sometimes in the painful relief of exposing an old wound. "That time... It's a year to the minute since old man Fisher died next door."

"Too much of a coincidence, right?"

"Yes, although living with you has raised my threshold for weird. And I'm just afraid that Tamsyn deciding to arrive now..." He paused. Lee had taught him not to fear alternative views of reality, but still he thought of himself as the prosaic one in their relationship, the man with his feet on the ground. "That doesn't have anything to do with the pastor, does it? Or Fisher?"

"Oh, God, no. None of these old men's dark spirits can touch Tamsyn. Listen, Gid—your dad was a gate-keeper, just like mine. The veil can get thin around the anniversary of a death, especially at solstice. He was just keeping the watch."

Gideon's throat tightened. He couldn't grieve any more than his mother could, but Lee's words shone a light on what had been best in the old man—his courage, the unflinching rectitude that had kept him at his station until the threat was gone. He took Lee's outstretched hand. The roadblock in the corridor was clearing at last, Jennifer opening the outside door to let in a wash of wintry seaside air. "Come on, then," he said. "Let's go get our solstice baby. But I'm warning you, if she's born feet-first with eyebrows that meet in the middle, I'm taking her straight to the zoo."

***

The traffic on the A39 began to congeal as the rush hour got underway. By the time Gideon had negotiated the queue as far as Treluswell, he was down to fifteen miles an hour, trying not to rev too hard into the gaps as the drivers ahead of him made their blind-faith dash into the double roundabout. He'd never been so tempted to slap on his lights and his siren, but that was strictly forbidden off-duty. He tried one of Lee's calming breaths, drummed his fingers on the wheel. "All right in the back there, Ma?"

"Yes, dear. Although we're going very slowly."

"I know."

"I think you'll need to get a different car. This one's very high. I won't be able to get into it much longer, especially if I'm carrying Tamsyn Elizabeth."

"I'll get you both a set of little steps made."

"And I'm not sure Lee's Escort will be suitable, either. They were saying on *Super Drive* that other makes do much better in terms of child safety."

"You've been watching *Super Drive?*"

"Gid, I think we're gonna be late."

Gideon shot Lee an anxious glance. He was bolt upright in the passenger seat, staring through the windshield at the rain-blossomed brake lights ahead, and Gideon feared his efforts to block Elowen's labour pains weren't meeting with complete success. "It's okay. I'll hang a left at the roundabout, take us over by the back roads."

"Isn't that a longer route?"

"Ten minutes or so. Much quicker in this traffic."

"Okay. Sorry. I'm making a fuss."

Gideon took a read of the emotional pressure building up in the Rover. Between Lee and his ma, he was surprised the windows hadn't blown out. "Not by comparison with that old lady in the back seat. She just told me I had to buy two new cars."

"Well, maybe we *should* get rid of the Escort. I saw that episode of *Super Drive* as well. Maybe we should..." He faded out, tugging at the seat belt across his chest. "Shit. Did Zeke say how far along Elowen was? How far she's dilated?"

"Not really his area of expertise." Gideon smiled wryly, flicking on his indicator and trying to edge across into the left-hand lane. "Not that it's ours either, technically, but..."

"It bloody will be when he's having one of his own." Lee wound down his window, leaned out and waved his arm at the truck-driver refusing to give way. "Back up, you fucking idiot!" He caught Gideon's look of amazement. "Sorry! Sorry, Mrs Frayne. I just don't want our experience of being parents to start with us missing the birth. I know we've jumped through all these checks and social worker's hoops, but what if we miss it, and they decide we're not—"

"Okay. Go ahead."

"What?"

"The blues and the twos. Hit 'em."

"Are you serious?"

"Never more so. It's that button there, and that switch."

The old two-tone siren was a wail these days, but the effects were the same. The Rover came to brilliant, noisy life. The guy in the truck decided to quit blocking the lane. Up ahead, drivers began to inch their cars aside to clear a path. Lee sat back to watch these effects, suddenly less of an anxious parent-to-be than an excited ten year old. Gideon chuckled, finally getting out of second gear and into the roundabout. "Better?"

"I've always wanted to do that."

"You should've said. We could've taken her round the village at home, chased Darren Prowse and his mates."

"It's for emergencies only, though, isn't it? For when people really need help, not when some copper's just late for his tea."

"How do you think I always get home on time?" Gideon turned right onto the narrow back road that would lead them through fields and woodland to Truro. He gunned the Rover's engine in satisfaction. "Besides, if this doesn't qualify as an emergency, I don't know what does."

***

Ezekiel was stalking the waiting room outside the maternity ward. His fiancée had done much towards humanising him, but under pressure he sometimes resumed his heron-like posture, hunching up his shoulders against the onslaught of the modern world. He was running his father's Methodist ministry full-time now, and tonight would have suited clerical black rather than the smart shirt and trousers Eleanor had picked out for him. "Gideon," he said, as soon as the doors swished open to admit his brother, Lee immediately behind him with the old lady clinging to his arm. "Elowen is fine. The nurses believe she'll be in labour for some hours yet. She can have visitors, but only two at a time." He put out a hand in warning. "And Michel Duroy is in there now."

Gideon skidded to a halt. Zeke was growing increasingly tolerant of his unconventional family, which Gideon and Lee were about to make weirder still by adopting Lee's niece as their own child. He was softening up in the pulpit as well, disappointing his congregation with lack of hellfire. Gideon was grateful that his first words had been the ones he and Lee had needed to hear, not a reproach for arriving like a blue-lit avalanche or for dragging Mrs Frayne out with them on such a night. He clearly still had something on his mind, though—something bigger than even than Michel Duroy. "Okay," Gideon said, exchanging a glance with Lee. "Wow, he travelled fast. You go on in, love—Ma and I will see Elowen when you're done."

"No. I'll wait and go in with you."

"Lee, you're gonna explode if you have to wait one more minute to see what's going on in that room." Gently Gideon detached his mother's death-grip. "Let the man have his arm back, Ma. You come and sit down over here. Look, they've got some car magazines for you." With a pang, he watched Lee dash off down the corridor. Then he braced up and turned to face his brother. "Sorry you got called out before we did."

"That's fine. I said I was happy to come, didn't I?"

"Yeah, you did. So what's wrong?"

"The undertaker phoned me, Gideon."

It was a rare sensation—that inward drop, like a lead weight into water. Cold pallor followed by a painful blush. "Oh, *fuck*."

"Is no situation so sacred that your first reaction will not be to swear?"

"Shit! I'm so, so sorry." Gideon was glad he'd left his cap in the Rover. He'd have knocked it halfway across the room with the mortified clutch of his brow. "You called me barely a minute after he'd gone, and..."

"And I told you about Elowen. I understand, although it was rather a large omission. That's not what I want to talk to you about. Come and sit down."

Gideon followed him to a pair of seats just out of Ma Frayne's earshot. He was trying earnestly to think of anything he might have done that could possibly be worse than forgetting to tell his brother that his father had died. "Seriously, Zeke. Forgive me. You must be gutted."

"Must I? Why? I modelled myself on him because he was all I had. That doesn't mean he was good, or that I was any good by the time I'd... finished my modelling." Before Gideon could absorb this startling pronouncement, Zeke had caught his arm and drawn him down to sit beside him. "Were you expecting Michel?"

"Michel? Not specifically, no. At least, we knew he was coming to visit at some point to talk to Elowen about work, but..."

"He hadn't arranged to be here for the birth."

"No." Unease stirred in Gideon's gut. "It's nice that he's gonna be around for it, though—isn't it?"

"Yes. Commendable, even, since he's the father of the child."

Gideon pressed his lips together. He was starting to learn that Ezekiel usually meant well, but his principles had been grating off Gideon since they were children. "The *biological* father. That's an accident of DNA. Lee and I will be Tamsyn's—"

"I'm not disputing that. I wanted to ask if you'd had the adoption papers formally drawn up."

Gideon flinched. He and Lee had learned to handle their rare disagreements with grace and love over the last six months. Their quarrels had been trivial, the day-to-day frictions of newlyweds settling down for the long haul—except for one point of profound moral dispute, which Gideon had dealt with by failing to deal with it at all. Elowen was Lee's sister. Gideon had only just met her, so who was he to lay down terms? "We were waiting," he said gruffly. "We thought it was best for Elowen to make the first move."

Ezekiel accorded him a sidelong glower which told him more plainly than words that he knew there'd been no *we* about it. That Gideon had wanted everything signed, sealed and recorded in the Civil Register, but had caved without question in the face of Lee's distress. *How can I ask her, Gid? It's her baby. This is so difficult for her.* "I'm not sure that was wise. Lots of women change their minds."

Irritation came to Gideon's rescue. "God's sake, Zeke. You always have to be the ghost at the feast, don't you? What would you know about *lots of women?*"

"That's rich, coming from you."

Gideon's mouth fell open. Ezekiel never took the low road. Before he could think up a retort, Eleanor appeared behind the glass doors. She came in quietly, and went to kiss Ma Frayne before turning to greet Gideon, but the message for her fiancé was written all over her face. *Did you ask him?*

Gideon sighed. She was a nice, kind, straightforward woman who took a very plain view of the world. "Hello, Eleanor," he said, wiping the annoyance from his tone. "How are you?"

"Fine, but never mind me. I just went down the corridor to get a cup of tea, and here you are. Where's Lee?"

"He's with his sister. Did you put Ezekiel up to this?"

"Up to what?"

"Asking if we'd had Tamsyn formally adopted."

She was too honest for a sidestep. He'd stung her, though, and she flushed in anger as well as embarrassment. "I didn't *put him up* to anything. I just know that I couldn't let *my* baby go, not once I'd seen her. No matter what I'd promised before."

A shriek cut across their confrontation. A door at the far end of the delivery suite flew open, and Lee and Michel Duroy came backing out into the corridor. Lee was white as a cod, Michel's hands up in a gesture of surrender. A plastic water bottle shot through the air, narrowly missing Michel's head, and impacted off the far wall. Another scream split the air, and then a groan like a soul in perdition. "Fuck off, both of you! Fuck the fuck off out of here!"

"Good God," Ezekiel said. "Is that..."

"Our sweet, nicely spoken sister-in-law, doctor of archaeology. Yes." Like his brother, Gideon had risen to his feet on instinct, ready for battle, the pair of them archetypal males despite their differences, and just as useless here. They both turned gratefully to the old lady, who had set aside her magazine and come to join them. "Now, boys," she said soothingly. "Your father called me a foul-mouthed hellion when I was having you. They encourage the girls to scream and shout these days, and it does them good. It's not as dreadful as it sounds."

"God, I hope not." Gideon swallowed dryly. He wasn't too worried about Elowen. He'd done the classic local-hero cop thing of delivering one woman's baby in the back seat of her car on the verge of the A30, and the *Herald* had made much of the new mum's wish to name her infant after her saviour, only to change her mind in horror when she'd heard what he was called. Michel too could look after himself, even if his six-foot Gallic gorgeousness wasn't doing him much good now. He shook off his paralysis and ran to Lee. "Right, you. Away from the door."

"I can't. Feels like she's dying."

"Well, she's not." Gideon detached him from the wall he'd backed up against, force-marched him a few yards down the corridor. "She's just having our girl."

"We're never having another one."

"I thought you mentioned wanting six of 'em. Plus the dog you already have, and a goldfish."

"I'll settle for the bloody dog!"

Gideon turned him so that the tides of Elowen's pain could break against his own broad back. Lee hung on to him for a moment, then pushed away. "I'm all right. Go to her."

"The midwife's with her. I'm not sure there's anything I can do."

"You always make everybody feel better. Please."

Cautiously Gideon returned to the doorway. The midwife glanced up. She knew Gideon from his pre-natal visits to the hospital with Elowen, and she spared him a brief smile. "Your turn to get your head cracked open with a bedpan, is it? Normally I only have one anxious dad to cope with, not three."

Two! Gideon kept the jealous thought to himself. Michel had just come here on a visit, and if he was now pacing the corridor with every appearance of a worried father-to-be, that was only natural. Such concerns were trivial anyway, compared to Elowen's struggle. "How is she doing?" He hadn't meant to speak as though she wasn't there, but she had turned her face away from him and was clutching the sheet round her chin. "Does she have much longer to go?"

"We thought things were happening a few minutes ago, didn't we, chick? But our contractions have subsided. Could be a few hours yet."

A few hours... Poor little bugger. Gideon's head spun a bit at the prospect and he asked, only halfway meaning to voice the question aloud, "What time is solstice?"

"Solstice?" The midwife gave Elowen a reassuring pat and straightened the blanket. "You're not into all that astrological stuff, are you? My son's just as bad. Three minutes after eleven this year, he says it is. I don't know what he expects is going to happen."

Elowen shifted in the bed. Her face contorted. Gideon had promised to help her—had taken turns with Lee to breathe with her in half a dozen ante-natal groups—and he took a step forward, but she waved him frantically back. "I don't want you, Gid," she rasped. "Or Lee, or Michel, or bloody Ezekiel, or any other bloody man, for that matter! How have I ended up here, flat on my back... surrounded by bloody *men*?" She began to sob in sheer weariness and fright. "I want my mum."

Gideon's heart shifted in his chest with pity. Her mother had died twenty years ago. "I know. Will mine do?"

Her face crumpled. "Yes. I want Ma Frayne."

Gideon didn't have to call her. She'd risen at the prompting of some instinct beyond family ties or reason, and was making her way down the corridor without stopping to think about her stick, her walking frame or the need for an arm to lean on. She pushed past Gideon into the room, her hands outstretched. "Oh, poor girl. My poor sweetheart. I'm here now."

Chapter One
July 2015

The clifftop garden was awash with colour and light, merry as a fairground in the sunshine. Gideon made his way with difficulty up the slope, balancing two cardboard cups of cider. He subsided gratefully into a deckchair beside Sarah Kemp, who was watching her daughter and the other kids tear around the lawn with Isolde, a sheepdog who nominally lived with Gideon and Lee but spent her time guarding the kitchens and offspring of half the other villagers of Dark. Gideon handed Sarah one of the cups. "There you go, your ladyship. Everything all right?"

"Heavenly." She waved in the direction of the romping children. "Would you look at that? That dog of yours is herding the brats away from the cliff edge."

"Whoever would've thought she'd have the brains, eh?" Gideon stretched and hid a yawn behind his hand. Even the smell of the cider was making the garden flutter and dance. "You should see her at home. Bites me on the bum if I'm late taking Tamsie for her bath."

Sarah chuckled. "Nanny dog." She leaned forward and pitched a Bodmin mother's moor-crossing yell at her two younger offspring. "Shaun and Jenny Kemp! You climb that bloody apple tree, I'll come and string you up from it! God," she continued to Gideon, smiling, "they love it here. It was nice of Jago to ask us."

"He knows how much help you were when we first brought Tamsyn home."

"Well, when you've had three of 'em, you either know what to do in most emergencies or you've stopped caring. He's a nice bloke, your Lee's Jago, isn't he?"

"Yeah, he is." When Gideon had first met him, he'd been certifiably insane. Now he was married to Mrs Ivey, his housekeeper, and had moved back into the beautiful old family farmhouse here at Drift, every inch the hospitable lord of the manor, his madness reduced to colourful eccentricity. "Think he might've bitten off a bit more than he can chew here. All he wanted to do was throw a quiet farewell party for his niece..."

"And half Cornwall smelled free food and came clambering over the walls. Where is Elowen, anyway? I haven't seen her since I got here."

"She's taking her turn to walk Tamsyn." Gideon suppressed another yawn. He'd been up half the night, wearing a track in the living-room carpet at Dark, gently jiggling his howling daughter against his shoulder. "No, wait. There she is with Michel. Lee must still have the baby, poor sod." He frowned. Elowen and Michel were in close conference, her hand clasped tight round his arm. She led him off towards the orchard, and they disappeared among the shadows of the trees.

Then a high-pitched wail carried over the voice of the breeze, and Gideon forgot everything at the sight of his husband emerging from the porch, Tamsyn cradled against his hip. Zeke had been wrong, back in that darkest night of December. Eleanor had been wrong. Michel Duroy had vanished like the morning mist as Elowen had surged into the final stage of her labour, and at three minutes past eleven precisely had opened the gates of the world to her daughter, clutching Lee with one hand, Mrs Frayne with the other, Gideon down at the business end to make the catch. She'd delivered Tamsyn right into his hands, head-first, two separate little eyebrows drawn with the delicate perfection of butterfly's antennae. Two day later, Lee and Gideon had taken their baby home. "Bloody hell," he said, setting his cider cup down, deciding that sleeplessness and worry were more than enough to make him feel three sheets to the wind. "Still blowing up a storm, isn't she?"

"Did you try clapping your hands behind her head?"

"Yep. Tried putting her in the car and driving her around like you said used to work with Lorna. Normally all we've got to do is walk her up and down the kitchen a few times and she goes out like a light."

"Well, if you don't mind my saying so, it serves you bloody right," Sarah said comfortably, propping her feet. "No natural baby was ever as good as that one. First everybody in the village loves your dog, and then they're falling all over themselves to get at your baby. No-one ever volunteered to baby-sit *my* brats, I can tell you that. What's your secret?"

Gideon had given this thought. He'd come to a conclusion, too. Sarah Kemp was one of the few people with whom he'd have shared it. He and she had walked through the valley of the shadow of death where kids were concerned. He noticed that she never took her eyes off Lorna, even in the sunny garden with Isolde romping by her side. "Most babies cry because they want something, don't they? A feed, or a clean nappy, or a cuddle to take their minds off this tricky business of being alive. And they can't communicate whatever it is, so they cry."

"That's about right." She leaned forward, watching Lee, who was now showing Tamsyn the dance of the wisteria blossom around the front porch, still to no avail. "Oh, I see. And Tamsie doesn't have that problem—because of Lee."

"Not usually, no."

"Aren't you afraid for her, Gid? If she's like him, I mean. He's a grand lad, and I owe him everything, but... it's been hard on him, hasn't it? Terrible, at times."

Gideon frowned. So far the bond between Lee and his girl had only been a blessing, a wonderful means of knowing what the puce-faced scrap in his arms required before she knew it herself. He'd been too busy, too besotted, to consider further implications. To think about why his child might be crying when all her obvious needs had been met. "Yes, it has," he said, taking the edge off his words with a quick smile. "I tell you what, Sarah—I'd better go relieve the guard. Lee looks knackered. You're right—we're *not* used to much of this."

"Well, you're gonna be on your own with it from now on." Gideon tried to look serious at the prospect, but Sarah grinned. "When is Elowen off, then?"

"Later today. She and Michel are taking the ferry to Roscoff so they can start their big project in Carnac."

"Don't you pull that face. You're thrilled silly, aren't you?"

Gideon turned away to avoid having to answer. The last few months of his life had been extraordinary in ways he hadn't anticipated. Something had happened to delay the start of the Carnac dig. With time on her hands, Elowen had decided she wanted to breastfeed, and everything Lee and Gideon had read or learned backed her up on the benefits of that. So from December till May, four people had been living in the one-bedroom flat in Dark, Elowen sleeping on a single bed in the nursery.

Gideon hadn't minded. She was funny and sweet, disconcertingly like her brother. Her studies for her new job had kept her working long hours in the Bodmin library, Lee taking care of Tamsyn at home, and they'd all come together peaceably in the evenings. Gideon had persuaded himself that her presence was just like an extra dose of Lee's. Still, he'd drawn a huge breath of relief when Tamsyn started showing a vigorous preference for formula, and Elowen had moved back to Drift. She still visited twice a week, and Gideon and Lee had brought the baby down to the farmhouse for a day each weekend, just like a normal, close-knit family, except...

Except that having Elowen around had weighed on him constantly, a lonely fear he could neither define nor share with Lee. He'd put it in a box so that his perceptive lover—who would never pry, but couldn't help seeing obvious troubles—wouldn't stumble over it in his frequent trips around Gideon's mind. He could put it aside today. Zeke, Eleanor, his own paranoid self— they'd all been wrong. Michel had come to collect Elowen and accompany her back to France, and all would be well. Gideon thought he might try and spirit away his little two-person family early from this party, pleading weariness and the ear-splitting nuisance of his daughter, who for once in her life wouldn't stop crying, as if shadows only she could see were lurking in the bright blue Penwith skies. "Lee?" he called softly, pushing through the wisteria and up the steps of the porch. "Fancy putting our infant child to bed and having the noisy kind of sex we used to have before your sister moved into the room next door?"

"Gideon *Frayne!*"

He stopped dead. "Oh, crap. Hi, Zeke. We're just doomed, aren't we?"

"We wouldn't be, if you had an ounce of decency in you. I take it you're looking for your other half."

Well, I'm not looking for you, crow-face. Gideon kept it to himself. Even Ezekiel couldn't quite pull off the ministerial look, emerging from the house with a pint of cider in his hand and a T-shirt that could almost stand accused of being pink in the right light. He was proving to be a good uncle, too, taking Tamsyn out on solemn nature walks, telling her the Latin names of all the wild flowers, and failing to combust when Gideon and Lee had chosen a Pagan priest from St Just to conduct the child's naming ceremony. "I am. Have you seen him?"

"I think he set off on the path towards the church. Tamsyn is still crying, Gideon. Does she have a fever? Another tooth coming through?"

"No. Believe me, we've checked her from head to foot about forty times. She's just really upset about something."

"Lee didn't look happy either. You'd better go and see to them."

Gideon didn't need telling twice. The cliff path was steep and he wouldn't have thought Lee would tackle it with Tamsyn in his arms, although she'd joyously yelled her way along many a treacherous track in her papoose across Gideon's shoulders, Lee following watchfully two steps behind. He set off, shielding his eyes against the sun. As far as he could see, the narrow ribbon of stone and dried mud was empty all the way to the churchyard in the fields below. The vacancy—its worst implication—struck him like a glancing blow, but his mind couldn't process it. Instead he started to run, giving thanks at every stride for his recovered health. He was back on full active duty once more, the classroom left behind in favour of the streets and the wide world where he belonged.

He made short work of the path, blind for once to its blaze of red campions and gold-green alexanders. The little grey church was dreaming in the sun. Built in a time when magic still swept this outpost of England along with the wild west wind, it held within its granite walls a concentration of the peace that reigned outside it, and maybe Lee had taken his squalling brat to see the wildwood faces carved into the pews. The door stood open a few inches to permit the ingress and swooping egress of juvenile swallows.

No. Gideon stopped on the steps. Lee wasn't in the church. He didn't know where the conviction came from and didn't care to analyse it, but he would have sworn in court that he was alone here. The growing instinct was handy, telling him where he could track Lee down to offer him a cuppa or a kiss when they were at home, but other than this domestic function, Gideon had no interest in developing gifts beyond his own good senses. That way madness could lie, even for an experienced voyager between the worlds like Lee. Dodging the dive-bombing efforts of the swallows, he retreated. He would just take a turn around the outside, check the rest of the churchyard and meadow.

Relief and chagrin swept through him. So much for that treacherous sixth sense—Lee was right there, carrying Tamsyn down the long straight path that edged the field on the landward side of the church. Gideon called to him and waved. He felt weary all of a sudden, a rare ache passing through his leg, reminding him that he'd almost bled to death on the cobbles of Bodmin last February. That was a dark thought for a summer's day, and he climbed the gravel path to the north-side gateway, a traditional Cornish cattle-grid made of huge granite spars set lengthwise between two stone benches. He sat down, rubbing his thigh. Movement caught his attention down among the graves. There was Jago, head lowered, hands in his pockets.

Not everyone was filled with sunshine on this festive day. Elowen and Michel seemed troubled, and Jago had chosen what should be the height of his party to visit his brother's grave. Gideon got up, determined not to disturb him if he could avoid it. He glanced up the field path to find Lee, to lose his crawling sense of unease in his lover's bright answering smile.

The field was empty. Gideon scanned its grassy expanse, but only the wind was moving there, pressing the blades into a tumult like a silky sea. The unease blossomed into downright fear: as far as he knew, there were no gaps in the hedgerow where Lee could have stepped through, even if for some reason he'd wanted to return a different way.

"Gideon?"

Jago was signalling for him to come down. Gideon ran to join him, the ache in his leg forgotten. "Jago, did Lee come through this way with the baby? I saw them on the path above the church, but they vanished."

"What? You can't have done. I just left them up by the house."

"Oh. Okay, that's weird. Were they all right?"

"Yes, but I felt strange, and I wanted to come down and talk to my brother about it."

Gideon nodded. They were standing at the foot of Cadan Tyack's grave. Gideon had learned to overlook the usual boundaries when it came to his in-laws. "Sorry. I'll leave you alone."

"No, we should go back. Cadan thinks so, anyway." He set off, and Gideon fell into step by his side. "That's a death gate, you know. Up there where you were sitting."

Gideon did know. The vast coffin-shaped stone between the two benches was an inescapable clue. He'd overheard visitors exclaiming at it in horror, but he liked the frank West Penwith acceptance of time and change. He liked the idea of weary mourners having a chance to lay down their load and eat bread and cheese in the sunshine. "Yes. The path's the old route down from the village, isn't it?"

"More than that. It's a corpse road. Run straight as arrows for miles across the country, they do, so wandering spirits won't be obstructed in their travels." Jago glanced at him fearfully. "Do you have it too, then? A gift like Lee's?"

"No, not at all." Gideon was surprised at his own vehemence. If he had no gift, he had still less of an explanation for his encounters with Lee's father, with Morris Hawke and the bloody Beast of Bodmin. But today he just wanted to be normal. "What makes you ask that?"

"You saw into *my* heart."

They had reached the patched-up hole in the eastern wall of the church. Jago seemed disposed to pause. Gideon laid a gentle hand to his back to move him on. "Jago, you made me a very full confession of the contents of your heart. Dropped half the village in it, too." As a man, Gideon had no doubts that he'd done the right thing by forgetting that Jago and his friends had clubbed a vicious child-napper to death and concealed the body not three yards from where they were standing, but the copper in him sometimes gave him a hard time. "I'd really like never to hear it again."

"All right. But there's a tradition that seeing someone on a corpse road means they'll be gone within a year."

"Oh, my God. Look, Tamsie's already got my nerves in shreds from crying all night. Can you do me a massive favour and keep any local legends of doom to yourself?"

"I'm sorry, Gideon."

"That's all right. Just... Oh, there he is. He must've found a different way back up the cliff."

But Lee was making his way down the path, not up it, and he didn't have the baby in his arms. Instead a small, odd deputation was following in his wake. Elowen was directly behind him, struggling to keep up. She stretched out an arm to grab Lee's jacket. He shook her off, the gesture so uncharacteristic that Gideon's alarm bells began to shrill. Behind them came Michel and Zeke, apparently vying for position. "Bloody hell," Jago said. "What's going on up there?"

"I don't know, but I don't like the look of it. Come on."

They met at the foot of the track. Lee came to him like a hard-hunted fox to its earth. He stopped three inches shy and stood motionless. "Lee, darling," Gideon said without thinking, something in Lee's face shocking the word out of him—a bedroom endearment, a sleepy last word after love. "What in God's name's wrong? Where's Tamsyn?"

But Lee couldn't speak. Nor could Elowen, who had jolted to a halt at his side and was sobbing without restraint. Michel made a kind of croaking sound, but he was out of breath and looked sick to his soul. And so it was left to Ezekiel to step forward, lay his hand on Lee's shoulder and say, "You have to stay calm, Gideon. Elowen's decided she wants to keep the child."

Stupidly, Gideon's first reaction was relief. He'd imagined his little girl hurt, knocked down by nonexistent traffic, fallen into the barbecue fire. This was just an aberration, a fault in the wiring. "She can't," he said reasonably, as if that would fix everything. "Where's my daughter?"

"Sarah Kemp and Mrs Ivey are looking after her."

"Right. Lee, come on—we're collecting her and going home."

Elowen caught her breath on a deep, gulping sob. "No. Michel and I have made all the arrangements. She's coming with us to France."

"Elowen, excuse me, but bollocks to that. What the bloody hell are you thinking?"

She looked up at him, pallidly defiant. "She's still legally mine. You can't stop me."

The trouble with being six feet tall and built like a house-end was the courtesy rules that applied. A kind of sliding scale governed them. The stronger you were, the punier the other guy, the gentler you had to be. Especially when the other guy was female. Gideon was old fashioned. He had never threatened violence to a woman in his life.

There was a time and a place for everything. "I *could* stop you," he said consideringly. "I could pick you up and throw you off that cliff." Michel's mouth fell open and he took a step forward. Gideon turned on him. "And as for you," he roared, "don't you so much as fucking look at me! Because you I *will* take down, mate, right here and now!"

"Gideon!" Ezekiel stepped between them. "A dreadful thing has happened. But to fight it out here is unseemly, and won't fix anything. Come back to the house."

His brother's hand, planted flat to his chest, was a force to be reckoned with. Gideon had never thought about him in physical terms. The ten-year age gap had prevented them from scuffling as children, and since then he'd been so buttoned up and godly that even the possibility of a brawl had never occurred. Yet here he was—an inch or so taller than Gideon, and probably stronger still inside his lean frame. That was good. Gideon's sliding scale reset itself to zero. "Blessed are the peacemakers, eh, Zeke?" he said shakily. "Not this time."

He drew back his fist. But his blind flying punch didn't connect: was stopped and absorbed by Lee, who grabbed his hand and drew it against his own chest. He gave a muffled grunt as the force of the blow expended itself. "No, Gid. No."

They dropped to their knees on the turf. Instantly Gideon tried to struggle upright, but Lee's arms closed around him like cables. "Zeke," Lee rasped, his voice a hollow echo of its usual rich sound. "Get everyone away from him. Please! Just let him calm down."

***

The house was quiet, the garden emptied of its guests. Mrs Ivey had steered Jago out of harm's reach into the kitchen. Sarah had taken the children home, parting from Gideon with a silent, white-faced kiss. Lee had held it together as far as the front door, and then at the sound of the baby's wails from the first floor, had left off his loving custodian's hold of Gideon and run for the stairs. Gideon was sitting opposite Elowen in the living room. It was as beautiful as ever—armfuls of dried flowers in the old tiled hearth, the family photos smiling down from the walls. Gideon wanted to torch it. "For God's sake, Elowen. You were so sure."

She had managed to stop crying. Her voice was still raw, her face swollen. "No. I was never sure."

"Are you kidding? You practically threw your foetus into my arms the first time you saw me."

Michel and Zeke had positioned themselves on the sofa, a pair of unhappy bookends. One guardian each, Gideon supposed, or possibly two to deal with him if he lost his rag again. He was already deeply ashamed of the first time. And he'd been right in his assessment of Michel as a decent man: he got up now and came to stand by Elowen's chair. "This is in a great part my fault," he said, his accent heightening the flawlessness of his English. "When Elowen became pregnant, I didn't make clear to her my feelings. And I hadn't anticipated having a child. So she made her own arrangements, and I must ask you to speak to her civilly, Gideon, even though you are so distraught."

"All right. Yes. I'm sorry, Elowen."

She sniffed and gave a miserable shudder. "Call me what you like. I don't blame you."

"I don't want to call you anything. Just... explain to me, please. Why are you taking Tamsyn away from us?"

"Because I'm her mother. I love her—far more than I'd ever thought I could, and now Michel wants to be with me, things are different. She'll have a father too."

"What about this amazing bloody job you were so desperate to have?"

"He's holding it for me. I can start when Tamsyn goes to nursery school."

Her nursery school's in Dark, just down the road so she won't ever feel too far from home. Gideon could have recited chapter and verse of such small arrangements, but Elowen already knew them. He swallowed the taste of helpless misery. "You're really going to do it, aren't you?"

"I have to. You and Lee can adopt another baby. It'll be easier for you this time—you've already been through all the checks. But Tamsyn's mine."

"I wish you'd thought of that before you'd let us start to love her."

"Gideon, you're killing me, okay? You can say as many heartbreaking, bitter things as you want—and I deserve them all—but I'm not about to change my mind."

"I can't accept that. Look, you've only known me for a few months, and we've got on well enough together, but... Please, Elowen, think about Lee. Tamsyn's his whole life."

"Oh, bollocks!" Michel laid a restraining hand on her shoulder, but she swung on him impatiently. "Well? He doesn't mince his words to me, does he? I didn't live in that flat with those two for all that time and not work out who Lee's *whole life* is. He has you, Gideon. I'm not talking about this anymore, all right? I'm going to fetch my baby."

She left the room. Ezekiel got up, but Gideon didn't need the move he made to prevent him from following. A terrible passivity had taken hold of him. "Okay," he said faintly. "You can say it if you want, Zeke."

"Say what?"

"*I told you so.*"

Ezekiel sat down on the arm of the chair. "About what?"

"Bless you for pretending to forget. The adoption papers. We never did get them signed."

"Shame on me, if I were to lay such a burden on my brother's wounded heart!"

Gideon looked at him in astonishment. The Methodist chapel at Dark must be a very different place these days. He rested his brow against Zeke's shoulder. It would have been nice to give it all up right here. He had a big brother, restored to him after all these years, and not half so much of a po-faced bastard as he looked. But Gideon's two Tyacks—the mother of his child, and his own poor Lee—were already somewhere upstairs in tears, and it was just too ridiculous for him to break down too. In a world where small mercies had suddenly loomed large, he was grateful that Ma Frayne was off with her bridge club today and not here to add her wail to the chorus. He sat up, awkwardly patting Zeke's arm. "I'm all right. Jesus, though, Michel—I still can't believe this."

Michel's eyes were red too. "*Je suis vraiment desolé*, Gideon."

"Not half as fucking desolate as we are. Can't you talk to her?"

"How can I? When I came over in December, it was to tell her that I wanted to be with her, to keep the child if we could. She said no at the time, but..."

"But she's obviously given it plenty of thought since." Gideon rested his elbows on his knees and sat listening to the shattered world around him. Zeke's breathing was unsteady. Michel turned away towards the window. To cap it all, the poor dog, forgotten in the fuss, crawled out from beneath the sideboard, crept to Gideon's feet and began a low, miserable whine.

Not a dry eye in the house, apart from Gideon's. Anger had carried him this far. Perhaps it would bring him out the other side. Someone had to stay calm around here, and it had better be the copper. Wishing he was in uniform—his armour, his outer carapace—he got to his feet. "I'd better go and check on Lee."

But a door clicked on the floor above. Lee appeared at the top of the stairs. He had Tamsyn's rucksack over his arm, and the baby—quiet now at last, looking around her with wide green-silver eyes—cradled against his shoulder. Elowen followed him anxiously down into the hall, the carrycot in her hand.

Gideon resisted the impulse to snatch it from her. He went to intercept Lee. "What are you doing?"

"I'm handing Tamsyn over to Elowen and Michel. And they'd better take her now, because..." He swallowed hard and turned away from Gideon to face them. "Because otherwise you'll have a fight on your hands, and this time I won't hold Gideon back. I'll help him."

"Lee, we can't let her go like this."

"Think about the options. Think about them."

Gideon did. A living-room brawl, the baby shrieking in terror as the adults around her erupted like volcanoes. Police called, arrests made for domestic affray. Even the best option—Gideon's fantasy, flashing through his brain in vivid colours—a farce, bundling the child into the back of Lee's Escort and driving her away from here, tearing up the singletrack lanes to escape. Abduction in the eyes of the law, because Tamsyn wasn't theirs and never had been. "Oh, God."

"It's all right." Lee sacrificed one hand from his hold on the baby and took Gideon's, drawing him close. "Do you see how calm she is now? This isn't the end."

"You... You *saw* that? You told her?"

"No. I didn't foresee any of this—possibly because I'd have gone batshit crazy. She told *me*."

He put Tamsyn into Gideon's arms. How awkwardly Gideon had handled her at first! His hands had looked massive beside her tiny limbs, and his terror of breaking her had only ebbed through the constant daily routines of care and love. Now she felt like a piece of himself coming back to him. Her strange gaze focussed on him, and she made a solemn grab for his nose. "But we'll have to go back to the flat first," he said dully, capturing the little fist and kissing it. "To Dark. All her things are there."

"That's all right," Michel said. He was crying outright, as if all this hadn't come about because of him. "We've bought everything she needs. We thought it would be easier on you and Lee if we did this here, rather than taking her out of your home."

"Oh, yeah. It's a piece of piss this way." Gideon studied the rosy face turned up to him. His heart was beating too fast, and a cold, racing nausea like an underground stream was chilling his guts. "How am I meant to say goodbye to her?"

"Give her here," Lee said softly. "This is just for now, love."

"I can't let her go."

But Lee's arms were outstretched for her, and it was such a habit to transfer the solid little weight that he did it unthinkingly now. Lee planted one kiss—silent, eyes closed tight—on her brow, then handed her straight on to Elowen, who shot Gideon a look of pure fear at having got her desire. "We should go," she whispered to Michel. "Come on. Now."

Gideon walked away. He slumped down on the window seat in the living room, the lovely broad space looking out over the cliffs. It was cushioned in faded green velvet. One of the house rules was that Isolde wasn't allowed onto it, a prohibition she steadfastly ignored. Gideon curled forward and laced his fingers around the back of his head. The dog's scrabbling, plumping weight promptly landed beside him. He was distantly aware of her warmth.

The porch door opened, then the outer one. By pressing his wrists to his ears, Gideon could block out most of the conversation. He didn't have to hear whatever words Elowen had chosen to end his brief experience of fatherhood and take the child away. Then Lee's voice cut softly though his self-imposed deafness. "I don't think I ever had a really bad word for you, Elowen—not even when we were squabbling kids. But you *bitch*, for hurting him now."

"Lee, don't." That was Ezekiel, sounding less reproachful than tired. "Just look after him. He's devastated."

"I will. I promise."

Gideon wasn't devastated. He was the only calm one. That was the whole point of him: he was stronger, calmer than anyone else. That was why he was a policeman. Always the last man standing. But the outer door closed, and Lee came to sit beside him on the faded green cushions not occupied by the dog. Lee said, "Come here, you. Come here," and Gideon proved himself no better or worse than anyone else by bursting into tears in his arms.

Chapter Two

"I can't get down the hallway. I'm sorry, Gid."

The days of their orderly two-man flat were long gone. Lee was a good stay-at-home dad but he'd been working on the scripts for a new season of *Spirits of Cornwall* at the same time, and their rush to leave for Drift had left a trail of devastation, Tamsyn's toys scattered over the carpet, the heated clothes-rail on its side where Gideon had tripped over it and hopped out of the house, swearing under his breath. None of this was the problem. What had brought Lee to a halt was the sight of the open nursery door. Isolde, who'd been a distraction and a comfort on the way home, gave a whine of outraged herding instincts and abruptly made matters much worse, picking up a discarded stuffed rabbit and trotting hopefully through with it into the empty room.

"It's all right. Close your eyes." Gideon steered Lee straight past. He took a deep diver's breath and half-pushed, half-guided him through all the silent relics, all the way to their bedroom door. He slammed it shut behind him with his foot, gently shoved him in the direction of the bed, then went to draw the curtains. The afternoon was changing to a beautiful summer's evening on the moors—the last day of July, he remembered in an irrelevant flash—but the outside world could do no good to him today, and he shut it out angrily. Folded up Tamsyn's extra cot for good measure and packed it into the closet. He turned to the bed, where Lee was watching him wide-eyed, already unfastening his shirt in a gesture of comprehension and welcome. "We always did everything too fast, didn't we?"

Lee nodded. He was pale, the marks of grief still fresh on him, his cock rising hard in his jeans. "Yes. Moved in together way too soon..."

"Got married five minutes later."

"Started our family five minutes after that. Yes."

"But none of it *was* too soon, was it? It was all bloody perfect." Gideon went to kneel over him, and he went down flat on the bed in passionate surrender. "We made it perfect. We can make anything good, love—even this."

"That's right. We can just be together by ourselves again. Can we get under the duvet, Gid? I know it's hot, but..."

"Yes." Gideon didn't want to see daylight either. Wanted to burrow and hide. "We didn't get Tamsie because our lives were empty. They were full to overflowing, and she just came along. Oh God, Lee, I feel like I'm dying."

"I know. Get in here and fuck me. Bury yourself in me."

Gideon dragged the quilt up over both of them. Lee struggled over onto his side, snatched the lube out of the bedside drawer and passed it back. He pushed his jeans down with an impatient movement that would have turned Gideon on at a funeral. "Don't undress," he whispered. "Just unzip and do it."

"I should shower. I even *smell* pissed off and miserable."

"You smell like home." Lee buried his face in the pillow. A silent sob racked him, and all Gideon could do was obey—untangle himself from jeans and underwear, coat his cock quickly with lube and thrust up and in. Lee gave a shattered moan and tried to draw his knees to his chest, Gideon reaching quickly to aid the movement, the impulse to curl and disappear. He could help with that: be his lover's refuge, his cave, just as Lee was offering him this last-ditch comfort of the flesh. They rocked together in the hot dark. They tried to make it last but the pang of this collision was too bittersweet. Gideon's movements became fast and urgent. He fought a terrible fear of pitching too soon and bailing out—cried out in relief as Lee shuddered in the grip of a hammer-blow climax, releasing him.

A short-lived, bone-deep respite. Gideon stayed where he was when they were both spilled out and done, only withdrawing when they ran out of breathable air beneath the duvet. They surfaced reluctantly, clambering into each other's arms. Gideon traced the lines of Lee's face with a fingertip. He caressed the swollen eyelids and mouth. Lee was crying helplessly and with barely a change of expression. No crumpling or contortion. Gideon knew the feeling from a distant childhood memory, the kind of tears that wouldn't stop because the lungs had gone shallow and tight, not allowing room for a calming breath, a chance to catch the reins. "Jesus, sweetheart," he rasped. "It's not too late. I could catch them at the ferry port. Let me go after them."

"No. No." Lee snatched a tissue out of the box by the bed, his attempt to pull himself together passing like a blunt knife through Gideon's heart. "All we'd end up doing is... fighting a pitched battle over her cradle."

Better that than an empty one. Gideon bit it back with an effort that nearly choked him. "I'd rather be fighting. I'd rather be chasing Elowen around bloody Dover with a police dog than..."

"Than what?"

"Than seeing you like this. Please."

"No." Lee handed him the last tissue, waited until he'd blown his nose, then put both arms around his neck and held on.

"You've done enough, big man. Would you really have punched Michel's lights out?"

"Hell, yes. And Ezekiel's." He shuddered. "And your bloody sister's."

"Before or after you'd chucked her off the cliff? Oh God, Zeke was right. Why didn't I get the paperwork done?"

"We both decided that, not just you."

"Nope. You suggested it, and I said, *no, she's my sister—there's no need*. It would take a saint not to say—"

Gideon wasn't a saint. He put a hand over Lee's mouth. "Don't. I haven't even thought it. No-one has."

"Ah, Gid." Lee moved the silencing hand, kissed its palm. "Your whole family is *bristling* with I-told-you-so."

Gideon bristled in his turn. "Did one of them say something?"

"No. They don't have to. You should know that by now."

"All right," Gideon said wearily, lying down beside him. "I *did* tell you so, you twat."

Lee gave a snuffling giggle in spite of himself. "Thank you. Why didn't you insist?"

"I didn't feel it was my place."

"Of course it was. Everything to do with Tamsyn's just as much your place as mine. I bet you'd have insisted if we'd been adopting from a stranger."

"Yes, but—"

"But nothing." Lee found his breath, got a grip on the runaway tears. "Listen. Forget the whole genetic thing. Tamsyn was gonna be our daughter, not my niece."

"How would you have felt if I'd put my foot down, though?"

"I'd have listened. I trust your feet. You're my Gideon—my husband, my other half. The only one who *can* insist on things with me."

Gideon drew him close. Shock and exhaustion were meeting post-coital tides in his bloodstream. He wasn't used to crying, not the way he had back at Drift—it made him feel punched in the face, or as if he was coming down with a cold. He fought the first tug of sleep. There were always things to do these days before he closed his eyes. Nappies, feeds, a final check to see that his cheerful infant hadn't taken to suicide by pillow or begun escape work on the bars of her cot. He twitched violently, and Lee restrained him, kissing his brow, soothing. "All right," he rasped, struggling back to surface. "But the same applies to you. We've got to insist with each other when it's important, even if we... break each other's hearts."

***

Someone was hammering at the door. That sound had haunted Gideon's world almost since the beginning of his time with Lee. Malevolent ghosts, the unearthly bang in the seafront Island house that had presaged a haunting, the temporary dispossession of his lover's very soul... Stiffly Gideon got out of bed. Lee was still sleeping deeply. Gideon could see the flicker of the pulse in his throat: he was there, alive, safe. At least one half of Jago's bloody churchyard prophecy hadn't come true.

And never would, if Gideon had any say in the matter. The frantic knocking started again. Lee had once warned him never to say *come at me, bro* to things from beyond the veil, never to fling wide the door and say *bring it on, then, if you remembered to bring it*, but he'd been denied his punch-up on the clifftop, and whoever had chosen this moment to disturb what was left of his domestic peace was certainly asking for trouble.

Or it's Elowen. Oh God, she's thought better of this insanity and brought Tamsyn home. He fumbled the latch, almost hit himself in the face with the door as he pulled it open.

There was no-one there. A great bronze-gold sun was poised over Minions Hill, and on the eastern horizon, beyond the quiet village and the tors, the moon had just risen. A blue moon, Lee had said, because it was the rare second one in the month, but to Gideon's salt-scoured gaze it looked red, as if someone had splashed blood across the ancient, changeless silver. "Fuck you, then," Gideon whispered, whether to sun, moon or ghosts he didn't really care. "Just leave us alone."

"I can't. It's back. It's back."

Gideon had been looking too high. Three steep steps led up to his front door, and the dry, cracked, goblin voice had come from pavement level.

From a child, although he wasn't sure that Darren Prowse had ever qualified, with his wizened little old man's face and jail-bait view of the world. "I tell you what, mate," Gideon said experimentally, just to see if he could keep his temper. "You have chosen the worst bloody time you could to play any kind of prank on me."

"I know. I know. Sarah Kemp said that cow had taken your Tamsie away. But it's *back.*"

"What's back, Darren? Think carefully before you answer me."

"The Beast! The fucking Beast of Bodmin Moor!"

Gideon looked down at him. He was a perfect mix of savagery and hysteria, tears and snot flying as he tried to fight off the trauma of his last-but-one Halloween. He was rootless, shiftless, and, since his mother had finally tired of Bill and moved out, utterly unloved. "Darren," he said slowly. "There is no Beast.

I know you were scared half to death by Joe Kemp, but he was just a very bad man."

"I know that! I ain't scared of any bloody *man*, bad or good. But no man did that to John Bowe, you stupid bloody plod!"

Gideon wasn't sure sometimes whether he was a good man or a bad one, but he was about to make this brat very scared of him in a minute. Then he saw the terror peeping out of the poor kid's reddened eyes, and instead he put out a hand to him. "Come here."

To his surprise, Darren dropped his precocious adulthood on the pavement and climbed him like a monkey. Or a rat up a drainpipe, he reflected, automatically rocking him—he was almost fourteen years old, but still weighed no more than a sack of potatoes. Gideon didn't take the attention personally. The boy would have shinned up a pole if there'd been a convenient one to hand. He was just escaping from the flood of his own fear. Gideon's arms had grown used to holding children, though, and despite the obvious differences between this little rodent and his own sweet-smelling bundle, he embraced him. "All right. Nobody can hurt you now. Take a deep breath and tell me what's wrong— the truth, if you can manage it for once."

"John Bowe. The farmer up at Carnysen, Bligh and Dev's brother."

"I know who John Bowe is." Everyone did. The Bowes were that modern contradiction in terms, a truly wealthy farming family. Their land was Dark's breadbasket, acres of rolling wheatfields from Minions all the way down through the fertile valley to Carnysen farm. Gideon could see the edge of the nearest barleyfield from here, gleaming in a mix of sun and moon. "What about him?"

"The Beast. It tore him apart."

The wretched brat had something in his pockets. Gideon set him down. He stood panting, eyes still wide, while Gideon extracted a wire-loop snare. "What are you doing with this?"

"Harvest tomorrow, isn't it?"

"Right. So you thought you'd set snares for the rabbits running out of the corn."

"Why not? Who cares for 'em? Who cares for me, or my dad, or our little Jackie or Sam?"

That was a fair point, really. And Gideon had never heard the child express concern for anyone other than himself, so he handed the wire back. "Don't let anyone see you, then. And that wire's rusty and blunt. That's a cruel way to kill beasts—if you'd come and do some gardening for me like I asked you to, I could give you the money to buy some new ones."

"I'm never going up there again. Are you not *listening* to me, copper? John Bowe is lying there. In bits."

Sometimes surrender was easier. Let Darren get whatever this was out of his system, prank the village bobby to the fullest extent, and maybe they'd both feel better. Half an hour's distraction wouldn't hurt, anyway. Leaving the child on the doorstep, he went inside to collect his mobile. Lee was still sleeping, with a look of beaten-down exhaustion it hurt Gideon's heart to see. He scrawled him a brief note and left it on the pillow. Took thirty seconds more to pick up the scatter of toys in the hallway, carry them into the nursery and close the door. Isolde whined as he shooed her out of the room, but she knew her duties well these days, and bustled off at his gesture to guard the bed she still could. "All right," he said, emerging into the uneasy sunset light. "Show me. And I warn you, it had better be good."

The route up to Carnysen field was a poignant one. It led along the back of Sarah Kemp's house, then the lane behind the terrace where Bill Prowse kept his little criminal empire. Lorna

Kemp—the brand Gideon had snatched from the burning almost two years ago—was helping her mum in the kitchen: he experienced the smell of their dinner cooking and the little girl's chatter like a warm caress. Sarah was smiling but watchful, her mind clearly fixed on the subject of lost children. Bill hadn't changed the wallpaper in his spare room. The lurid green-and-blue roses still shone their sickly light across the garden. Gideon's duties and promotion to sergeant had kept him over in Truro a lot recently. A constable had replaced him, but she lived over in Bodmin town, and it wasn't her door that got hammered on when ancient demons reared their heads. He had a sense of homecoming, as if he'd been away too long and it was time.

Ancient demons, or annoying little brats whose lifelong malnutrition had finally affected their brains. Darren was positively dancing in the lane ahead, Gideon's distraction too much to bear. He picked up his pace a little out of mercy to the boy. Honeysuckle was arching over the holloway track that climbed the side of the hill. Huge yellow-headed alexanders were nodding in the verges, their combined somnolent scent like a drug to his weariness, to the dull grief that went through him when he recalled that he'd brought Tamsie here not two days ago, to crawl in the soft grass and get her Cornish girl's inheritance of sunshine and fragrance-laden summer air. He was thinking about that, not dismembered bodies or beasts, when he climbed the stile into the field.

It was long and narrow, like all the Bowes' land curving round in a scythe-shaped arc that led up to the farmhouse a mile away. In the low light, the conjoined fields gleamed like a blade, their rich heavy yield awaiting the threshers. The sky had been clear and fine for weeks. Like everyone raised in the moorland villages, Gideon was half farmer by default, and he cast an anxious weather-eye at the copper-green cast on the western horizon. A lot of livelihoods depended on the Carnysen grain.

Which made it all the more annoying that some fool had been out here trampling it down. Gideon was as intrigued by the crop-circle phenomenon as the next man, but it had better not start out here at Dark. The place attracted fringe-dwellers, with the Hurlers and the Cheesewring and the mysterious tors. Really it needed its own full-time constable, to keep the lunacy under some kind of control, and offer education as to why it wasn't all right for strangers to come up here, leave the footpaths and tramp into other people's wages, rent and grocery funds.

"There. There. Do you see?"

Gideon caught hold of Darren's T-shirt and pulled him back before he could compound the damage. "I see someone's been buggering about up here, yes."

"That bit there, where the corn's flattened down. Do you see?"

It was only a small patch. "What are you talking about, Darren? That's just a dead hare, or a..." He took a few steps into the field, careful not to harm any more of the grain. Then he stopped, looking down. "Oh, Jesus."

"I told you. I told you. That patch there, and there, and—"

He was tipping back into hysterics. Gideon turned him sharply round and shoved him towards the stile. A strange huffing sound from the track caught his attention. Leaning through the hawthorns, he saw Bill Prowse lumbering up the hill towards them, bright red in the face and as incongruous in this landscape as a hot-dog stand. Gideon had never in his life thought he'd be pleased to see him. God only knew what had gone through Bill's mind on seeing his eldest pass by the house in company with the village bobby, what grassings-up he'd imagined. "Bill," he yelled, hoisting Darren bodily over the wall. "Take him home. Do it now, and for once in your life look after him."

"What's happened? What's he been telling you?"

"Nothing. I just want you to..." Gideon had to stop to take a deep breath. He'd seen quite a lot in his time as a copper, but he'd never encountered one of his neighbours as nothing more than an arm in a chequered sleeve, expensive wristwatch still attached. *Motive not robbery, then...* "I want you to get out of here, and Darren, you keep your mouth shut." That was a hopeless request, but Gideon had to try, or he'd have the whole village up here gawping. "Do you both hear me? Go!"

Chapter Three

At half past six in the morning, Gideon made his way back home. Behind him on the peaceful hillside, as much of John Bowe's cornfield as practicable had been marked out with crime-scene tape. He could still hear it fluttering in the early breeze, a festive sound for a Lammas dawn. First of August, he thought distractedly. Lughnasadh. The beginning of the Guldize festival that would continue here in Dark across the barley and wheat harvests and on to Allantide. The day was going to be a scorcher—he need not have worried about the sulphurous cast to the sunset after all. The honeysuckle swayed, and he inhaled its untainted freshness. Once the morning wind from the moorlands died, the village would roast on its harvest-time anvil.

Ezekiel's car was parked outside the flat. That didn't seem odd, by comparison with everything else Gideon had seen over the last few hours, and he entered quietly, closing the door behind him.

Voices were coming from the kitchen. He identified his mother's. Rubbing his eyes, he walked into the sunny room, where Zeke and the old lady were seated at the little breakfast bar, and Lee—pale, almost translucent in the brilliant light—was handing round toast and tea. He took one look at Gideon. "Morning, love," he said, came up and kissed him on the cheek. "Your breakfast's ready. Or would you like to go and have a shower first?"

Gideon was covered in soil-dust and bits of corn. He'd spent all night under arc lights, picking his way up and down Farmer Bowe's furrows along with the forensic and SOCO team. "No, I'd love some breakfast. But you don't look as if you should be on your feet."

"I'm fine." Lee pulled out a stool opposite Ma Frayne and Zeke. "Here, sit down."

"Do you see?" the old lady said wonderingly. The question was aimed at Zeke, who was as unshaven and dishevelled this morning as the world was ever likely to see him. He turned to look at her.

"See what, Mother?"

"This is what marriage is. Men with women, men with men, women with women—anything. The people live together, love each other, care for each other."

"Yes, Mother, but—"

"But nothing, Ezekiel, ever again. Do you see how your brother and your brother-in-law watch out for each other, even though Gideon has been working all night, and they both are plainly sick with exhaustion and grief?"

Gideon wondered if he'd curled up in a corner of the cornfield and accidentally fallen asleep. His mother, in comparison to poor Zeke—reddening under the onslaught—looked fresh as a daisy, and full of business. "You're a tremendous ally, Ma," he said. "But Zeke didn't say anything to the contrary. And although we're pleased to see you..."

"It's six in the morning, and you want to know why we're here." Zeke flashed Gideon a grateful look. "I went to see Mother last night, to tell her what had happened before she heard it from anyone else. And it seems she had an... inspiration of some sort in the night, and I'm afraid she wouldn't rest until she'd phoned me and persuaded me to drive her out here to see you. Still, we wouldn't have come if we'd known..."

This was going to be interesting. "Can I ask what you do know?"

"Well, that there's been a murder. One of your local farmers."

"And is that because Mystic Meg grilling sausages over there told you, or—"

"No. I'm afraid some of your neighbours were already out on the streets when we arrived, despite the early hour. They were rather agitated, and deeply embroiled in gossip."

"I swear, one day I'm gonna swing for Darren Prowse."

"Is it a problem? Is there anything we can do?"

Gideon released a sigh. "No. Everything's under control up there. Darren found the body, and I got the Truro and Bodmin lads over straight away. The scene's secure. They just sent me off to shave and have a shower, because..."

"Because the poor sod's on duty in an hour." Lee placed an aromatic plate of sausages, toast and tomatoes in front of Gideon, his usual ladies-first courtesy overruled by the impulse to feed his weary husband. "Isn't that right?"

"Oh, surely not," Ma Frayne protested. "Hasn't he been on duty all night?"

"Not officially, Ma." Gideon flickered her a reassuring smile. "Got to put on my uniform and tour the streets of Dark like an old-fashioned beat bobby. My constable took one look at the bits of poor John Bowe and decided she didn't want to be a copper anymore."

"That's ridiculous."

"I'm not so sure. The forensics assistant fainted, and he's been on the job for years. She'll be okay. Just needs a bit of time off."

"But what about you, Gideon?"

"Oh, I've got my other half to protect and serve me." Gideon caught Lee's hand in passing, pulled him gently down to sit next to him. "Where's your breakfast?"

"I'm okay. Not much of an appetite this morning."

"Share mine. Please." Gideon speared a piece of tomato, and was about to pop it into Lee's mouth on the fork before deciding the spectacle might be too much for his ma. He loved her advocacy, but poor Zeke was getting his arse kicked for the perceived lack of it, a punishment he these days scarcely deserved. In his stiff-necked way, he'd become a good friend to their relationship, and this morning looked as bereaved as anyone could wish. Gideon let Lee take the fork for himself. "So, Ma, I've got to know. What's the big idea?"

"Ezekiel and I will follow Elowen to France. He's a church minister, and I'm Tamsyn Elizabeth's grandmother. I'm sure she won't refuse to see us."

She was fragile today, underneath her valiant uniform of cashmere and pearls. Gideon wondered if she'd spent a sleepless night hatching her plans. "I'm sure she won't. But what are you going to do then?"

"Well, in some of the police dramas I like to watch—you'll know about this, son—they sometimes do a thing called *good cop, bad cop*. Ezekiel will take a very stern approach with Elowen, and tell her that because Tamsyn lived alone with you and Lee for five months, that established a precedent—you know, like when you have a job but no contract, the employer still has certain duties to you."

"Is there any such law?" Lee asked, ignoring Gideon's second quarter of tomato. His face had gained a faint wistfulness during the old lady's speech. "Gid?"

"Not that I know of, but..."

"But that's just the beginning," she went on. "If we can make her just a little bit afraid—nothing dreadful, Lee, just Ezekiel pretending to be the bad cop—then I can tell her how much it's breaking my heart to lose my granddaughter. That I'm a poor old lady who doesn't know how much time she has left. Which is a great exaggeration, of course, but, you see, at this point..."

She pulled out a handkerchief. The exaggeration wasn't a very great one, now she'd heard herself say it. "At this point you're being the good cop," Gideon finished for her gently. "Yes, I see."

"Well, what do you think?"

"Does Ezekiel mind doing his part?" Gideon looked up and found his brother's eyes already on him, saying more clearly than words, *Gid, if you'd just spent the night with her I have, you'd agree to anything.* "Okay. I'm probably just tired, but this doesn't sound as crazy to me as it should. Lee, what do you reckon?"

"No."

All three Fraynes turned to him in surprise. His hands were clenched together on the table. He had taken on what Gideon had come to think of as his winter-sea look—silvery and distant. It was often the sign of an oncoming vision. Gideon took hold of his wrist. "Are you all right?"

"Fine. Just... no."

Ezekiel shifted uncomfortably. "Look, Lee, I know she's your sister. And I don't think we'll be able to manage it exactly as my mother says, but it has to be worth a try. I'm willing to, anyway."

Lee shoved his chair back. He banged down one palm among the breakfast dishes, the sharp gesture so unlikely from him that everyone started back, and Isolde gave a frightened yelp from her basket. "I said no. It isn't the right thing to do. Isn't it enough that I've spoken?"

Gideon got up to follow him out of the room. "Oh, Gideon," his mother wailed, clutching at his sleeve. "Do try to persuade him! I thought it such a good idea."

"Sorry, Ma. If he's this set against it—yeah, it *is* enough that he's spoken."

"Don't *you* get a say?"

Gideon wheeled back to face his brother. A hot snake of pain was rising in his throat, devouring justice and sense. "Don't you dare try to drive a wedge in there, Zeke. Don't you dare."

"Oh, Gideon, he isn't! I know he hasn't been good to you in the past, but—"

"Mother! Please stop apologising for me. I've done my best to make amends to Gideon and Lee for the way I expressed my convictions, but..."

This was all going downhill fast. Gideon took his mother's hand—reached out and awkwardly grasped Zeke's shoulder. "Sorry. Sorry, okay? He's a mess this morning, and so am I. I have to go after him."

He found Lee in the nursery, huddled up in the armchair where he and Gideon had taken turns to bottle-feed Tamsyn. Gideon knelt in front of him. He set aside the little girl's favourite blanket, as if that would make any difference in this bombed-out city of memories. "Oh, sweetheart."

Lee took fierce hold of him. He pressed their brows together. "I was rude to your mum. I love her, and... I was rude to her."

"I love her too, but she rucked up here at half six in the morning on the day after we lost our kid. She can expect to feel the edge of our temper." Gideon kissed him, let his eyes close in the sunlight streaming through the window. "And quite a temper it is—get you, all sexy and assertive, putting your foot down. I think Zeke thinks you're oppressing me."

"Ugh. There was nothing sexy about that. I just miss Tamsyn, Gid. I *miss* her."

"I know. It feels like a hook in the gut. Is there no way you'd let Zeke and Ma try out their crazy plan?"

"I can't. It's a wrong thing to do, and not because I'm frightened of upsetting my bloody sister. I can't explain it—not to them, not to you."

One hook at a time was enough. Gideon let him off this one in silence, rocking him. When his death-grip eased and his breathing quieted, he said, "All right. Look, are you okay? I really do have to go back to work."

"I know. I have to go with you."

Gideon sat back. "Oh, no. Not this time, sunbeam. This is a bad one. And all I'm gonna do is go back up to the field to see if they need me for anything more there, and then I think I'd better call a meeting at the village hall, see if I can talk everyone out of whatever panic Darren Prowse is trying to start."

"The thing is, I've been invited."

"What? *Please* don't tell me John Bowe's disembodied soul is summoning you to—"

"No, no. I just had a phone call this morning, even earlier than our early-bird visitors. It was your HQ at Truro. They want me to go and have a look at the scene once it's been cleared up, see if I can get any read on what's happened."

"Wow. Don't they usually wait until I'm bewildered and desperate before they call in the psychic?"

"Nothing to do with you, Robocop." Lee brushed a kiss to Gideon's mouth, just a moth-wing touch but enough to make him want to sling Zeke and Ma out of the house and slam the door. "Apparently they've hired an officer whose special remit is to look into cases with any kind of... well, I forget what they called it, but anything out of the usual run of things. Folklore connections, Pagan, paranormal, that kind of thing."

"Ah. The weird shit."

"That's it. And this weird-shit sergeant reckons a ritual slaying in a cornfield on the eve of harvest festival might just be the making of his career, so I've been drafted."

"Wait up. Who said anything about a ritual?"

"He did. So you can see what kind of kook we've got on our hands. Looks like I'll be putting out fires, too... All of which is far less important than the fact that I upset Ma Frayne. Better let go of me, gorgeous—I've got to go make things right."

"No, Lee, dear." Ma Frayne came tentatively through the nursery door. "It's for me to make this right. I wonder if you can understand—I was married for fifty years to a man who would have said that something like this was God's will. But now he's gone, and I've come to know what a load of..." She hesitated, and Gideon held his breath: not *bollocks*, surely, not from the cashmere and pearls. "What an *error* that is, I feel obliged to try and fix things, whether God likes it or not. With the result that I've become a most interfering old woman."

Lee held out a hand to her. She wobbled over and took it, subsiding onto the edge of the cot. "You're not," Lee said. "You're a perfectly normal grandma. Look, Gid and I are just shell-shocked. Can you give us a couple of days to think about what we should do?"

"Yes. Yes, of course."

"Is Zeke all right?"

"I've tired him out. He's gone into the garden with Isolde."

Gideon glanced through the window. He'd made serious efforts with the little moorland garden so that Tamsyn would have flowers to marvel at, a pond, a swing. Zeke had taken up an unlikely perch on the wooden board hanging from the hawthorn tree. Isolde was sitting on his feet, her big mournful head laid in his lap. "Jeez, what a screw-up," Gideon breathed. "Right. I'm going out to try and make things right with him, and then all of us—you included, Lee—are going to sit back down and finish our breakfast."

***

The officers stationed at Carnysen field were more used to crowd control after football matches and at Golowan when the fire-dances got out of hand. To his dismay, Gideon encountered the first of them frog-marching old Mrs Waite down the lane. "Michael," he called, recognising the young constable. "What's going on here? That's our village shopkeeper."

"So she tells me, Sergeant Frayne, but she kept trying to get under the tape. We can't seem to make any of them understand..." He paused at the sound of further ruckus beyond the stile. "That this is a crime scene. Soon as we chase one of them away, half a dozen of the others are trying to climb the fence."

"Gideon!" Mrs Waite gave an improbable wriggle and escaped the constable's grasp. She shot to Gideon's side. "I'm trying to tell him, I have to be in there. I'm godmother to young Dev Bowe, and he's in there, crying and sobbing over John—what's left of him, God rest him—with no-one to comfort him."

"That's the problem, Sergeant! We try to keep 'em out, but they've all got reasons for being in."

"That's because they all know each other," Gideon said, dusting Mrs Waite off and straightening the straw bonnet she'd assumed for her mercy mission. "Now, you listen to me, Elsie. It's terrible to hear Dev crying, but there will be somebody on the scene to help him, somebody professional. Michael, tell me there's a counsellor in there."

"There is, but he can't get started because of all the fuss."

"You hear that? You're hindering the police, Elsie. Obstructing the course of justice. The penalties for that are heavy, and what would Dark do for its groceries if you're in the nick?"

"Oh, Gideon." She gave him a painful jab in the ribs. "You're such a joker."

"Am I? You try me and see. Someone will look after Dev, I promise. Now go home." He watched her bustle off down the track, then turned back to the constable. "Right. Next?"

Next were the Prowses, of course, Darren and Bill and a handful of ne'er-do-well cousins from Bodmin. They were variously engaged in harassing the officers trying to guard the stile, and ducking over and under the uniformed arms to snap photos with their mobiles, no doubt for a quick sale to the local gutter press. Gideon, freshly showered and uniformed himself—heartbreak on temporary hold—waded in. He jumped onto the stile, straightened his cap and made a quick assessment. "Right, you lot," he called, and the various well-known faces, Prowse and Kemp and Priddy, turned like odd flowers to a familiar sun. "What do you mean by crowding around here and making a nuisance of yourselves? A man's lying dead in that field."

Jack Wilson stopped his efforts to break through the hedge. He was one of Dark's more sober citizens, his presence here an indicator of general emotional pressure. "We know that, Constable," he said, and Gideon as usual ignored the slip: he'd been their constable for so many long years before his promotion. "It's John Bowe, and something appalling's happened to him. Why isn't anyone telling us what's going on?"

"Because nobody knows yet, Jack. Simple as that."

"The Prowse kid says he was dismembered. That some kind of beast tore him apart."

Nothing worse than half a story, unless it was half a limb. Gideon thought he could see one now. He gestured to the plain-clothes officer frowning over the coroner's shoulder. "Detective Inspector Lawrence? Could I have a word?"

Lawrence had worked with him on the Lorna Kemp case. She gave Gideon a look that suggested he had cornered the market in weirdness, and made her way gingerly out through the corn. "Morning, Sergeant. I gather you had the pleasure of finding Mr Bowe."

"It was one of our village lads, actually. He's a bit shy, and..." Sharply he gestured Darren away from a shiny digital tape-measure someone had foolishly left untended at the edge of the field. "Well, it might be best if I interviewed him. Would that be all right?"

"Please. Knock yourself out." She glanced around impatiently at the crowd. "Always nice to get a good turn-out, but this is ridiculous."

"Popular neighbour, ma'am, and this is the start of the harvest. A lot of people expecting to start work in the Bowes' fields today."

"I don't see why they shouldn't. Not this one, obviously, although we're about to get the wagon in here and clear up. Can you help us with the audience?"

"I'll be glad to take them off your hands. Anything I can tell them yet?"

"I'm afraid not, but try and nix any bloody stories about the Bodmin Beast. We had more than enough of that last time around."

"Yes, ma'am."

"I suppose you already know that Sergeant Pendower, our esoteric-crimes consultant, is coming up to meet your other half later."

"Esoteric crimes, ma'am?"

Her expression became weary, and Gideon wondered how much she'd already had to put up with from Sergeant Pendower. "Someone in Truro has decided—and I have to say, this is partly your doing, Frayne, what with the Lorna Kemp case and then that business in Falmouth—that what this county needs is an expert in paganism, folklore and the wheel of the ritual year. I don't suppose you asked for one at our last general consultation, did you?"

"No, ma'am. I asked for an expert in drug abuse and the effects of unemployment."

"Right. Well, Sergeant Pendower is what we have. Please cooperate, but bear in mind that his work—and Lee's, if he chooses to help us out—is quite separate from our main investigation." She paused a moment, hands behind her back, the picture of British reticence in the face of strong emotion. "Nobody wants to pry, Gideon, but... bloody bad business, that, about your little girl. Everyone at Truro feels the same. If you need some time off as compassionate leave, let us know, just..."

"Just not right now, eh?"

"If you could possibly manage it, no."

Gideon could stand here and burst into tears at this touch of awkward sympathy, or he could start chucking his weight about. There really wasn't anything in between, so he drew a deep breath and turned to face his villagers. "Right, everyone," he barked. "This isn't how we act when trouble comes to Dark. We don't hang about and get in the way of the people trying to help us. All of you have questions, and all of you will be heard, but not here—get down to the village hall, and I'll join you there in ten minutes."

He didn't need to ask twice. Immediately some kind of raggedy line formed in the lane. He wondered at their cooperation, then remembered something Lee had said a long time ago—at their first meeting in Sarah Kemp's kitchen, in fact, before they had so much as shaken hands. *Gideon's worked all his life to keep everyone safe in this village.* Gideon had been at a nadir, and the words had stayed with him. He cleared his throat, lowered his voice and addressed DI Lawrence again. "Don't suppose petty cash would run to tea and biscuits down there, ma'am?"

She was watching him, smiling faintly. "Go ahead."

Chapter Four

"There wasn't much blood," Bill Prowse declared. "That means poor John was dead before he got chopped up."

Gideon took his cap off and laid it on the table amongst the harvest-festival offerings, careful not to damage anyone's broad beans. He waited until the chatter caused by Bill's pronouncement had died down. An expert on most things, was Bill, by dint of long service in front of the TV. "Yes," he agreed carefully. "And that's horrific, obviously, but I hope no-one thinks the alternative would have been nicer."

He let them have a think about the alternative. He'd gathered a couple of dozen of them, and strictly no kids—Darren Prowse had been sent off, complaining bitterly, to the summer school that was meant to help reform his character. They all had their tea and biscuits, and were ranged before him on the plastic chairs as if for a talk on archaeology. Sarah Kemp got there first. "Ugh, Gid," she said, dunking her rich tea with no less appetite. "It's like he was butchered."

"Oh, right," said Frank Pawley, who ran a flourishing meat business on the high street. "Always look to us first, like this was Jack the Ripper. Like your brother-in-law was any better than he should be—"

"Frank!" Gideon thundered. He'd clearly chosen the wrong time for a straight-faced, lame-arsed joke. "Sorry. The point I was trying to make is that speculation is useless. The forensics lads haven't even finished clearing up the field, and until they do, and every scrap of DNA is scraped off John Bowe's barley stalks, bagged up and analysed, we won't know a thing more than we do now."

"So what have you dragged us here for?" demanded Bill Prowse, who'd been first through the door for his cuppa and the gory truth. "Waste of my time, this is."

"Nevertheless, spare me a few of your precious minutes. It's particularly important because your boy not only found John, but ran around scaring the crap out of everyone as much as he could afterwards. If I had a kid—" Gideon's words turned to acid in his throat and he stood for a moment, waiting to be able to breathe. "If someone in this village has flipped out and started hurting people, we shouldn't let our children be conspicuous. Agreed?"

He got a surprisingly fervent response. How many of them knew about Tamsyn? He couldn't handle direct sympathy, but was grateful for the compassionate vibration in the air. "All right," he went on. "I haven't brought you here to tell you what happened to John. I'm just here as your village bobby, same as I ever was. Something bloody catastrophic's befallen one of our neighbours, and I want to keep the rest of you safe. Who has to work on the Bowe land today?" The several hands went up. Harvest was a good chance for casual work. "Right. Obviously Carnysen field's out of bounds, but DI Lawrence says you can go and get started once the coroner's van and the other vehicles are gone. I'm going to add this. Come straight home once your shift is done, and curfew your kids. I want no-one under the age of sixteen out on the streets after seven, and no-one of any age, man, woman or child, out on the moors after dark. Is that clear?"

He was trading on his loss. He hadn't meant to, but under normal circumstances he'd have had to deal with an absolute barrage of protest, and this was a hell of a lot easier. He laid his hands on the table and for a moment let himself look as tired and sick as he felt. "Thank you," he said, breaking the unnatural silence, and was almost relieved when Jenny Salthouse raised her hand. "Yes, Jen?"

"What about Guldize, Sergeant? It feels barely Christian to be asking in the light of what's happened, but do we need to call off crying the neck?"

There wasn't a flicker of Christianity in Dark's version of the harvest-home rites, but leave it to Jen to serve it up on a doily. Still, she ran the parish council ably and well, and Gideon needed her on-side. "Where is it this year? Up by the Bowes' farm?"

"That's right. John said we could scythe the little field by hand and do it properly, all according to tradition."

"Then—much as I hate to say it—I think you'd better postpone. I don't think Bligh and Dev Bowe will want people frolicking up by the farmhouse tonight. And you'll be coming back right over the moor after sunset, so—"

"You *do* think it's the Beast, don't you?"

Gideon met Bill's eyes. He, Sarah Kemp and a handful of the other people in this room had seen too much, last Halloween but one, to deserve a flat denial. In any other village in the world, Gideon might have stood here and preached common sense. *There is no Beast. For God's sake pull yourselves together.* But the people of Dark lived with their moors and their legends and their ghosts, and no-one from the outside ever came to help them. They shaped the world around them for themselves. "I don't know what to think," he said honestly. "There's CID and forensics guys working up at Carnysen now, and I hope to God they'll tell us what to think soon enough—because until then I don't know who my enemy is, and until I do, I can't look after the rest of you properly. So will you try and protect yourselves, and offer every cooperation—including staying well out of the way—to the police?"

Bill gave a snort. Under the murmur of assent that followed, Gideon thought he heard himself being called a worse bloody preacher than his brother, but he could live with that, if only the rest of them would meet his efforts halfway. There was no Beast of Bodmin, not by any sane reckoning, but maybe they could all behave as if there was until John Bowe's killer was caught, and all would be well...

The hall door flew open. Gideon jumped as Lee appeared in the sunlit space, out of breath and pale. "Gid," he said, gesturing back over his shoulder. "Trouble."

***

As well as a Beast, several numinous tors and stone circles, Dark had its own local witch. She didn't fit the bill in many ways, living in a tiny modern terrace on the village outskirts and wearing nothing more outlandish than last season's M&S, but for as long as Gideon could remember, if you wanted your palm read, your toothache eased or your warts transferred to someone more deserving, you went to Granny Ragwen. Recently she'd developed Alzheimer's, and was only maintained in her own home by the efforts of her increasingly frazzled daughter, Madge. She'd lived quietly enough before her illness. You had to know by word of mouth where to find her. Now she'd taken to occasional tours of the high street, declaring to anyone who would listen that she had the mojo and she wasn't scared to use it, and so—Gideon guessed, anyway, jogging in Lee's wake up Pellar Street, counting heads and raised voices, trying to sort out his problems in advance—her fame had spread.

Poor Dev Bowe had found her, anyway. He was standing on the pavement outside her house with a group of the Carnysen farmhands around him. He was gesticulating, almost poking Madge Ragwen in the chest. Madge, never one to take abuse lightly and well used to having to defend herself, was poking back at him, yelling into his face. This was all understandable, or would be in a minute once Gideon got them dragged apart and their separate stories told. What he couldn't work out was the presence of the squad car parked neatly a few yards down the road, and the immaculately uniformed sergeant standing by it with his arms folded, as if he'd arrived in time for some fascinating local folk drama.

Gideon grabbed Lee's arm to slow him down. "Who the hell's that guy?"

"I don't know. Thought he was one of yours."

"Looks like he is, not that he's doing anything to... Oh, wait." He dropped his pace to a walk so as not to plough into the scene like a bulldozer. "I think he might be one of yours. Sergeant Weird-Shit, I presume?"

Lee gave a choked bark of laughter. "Oh, no."

"You go introduce yourself while I break up this brawl. Do I even want to know how you knew this was happening, by the way?"

"Granny Ragwen gave me a call."

"She doesn't have a phone, Lee."

"Nevertheless."

"Great." Gideon gave him a swift, hidden caress to the spine as they parted. They'd both managed to find a working-day mask, but Lee beneath his looked just about ready to die. It was half past nine, time for Tamsyn's second feed and a game of where's-the-dog, a ritual that never seemed to get old for the baby or Isolde. If Gideon was working late shift, he was often around to take part. *Where's the dog? Where's the six-foot policeman? Oh, here they both are under the stairs again.* Shrieks of joy, enough to make the neighbours think the child was being murdered... "Right," he said, stepping between Dev Bowe and Madge. "Back up, the pair of you. Dev, I'm very sorry for your loss, but if you try to dodge under my arm and lay a finger on a woman in my presence, I swear I'll arrest you."

"But her ma... Granny Ragwen..."

"Is an eighty-year-old lady with Alzheimer's. Yes?"

"There's nothing wrong with her! She just pretends! She's a witch, and she knows all about what happened to our John—she *said* she did!"

Madge, twice the bulk of frail skinny Dev, lurched against the flat of Gideon's palm. "She *said* she was courtesan to Charles the bloody Second yesterday, when I had to stop her taking off her knickers in the grocery store! What were you and your bunch of pitchfork-bearing oiks gonna do to her, anyway?"

Gideon glanced at the oiks. There were only three, and matters hadn't yet got to the pitchfork stage, thank God. He pointed at the least-aggressive face. "You! George Miller. I never saw you coming out of Ross Jones's house with a packet of dope in your hand, did I? Good—in that case, come over here and sit Dev quietly down on that wall, while Madge goes in and puts the kettle on for her ma, who's probably scared out of her wits." He waited until these instructions were obeyed, Madge inside and the door safely closed behind her. "I'm ashamed of you lads—really, properly ashamed. Where's Bligh Bowe?"

"Up at the field with the poliss," George sullenly replied. He was blushing to his ears, as if suddenly as puzzled by his presence here as Gideon was. "He's got no time for Dev anyway."

Gideon knew that. John had been the loving parent in the family since Farmer Bowe the elder and his wife had died last year. He'd been fifteen years older than Dev, a good guardian to the runt of the litter. He took gentle hold of the boy's chin and lifted it. "Come on, Dev. This isn't like you. Why are you really here?"

"Because..." Dev looked away, tears welling, a big improvement on the blank rage. "I don't rightly know. She did say she knew why my brother had to die at Guldize. And she does have all that stuff in her house—a skull, and a great big blackthorn stick."

"Have you been inside?"

"No. George told me years ago, after he'd been to get his palm read."

"That really *does* seem hypocritical." Gideon glanced at George, now puce. "Not many years back, a village thought itself lucky if it had a cunning-woman, someone to help with the weather and people's aches and pains. It was seldom they did any harm. And now they're dying out, which ought to please you fine young heroes. It had better not happen any faster here in Dark because of you. Do you understand?"

Dev nodded. Gideon waited until the other lads had done the same, then he sat down on the wall beside Dev and offered him a handkerchief. A few yards away on the pavement, Lee looked up from his conversation with the weird-shit sergeant and frowned, as if scenting trouble on the air. Christ, Gideon hoped not. He'd had enough to last him through Guldize, Allantide, Montol and Golowan. "Thing is, Dev," he said, "you've had a horrible shock. And although you might think you're thinking straight, you're a long way from it. Who's at home to care for you?"

"Nobody. John cared about me. No-one else."

"Well, your godmother was practically climbing a hedge to get to you this morning. If I let you go now, will you let George take you down to the shop? You could help her a bit, make yourself useful. That often helps more than you'd believe." *It's almost working for me.* "Agreed? And as for you other two, if I catch you near this house again, you'll be celebrating harvest-home from an overnight cell in Truro."

Well, that was another fire extinguished. For now, anyway— Gideon hadn't liked the look of Dev Bowe one bit. He went to shake hands with Lee's companion, scrambling through his brain for the right name. Sergeant Weird-Shit had fitted too well, not your traditional double-barrelled title but strangely assonant. "Good morning. Sorry about the ruckus. It's Sergeant Pendower, isn't it? Very good to meet you. Gideon Frayne."

"Rufus, please." Pendower held out his hand. He was a small, upright figure in his immaculate uniform, making Gideon aware of the barley-dust and pollen adhering to his own. "That was very interesting."

"What was?"

"How you handled them. A combination of sympathy and force. Pretending to fall in with their beliefs, and then the boot."

Gideon raised an eyebrow. "I'm with you as far as the boot," he said. "But..."

"Your speech about the village cunning-woman. Very good. Do you understand the meaning of the word *cunning* in that context?"

If I didn't understand, I wouldn't bloody use it. "Kenning. Conning in the French sense of *connaître*—somebody who knows things. A wise-woman."

"Yes. Marvellous! It's not often I meet someone who shares my fascination with the origins of words."

" I tell you what, Pendower—next time you see a street brawl break out between a lone female and a group of big lads, do feel free to jump in."

"Ah. DI Lawrence might have told you that my role's purely observational. Anyway, I could see that the cavalry was on its way." He turned to beam at Lee, who was watching him in polite astonishment. "While you were busy, I've been making the acquaintance of Mr Tyack. I was meant to meet him later, but I'm sure his presence here is far from a coincidence."

"Well, nor is yours, Sergeant," Lee said pleasantly. "Rufus here was just telling me how he met the Carnysen lads down in the village, rampaging round and looking for a fight. So he asked them—given the ritual aspects of this case—if anyone around here happened to dabble in such things."

"Wait." Gideon rounded on Pendower, who took a step back. "You *sent* those lads up here?"

"Of course not. They were going to go *somewhere*, though, and I—"

"You just directed the flow. Then drove up here in your panda car to watch the results."

Pendower looked delighted. "Panda car? I haven't heard that in ages. Yes, I was very interested to see how Mrs Ragwen would respond when directly confronted with an accusation of witchcraft. It's a pity that her daughter intervened."

Gideon met Lee's gaze. The days were long gone when Lee could convey only *calm down, Gid* with such a look. Now it said, through the growing intensity of their bond, *keep calm, and at some point today will be over, and I'll take you home and shag you by the fire.* "Never mind," Gideon said civilly to their new colleague. "I'm sure there'll be other opportunities for you to scare an old lady to death. What exactly is your remit here, if you don't mind my asking?"

"I'm sure DI Lawrence has already told you. I'm to work with Mr Tyack here in looking into any folkloric, esoteric or apparently paranormal aspects of this case." He beamed at Lee. "I don't mind admitting I'm a huge fan. Have you been watching Spirits of Cornwall, Sergeant Frayne? I don't know if you're aware of his approach, but..."

Gideon couldn't resist. DI Lawrence clearly hadn't told Pendower everything. He picked up a look of resigned permission from Lee, and smiled broadly. "I know a thing or two about him, yes. He's my husband."

Pendower blinked. Gideon could see the cogs whirring, Cognitive dissonance, he'd learned it was called, when evidence came along to clash with an established world view. It wasn't a homophobic response—just an insular Cornish one, and left untended could result in the blossoming of UKIP posters in front gardens around election time. "Husband," Pendower echoed, as if he hadn't quite heard right, or Gideon had just got his words mixed up and made an embarrassing mistake.

No time like the present to do a little weeding. "That's right. Lee did me the honour of marrying me last July—didn't you, love?"

Lee stepped forward, hands in his pockets. "I did that."

Pendower was blushing furiously. But he tugged his jacket straight, adjusted his cap, and after a couple more displacement actions was able to say, with some grace, "Well, my best congratulations to you both."

"Thank you." Gideon glanced at Granny Ragwen's firmly closed front door. "Right. I gather you wanted to take a look at the field where poor John Bowe died."

"I... Er, that's right. To see if Mr Tyack can pick up any psychic impressions." Pendower collected himself. "He really is quite marvellous. I can dismiss most alleged clairvoyants as frauds with no effort at all, but... Well, I don't need tell you. You'll know all about him, of course."

"Some. But he keeps surprising me. Shall we move on? The coroner ought to be finished by now."

"Oh, no. I really must interview Granny... er, Mrs Ragwen."

"You have to be kidding. You don't seriously think an unhinged eighty-year-old had anything to do with this?"

"Directly? Of course not. But if she's a self-styled witch, who knows what kind of influence she has over impressionable minds in an isolated place like this?"

Gideon looked him over. Neither of them could pull rank—it was sergeant-to-sergeant, and a clash out here on the pavement would be unseemly, after Gideon had just broken one up. "I'll interview her, if someone has to," he said. "You're welcome to observe."

"I'm told you've also made arrangements to interview the child—a shameless delinquent, as I gather—who found John Bowe. Has it ever struck you, Sergeant Frayne, that you're not protecting these villagers of yours so much as allowing them to run rings around you?"

Yes, it's struck me. I know the rings, and I know where and when they'll spiral in and run back to me. Gideon kept his mouth shut. On some deep level he no longer cared. After Tamsyn's feed and playtime, Lee would take her to the park to wear her out. The one text a day he allowed himself to send would often be a picture of the odd little soul with her latest discovery, a snail or a worm or a lovely lump of moorland dirt. "Okay," he said tiredly, ignoring Lee's glance of alarm. "Like DI Lawrence would say, knock yourself out. But be gentle, Pendower, or..." He struggled to find a threat. Then a good one occurred. "Or I'll let you interview the Prowse child yourself.

Chapter Five

There'd been no need for the warning, or so it seemed at first. Granny Ragwen was having one of her rare intervals of lucidity. Madge was nowhere to be seen, and the old lady, smiling and affable, had set out on her little table three teacups, saucers and plates. It didn't strike Pendower to wonder how she'd known to set a place for Lee, who had done his best to escape but been dragged in by his adoring new friend. "That was a fuss and a half, wasn't it?" she said placidly, resuming her seat in her armchair. "Still, it was better than last time. Burning torches they had then." She paused and added, just as Pendower was pouring his tea, "Back in Bavaria."

He looked up at her from under the brim of his cap. Gideon was suddenly irresistibly reminded of Sergeant Howie encountering his first native on Summerisle, and he pressed his lips together, glad that the tiny dimensions of the living room had forced him to perch on the window ledge behind Pendower's shoulder. Lee, much better at keeping a straight face, only nodded from his seat by the table. "It *was* a fuss and a half," he said, "and not one you should've had to put up with. Are you all right?"

"Why should I be anything else, with Madge and you and the constable there to protect me? And after all, those poor boys were only lads from Carnysen farm. They had a right to be angry today."

"Yes, Mrs Ragwen," Pendower said, mopping up spilled tea from his saucer. "But why were they angry with you? Did you have any dealings with John Bowe?"

"Me? Goodness, no. I hardly saw him in my life, apart from the usual matters."

"Would you mind telling me what those are?"

"Must I?" She gave Gideon a wide-eyed glance. "Am I on my oath, Constable?"

"Not at all," Gideon told her. "This is just a very informal interview. But we really would appreciate anything you can tell us about John."

"Very well." She was kneading a piece of blue-tack between her fingers. In anyone else Gideon would have taken it for nerves, but she was neat and calm as ever, an innocuous old lady in crimplene slacks and floral blouse. "Some of the modern-day farmers are a bit ashamed, that's all. But Farmer Bowe would come to me for cattle charms just like the rest, and to ask me for good weather for the harvest." She leaned forward to look at the sky. "The sun should hold out nicely for them in the fields today. Right up till sunset, and then..." She gave Lee an enquiring little glance, as if he too should know. "Then there'll be a storm."

"Wait," Pendower said, taking out his notebook. "You scarcely knew John Bowe, or so you tell me in one breath. And in the next he's coming to you for charms and weather spells, and goodness knows what other superstitious claptrap, and the other farmers do the same?"

The blue-tack took on tiny human form. "Of course they do, officer," she said mildly. "When did you ever hear that a Dark harvest failed?"

"So you are, by your own confession, a witch?"

"Oh, Constable Frayne, he is fierce, isn't he?" As if startled, she dropped the little figure into the fireside ash. Gideon struggled not to notice that it had acquired a jaunty sergeant's cap and a tiny but accurate face. "Worse than old Matt Hopkins, I declare. Wait a moment while I pick this up—Madge'll want it for the posters in the children's room. My, it is dusty in here, isn't it?"

Pendower sneezed violently. "Yes, it is. You were saying, Mrs Ragwen—you consider yourself a witch, with the power to heal cattle and alter the weather. What else do you think you can do?"

She fidgeted around in her chair. One hand strayed towards the waistband of her trousers, and Gideon prayed they weren't in for a repeat of the grocery-shop incident. "It's funny," she said. "Ever since I got what they call the Alzheimer's, I think I can do all kinds of things. Then I calm down again and I remember I'm just a tired old lady with a few little tricks up her... Ah, there you are." Triumphantly she withdrew a long white feather from the cushion at her back. "Madge is good to me, you know—always buys these with the goose-down. But sometimes the feather-ends don't half proggle your arse."

"Mrs Ragwen! *Sergeant* Frayne is right in that these are informal proceedings—for now. But I do need your cooperation. Do you believe, and have you at any time convinced anyone else to believe, that the fields around this village require any kind of sacrifice for their harvest?"

"A *sacrifice*? Gracious..." She drew the feather absently across the face of her little blue-tack man. "What an imagination you have, Sergeant! I had a friend once, you know—Doreen, they called her, from all the way over in Sussex, but no worse a woman for that. And she wrote a kind of poem, and the young ones today—the girls you'd call witches, I suppose, Sergeant—have taken it up. *Nor do I demand aught of sacrifice*, it said, *for all acts of beauty and pleasure are my worship*. Well, Doreen died, and some of the young 'uns have come to believe it's a very old chant." Back went the feather in the opposite direction, sweeping, delicate. "Which it's not, and Doreen never said it was, but it's none the less true for all that. Do you take my point, Sergeant?"

"Not at all. And I'd be very much obliged—" Pendower broke off with another enormous sneeze, followed rapidly by three more. "Good grief," he rasped, sitting up. His eyes were streaming. "Do you have a cat in here?"

"I wouldn't dare keep a cat these days, would I, Sergeant—not with accusations of witchcraft going around. Allergic, are you?"

"No. Well, yes, but normally it's pollen, and I haven't had an attack like this in years... Oh, excuse me. I'll have to go and get my medications from the car."

He stumbled out. Lee followed, his face a little too carefully composed, and Gideon got to his feet. He paused by Granny Ragwen's chair, folding his arms. "You're really not doing yourself any favours, you know."

"I know. But isn't it fun?"

"*Did* you have anything to do with what happened to John?"

"Of course not. All I said down in the village—and I might have been having one of my turns—was to stay off the moors after dark. I bet you've been telling 'em the exact same thing."

Gideon couldn't deny it. He put out his hand for the little blue-tack man, and when the old lady surrendered it, rolled it into a harmless ball, hoping his motives were pure. "There. For your grandchildren's posters. Do you think you can stay out of mischief till all this is over?"

"Look out for the Beast, Constable."

Ice went down Gideon's spine. "I'm sorry?"

"I'll do my best. That's all I said. I'll do my best, Constable."

Out on the pavement, Pendower was wiping his eyes. Lee was patiently holding a box of tissues. The sneezing was beginning to let up, and Pendower managed a nod in response to Gideon's polite enquiry. "I'm a little better now. Must have been something in her carpet."

"Very dusty, these modern terraces," Gideon agreed. "I hope you feel you've eliminated Mrs Ragwen from your enquiries."

Pendower eyed the net curtains, and the trim little figure moving about innocently behind them. She seemed to be shaking a feather duster, and something about the action made him shudder. "Not at all. She's a very disturbing person. But I'm prepared to leave it for now." He glanced at his watch. "I have to be back in Truro this afternoon, Mr Tyack. If your offer to look over the scene with me still stands..."

***

"You'd think," Lee said innocently, surveying the field of trampled corn, "that your allergies would be worse up here, Sergeant, not better."

"Yes, they would be, if I hadn't had my pills."

Gideon watched the pair of them from the discreet position he'd taken up by the stile. Technically he had no business here, and Pendower clearly wished he'd go and make himself busy with the half-dozen interviews he had scheduled for the day, but Lee had gone pale at his offer to get out of his hair. So here he would stay, quietly waiting, as long as he was needed. He knew it could take a long time.

Pendower, not acquainted with Lee's methods, was expecting faster action. He'd followed at Lee's heels for his first pass down the barley rows, from one length of fluttering tape to the other. Now they were back within Gideon's earshot again. Lee was standing with his hands in his pockets, his posture relaxed. He'd made a big effort after sending Zeke and Ma Frayne on their way, Gideon could tell—was showered and fresh in his jeans and clean white shirt. His grey waistcoat lent grace and class to the outfit, displaying his broad shoulders and neat build. Gideon could have watched him all day.

His was a specialised point of view, though. Pendower was starting to pace. "How will you go about this, then, Mr Tyack? Will you dowse the land, try to get a read on any electromagnetic currents?"

"No. Probably I'll just stand here for a while. Why don't you go and talk to Gid?"

"Well, I'd like to watch your methods, if..."

"Seriously." Lee's voice edged out of its normal good-natured timbre. "Could be a while. Might be best if you let my, er... aura expand."

"Oh, is that how you begin? Do you believe you have an aura, a personal energy field you can expand or contract at—"

"Pendower?" Gideon called. "Come over here for a second. I forgot to tell you something about Granny Ragwen."

God, the man was like a baby bird, running from one parent to the other in the hope of a beakful of worms. Gideon wondered what had made so dry and level-headed a copper turn to the weird shit as his speciality. Was he seeking proof, or a chance at demolition? "You're interested in the origins of words, right?"

"Yes, very. I wrote a paper on etymology as part of my degree thesis. Place names, surnames... They're often a clue to local myth and legend when all other evidence has gone."

"In that case I've got a good one for you. Do you speak Kernowek?"

"Only a few words. A shame, since it's part of my heritage, but I never had time."

"Me neither. Lee's taught me a bit, though."

"Oh, right. I heard him on *Spirits of Cornwall*, reading part of one of the old mystery plays. He really is talented, isn't he?"

"You have no idea." Gideon let it sound as suggestive as Pendower's ears chose to hear. He realised he was enjoying making the poor man blush, and stopped himself: that kind of distraction from personal grief was both short-lived and unfair. "His family taught him as a second language. They're staunch Celtic Revivalists."

"Ah. Marvellous. But what did you want to tell me about Mrs Ragwen?"

"Her surname means *white witch*. It's pretty much a direct translation."

Pendower came to hungry attention. He whipped out his policeman's notebook. "I don't think I quite see it. No, wait—*ra*, as in W-R-A..."

"And *gwen* for white. Yes. So I don't have to pretend to fall in with her beliefs, as you put it. My beliefs or yours are irrelevant to her. Her bloodline's older than the hills around here."

Pendower was scribbling frantically. He looked up, eyes shining. "That really *is* marvellous."

"Yes, isn't it?" Annoyance surged in Gideon's chest despite his best intentions. He'd meant to inspire this little collector with a bit of respect for the Dark village elders, but had only handed him another juicy fact for his archive. "So best tread lightly around her," he added, gathering all his best gravity of demeanour, "or she might just turn you into a toad."

"For heaven's *sake*, Frayne! This is a murder inquiry. And even if my involvement is only peripheral—"

"Yes. Sorry."

"I'm having serious doubts over your impartiality. I reviewed the Lorna Kemp case notes before I came out here. Joe Kemp's body never was found, was it?"

"No. Why—"

"And there's only your testimony, Mr Tyack's and that of a traumatised child for the circumstances of his disappearance. The people around here look up to you, don't they? You wouldn't be the first village copper to take matters into his own hands with a child molester on the loose."

"Joe wasn't a molester. He kidnapped Lorna to punish Sarah for rejecting him."

"Well, whatever his crime, the Beast didn't like it. That's the gist of your report, although you've done your best to sound rational. Kemp got away from you, and vanished after what you ultimately describe as a wild-animal attack."

"That was the only conclusion I could draw." Gideon was drawing another one now. He could hardly believe it. "Hang on. Are you saying I made away with Joe myself, and blamed his death on a local legend?"

"Why not? The framework was in place. People around here talk about this Beast as a reality. I might have done the same myself, in your position."

"Did you say you wanted to watch Lee work?" Gideon asked distantly. He was wondering if he could punch Pendower in the face, sling him over the hedge and blame that on the Beast too. "Because I think he's found something."

Pendower whipped round. His face lit up strangely. "This should be interesting. Is he on a scent?"

"He's not a bloodhound, Sergeant."

Lee had set off between two rows of corn. Gideon saw his target straight away—a thread of blue wool, snagged on a barley ear and dancing in the wind. The forensics team must have missed it. Lee was too experienced a police consultant to need Pendower's shout of warning: Gideon hushed him with a gesture, following him to the edge of the crop. Lee would check it over without touching, and then either leave it in situ or, if it was likely to blow away, ask Gideon for gloves and a bag.

He leaned close to the strand, closing his eyes, inhaling the air around it. Then, to Gideon's astonishment, he snapped it off the stalk in one impatient gesture and strode back along the furrow. "Sorry, Gid. This isn't relevant to your investigation."

"Bloody hell. It had better not be. Do you know who it belongs to?"

"Afraid so."

Gideon thought he knew too. The wool was a particular shade of blue. With a sinking in his gut, he stepped back to let the pantomime play out. Lee wrapped the wool around one forefinger and extended it to Pendower. "You'd better have this back, or your jumper might unravel."

Pendower wasn't wearing a jumper. Like Gideon, he was in his warm-weather uniform of short-sleeved shirt and utility vest. In the cool of the morning, though, arriving with DI Lawrence and her team... "Goodness," he said shakily, attempting to retain his fascinated mask. "Can you really tell that just from being near an object? Touching it?"

"No, you idiot. From smelling. I like your cologne, but if you don't mind my saying so, you overdo it just a touch."

Pendower undid the wool. He was blushing to the eyeballs, and Gideon didn't think he needed say anything to add to his humiliation. He was puzzled, though. "Did Lawrence give you permission to leave that?"

"Not permission, exactly. She told me I could if I wanted."

"To test Lee, right? What did Lawrence say to that idea?"

There was an honesty in Pendower underneath his tricks and bullshit. Caught out squarely, he looked up in wry acknowledgement. "She said, *good luck with that*. Believe it or not, Mr Tyack, I'm actually really sorry."

Lee pushed his hands into his pockets. "I believe you, Rufus. It's not the first time. One client planted a pair of her boyfriend's Y-fronts in an underwear drawer when I was supposed to be helping find her missing husband. But her husband wasn't missing, just off on a bender with his mates in Camborne, and there was a bit of a furore after that." He smiled faintly, turning to look out across the field of silkily dancing corn. "The thing is, I'm not asking you to believe in anything. Your faith doesn't matter to me one way or the other. All you have to do is judge by my results, and if I'm not getting any, I'll tell you right away. Speaking of which, Gid—I'm really sorry. I'm drawing a total blank here. Maybe that's because it's getting dark."

Gideon took his hand to steady him back out onto the field's edge. The sun was just rising to noon above Minions Hill, the day gathering its full brilliance. "All right, love," he said calmly. "Got one coming on, then?"

"What? No, I'm fine. Did you ever wonder..." Lee swayed, and took hold of Gideon like a scaffold, an oak tree in a storm. "Did you ever wonder why it was *called* Dark? The village, I mean?"

"Sometimes, yes." Gideon gave Pendower a look that backed him up five paces. "Come here. You're okay."

"Seems stupid. It's so full of light most of the time. Sunshine and leaves, and you're part of it. You're the same as the moor, massive and lovely and laid out in the sun. Sometimes I have nightmares that I left Sarah Kemp's house five minutes earlier on that day when she called me in about Lorna, and I never met you."

"Didn't happen." Opening his arms, Gideon let him huddle close. "Met you, married you. Everything's all right."

Lee looked up at him. His pupils were constricted, gaze washed out to sunlit silver. His attention seemed to pass blindly through the bones of Gideon's skull and into the closely guarded innerspace where the lightest touch was sweet anguish, inexpressible pleasure and pain "How, though? How did I find you? I love you, Gid."

"I love you too," Gideon choked out. He couldn't do this here, not with Pendower watching. But nor could he spirit Lee away to a place that would be private and safe for such naked declarations. Lee's vision had to play itself out right here, and Gideon knew he'd have hell to pay for interrupting. "What do you see?"

"Leaves. My head is full of leaves and light. But there's a cold wind blowing, and it's starting to get dark. Turn me so I can face into it—just for God's sake don't let go."

"You know I won't." Holding his shoulders, Gideon eased him round, warming and shielding his spine. "Is there a monster I need to unmask?"

"No. It's a lamb. But the lamb will devour the wolf and... he slew John Barleycorn."

Wow. This one was wild. Gideon squeezed Lee's shoulders. "Breathe."

"It's hard. Hard to breathe the darkness. Everything's black now. The leaves are withered, and the moor's gone, and there's no water, no water anywhere. No fields, no trees." He shuddered. "It's coming. It's going to hit."

This time Gideon felt it. Back in All Saints Hall two Christmases ago, he'd sat in the audience and watched while an unseen force made a fist of itself and knocked Lee down. He had a fraction of a second to brace—to hold his lover fast and tight under the impact and then to catch him, one clean grab as he dropped like a stone. "Got you!" Gideon gasped, lowering him onto the turf. Lee's head was back, his muscles in spasm. "Come home now, sweetheart. Come home."

"What's wrong with him?" Pendower demanded. "Is he having a seizure? Should I call for help?"

"Not just yet." Gideon restrained one wild, flailing movement, remembering that they'd missed Lee's last two MRI appointments, one in the flurry of their wedding preparations and the second because Tamsyn had been ill. "Get your phone out. Jesus Christ, Lee. Easy. Easy."

Pendower crouched beside Lee in the grass. "What can I do?"

"Just help me hold him so he doesn't hurt himself. And don't look so scared."

"But he seemed so calm—so normal..."

"He *is* normal. He just has visions." Gideon rolled Lee onto his side. "Mate, if you don't come out of this in thirty seconds flat, I'm calling Commander Summers from Hawke Lake to get you medevac'd. Do you hear me?"

The dark wing passed. Gideon felt it like a pressure-change in the air. Lee jolted once more under his hands and went limp, breathing hard. He half-turned his face into the grass and said, distinctly, and apparently to the daisies and the moss, "The shepherd. The good shepherd of Dark."

"Who's the good shepherd?" Gideon stroked his damp hair. "Is it my brother? Do you want Zeke?"

"No." Lee lay still for a few seconds longer. Then he pushed onto his elbows and sat up. "I just want our baby. You're the good shepherd of Dark, Gid. It's you."

Gideon helped him stand. Between them they brushed off most of the bits of barley from his hair. He glanced regretfully at the grass stains on his shirt, then at Gideon's vest. "Shit. Did I drool on your uniform?"

"Only a bit." He was trying desperately for normality. Gideon propped him discreetly as he could, aware of Pendower in the background, frantically scribbling down notes. "Do you want to try and tell me what it means—the lamb and the wolf?"

"Is that what I said?"

"And something about John Barleycorn, and the fields going dark."

His colour faded from parchment to grey. "Do you remember... last time something like this actually knocked me on my backside?"

"Yes. You were dramatically sick about a minute later."

"Minute's up, nearly. If you let me go now I'll get to the fence. Don't want to contaminate the scene."

Gideon patted him on the back. "You're a true pro, you are. Want me to look after you?"

"No. Just keep Sergeant Weird-Shit out of my face. Please."

He stumbled away. Pendower watched him go, pen poised over a page of his notebook. His expression was hard to interpret. Was there a trace of disappointment there? Lee reached the fence and doubled over. Gideon moved to block Pendower's view. "This is the reality of it," he growled. "The work he does. It isn't always pretty."

"Yes, but..." Pendower flipped a few pages back in his notes. "It doesn't seem to make much sense, either. A lamb eating a wolf? And John Barleycorn's just an old rhyme. This isn't how he comes across on his TV show. I've seen a couple of his stage acts, too. He can cold-read an audience with no props at all."

"Those are controlled environments. Think about what happened here, Pendower—what we asked him to open himself up to."

"I'm not questioning his courage. What was the point of it, though? He didn't give us anything useful at all. Or if he did, it's so cryptic that even he doesn't know what it means." He turned another page or two, shaking his head. "And... wait. He said something about a baby."

Weariness swept over Gideon. "Yes, Sergeant. He's my husband, and we had a baby. It's almost like we were human beings, isn't it? But we lost her."

Pendower blanched. "Oh, God. Did she die?"

"No, she..." Gideon flinched as Lee dropped to his knees by the fence. "I can't talk to you about it now. I have to get him home."

"Right. I'll, er... I'll go fetch my car, shall I?"

First bloody useful suggestion you've made all day. "Please. Bring her all the way up the lane, as close as you can."

Lee was done for. Gideon measured his exhaustion in his lack of protest at being hoisted up, his passive acceptance of an arm around his waist to help him across the field. If Pendower hadn't been there, busily parking his patrol car, opening doors and vaulting back over the stile, Gideon would have cashed in on the situation and lifted him bodily, carried him off the battlefield like the soldier he was. Damn Pendower anyway, the pen-pushing little bookworm—what could he ever know about the risks and rewards of clairvoyance?

Two years ago, Gideon had known nothing about them either. Except that he hadn't been sufficiently open-minded to write down Lee's pronouncements in a book. He'd called him a charlatan and warned Sarah Kemp not to give him any money upfront. He accepted Pendower's help to steady Lee over the stile and into the back seat of the patrol car, where he curled up. He was shivering in spite of the warm breeze. Gently Gideon closed the door behind him.

"Is he okay?"

Gideon turned to face Pendower. The sergeant was too old and solid a man to be suspected of a crush, but Gideon knew the look—an idol turning out to be human, just as nerve-strung and fallible as himself. "I don't know. That was hard for him."

"Yes, I can see that. Sergeant Frayne..." Pendower adjusted his cap nervously. "Can I ask you something? As a fellow officer, I mean, someone I can trust even if I don't really know you..."

"You're going to ask if Lee's for real. If he has a genuine gift."

"Yes."

Gideon lowered his voice. "Let me tell you about his gift. If it was a bad tooth or a tumour or something I could get taken out of him, I'd do it tomorrow. It rips him to shreds. So just be grateful for anything he shows us, and don't ever set another trap for him."

"I'm sorry. I... Can I give you both a lift home?"

"That would be good. Thanks."

Chapter Six

"Sergeant Pendower," Lee said fervently, as soon as the door was shut behind him, "is a pain in the arse."

"I couldn't help noticing that myself. It's a shame *you* don't like him, though—he thinks the sun shines out of yours."

"That's just where you're wrong. He thinks I want the world to believe it does, but really I've got a torch rammed up there to fool them. He wants to get in there—dissect me, if necessary—and find the torch."

Distracted by the imagery, it took Gideon a moment to catch on. "If you mean he thinks you're a fake, he's had his convictions seriously rattled."

"Still. He *wants* me to be one."

"I don't think so. He's your biggest fan."

"Nope. He's just impressed by how well I hide my torch, and my amazing remote-control system for switching it on and off. And the ironic thing is, I know all this because I *am* a genuine psychic and can read his tiny mind like a very short book."

Gideon checked the lock. Their home was a much-besieged castle, and their guard dog was on secondment to the Kemp house. He was glad Lee was talking, but his colour didn't match the vigour of his words, and Gideon wanted him off his feet and securely in bed. "All right, Mr Tiger. Go lie down, and I'll bring you a cup of tea and a sandwich."

"I don't need to lie down." He shuddered. "Couldn't manage the sarnie yet, either. What time is it?"

"Just after one."

"Jesus. We haven't even managed a whole day yet without her."

Gideon reeled him in. He pressed his mouth to the top of his skull. "Tell you what," he said after a moment, almost managing to smooth the rasp of pain from his voice. "If I took my lunch break now, and hopped into bed with you and shared the sarnie, would you submit?"

Lee met his eyes. He dredged up a pallid smile. "That does put a different complexion on it, yes."

They'd been planning to stop for groceries on their way home from Drift. That, together with so many other small daily intentions, had gone to hell. Gideon did the best he could with the end of a loaf, cheese and pickle. By the time he'd made tea and carried everything through on a tray, Lee had obediently got beneath the duvet. He'd showered the Carnysen barley-dust out of his hair, and borrowed the dressing-gown Gideon had left in the bathroom. He looked good enough to eat, but for once Gideon wasn't hungry either, not in that way. He hoped he hadn't made his bedroom lunch break sound too seductive. "It's all right," Lee said, holding out a hand to him. "I couldn't manage the afternoon delight either, not now. Just come here."

Gideon set the tray down, kicked his shoes off and crawled in under the quilt. As often when he'd thought Lee too worn out to offer comfort, he found a strong arm extended to pull him in. He subsided with a faint moan. To breathe his own scent mixed with Lee's through the dressing gown's fabric was a primal reassurance.

He closed his eyes on Lee's shoulder and listened to the thump of his heart. "How are you feeling?"

"Better now. Sorry for the performance."

"We should make you a hospital appointment, get you caught up with your scans. That looked more like a seizure than..."

"Than my usual fit of the vapours? Yeah, it felt like one. But I don't think it was anything to do with me, if you know what I mean. It came from whatever happened in that field." He ruffled Gideon's hair. "And I know I have to start trying to untangle whatever did happen from the wolves and the lambs in my brain, but..."

"It's okay. Don't rush it."

"Did you really threaten me with Flyin' Flynn Summers as a punishment for not waking up?"

"Not exactly a punishment. More an inducement."

"I'll say."

Gideon slid a hand into the dressing gown, smiled as a warm nipple tightened against his palm. Just an autonomic response, but he and Lee had raised one another from the dead before. "You're disgusting. And Summers is as married as you are, so forget him. Did you see the guy he brought with him to the services benefit night?"

"What, the ex-army doctor, all brooding good looks and haunted past? Can't say as I noticed him, no."

"Whatever."

"Whatever. Stop distracting me. You know I've got to try and get something out of all this before it fades. Do you remember anything I said?"

"Pretty much all of it. You said, very clearly, that the lamb will devour the wolf, and he slew John Barleycorn."

"The lamb *will* devour the wolf? Not that he's already done it?"

"No. You said *will*."

"That's important. Be careful, Gid—the lamb hasn't finished his work."

"And it's a he, this lamb? A person?"

"I want to say yes. But when I think about it, I'm getting a sense of division—two people, maybe, or one and... something else. Tell me, love—as sensible men, you a copper and me just a deckhand and a bartender when I'm not making creepy pronouncements in cornfields—do we believe in the Bodmin Beast?"

Gideon let the sunlight filter through his eyelashes. Beyond these self-made rainbows lay the moor at its sunniest best. Tourists came for hundreds of miles to walk its shining expanse. It was peaceful, benign, devoid of any creatures larger than the ponies that cropped the turf around the Hurlers. "As sensible men who lived through the Lorna Kemp case... I don't know. Is that important too? Something to do with the rest of your vision?"

"There was more?" Lee gave a shiver of disturbance. "I really went to town, didn't I?"

"You talked about the moor going dark. Everything turning black, and losing the trees and the water. Don't you recall?"

"Yes, I do. I just... didn't realise I'd said any of it. I thought it was just a projection of how I was feeling."

It took Gideon a second to understand. Then he sat up, disentangling carefully. "About Tamsyn? That's how you feel inside?"

"Oh, Gid. I'm trying my best, and I know you are too, but..."

"You know, when we were up there in the field, Sergeant Weird-Shit asked me what was wrong, and for some unknowable reason I told him the truth. I said we'd lost our child. And he asked me if she'd died."

"Oh, Christ."

"I know. And I told him she hadn't, but... in one sense I feel as if we're acting like she did. I don't quite understand why we're not on the ferry right now with Ma and Zeke, doing everything we can to get her back. She didn't die. A couple of idiots took her from us."

Well, that was off his chest. Gideon waited to feel better. Instead he watched his lover's face turn bleak and cold with despair. "I told you," Lee said hoarsely. "It's the wrong thing to do."

"Probably, yes. But I still don't really know why."

"You think I'm hanging back on purpose. That it's because of Elowen, and I'm... I don't know—dressing it up as some kind of vision."

Gideon got out of bed. He looked out at the smiling, gorse-shimmered moor. Most likely Lee didn't remember telling him he was part of all that beauty either. He turned back to face the room. "Fuck," he whispered, running a hand over his hair. "I did not say *any* of that."

"You wouldn't, would you? You're too kind. Don't worry, I haven't been poking around in your mind. It's just what any sane man *would* think."

Gideon grabbed a fresh shirt out of the wardrobe. He smelled of hard graft and misery, and he had interviews to conduct. He strode down the hall to the bathroom: closed the door behind him with great deliberation, letting the aborted slam ricochet through his shoulders instead. He pulled his sweat-damped shirt over his head and stood staring blankly at himself in the mirror. Tears did not suit him. They contradicted everything about him—his sturdy frame, the air of calm reassurance he'd cultivated over all his years as a street bobby until it had become part of him. He evicted a handful of Tamsyn's rubber ducks from the sink, turned the tap on hard and muffled one great sob in the water, splashing it into his face.

That was better. He continued the treatment until the surge of grief had passed. Then he dried off, blew his nose and put on the clean shirt.

Back in the bedroom, Lee was only a shape beneath the quilt. Now Gideon had to repress a painful rush of compassion—and, against all odds and sense, the urge to laugh. The poor sod looked like Isolde when the world had become too much for her and she'd crept beneath the sideboard to escape. Cautiously he lifted a corner of the quilt. He caught a glimmer of silver, and then—his imagination, surely—the faintest growl. Maybe he *should* call Zeke, who had performed impromptu exorcism on Lee's beleaguered spirit before...

No. This was just ordinary human misery, put beyond manners and even affection. It wasn't written into their marriage vows, but it had been one of Gideon's first assurances to his new lover, something Lee had desperately needed to hear: *you don't always have to be nice for me to like you.* So Gideon went to the telephone table in the hall, tore off a sheet of notepaper and wrote three words—the obvious ones, unashamed to be corny and straightforward in this emergency—and enclosed them in a quick scrawl of a heart. He folded the paper and slipped it under the duvet. "I've got to go out now," he said levelly. "I'll just be around the village if you need me. I'll be back by eight."

***

The door opened before he could turn his key in the lock. Lee was standing off to one side of it, eyes downcast, the harvest sunset making a burnished statue of his immobility. He'd turned in his second huge effort of the day and was dressed in clean jeans and the same shirt he'd been wearing when Gideon had first set eyes on him at Sarah Kemp's. It was an old one, faded with laundering, and a favourite of Gideon's because of the associations. Wordlessly he held up a folded piece of paper. Gideon recognised the note he'd left. On its blank side Lee had returned him the same message, one word added at the end. *I love you too.* "It's all very well liking me when I'm not nice," Lee said quietly, drawing him into the house. "Nowhere is it written that you have to love me when I'm being a complete dick."

"You're wrong. That's exactly when I have to love you. And you weren't being a dick—just tired and unhappy."

"Well, let's not split hairs." Lee tucked his arm through Gideon's. He bumped his brow once off his shoulder and led him through into the living room, where a handful of fire was cheering the beginnings of a cloudy twilight. "Are you hungry? Or have all your villagers been plying you with cake?"

"Mrs Waite offered me her killer sponge, but I declined. I'm starving, actually—especially if that's your chicken casserole I can smell."

"With roast potatoes and carrots. It'll be ten minutes or so. Go and get changed, and I'll fetch you a drink."

The flat was pristine. They'd been living in chaos for months. Lee must have got out of bed and spent untold hours in tidying away their books and papers, dusting shelves and hoovering dog hairs and baby crumbs out of the sofa and carpets. The bed was neatly made and turned back to air—just in case of lingering silver-eyed demons, Gideon thought with pained amusement, stripping out of his uniform. The bathroom had been cleared of Tamsyn's toys, the whole flotilla and menagerie it had taken to amuse her during a five-minute wash. He showered and picked out a favourite outfit of Lee's, the shirt and trousers he'd worn to their anniversary dinner in July. If love and goodwill could fix this hole in their lives, the job would get done.

Eventually, somehow. In the little dining room they seldom used, Lee was lighting candles at the table. Beneath his smile he looked tired enough to die. He pressed a soft kiss to Gideon's cheek, and they went through the pantomime of pulling out chairs for one another until the game broke into laughter and they both sat down.

The casserole was good. They'd each perfected a few simple recipes, and this was Lee's speciality, although more often of late they'd eaten ready meals on the sofa, the baby propped between them and trying to hijack each forkful as it passed. Zeke had said they were spoiling her, not teaching her proper table manners, but they'd have got around to it in time. And eating like this—just the two of them sharing the table, napkins and nice silverware— wasn't any worse or better than the alternative, just different. They'd have found the balance eventually, between doing everything with their kid and separating out the strands of their own adult lives. These things took practice, the trial-and-error stages most parents could take for granted. They both ate conscientiously, doing justice to the meal and the strength it brought. "That was gorgeous, love," Gideon said, giving them both permission to stop. "Thank you."

"My pleasure. How did your interviews go?"

The other menu option had been bitter herbs washed down with tears. Gideon was fairly certain of that, just as he knew Lee had chosen daily small talk over another anguished wrangle about their child. "Routine. No surprises. Even Darren and Bill Prowse seem to have been where they claim they were when John was killed, and everyone else can account for themselves too. Nobody saw or heard anything out of the ordinary at all."

"What about Bligh and Dev Bowe?"

"Oh, no." Gideon shook his head in comic reproof. "The village bobby doesn't get to do those interviews. CID deals with immediate family."

"CID doesn't know them from Adam."

"Well, that can be a good thing—no preconceptions. I'll probably be allowed to have a chat with them once they've been eliminated."

Lee's eyebrows went up. "What—as suspects?"

"Yep. First port of call in a murder enquiry, the loving relatives. Let's face it—if ever Zeke was found murdered, I'd be the likeliest perp, wouldn't I?"

"After me."

They both smiled. Their bitching about Zeke was mostly groundless now, a habit. "I hope he's all right," Gideon said unguardedly, his pre-dinner beer suddenly going to his head. "I'll give him a call. He was nearly as upset as we were, and maybe Elowen would phone or text him even if she felt she couldn't contact us. You know, just to say how Tamsyn was doing."

"Gid..."

"Look, I accept that rushing off to France is the wrong thing to do. That doesn't mean we can't keep in touch. Or..." He paused, a new fear twisting in him. "Is even that too painful for you?"

"For *me*?" Lee got up. He took Gideon's hand and drew him upright. "Come with me. I have to tell you..." He swallowed hard and caught his breath. "No. I have to *show* you something. Please."

Gideon followed him into the living room. The sky to the northwest was still bright, red-gold light shafting through strange heavy cloud sculptures. The fire gleamed brightly, somehow necessary despite the evening's warmth. "You even cleaned the hearth," he said uneasily. "The whole place looks great. You didn't have to do it, though—not as an apology."

"I know I didn't have to. Sometimes if you're tired and unhappy, a clean house helps." Lee had retained Gideon's hand in his own. "You read that so easily, didn't you—why I did it?"

"I suppose so, yeah. But it's obvious, isn't it?"

"Maybe. Where did I put the TV remote?"

"On the edge of the bookcase. How am I supposed to find it there?"

"Think about it, Gid."

The bookcase was behind him. All he had in his mind was an image of Lee turning round and setting the remote down on the shelf. "Oh. Did you, er... Did you *send* me that?"

"No. You picked it up all by yourself because you weren't thinking about it. You do it half a dozen times a day. You read me all the time, and I want you to do it now, because I can't be on my own in here with this—this *feeling*—anymore."

"What feeling? About Tamsyn?"

Lee nodded, his eyes darkening with frustration. Gideon ran a thumb over his cheekbone. "How do I share that with you, though?" he asked. "I... I *am* thinking about it now, and I'm not picking up anything at all. Maybe I've developed a bit of married-man's telepathy, but—"

"Oh, you've got no idea. You heard old man Fisher. You saw Morris Hawke. And before you tell me that I was channelling those things through to you, you saw and talked to Gwylim Kitto all on your own—not to mention that the bloody Beast of Bodmin came and scratched on your door to ask for help before I'd even met you."

"What?"

"Don't you see that yet? You thought it was chasing you. And in a way it was, but not to hurt you—to get you out onto the moors where you belong and do what you're best at. Helping people. Finding lost souls."

Gideon stood silently, feeling the mesh and the press of Lee's fingers between his, the grip tightening and releasing in a slow rhythm. He remembered sanding down the front door of the old parish house before it had gone on the market, because horror-movie claw marks scored from top to bottom weren't much of a selling point. He remembered making love to Lee on the inside of that door—their first exchange, while beyond it, incomprehensible forces of moorland night snuffled and scratched and strained the barricade. What had Lee said to him? *We have to seal the gate...* "Please tell me," he said at last, "you don't believe some fairytale monster ripped John Bowe apart as a calling card for me."

"I don't know. But you're important in all this—so much more than you ever let yourself know. You're the good shepherd—the guardian. Let me go for a second while I close the curtains."

"Oh, no."

"What?"

"We don't have to... shut the place up, do we? Start taking down the paintings?"

Lee smiled, a bright unexpected flash. "Oh. No, not at all. That was Hawke, and he more than met his match in you. I just don't want our neighbours to see us rolling around on the rug."

Gideon stared in astonishment. Good though the casserole had been, Lee would have had to serve it with a Viagra cocktail to get any action tonight. While he was still wondering how to break the news, Lee came and stood in front of him. He undid the buttons of the old plaid shirt. There was nothing intrinsically sexy in the action: he could have been getting ready for a bath or for bed. But when he was done, he looked up and met Gideon's eyes. In the newly darkened room, the firelight could have full sway. Lorna Kemp had done well when she'd swapped out the unpronounceable Tyack for Tiger. In the flickering shadows,

Gideon could almost see his stripes. "You're so bloody beautiful," he whispered, undoing the last button, the one deliberately left fastened for him. "God give me strength to make the most of you."

"You always do. The most of me, the best. I want you to come inside of me."

"Oh." Gideon's performance anxiety evaporated like snow on a hotplate. Lee's occasional blunt statements of his needs and desires had instantaneous, intoxicating effect. "I'll go get the lube, shall I?"

"No, big man. For once I don't mean it like that. Just come here."

They went down on the hearthside rug awkwardly, almost shy with one another in the intensity of Lee's new meaning. Gideon rolled under, closing his eyes in the gentle storm of kisses Lee was unleashing on his brow, his throat, finally on his open mouth, tongue pushing urgently. Lee grunted and lifted his hips, the signal clear for Gideon to slide a hand down and unzip and unbutton them both. "I love you," Gideon managed between kisses, tugging his cock and Lee's out of their clothing. "And I'll go along with whatever new project you've got in hand, but... you are gonna get yourself screwed tonight, son, if you carry on like this."

"Don't mean to tease you." Lee reached down and captured both of them in a warm grip, holding them length-to-length together. "I need you hot, though, so you can..."

"Can what?"

He laid his brow softly to Gideon's. "So you can let go all your notions of what you think you can and can't do and just... come in."

Gideon had no idea what he meant. He didn't really care. It was enough to lie here under his weight and heat and let the world drop away. He saw a beach in his mind's eye, a silver sea and a broad stretch of sand. He was floating over the cliffs, which should have alarmed him but didn't. The air was sunny and full of the scent of gorse. "What are you playing at, lover?" he asked lazily, writhing his hips up against Lee's grasp, instinctively curling a hand around the back of his skull. "Where are we now?"

"My borderlands. The edge. I need you to come inland."

There was a holed stone on top of the cliff, like a displaced Mên-an-Tol but much larger. When Gideon drifted closer— effortlessly, as if drawn down through the air whilst at the same time comfortably inhabiting his body by the fireside—he broke into laughter. The stone was a hybrid megalith and Stargate. "Do we go through there?"

"Well, it works as a symbol, doesn't it? Our heritage and our wasted youth. I bet you watched it too."

"If the pastor wasn't home. Even Zeke used to creep in sometimes."

"All right, then. Come on."

He didn't have to do anything. He let the stone, with its hieroglyphs and ancient air of sanctity, leap up and swallow him. And then he was inside Lee's mind.

No. Nothing so dramatic as that. He was still aware of himself and his other half. He could see, clearly as if they were his own, all the lights and the landscapes of Lee's interior. He drew breath after exhilarated breath and it wasn't enough. He wanted to immerse himself in this dazzling country, drown in it. "Easy," Lee said, releasing his hold and crushing their bodies together so Gideon would feel the demands of his flesh in the fireside world. "We're not meant to see this much of one another, not in this life. And this is just the edge."

"I love your edge. Why shouldn't I see it?"

"Because our nice thick, opaque skulls are there for a reason. We have to understand one another from the outside. But just this once I need you to look further. Come inside."

They were back in the flat. Gideon jolted under the impact of arrival. It was weirder to occupy the next room and this one at the same time than it had been to fly over Lee's beach. They were standing in the nursery, hand in hand. Tamsyn was safe in her cradle, sound asleep. And surrounding her—head and foot of the crib, window side and door side—sat four strange immobile versions of Isolde. Each of them was facing outwards, and, grotesquely, each one wore a paper mask with the crudely drawn face of a lamb. "What is this?" Gideon said hollowly. "That's our dog. Why are there four of her?"

"I'm not sure. Possibly it's a directional thing. I didn't have a religious upbringing, but you remember the prayer your father taught you—*Matthew, Mark, Luke and John, bless this bed I lie upon...*"

"I remember. *Four corners to my bed, four angels round my head. One to watch, one to pray, and two to bear my soul aw-...* No!" Gideon leapt for the surface, pulling Lee with him. The nursery folded up into a paper dream beneath them and they soft-landed back beside the hearth. "No, not that. What did it mean?"

"I don't know yet." Lee was holding Gideon's face between his hands, his grasp a warm chalice of life. "Breathe. I'm sorry I did that to you."

"My God, are these the things you *see?*"

"You've known that from the beginning."

"Yes, but you never showed me... Why was the dog wearing a mask? Why—"

"Gid, finish what you're doing. Please."

He'd almost lost track. But his half-forgotten body gave a hungry surge, and Lee cried out in relief as he rolled on top. "I saw inside you. I was right there."

"Yes. Nobody else on earth, love."

"I wanted to stay."

"We can't. We can't." Lee arched his back, closed his thighs hard around Gideon's. "We have to make do with... this."

With seeing each other, working each other out, from the outside. It would take a lifetime. And that was what Gideon had signed up for with this man. He settled for it—grabbed for it joyously, hauling Lee into his arms. Clamped together, shoving hip to hip in the restrictive tangle of their clothes, they rode out the next thirty seconds in a hush broken only by muffled grunts and Lee's half-suffocated gasp for air. Gideon held out for the buck and heave of the body underneath him, the clench of Lee's fingertips into his arms. For the wet rush against his belly, irresistible trigger for his own hard coming: he pinned Lee down, pressed hot kisses to the side of his neck and growled out his name.

They drove each other to breathless silence. Beached and delivered at last on the far side of the act, Gideon fell back onto the rug. He made a cushion of his shoulder and welcomed Lee there. "God almighty. Why was that..."

"So hot?" Lee wrapped an arm around him and lay panting, aftershocks still rippling through. "Because you did it. I asked you to come inside, and you... you did."

"It was no effort."

"Not to you. A thousand men would've turned away—not from the beach and the Stargate, but... that nursery. The dog and the masks. Do you see why I had to show you?"

"Yes. I get that it would be wrong to try and bring Tamsyn home just now, that there's some great danger. But I can't read it any more than you can. Why was the dog wearing the mask of a lamb?"

"I don't know yet." Lee drew back Gideon's shirt and anxiously examined his shoulder. "I bruised you a bit."

"Only very discreetly. No love-bites above the uniform collar..."

"As per regulations. A lamb's mask on the dog... Could be simple wolf-in-sheep's-clothing symbolism, but Isolde would never hurt her."

"No. She was guarding her, from all four sides, or telling us that we had to. Seems like a lot of this depends on working out who or what this dangerous lamb might be."

"And I'm not being an awful lot of help." Lee raised his head, inhaling deeply. "Smells like somebody's roasting one at the moment. Did I leave the cooker on?"

Stiffly Gideon sat up. "Don't think so. That smells like woodsmoke—a bonfire, maybe."

"Hang on. I'll go and have a look."

Gideon watched as he went to open the curtains. It had been a long, tough day, and now they *had* survived more than twenty four hours without their daughter. He wasn't feeling any better for crossing the barricade. He wondered if he could steer himself and Lee off to bed while the tide of aftermath sleepiness was still upon them. That would get a few more hours beneath their belts, and surely tomorrow would be easier.

"It is a bonfire," Lee said, standing on his toes to look out across the hill. "Either they're burning down Carnysen farm, or..."

"Or some idiots have decided to go ahead with the Guldize celebrations anyway." Gideon scrambled to his feet. "I can't have poor Dev and Bligh bothered by that kind of thing tonight." He could have used a few hours' sleep to revisit Lee's beach and cliffs. Who else would have such a beautiful borderland around his mind? The modified Mên-an-Tol had been for Gideon's benefit, a construct to overcome his disbelief, but everything else was just Lee, the windswept liminal freedom Gideon had experienced from their first hours together. He'd learned something from his brief visit, though—it didn't occur to him to try and leave Lee at home. The kind of love that tried to swaddle up grief in over-protection would do him no good, and why would Gideon deprive himself of such a comrade? "Come on. Are we presentable?"

"Just barely. Change of pants might be good. Is it okay for me to tag along?"

"Tag, my arse. This isn't a police matter—just a neighbourly visit. I bet you a fiver Bill Prowse and his mates are involved somehow, and if so there'll be fisticuffs. So I'm sending you in first."

Lee smiled, palpably pleased at the thought of violence. "I can't wait."

Chapter Seven

A neighbourly visit was one thing, but Gideon would never be anything less than the arm of the law to the people of Dark. He'd driven Lee's old Escort up here, not the patrol truck, but even so, heads started turning as soon as he pulled up in the Carnysen farmyard and got out. Lee came round the bonnet to stand beside him. "Looks pretty orderly, for one of Bill's riots."

"Does, doesn't it? I don't think I even see him here."

"Must be swingers' night in the Camborne layby."

Gideon gave a helpless snort of laughter. "God's sakes. I do see Bligh Bowe over there, which is weird. He doesn't look too upset."

"Okay. You go do your neighbourly thing with him, and I'll just melt into the crowd, if that's all right. See if I can find any stray lambs."

Just you be careful. Gideon didn't have to say it. There were lots of things he wouldn't have to say to Lee anymore, he realised: a whole expansion of their nonverbal range. Lee nodded, dark eyes lambent in the bonfire's tawny blaze. Then he slipped away, climbing lithely over the drystone wall into the field.

There wasn't much chance of finding Bill Prowse here tonight. The Dark Guldize involved some hard manual graft as part of its celebrations. Only the bystanders had noticed Gideon's arrival. The men and women busy in the farm's home meadow were too involved in their labours to look up. Everything seemed peaceful, so Gideon took a slow track around the boundary wall, enjoying the festivities for a moment himself. According to the rules he'd laid down in the village hall that morning, he was going to have to break them up. And that was a shame, because this was one of the most ancient and compelling sights anywhere in the world, let alone Cornwall: a row of men and women hand-scything a field of corn.

The blades sliced rhythmically through the stalks, catching the last light of the sun. Gideon took note of the dozen or so faces made pure by concentration, and shook his head—these same people could express fifty different opinions on any given topic in the pub, but set them to work on any one of their beloved heritage tasks around the wheel of the year, and they turned into a corps de ballet. Slice and straighten, step. Slice and straighten, step. The scythes were either cherished heirlooms from farming ancestors or lovingly handcrafted blades created in metalwork classes at the village forge. An odd pang went through Gideon's chest. Like any place on earth, Dark had its heroes and villains, but they were good people on the whole. He'd grown up with them, known their elders all his life, watched his own generation have children, fall in and out of love, debt and divorce. Ordinary people, not to be found anywhere else in the world.

Not just a dozen or so. Exactly thirteen, including the leader who marched ahead of the line, swinging his scythe boldly from side to side as if harvesting the blood-red air. He was stamping his feet, giving the beat to the Guldize chant, the reapers and all the gathered crowd roaring it back to him. The number would interest Lee, although doubtless it only meant that thirteen people had happened to turn up with their blades. The song itself echoed

Lee's vision in the field where John Bowe had died. *Three men came from the west, their fortunes for to try, and these three made a solemn vow, John Barleycorn must die...* A cold-footed goose picked its way over Gideon's grave, and he looked around him, seeking the source of the unease. The clouds massing over the hilltop had taken on a bruise-coloured weight as the sinking sun lit them from below, but nothing was out of place, apart from...

Gideon sighed. Sergeant Pendower, still neatly turned out in his uniform, was perched on the fence beside Bligh Bowe, rapidly scribbling notes. There wasn't any point in asking him why he hadn't tried to stop this gathering, on a curfew night with a dangerous killer somewhere on the loose in the fields. Instead Gideon went and leaned quietly on the fence on Bligh's other side, and waited until Pendower noticed him. "Oh!" he said at last, and narrowly caught himself from tipping backward into the field. "Sergeant Frayne. I didn't think you'd be here tonight."

"Nor did I, seeing as it wasn't meant to happen. Bligh, I'm terribly sorry for your loss today. Do you want me to clear this lot off your land?"

Bligh bent down and picked up Pendower's notebook. He was a stocky man in his thirties, almost as comely as his brother had been, with the blond good looks so rare on the peninsula. He was smiling politely, but he looked as though he might have been telling Pendower the history of the Guldize festival for rather a long time. "Hello, Gideon," he said, handing the notebook back. "No, don't worry. Fact is, I asked the lads to come and cut the field, just as they always did. I didn't think John would have wanted it to be called off."

"OK. But you seem to have the full party going on, bonfire and cider and people wandering in and out of your kitchen... Are you all right with that?"

He shrugged helplessly. "It was all set up. When people started turning up along with the reapers, I just thought I ought to go ahead. They got the harvest in off the main fields in record time today, knowing the weather was going to change. I owe them."

Beneath his moorland farmer's stolidity, Bligh was nervous as a cat. Hardly to be wondered at after the day's events, but Gideon's senses twitched. "Pendower," he said conversationally, gesturing over the field in the opposite direction from the one Lee had taken. "Lee's just over by the hedge there, seeing if he can pick up any—er, Pagan vibes from the land. I'm sure he'd like your input." A little ashamed, he watched Pendower scramble down from the fence and set off as fast as dignity allowed. "Sorry," he said to Bligh. "Sergeant Pendower's doing some kind of research project. Hope he hasn't been a nuisance."

"No, no. Just asking about the farm, how long we'd lived here, where we came from—that kind of thing. Seemed very interested in our names, as well."

"Ah. Names are his speciality." Gideon was suddenly sure that Bligh had been relieved to talk to a police officer about anything other than his brother's death. Well, Gideon wasn't about to talk to him about it either. "You'll have had CID with you all today, I suppose."

"Yes. Went over the house from cellar to rafters, they did. And kept me and poor Dev stuck indoors all day, answering a hundred questions. I couldn't even see the point of half of them."

"Not quite all day for Dev. I met him up at Granny Ragwen's this morning."

"Oh, God." Bligh ran a hand over his face. "Yes. He told me about that, as best he could. He was very upset."

Gideon gave him a moment. They watched the field together, the progress the reapers were making towards the last few rows of corn. "I'm sure he's devastated," Gideon said gently. "He's a lot younger than you and John, isn't he?"

"Yes. Fifteen years. He was our mum's autumn rose—that's what she used to call him, anyway. Her last lamb."

"How is he tonight? Isn't all this noise bothering him?"

"No. I had the doctor out to see him this afternoon, he was so bad. Gave him something to make him sleep. Can I tell you something, Gideon? I said the same to the CID, and it's important."

"Go ahead."

"Well, John and I were old enough to cope when Mam and Dad died. But Dev—it knocked him for six. We've tried to keep it quiet, but a couple of months after the funeral, he was diagnosed with schizophrenia. He hears things and sees things sometimes, and he talks about them. So... please, anything he comes out with to you, will you take it with a pinch of salt?"

Over the years, Gideon had learned to take witness statements without any seasoning at all. He nodded gravely. "I'll bear it in mind. Poor Dev, though. It must have been tough on you and John."

"Yes. How I'm gonna manage him on my own, I'm not sure."

"Shall I have social services pay you a visit?"

"Please. But ask them not to set too much store by what he says about me and John. He's sometimes... very hostile to us, and God knows neither of us ever gave him any reason."

Gideon laid a hand on his arm. Something was off, but this wasn't the time to root around after family secrets, and as far as Gideon had seen, the elder brothers had done their best with the boy left on their hands. "No, I'm sure of that. Don't worry, okay? You've got enough to deal with." Making a mental note to see Dev Bowe as soon as was decent and let him talk his heart out, he returned his attention to the field. "Looks like you have a winner."

"Oh, that's right. It's gonna be Joe Poldue." Bligh's face lit with a smile so full of longing and regret that Gideon's sinuses prickled in sympathy. Missing his brother, Gideon supposed, at this height of the ceremony, and the Dark village version was moving in itself—a kind of a race to be last, although any signs of slacking would have been dishonourable, and all the reapers took down their final row of corn with as much strength as they could muster. Someone had to lose, though, and thus it was often the oldest or the least physically able among them who cut down the last shock of corn. Old man Poldue, whose tobacconist's shop had been teetering on the brink of closure for as long as Gideon could remember, stood up straight in the firelight, proud as if he'd just whipped Excalibur out of the stone. Instead of a sword, he was waving a handful of barley over his head. "I have 'un! I have 'un," he cried, broke into a fit of wheezy coughing and got out the magical third repeat into the expectant silence. "I have 'un!"

The other reapers laid down their scythes, a gesture of surrender and respect. The onlookers came running to the fence, and Gideon, who had grown up with the rite and knew it better than his father's prayer book, couldn't resist joining in with the roar of response—*What do you have? What do you have? What do you have?*

"A neck! A neck! A neck!"

Now would commence the mayhem. Poor old Joe would have to try and get his prize, the final neck of corn, into the farmhouse kitchen without being seen by the sharp-eyed maiden appointed there to keep watch. This guardian—Jenny Salthouse this year, already at her station behind the door with an upraised bucket in her hands, grinning from ear to ear—was authorised to soak the winner to his skin if she managed to catch him. "Does Joe know about your back stairs?" Gideon asked Bligh quietly, not wanting to lose his home's last baccy and old-fashioned sweet shop to pneumonia. Bligh only nodded. Tears were rolling down his face. Saddened, still convinced on some level that there was more to his grief than met the eye, Gideon patted his shoulder. "I'll be closing this party down soon anyway. I want to see everyone back to the village myself. Shall I pull the plug on it now?"

"No. No, the cider's ready in the kitchen, and they'll want to weave the neck. Give 'em a little bit longer." He looked up suddenly. "You do understand, don't you—if it had been up to me, all this could have gone on forever."

"What do you mean?"

"The ceremony, and... all the old ways. The fields and the land."

"Well, you and John have hosted it for years. You've been very generous, and maybe you'll feel like going on with it next year. If not, it's past time someone else took a turn." Gideon surveyed the cornfields, laid out in fresh-mown splendour under the sun's last light. "As for the land—that'll go on without any help from either of us." A rumble of thunder shook the distant tors. "Weather's on the change, just like Granny Ragwen said. I'll go help supervise operations in the kitchen."

He was on his way across the farmyard when the first drops of rain began to fall. Almost immediately they dried, leaving only a constellation of dark marks in the dust. He wished the downpour had started: this start and sudden cease was like a car being revved and then jerked up on the handbrake. The air became arid and still. Thunder rolled again, louder this time, and all around him the scurrying reapers and revellers came to a halt, exchanging wide-eyed looks. Gideon drew a deep breath. Then he turned back to Bligh Bowe, and said without thinking, without taking a second to wonder at the impulse, "Bligh? I want you to help me get everyone indoors. Right now."

"What? It's only a shower, isn't it?"

"No. It's more than that. Can you help?"

No. Bligh's attention had been caught by some indefinable shift in the atmosphere, some scent borne in on the cold breeze rising from the darkest flank of the hill. He was transfixed. Gideon looked around and saw to his relief that there was someone who *could* help—someone equivalent to ten Bodmin farmers, Gideon's own household cavalry, vaulting the wall with easy grace. "Lee," he said, reaching out to grab his hand. "Something's happening."

"Yes, I know. I thought it was just the weather, but..."

"No. We need to get everyone to shelter—the kitchen or that open barn, whichever's the closest."

"Okay. Where's Pendower?"

"God knows. Interviewing a scarecrow, I should think." Gideon spun round, releasing him, vaguely aware that he shot off into the darkness, shouting for attention. He should be doing the same himself. But what was the shadow that had dropped over Carnysen farm? Not just the sunset, although that had happened abruptly, the red orb devoured by the jagged horizon and clouds. He stood frozen, listening, trying to analyse the ozone-laced wind. Something foetid and fearful, something that whipped him back to a Halloween night on the moors by the Cheesewring, when he should have been alone—and he'd felt like the loneliest man on earth—until the night had thickened and put forth a deeper darkness, darkness with a throat and a voice...

That bone-vibrating growl had to be thunder. Small hairs on his nape tried to erect, and all around him he saw his fellow primates undergoing the ancient reaction, fluffing out their nonexistent coats to conserve warmth in crisis, wheeling about to try and find the source of danger. Lightning flashed, a long, anguished strobe that turned human shapes to paper-thin cutouts, dancing moorland maidens suddenly cast into stone. In the farmhouse, the lights flickered and went out.

Gideon grabbed Bligh Bowe. Lee had started a good small panic at one end of the farmyard, but another one was needed right here. "Bligh! Can you get people into the house?"

"It's dark in there. Dark."

"It's just a power cut. Your generator ought to kick in."

"It's broken. Just emergency lighting for outside."

"That'll do." Off among the outbuildings, an engine coughed and roared, and neon strip bulbs flared along the rafters of the open barn. Lee was gesturing people inside, encouraging stragglers with a propelling hand to shoulders and spines. "Look, someone's lighting candles in the kitchen. It's just a storm, but you're exposed up here, and I want everybody indoors right now. Do it!"

Finally Bligh broke paralysis. "Hoi," he yelled unsteadily, gesticulating towards the house. "Get inside, all of you. Come on!"

That accounted for everyone in the farmyard. The reapers were beginning to scramble over the fence from the field, but Gideon had barely counted six out of the baker's dozen when the storm hit. He darted into the blackness, aware of Lee as a sudden muscular warmth at his side, stopping to boost him over the wall and reaching to be hauled up himself. Lightning split the sky again, revealing a frightened cluster around Joe Poldue, the old man still clutching his barleycorn neck. "It's all right," Gideon called, making a half-blinded dash through the stubble towards them. He almost believed it himself. He had plenty of help now—not just Lee but Bligh Bowe, who had recovered himself enough to come running to the rescue, and there in the background was Pendower too, actually putting away his notebook and laying useful hands on Gideon's flock. "Go with Lee and the sergeant, all of you. Bligh, can you get that gate open for them? Joe can't climb the wall."

Pitchblack again, and a growl of something not thunder twisting up out of the field, stitching earth and sky together in a nightmare howl made worse for Gideon because he'd heard it before. Instinctively the group clustered together. Finding Lee within arm's reach, Gideon allowed himself a heartbeat's comfort of clinging to him. "What the bloody hell is that?"

"If you don't know, no-one does."

"How do I stop it?"

"You can't." Lee's arms closed round him: a short, hard embrace. "It's not here for you."

"Is this what you saw—the black fields?"

"No. This is just a warning. Christ, Gid, look!"

The next lightning flash showed Bligh Bowe and Poldue. Bligh was trying to take hold of him, to steer him towards the gate. But something had caught Poldue's eye—something beyond Bligh's shoulder—and he thrust the sheaf of corn into Bligh's arms and turned and fled into the dark.

Gideon ran after him. He knew he'd made the wrong choice when a vast hot presence passed him, buffeting his shoulder and knocking him flat to the ground. The screaming howl came again, this time joined by a terrified human voice. He tried to get up, but Joe was clinging to him like a leech. "Don't leave me, Constable! 'Tis the Beast!"

"'Tis not the... Oh, for God's sake." Gideon cleared his throat of corn-dust and centuries-old vernacular and tried again. "It's a storm. Stay right here, Joe, and I promise you'll be all right. I'll come back for you."

"I'll look after him."

Gideon glanced up. Pendower was crouching on Joe's far side, gently detaching his fingers from Gideon's collar. He looked as if he'd been knocked through a hedge. There were scorch marks on his shirt. He'd lost his cap, and his hair was as much of an electrified mess as his short copper's crop would allow. "Bloody hell," Gideon said. "What happened to you?"

"I think I got struck by lightning. But I can hear something else, like..."

Like a beast on the rampage. Gideon took his shoulder and gave him a firm shake before he could say it and terrify Joe still further: the old man was whimpering now, trying to clutch at them both. "I don't know what it is. I just need to know you're not too freaked out to help."

"Of course I'm bloody well freaked out!" Pendower grabbed Joe's arm and hauled it over his shoulder. "I've got him, though. You go and..."

He broke off, coughing. Gideon couldn't wait. Either he ran in the direction of the bestial snarling right now or he too would take to his heels and vanish into the moorland night, forever disgraced to himself and the community he was sworn to serve. He pushed upright, found his balance and set off.

There was barely enough light to see by. Something had hit the bonfire full on and scattered it to fragments, consuming themselves and dying in the field's far corner. He almost fell over Bligh Bowe. Dropping to his knees, he thanked God that he'd found a whole body. Somewhere close at hand, something vast was still huffing and growling: deliberately he turned his back to it. *No. If I conjure you somehow, if it's me you bring your messages for—like a proud cat with a dead mouse—I don't have to listen.* He leaned over Bligh, who was flat on his back as if hurled there. His throat was intact but there was no pulse in it. Gideon checked his airway and began CPR.

He kept it up for a fathomless stretch of time. Behind him the air went quiet, as if some great watching force had finally seen what it had been looking for and could depart. Rain pattered on his neck, and then, with a pinging sensation like cold elastic bands being snapped, big storm-born August hailstones. A hand closed on his arm. "Sergeant Frayne?"

He stopped his chest compressions and sat up. "Yes?"

"Paramedics. You can step aside."

Gideon hadn't heard them arrive. Falling back a step or two, he saw that the lane was ablaze with swirling blue lights. The real storm was breaking over Carnysen now, hail slamming into the empty furrows, thunder beginning to peal. The mobile mast on top of Minions Hill would soak up most of the lightning, but after that the farm was the highest point. Anyone left outdoors would be in real danger, a peril Gideon could understand and fix. He waited until the medic looked up and confirmed what he already knew—*sorry, Sergeant, he's gone*—and then he turned away.

He found poor Jenny Salthouse crouched beside the wall, her arms folded over her head. He picked her up gently, sheltered and calmed her until she rediscovered the use of her legs and went stumbling off to the gate. That was one. He scanned the field for more. The hailstones were melting into heavy summer rain, soaking his eyelashes, half-blinding him. The ambulance lights were sweeping the field like swallows' wings. It was empty now, surely, everyone under cover in the house or barn.

Wait. Had a sheep got in here somehow? There was a huddled white shape on the ground, about twenty yards from where he'd found Bligh. A few strides nearer, and the sheep became a person—a girl, it looked like, tangled up in a heavy white nightgown, although no women lived at Carnysen, no daughter or sister to have found her way out here and been overwhelmed by the storm. Lee was kneeling beside the prone body, his stance hard to read. Shielding or restraint? He sat up suddenly, waving. "Gideon! Over here!"

With a cold shock, Gideon recognised Dev Bowe. He was curled on the ground, his face an unconscious blank. His skinny limbs were tangled in the folds of a cotton nightdress, complete with lace and frills. "Bloody hell. What's he doing out here?"

"Don't know. I found him like this. He must've come down in all the chaos and been frightened, or..." Lee stroked the boy's hair, the action diagnostic as well as kind. His expression darkened. "I don't know."

"Are you all right?"

"Yes, fine. Is Bligh..."

Gideon shook his head. Dev didn't need to find out just now that he'd lost a second brother. "Let's get him indoors. Here, I'll carry him."

He scooped him off the ground. He weighed little more than the sheep Gideon had initially taken him for, and a weird pang of pity went through Gideon's marrow. What had possessed the lad to run around dressed like this? A nightie was one thing—no weirder in principle than Elowen borrowing Lee's pyjamas—but Gideon had a feeling that this great meringue of lace and cotton had belonged to Dev's mother. He focussed on Lee, who was running ahead to pull open the gates. He wanted to be home with him, to lose the weirdness and fear of this night in his arms, in the warmth of their new communion. But police lights were meshing with those from the ambulance now, patrol cars wailing and bumping up the farm track, and God alone knew when they'd be allowed to retreat to their own bed tonight...

The crowd from the kitchen and the barn were emerging cautiously. Lee began to ease his way through, clearing a path for Gideon and his strange burden. Gideon picked out the first intelligent face—Jenny Salthouse, recovered from her fright now and clearly mortified at having been so overcome. "Sergeant," she said, pushing towards him. "I'm so sorry I was a nuisance. It was terribly noisy, that's all, and I thought I heard something—felt something, anyway... My God, is that little Dev Bowe?"

"Yes. I need Mrs Waite up here, fast as she can come. Do you have her number in your mobile?"

"Of course. All the WI members."

Gideon held back a smile. She could probably raise an army. "Just one will do."

"Right. I'll call her now."

"Tell her to get a taxi. I'll pay." Gideon swung round at another sudden bustle in the crowd, and saw Pendower limp out from behind the barn, swaying beneath the weight of two small children. "Good heavens, Rufus," he said, because the man looked entirely human now, all signs of his authority left behind him in the mud. "Where on earth did you get those from?"

"Little beggars sneaked out to watch the Guldize. That'll teach 'em." Pendower squinted into the barnyard dazzle. "Oh, hell, here comes DI Lawrence. What am I supposed to say to her? What *happened* here tonight?"

Gideon thought for a moment. He needed a story of his own, more badly than his colleague could know. "Well, there was a storm. Perhaps it was ball lightning."

"*Ball* lightning?" Pendower echoed, and Lee turned round in the kitchen doorway and took him in, scorch marks and refugee children and all. "More balls than most, Sergeant," he said admiringly, and Pendower blushed pink as a sixteen-year-old girl being offered her prom corsage.

***

"It isn't very good, really, is it, Sergeant?"

Gideon didn't need to ask what. He stood at attention by the Bowes' empty fireplace, soaked to the skin and off duty, still very much accountable to his boss. "No, ma'am."

"A second Bowe brother dead, at a gathering which I specifically advised was not to take place. This village is under your jurisdiction, Sergeant."

"Yes, ma'am."

A tremendous throat-clearing rang out from the corner of the room. DI Lawrence turned in her chair. "Sergeant Pendower," she enquired politely, "did you catch a cold out there, or do you have something to say?"

"No, ma'am. I believe I was struck by lightning."

Gideon compressed his lips. He looked at the dark-raftered ceiling with its array of shining copper pots and horse brasses. This was a house of death. Poor Dev Bowe was lying upstairs, bereaved and sedated, and Gideon was about to get the giggles. He controlled himself fiercely. It was just that Pendower's hair was still on end, and his solemn little mug beneath it was too much of a contrast.

"I do have something to say, though."

Uh-oh. Here it came. Gideon didn't suppose he'd been a model of police procedure tonight, running around manhandling people into his idea of safety, never pausing to call for backup or help until the crisis was over. He braced up. But Pendower cleared his throat once more, drew back his shoulders and looked DI Lawrence in the eye. "I don't think Gideon—er, Sergeant Frayne—was in any way responsible for what happened here tonight, ma'am. If anyone should have prevented the gathering, I should—I was here from the beginning, and Sergeant Frayne came in on his off-duty. Furthermore, he acted with great resourcefulness and courage when the storm broke. Many more people would have been injured without his help."

Wonders would never cease. Lawrence looked from one to the other of them in astonishment. "Well," she said at length, "point taken, Pendower. Nevertheless someone *was* killed, and given his identity and the location, that death is at least as suspicious as his brother's."

"Hardly, ma'am, if you don't mind my saying so. John Bowe was torn apart. Every indication suggests that Bligh overtaxed himself and died of a heart attack."

"But I *do* mind you saying so, Sergeant." Lawrence got irritably to her feet. "Kindly don't jump to conclusions. We haven't even seen a preliminary path report. Frayne, have you taken steps to secure the village?"

"Yes, ma'am. One patrol car at Upton Cross, one on the A38 route. Can I ask that we review the roadblock in the morning? People have to get to work."

"They can go to work when they've been interviewed and eliminated from our enquiries—every single person here tonight, and for preference anyone conspicuously absent. Furthermore, anyone with a grudge against this family now has only one target left. Sergeant Frayne—"

"Officers posted at the main gate and both house entrances, ma'am."

"Very well. I'm assuming Dev Bowe is safe for now?"

"He's upstairs with his godmother. Lee's there too."

"Ah. In what capacity?"

"Concerned neighbour, ma'am. Unless anything else becomes necessary."

"I see. Well, I'll have to interview him too, and the nice old lady."

"I'm sure they'll understand."

"And I'd like to see the boy for myself. You say he was found in his deceased mother's nightgown?" Lawrence shook her head.

"Strange business, Frayne. Very strange indeed. You'd best come upstairs with me, and..." She spared Pendower a glance. "You too, Sergeant, I suppose. This case must be right up your street."

"Yes, ma'am, but... I think I'll stay out of Mr Tyack's way. I had doubts of his ability, and I'm afraid I made them rather clear. I'm sorry about that now, and... anyway. I don't think I'd be welcome."

"Don't be daft," Gideon rumbled, still dangerously close to laughter. Shame it had taken a lightning bolt to turn Sergeant Weird-Shit into a nice guy. "Lee isn't one to bear grudges. And he's been doubted by bigger things than you."

Chapter Eight

Lee was sitting in an upright chair by Dev Bowe's bed. He was holding Dev's left hand between both his own. When Gideon came in, he said, as if they'd been alone in the room together, "Oh, Gid. Don't ever let me be this empty."

Gideon forgot about Lawrence and Pendower in his wake. He forgot Mrs Waite, perched anxiously at the other side of the bed. "I won't," he said, leaning over Lee and taking him into his arms. "I promise." He pressed his brow to Lee's skull and felt there the strange shifting currents, the direction of the stream. "Don't let him drain you, all right?"

"He isn't. There's just a natural energy gradient. He's got nothing, and I... I've got you."

"Er... Sergeant Frayne?"

Gideon let him go. Lawrence had her arms folded and was looking at her feet, good equal-ops boss as she was. "Yes, ma'am?"

"I'm reversing my usual order of business here, but it might be useful if Lee could give us any insights he has prior to our investigation. We won't let them colour our findings, but since he's here, and he seems to have some kind of connection with this poor boy..."

"Yes, ma'am. It's all right for you to ask him yourself."

"Ah. Well, Lee—"

Lee snapped his head up. He focussed on Lawrence with an intensity Gideon knew well: blind and visionary at the same time. "No, he wouldn't be better off wearing something else. Those are your own concerns you're addressing, Detective Inspector— you're a nice person, but you don't like seeing a man in women's clothes. Why shouldn't he wear his mother's nightdress, if it comforts him?"

Now it was Gideon's turn to look at his feet. Poor Lawrence was open-mouthed, too honest for denial but clearly mortified. "That... That is his mother's, then?"

"Yes." Lee's voice altered. "I put it on every night once John and Bligh have gone to bed and no-one will see me. She was a *really* good person, better than any of you lot. She understood about the black fields. That's why my brothers made her go away."

"Hoi," Gideon said warningly. Dev's face was still serene and blank, but his hand had closed tight on Lee's. "Remember who you are."

"Okay." Lee drew a deep breath, swimming for the shallows. "My name is Locryn Tyack-Frayne, and Gideon is with me, and nothing can dislodge my soul. Rufus Pendower is dying to start making notes. Elsie Waite is afraid we'll think less of her for not wanting to take Dev in. She has to keep the shop open, has to earn a living. It's all right, though—the doctor's on the phone downstairs, trying to get him a bed on Fletcher Ward at Bodmin hospital."

"Bloody hell!" Pendower whispered. "I *am* dying to make notes." He pulled out his pad, and Mrs Waite gave a guilty sob that confirmed her feelings too. "How is he doing this, Gideon?"

"Dev's trying to pull him in too far. So he's using us as handholds, as anchors." Gideon had no idea how he knew this, but Lee gave a fraught little nod. "He's sorry. He knows it isn't good manners. He'll try not to look at anything you don't want him to see."

"Christine Lawrence is embarrassed. She's making a mental note to attend the next diversity-awareness day."

"Great," Lawrence growled. "What do you mean, the brothers made old lady Bowe go away? That was a carbon-monoxide accident at their caravan."

"No, it wasn't. Brothers fixed the gear."

"Oh, you have to be kidding me. Why would they do that?"

"Because my mother—*Dev's* mother—knew about the dark. The black fields."

Lawrence shook her head. "This is crazy. Frayne, I know I asked Lee to do this, but I think we'd best stick to our usual procedures. Maybe you should take him home."

Gideon wanted nothing better. Something was tugging at the edges of his mind, though. He laid a hand on Lee's shoulder. "You said Dev feels empty, love."

"Yes. Like a shell."

"Do you know why that is?"

"Because he has to leave room for... Oh, God." Lee jolted upright, tearing his hand out of Dev's. "Sorry, DI Lawrence. You're right—this is nuts. I must be picking up on his nightmares, or the way his schizophrenia expresses itself. I'm not gonna be much more help to you here tonight."

"That's quite all right." Lawrence sounded relieved. A lot of people did, when Lee switched off his searchlight and the world could regain its familiar shadows once more. "If you come up with anything definite, feel free to give me a call. I will pull up the records for that carbon-monoxide case, but..."

"It's paranoia, probably. He's very ill."

"Yes, poor lad. Best we leave him to the doctor for now. Mrs Waite, Sergeant Frayne will have a chat with you in the morning, if that's okay."

"All right. I'll stay with Dev until they take him to hospital." Her expression became resentful. "It's not that I'm not fond of him, you know. Your Lee must be awful to live with."

"Horrible," Gideon agreed, putting an arm around him. "I don't get away with much. Mind you get a taxi to take you back home."

Down in the hallway, the doctor was just hanging up the phone. "Right," he said placidly, as if he got called out to murder scenes every night. "That's the admission sorted out—I've managed to swing a bed for him in Fletcher Ward." He politely ignored Sergeant Pendower's gasp of delight and the frantic scratching of his pen across another sheet of notes. Gideon could guess the gist—*Tyack not only identifies primary concerns of everyone present in the upstairs room, but correctly predicts psychiatric facility. Marvellous!* Well, as Lee and Paul Simon had pointed out before, proof was the bottom line for everyone. "To be honest," the doctor went on, "from the look of the lad, he should've been in some kind of care before now. Anything more I can do for you tonight, Detective Inspector?"

"No, that's all. Just have the hospital call me when he's well enough to be interviewed."

"Not sure when that'll be, but right you are."

He jogged off up the stairs. Lawrence watched him go, then turned back to Gideon and Lee. "I've been thinking," she said. "I'm sorry to raise such a painful subject, and I know this probably isn't the time, but... you two really did get handed a raw deal with regard to your baby. I don't want to say anything definite, but I'm sure one of our colleagues in France could find a reason to pay the child's mother a visit. Just to see if there are any welfare issues, you know."

Lee smiled wearily. He pushed his shoulder against Gideon's, and the wave of grief passed between them—strong, unstoppable, bearable because finally and perfectly shared. "Were you thinking of frog-marching my sister home?"

"No, not at all. Just a few routine enquiries."

"It's all right," Gideon said, taking hold of his hand. "We've decided to leave it for now."

***

My name is Locryn Tyack-Frayne, and Gideon is with me, and nothing can dislodge my soul. Yea, though I walk through the valley of the shadow of death... Gideon recollected his wandering thoughts. One manic preacher in the family was enough. All he needed to pray for was strength to justify Lee's faith in him.

He rubbed his eyes in the morning sunlight. It was past time he was out on the mean streets of Dark, tackling the string of interviews that would fill his day from this bright dawn until the late summer dusk. No bad thing, to be kept so busy, and Lee had said he'd be occupied all day as well, taking up his interrupted work on the *Spirits of Cornwall* script. Work was best for both of them. Still, Gideon had let him sleep through their alarm. Given himself five quiet minutes too, between pulling on his uniform shirt, checking his duty belt and heading out the door. He just wanted to sit here in the window of the bedroom where he and Lee had shared so much—sex, rambling small-hours discussions about everything and nothing at all, their first morning of waking up alone with Tamsyn and realising fully at last that they were parents—and watch his husband sleep.

He did it with an abandoned grace that showed nothing of the nightmares that stalked his daily world. He was lying on his stomach, the quilt tangled up round his hips. The sunlight took the smooth olive skin of his back and turned it to gold, the colour of the beach at the foot of his borderland cliffs. His hands were lightly clasped on the pillow, his breathing deep and regular. When Gideon listened to that, he lost track of all the evil and sorrow in his own life and the broader world around him. It was as if Lee stripped away his outer layers, all the roles he'd taken on, father and brother and husband and son. He didn't even feel like a copper anymore—just a man, sharing a sunlit silence with the other half of his soul.

And yet the qualities that made him a good copper were more at liberty than ever in this pared-back freedom. They were fundamental aspects of his nature. He watched and observed. He didn't assign weight to what he'd seen until he had facts at his disposal, and so he wasn't burdened by assumptions. He moved freely through his inner and outer Dark, gathering his own quiet harvest.

He'd been caught out rather last night. The little group in the farmhouse hallway had been distracting, Lee and the inspector and the doctor, and Pendower with his fanboy zeal. Gideon's good policeman's brain had continued to record through all the chaos, and he'd seen something, hadn't he? Something ordinary but out of place.

Lee's quiet breathing brought down the barriers, telling him to look again. John and Bligh Bowe had kept an orderly household. Like many of the old farming families, they preferred to leave the barnyard outside, and the inside of the house was tidy. The doctor had been scribbling on a notepad by the phone. Everything in the small, crowded space was where you'd expect it to be, except for the crumpled scrap of paper on the floor.

Look a little closer, Gid. Not just crumpled. Torn.

Gideon glanced up in amusement, but Lee was still out cold, his fingertips twitching with dreams. Obediently he returned his attention to the Carnysen farmhouse, and read off the five letters on the discarded scrap. B-A-R-A-G... Only the surname *Baragwanath* began like that, an unusual one even by Cornish standards. The rest of the note was in pieces, scattered along the skirting board. *Not just torn, Lee. Ripped to shreds.*

The computer in the living room was up and running. Gideon tapped *Bodmin* and his handful of letters into the internet hoping for an autofill suggestion, but nothing came up. He stood for a moment, paying attention to his aches and pains from yesterday. He had a few burns on his hands, which Lee had disinfected and bandaged before they'd crawled into bed. He imagined poor Pendower was feeling the results of his exertions too. Smiling at the memory of that electrified brush-cut, he consigned the torn-up note to his own inner search engine, where his subconscious could work away at it. He'd get access to the farmhouse as soon as he could and patch the rest together, but for today at least the place would be locked up. Almost impossible to believe that the family which had thrived there for so long had been cut down to one lost lamb.

Dev, the autumn lamb. He was such a fragile scrap, and yet if he hadn't been safely locked up in Bodmin psychiatric, Gideon would have arrested him by now. Loved ones *were* always first on the list of suspects, and Lee's vision in the cornfield remained vivid—that, and his warning. *The lamb hasn't finished his work...*

Gideon wondered if the work was finished now. It would all have to wait. He had to see the coroner for the preliminary report on Bligh's death, and then begin his interview rounds. He stopped off by the bed. Lee made a sound of sleepy welcome and tried to grab his hand, but he dodged it, chuckling. "Not now, handsome. I'll see you tonight."

"You're all dressed. What time is it?"

"Morning."

"Which part of it? I should get up too, make a start on my scripts." Lee pulled his mobile out from under the pillow to check the time, and frowned at what he saw.

Gideon reached to ruffle his hair. "What's up?"

"Nothing. Just... later than I thought."

"No need for you to leap out of bed, is there? You still look tired."

"You know what? I am. I slept all night, but my head was noisy. I might take one of my horse pills."

"Are you sure?" Anxiety prickled at Gideon's nape. Lee had a prescription of high-dosage sedatives left over from the days when his doctors hadn't been able to tell his gifts from a brain tumour. He hadn't needed to touch them in months. "They knock you right out, and I won't be around to look after you."

"Isn't that the one time when I *don't* need you to keep me out of mischief?" Lee shot him a scapegrace smile. "Be honest with you, love, I could use a break. Being awake has limited appeal at the moment."

***

Twelve o'clock found Gideon in Bodmin town, tracking down Sally Polwen on her break from the post office there. Like everyone else he'd spoken to that morning, she was shocked, sympathetic, and utterly unhelpful. Gideon wasn't quite sure why he was using his day's best energies on people who could no more kill than fly, but he had a job to do, and he owed it to Lawrence to eliminate the angels before chasing mythical demons and beasts.

After he was done, he granted himself twenty minutes for lunch, and on impulse went into the Petroc Library café. It was generally peaceful there, and he wanted a wander through the shelves. After grabbing a coffee and a sandwich, he set out.

He wasn't quite sure what he was looking for. He was pretty certain he wouldn't find it among the chicklit and harrowing life stories, though, and he left the brightly lit modern shelves and found his way into the cooler shadows of the building's heart, where dusty legal and accounting texts served out their time largely untouched. The elder gentlemen of Bodmin, unused to seeing a burly copper in the aisles where they too waited out their days, slipped out of his way like mice, but Gideon wasn't interested—never had been—in moving them along. He just wanted to look at some old books.

He'd liked it here as a child. The leather-bound volumes had smelled lovely to him, and he'd prowled here, inventing labyrinths and warzones, while Ma Frayne had exchanged her Mills & Boons and chatted to the librarians. He'd liked the names of the old solicitors, printed in fading gold on the spines of their legal texts, which had given him names for his own expanding population of imaginary heroes and villains. Borlase, Godolphin, Rawle.

Baragwanath, Keast & Co, the town's longest-established law firm, and just about its most obscure. Gideon wasn't even sure they were in business anymore.

Technically he was allowed an hour for lunch. He seldom took it, but if he did, that would leave him with thirty minutes more before he had to go back to the methodical plod-work. The offices had used to be tucked away down a side street by the chapel, a two-minute walk from here. He gave the Baragwanath book a thoughtful tap, raising a small cloud of dust.

He was on his way out when frantic movement from one of the desks caught his eye. He paused by the doorway. To his surprise, Rufus Pendower was sitting at a table in the reading room, surrounded by piles of volumes as venerable as Gideon's own. He was beckoning excitedly. Yesterday the sight of him would have annoyed Gideon, but his grim-faced courage in the Carnysen fields had altered things. He hadn't quite managed to smooth down the lightning-bolt hairdo. Gideon went over to him, forbidding himself a smile. "Afternoon, Pendower. Come to pay your overdues?"

"No, no. I've been doing some research. I think I've found something interesting."

Scattered explosions of hushing rang out. There were about ten people in the room, and none of them engaged in the perusal of anything more serious than the local papers, as far as Gideon could see. He and Pendower raked the desks with a well-practised officer's glare, and the objectors fell silent. "Right," Gideon said. "I've only got a few minutes. Can you tell me fast?"

"Yes, but do sit down. How's L-... er, Mr Tyack?"

"You can call him Lee." Reluctantly Gideon pulled out a chair. It was so unlike his tough other half to choose drugged oblivion over reality. "He's fine," he said, more to convince himself than Pendower. "He's working from home today, though. He needs a rest."

"Yes, I'm sure. The things he said, the things he saw in his visions—they set me thinking. They were ringing all kinds of bells with me from my graduate studies, everything I've learned about names and their origins." He drew a huge leather-bound tome across the table and laid it reverently in front of Gideon. "This is Mellin's lexicon of the Cornish language, drawn up in 1873. I thought Bligh and Dev were strange first names, so I looked them up, or rather I chased them through what I knew of their etymology. Bligh is a nickname from the Kernowek word *blyth*, or wolf. And the word for *lamb* is *deves*."

"No, it's not." Gideon knew this because he'd heard Lee singing nursery rhymes in Cornish to the baby. "The word for lamb is *on*."

"Well, okay. But *deves* is the plural form for a ewe, so—"

"So you're clutching at straws. That's a big stretch for a connection."

"Maybe not. Imagine you're Dev Bowe, and you're a paranoid schizophrenic who's just lost his parents. You're convinced your brothers have got something to do with their deaths, and you're alone in your room all day, drugged up, with access to an internet connection. If Dev thinks of himself as a lamb—and a ewe lamb, at that, not big and husky like his brothers, dressing up in his mum's nighties—he might have made these connections too. But that's not all. *Bowe* is quite an unusual surname too. It's usually *Bowes*, isn't it? Like the queen mother's family."

"I suppose so." Gideon's head was spinning a bit with all these suppositions. Pendower was a different man on his own turf, though, joining the dots with a confidence that drew Gideon helplessly along with him. "What's the significance there?"

"The oldest word for barley or corn in the whole English language is B-E-O-W. It's a direct anagram, and the pronunciation wouldn't have been far off. I never thought about checking into John Bowe's name because John is so ordinary, but..."

"You have to be kidding. John Barleycorn?"

"Exactly. Isn't that *marvellous*?"

"If the poor bastard hadn't been horribly murdered, yes."

"And to top it all off..." Pendower flipped open another volume at a bookmarked place and tapped the page triumphantly. "Carnysen farm itself—Carn Ysen, the hill of the corn. John Barleycorn of Corn Hill farm. What more do you want, Sergeant Frayne?"

Gideon sat back and folded his arms. "I'd like some evidence, for starters." He waited until Pendower had turned a pre-explosive shade of puce. "But I'll admit this is interesting stuff. Do you fancy coming along with me to check out another angle?"

"Well—yes, of course." Pendower looked mollified, then frowned. "But Lawrence doesn't want me involved with the real investigation."

"Who says what you've been doing isn't real? Besides, this isn't something I'd put before Lawrence, not until I know more about it myself." Gideon recounted his ideas about the torn scrap of paper, aware as he did so that Pendower's eyebrows were on the climb. "So I'd like to pop along and see old man Baragwanath, if he's still running the shop. Just in case."

Pendower stared at him. "You really are in no position at all to lecture *me* about tenuous connections, Sergeant Frayne."

***

Gideon hadn't taken Pendower along just to give him a breath of fresh air. The sudden arrival of one police officer might be enough to daunt your average guilty soul into a reaction, but lawyers were a different matter. He ushered Pendower ahead of him into the dingy little office and made sure to follow hard on his heels, the pair of them a polite, nicely spoken brick wall. "Good afternoon. I'd like a word with Mr Baragwanath, please."

The lady behind the desk jumped so hard that her calculator went flying. "You can't!"

"Is he out of the office?"

"No. I mean, yes, he is. He's dead."

Gideon wasn't in the business of frightening innocent receptionists. He picked up the calculator and handed it back, trusting that the noise and the poor woman's high-pitched shriek had done their work. "I'm sorry to hear that."

"Oh, it wasn't recent." She composed herself with an effort. "The firm's in the hands of his partner now, Mr Keast. But—"

But nothing. Gideon waited. The scrabbling sounds in the office next door, the unmistakeable slamming of metal file-cabinet drawers, eventually stopped. Then the door creaked open.

Oh, dear. This was no bloody use. Gideon sank down on one of the rickety chairs and indicated to Pendower that he should do the same. He vaguely remembered Baragwanath as a stocky, hard-faced old sod, the one you went to for dodgy conveyancing deals or a quick, dirty divorce. Just for once it would be nice if the world's badness could present itself like that, in an easily readable format. The man who'd just crept out of the office was barely five foot tall, and yellow-faced with fear. Just for once—today, for example, when Gideon was nearing the forty-eight-hour mark without his daughter—it would have been nice to have someone to beat up. "Mr Keast, I presume," he said, rubbing his eyes. "All hell's broken loose at Carnysen Farm, as you know. Tell me exactly what this firm's connection is to the Bowes, and all this will be over. Come on, sir," he added kindly. "You don't want to carry this around anymore, do you?"

For a second he thought the man would tough it out. As Baragwanath's underling, he must have had some practice. Then the receptionist made an unsubtle dash for the door, and to Gideon's horror, Keast began to cry.

Chapter Nine

"I never wanted to do it. But John Bowe offered him *so much*, and he said I'd get my share of it when the sale went through. I've slaved my whole life in this dump. Baragwanath never even made me a full partner, you know. I was just a name on the letterhead."

Keast stopped for breath, and to grab a tissue from the box Pendower had handed him. He'd let himself be guided back into his office, and, once seated behind his desk, had regained a little composure. He was still a sorry sight. Gideon was glad of Pendower's presence, scratching away in his little notebook as usual. He had the feeling he was going to need a witness. "What sale, Mr Keast?"

"Carnysen Farm. You must know that already, or why are you here?" Keast blew his nose. "Shit. I always knew we'd get done. Bloody typical of Baragwanath to up and die just when it all went through. Left me holding the baby. I was starting to think no amount of money could be worth it, and I'm right, aren't I? You've come to finish the game."

"For the sake of honesty, I don't know what you're talking about. You're not under arrest, so I can't read you your rights, but

I will warn you that the sergeant here will take down every little detail of what you say, and it will be held against you if it's bad." Pendower shot him a look that plainly told him he was throwing away his advantage, but Gideon couldn't keep up a front of bullying vagueness for long. Instead he did what he was best at. He leaned forward, examined Keast's face. "You're obviously miserable. You're not a bad person, are you? Why on earth are you behaving like one?"

For a moment he thought Keast was about to throw himself across the desk and into his arms. The poor bastard buried his face in a tissue, banged the palm of his hand against the cheap woodwork in a surge of grief. "I'm not! I wasn't, anyway. It was just... so *much*."

"All right. So much money for the sale of Carnysen Farm, which I didn't even know was on the market. Tell me why."

"Because of the purchasers. The confidentiality agreements they made us sign." Keast showed signs of recovering himself at the thought of them. "My God, you really don't know anything, do you? Why am I talking to you?"

"Because people have died. In my village! I won't have that. And when I make the connection back to you, you'll wish to God you'd taken the chance to tell me all about it in your own words."

Keast swallowed audibly. "I don't know where to start."

"The purchasers. Who was offering so much money for an old Cornish farm that you and your boss sold yourselves out to get a slice of it?"

"It was him. Baragwanath sold out. He only told me when it got too big for him to manage on his own, and then he offered me... he offered..."

"I don't need the price of your soul. Just a name. I'll bear in mind that you volunteered the information."

"Oh, God. They're a company called Mitchell Shale Gas."

"Shale gas," Gideon echoed. He sat back in his chair. "Wait. Shale gas, as in... For Christ's sake. *Fracking?*"

"Yes. I hadn't even heard of it until the old man told me. I swear."

Pendower snapped his notebook shut. "Bollocks," he unexpectedly announced. "Gideon, this joker's wasting our time."

"I'd love to think so. Er—Mr Keast is offering a voluntary statement, so keep it civil."

"Yes. Sorry. But there is no natural shale or oil in Cornwall. The geology rules it out. Not to mention that Carnysen's smack in the middle of the Bodmin AONB. You can't get permission to build a garden shed, let alone blast holes in the earth for oil."

Gideon turned back to Keast. His skin was crawling. "Tell me he's right."

"It's an isolated pocket of shale rock, packed with organic matter. Mitchell does surveys for radon gas too, and they found it by accident. It's a rich one—untold resources, right underneath the farm. Joe and Bligh Bowe still didn't want to sell up. Mitchell hired us to make them the offer, and..." He chuckled unsteadily. "So much for the old farming family. The next day John Bowe was here in the office with the deeds in his hands."

"This is still ridiculous. Mitchell would have had to jump through a thousand hoops from the council for planning permission. And even if they'd somehow managed that, there's the—"

"The Bodmin AONB?" Keast was calming down. Suspects often did, once well launched into a confession, their worst fears realised and their desire to tell their side of the story strong. "You're a bit naive, aren't you, Sergeant? If there's a good side to people, you'll try and find it. You say *council* and *planning permission* like they were magic words."

"Tell me why they're not."

"Don't mix up an Area of Outstanding Natural Beauty with a National Park. It hasn't got anything like the same legal protection. Old Farmer Bowe—John's grandfather—didn't like the idea of being bound hand and foot for planning consent back in the 1940s, so he just demanded Carnysen be left out when the AONB was set up, and the Bowes were a big noise around Bodmin back then, so the local authority allowed it. And as for your councillors and planners today, Baragwanath knew the right ones to approach. What's the matter—did you think people like that couldn't be bought? Anyone can be bought, Sergeant. Anyone."

A silence fell in the room. Shafts of dusty light drifted solemnly through the cobwebbed windows. Baragwanath, Keast & Co hadn't attracted much in the way of big business over the years. Mitchell's proposition must have hit them like a solid-gold brick. If someone had turned up on Gideon's doorstep and offered him Tamsyn back, what might *he* not have done?

Keast was right. He was naive. He always looked for reasons, human mechanisms of love or loss, to explain criminal behaviour. And often it boiled down to sheer greed. "Right," he said hoarsely. "I need you to tell me now—has this deal with the devil gone through?"

"Finally. Two days ago, the very day that..." Keast gave a shudder. "The day that John was killed. I had to act very slowly after Baragwanath died, make sure nothing happened fast enough to alert the AONB authorities. But yes, the land has been sold. And the grand thing about all this is that... now I've done it, now I've sold out this land and the moor and all the people who love it, I stand to come away with..." He took up a pen and tapped it on the desk top, a short, bitter tattoo. "With nothing. Even if you and your sidekick hadn't come along."

Light dawned on Gideon. "You're being blackmailed."

"Oh, spectacularly. By Councillor Robin Walsh, if you want final proof of the virtues of our noble town leaders. What—do you think I'd have said a word to you now, if I'd had anything left to lose?"

Gideon's phone began to ring. With a sense of unreality, he saw his brother's name flashing on the screen. He cut the call off and stood up. "Right. I don't actually know how to deal with you, Mr Keast, but I'll start by asking you to come down to the station with me so I can find somebody who does. All I care about is getting this monstrosity stopped."

Pendower stood up too. "It *is* a monstrosity. Gideon, this was Lee's vision—the dark fields, all the trees gone. And no water—all it would take is for the Mitchell company's drilling or blasting to hit an aquifer rock, and..."

"All right, all right. I'm not gonna let it happen." His damn phone was ringing again. This was twice in recent memory that Ezekiel had called him insistently. Perhaps he was just making up for the ten years when they hadn't spoken to one another at all, but... "Pendower, keep an eye on Mr Keast. I'm going to have to take this call."

He let himself out onto the landing. The offices were poised above a kebab shop, and the lunchtime smells that would normally have enticed him now made his guts lurch. *Hard to breathe the darkness. Everything's black now. The leaves are withered, and the moor's gone, and there's no water, no water anywhere. No fields, no trees...* "What is it, Zeke? I'm really busy."

"Mother's disappeared from Roselands."

"What?" Gideon had to struggle to extract sense from his brother's words. They were plain enough, but he hadn't heard that ragged edge of fear in them, the distant threat of tears, since before their decade's estrangement. "Don't be daft. She'll have got in a taxi and come over to Dark to visit Lee."

"I'm *in* Dark. That was the first thing I thought too. Nobody's answering at the house. And Dev Bowe just accosted me in the street—I'm wearing my dog collar—and said he was possessed, and I think he's right."

Gideon took a deep breath. That was what Lee had taught him to do when the world dissolved into hopeless chaos around him, and sometimes it worked. Maybe it would help his brother too. "Ezekiel? Take one nice deep breath and let it go. Then tell me what the bloody hell you're talking about."

"I *am* telling you. Mother's gone. Mrs Harle thinks she must've got confused and wandered off."

No. The old lady had become more eccentric of late, but it wasn't senility—just the spontaneous creature she'd been before her marriage enjoying a rebirth. "I don't think so. First off, Lee's not too well. He was going to try and get some sleep, so he might not have heard you knock. Don't you have your key?"

"Not with me, no."

"Shit. Have you called the police?"

"What the devil do you think I'm doing now?"

"Oh." Gideon tugged at the brim of his cap in frustration. "Right, but you also need to dial 999 and get emergency services involved. There's a twenty-four hour wait for missing persons but they won't put you through that—she's elderly and vulnerable. Wait, don't hang up. Is Dev still there?"

"Yes. He's trying to get into my car."

"He's meant to be in hospital. Can you keep him with you?"

"He's very insistent about taking me up to some field or other. Look, I don't have time for this. I have to find Mother."

"Ezekiel, do as I say. Call 999 and report Ma as missing and in danger. I'll alert the hospital about Dev. Start off with him if that's the only way he'll let you hang on to him, and I'll be there in twenty minutes. Okay?"

"No! No, it isn't okay. Where *is* she?"

He was on the verge of tears. Gideon was ashamed of having ever taken his harsh front for the whole man. "We'll find her," he said firmly. "I promise. I'll phone the Falmouth lads and ask them to make her a priority. I'm on my way, Zeke—just hang on."

Pendower had emerged from the office in time to hear the last part. He was herding Keast ahead of him, like Isolde with a recalcitrant sheep. "What's the matter? More problems at home?"

"Yes." Pendower must think he lived in a perpetual vortex of drama. "Never mind. Let's get this guy over to Tollgate Road, and then—"

"You go and sort things out. I'll escort Mr Keast to the station, and I'll make sure he tells the truth when he gets there." He riffled through his copious notes, smiling grimly. "All of it."

***

The main street of Dark was empty when Gideon arrived. The day was oppressively hot, dried leaves barely stirring on the pavements. He pulled up in the grassy layby at the foot of the Carnysen track. He'd wanted to go home first and check on Lee, but he could see Zeke's huge funereal Volvo halfway up the lane, more or less blocking it. Probably Zeke had got it that far before realising it would be impossible to turn it round further up.

Gideon got out of the police truck and stood for a moment, reading currents of unease in the hot air. Heavy heads of grass swayed around his knees, and the spill of dog roses over the fence—so deep a purple they were almost blue—almost overwhelmed him with their scent. He tried Lee's mobile again, then decided that whatever new crisis awaited him this afternoon, he would let the poor sod sleep and handle it himself. If Ma Frayne had found her way to their flat, Lee would have been phoning him. The Falmouth duty sergeant had taken the news as if the old lady had been his own mother, and raised the alarm accordingly. Nothing more could be done on that front, and meanwhile Gideon's brother was alone in a cornfield with an escaped lunatic. He set off up the track at a run.

Not alone, no. For a second in the heat-haze, Gideon thought his ma had come to officiate at some bizarre family picnic. Right in the very centre of the field where John Bowe had died, in a patch of flattened corn, Dev Bowe was sitting cross-legged, Zeke on one side of him, an elderly woman comfortably settled on the other. He was no longer dressed in his mother's nightgown—the scene was weird enough without that—but his shirt and trousers were too big for him, as if he'd stolen them from somebody's locker. And he was nursing a baby in his arms.

No. Gideon rubbed dust out of his eyes. He was clutching the charred remains of the neck, the last sheaf of corn Joe Poldue had cut the night before. He'd wrapped it in a sheet of white plastic from one of the bales and was rocking it. And the old woman was Granny Ragwen. "Where's that other nice young fella?" she cried, as soon as she clapped eyes on Gideon. "The one who was so allergic to my cat?"

"You don't have a cat," Gideon reminded her. "Zeke, are you okay?"

"Yes, except that this young man was very insistent about coming here. Has Mother been found?"

"Not yet. But she's all right." Gideon felt this as a powerful certainty. He didn't question it, and Zeke's raised eyebrows couldn't shake it. "What are you doing up here, Mrs Ragwen?"

"Why, I met the minister in the lane. He was going my way, and he let me take his arm."

"Hardly. She grabbed it and hung on. I have to go, Gideon. If Mr Bowe feels in need of spiritual aid, he's more than welcome to visit me at the chapel, or—"

"Zeke. Hush for a moment." Gideon crouched in front of Dev. Poor Zeke—they must have made quite a procession, the deranged boy clinging to one arm and the village witch on the other. "Dev Bowe, are you listening to me? Can you look up?"

Slowly Dev raised his head. His gaze was unfocussed and blank. "Do you see my baby?" he asked, his voice as dry as the wind in the corn. "Do you see her?"

"Yes, I see her. She's Breedie baby, isn't she? The one we take in after the harvest, and put her by the fire in a cradle so her mother can come and find her."

"Yes. The mother of all the fields. But the Beast came, and she was left out alone in the cold. I've got her now. People should look after their babies." His brow creased in pain. "You should have looked after yours, shouldn't you? Then maybe you wouldn't have lost her. Would you like to have a hold of mine?"

"Dev Bowe, have you been sectioned under the Mental Health Act? Do you know what that is?"

The boy shook his head. Granny Ragwen reached out and gave him a sudden thump to the shoulder, as if ashamed of him. "Don't you be rude to the constable! Did someone tell you at the hospital you had to stay there? That you weren't allowed to go?"

"No. They told me I should be a good boy and get some sleep." A terrible smile cracked his face, sharp as a scythe with cold cunning. "I can go wherever I want. I've already been somewhere, Sergeant Frayne—somewhere *you* wouldn't want me to go."

"If you haven't been sectioned," Gideon said quietly, "I'm arresting you now on suspicion of the murder of both of your brothers. You do not have to say anything. But it may harm your defence if you do not mention when questioned something which you later rely on in court. Anything you do say may be given in evidence. Are you able to understand what I've just said to you?"

"Yes, Sergeant."

"And do you think I'm wrong? Because it's ridiculous, isn't it—a little scrap of a lad like you, killing those two big fine men."

Dev shuddered. "Not fine. Not fine men."

"All right. Suppose I agree with you that they weren't. That I knew what they'd done, and I could make you a promise right here—my deepest, best promise, Dev—that I could put it right?"

"No-one can put it right. Dev tried. But John said he was mad, and locked him up in his room, and said a bad thing would happen to him just like it did to his mam."

"John killed your mother and father—what, to get the land?" Dev nodded, and the alien jolt of his head, the vulpine snarl that accompanied it, chilled Gideon's marrow. "Wait. Who am I talking to here?"

"Not Dev. Not Dev."

"All right. In that case I'm telling whoever's in there—Dev Bowe is just a little boy. I'm a policeman, and more than that, I'm..." Gideon cast around for words, memories, symbols that would make sense in this field, beneath the open sky. He remembered what Lee had called him. "I'm the guardian of this place—one of 'em anyway. I'm the good shepherd. And I *can* make the darkness go away."

The boy turned to Ezekiel. "Is that right? Is it true?"

A big leap for poor Zeke, who had no idea of what was going on. But he gave Gideon a glance and said slowly, "If my brother promises, yes."

"Then... can you take it out of me?"

"Careful, Zeke. He's mentally ill, not possessed."

"So much harm is done by godless men of this world who insist on the distinction. Do you *believe* I can take your demon from you, child?"

Zeke must have been conducting a service or a funeral. He was in clerical black, his collar gleaming in the sunlight, enough to inspire faith in anyone. The boy recoiled from him. "Dev does," he said. "Dev believes. But the truth is, preacher, I'm too old for you. It's a shame. I'm wearing this little body out."

"Then leave it. Please."

"It's not so easy as that. Can't you see how he's woven me in? Learning about all the names and what they mean, creating his own mythology. Did you know..." Dev snapped his arms tight across his chest and began to rock. "Did you know the old song is all about him too? About him and his brothers... Their father sent all of them away, each in his turn, to the Duchy agricultural school, all the way over at Camborne in the west." He began to croon. *"Three men came from the west, their fortunes for to try, and these three made a solemn vow, John Barleycorn must die...* John and Bligh tried their fortunes on this farm, didn't they? What a treasure they found!"

"Dev!" Gideon seized his wrist. "You have to fight this. How could your brother be one of those men and John Barleycorn at the same time?"

"Because he knew by then. He knew what he'd done. He was sorry, but it all had gone too far. The best sacrifice is a willing one. He went out into the midnight field on Guldize Eve on purpose to meet the Beast, and we were there. And as for Bligh, all we had to do was... show him our face." Dev gave a guttural laugh. "God, how he screamed!"

Ezekiel had gone pale. "Gid, tell me someone's coming to look after this... boy."

"Yes. They should be here soon, but—"

"But what good could they do him while he's like this?" Granny Ragwen had finally stirred from her easy crouch in the corn. She was as neat and prosaic as ever, in her M&S leisure wear, but she looked as though she'd spent several centuries sitting by cauldrons, waiting on her natural throne of earth for events to turn. She put down a hand to Dev. "Too old for the preacher, are you? You're not too old for me. Come along."

Dev scrambled to his feet. Gideon and Zeke got up too. "Careful, Mrs Ragwen," Gideon warned. "He's not himself."

"That's just the problem, isn't it?" She smiled back over her shoulder, leading Dev away through the corn. "What harm can come to me here, with you two big lads looking on? Come along, now, you creature of earth and sky. What are you doing in a little flesh cage? *I exorcise thee*, Dev Bowe," she went on conversationally, picking up his hand and lightly shaking it, "*that thou cast out from thee all the impurities and uncleanlinesses of the spirit of the world of phantasm*. That's one of Gerald Gardner's old blessings for water—or Doreen's, or Aleister's, depending on who you believe—but it works pretty well for beasts too. Do you hear?"

Dev came to a dead stop. He laced his fingers through Granny Ragwen's and bowed his head. The air tightened like a violin's overdrawn string. Unthinkingly Gideon drew close to his brother, the way he had before the age gap and their disparate natures had driven them apart. "What is she doing?"

"I don't know, but shouldn't you be stopping her?"

"You're the minister."

"You're the policeman, for God's sake!"

Their eyes met. They waited in silence, and after a moment the moorland around them became silent too. The larks ceased their burble, and the linnets left off their high-pitched defence of every gorse bush for miles around. "I don't think you should look at Dev or the old lady," Zeke said tonelessly. "I think for a minute you should just look at me."

Gideon swallowed painfully. "Okay."

A wind sprang up. It didn't come from the tors or the faraway Atlantic. Its breath was hot as a wolf's, and rich with pheromone messages of death and change. Its density altered, coalescing from air to flesh, and in this manifestation it circled the place where Gideon stood with his brother. In this manifestation it knew him: passed behind him once, close enough to swipe at his shoulder. He staggered and Zeke caught him, and a low growl filled the air. "You'd better go now," Zeke said to something behind him. "I don't know what you are, but I think you'd better go."

The growl spiralled up into a roar. Gideon had heard it before, just as he'd felt the passing of that vast force, breathed the ozone and blood-bright copper it left in its wake. Something swept once round the cornfield, a wing or a thunderclap. He clutched at Zeke and they braced each other, and then with a swirling, gale-throated howl, the thing was gone.

Granny Ragwen was on her knees with Dev. He was whispering to her, his face a mask of blanched-out fear. She got up unsteadily, brushing bits of corn from her velour. For the first time in Gideon's acquaintance with her, she looked a little discomposed. "Right," she said, straightening her beads. "He ought to be all right now. I'll wait with him here. But you have to go home now, Constable. He says he was angry when your Lee got inside of his mind. He says he's done something bad to him. You have to go."

***

Gideon took a flying leap across the stile, barely noticing it was there. He pounded down the lane to where Zeke's car was parked: reached out and hauled his brother past when he slowed to try and find his keys. "No! By the time you've turned it round we could be home."

"I don't know. Perhaps we should—"

"My truck's at the end of the lane. Come on!"

They reached the Rover together, stride for stride. To Gideon's disbelief, Zeke blocked his track to the driver's door. "What the hell are you doing?"

"Tell me you're fit to drive."

Gideon couldn't. Shame rushed over him. Not once in his career had he let his emotions incapacitate him. But Lee hadn't picked up either of the speed-dialled calls he'd punched in on his way from the field. "It's three streets away," he said faintly. "I'll run."

"Shut up and get in. He'll be all right, Gideon—Dev Bowe's insane."

"I don't know." Gideon scrambled into the passenger seat. His limbs were heavy and awkward, and he wasn't used to this side of his truck—felt trapped in a mirror world, everything in the wrong place. He gasped as Zeke tramped the gas and stalled. "For God's sake. Are *you* fit to drive?"

"Perfectly. Forgive my natural concern about my brother-in-law." He tried again, found a biting point and sent the truck roaring out into the road. "Doesn't this thing have a siren?"

Gideon reached across and switched it on. Snapped on the lights for good measure, trying not to remember a rainy December night when Lee had taken a moment out of crisis to light up with mischief himself at the broken rule. Bill Prowse's street flashed by, then Sarah Kemp's... And then Zeke was tearing down Moor Lane, and between one blink and the next Darren Prowse was in the middle of the road. "Zeke, *stop*!"

Zeke stamped on the brakes. The truck gave a squeal and laid a year's worth of rubber onto the tarmac, her rear end slewing through ninety degrees. By the time she came to a stop Darren's hands were planted on her bonnet, Gideon braced to the dash, staring down into his eyes. "Jesus fucking Christ."

"Gideon!"

"Sorry." He snapped out of the belt he'd somehow remembered to fasten and half-fell out into the road. "Darren, this is the absolute limit. What the bloody hell are you—"

"You can't go in there!"

The boy's voice was an octave up out of its usual range. He was sheet white. He transferred his grip from the grille of the truck to Gideon's chest, the exact same gesture of hopeless warding-off. Gideon detached him blindly. "Go in where?"

"Your house. I saw *him* coming out of it—that nutcase from up at the farm."

"Dev Bowe?"

"Yes! And I didn't mean to—but he'd already broken in, so I—"

Gideon picked him up bodily and dumped him into his brother's arms. "I don't care what you've done. Zeke, keep him out of my way." He began to run. He could see his own front door now, not twenty yards off, locked tight and intact with his whole world behind it. He didn't believe for a second that Dev Bowe could have harmed Lee. Lee's gifts didn't always work to order, but he'd have seen a danger like that on its way from a mile off, even in half-drugged dreams, surely...

Rufus Pendower was on the doorstep. This was bloody surreal. He caught sight of Gideon and dashed back down the garden path and into the road, holding up his hand like a traffic cop. "Stop!"

"Pendower!" Gideon met him halfway, barely avoiding a collision. "What's going on here?"

"I came to find you. But no-one's answering the door, and I could smell—"

Gideon shoved him aside. He could smell it too, pungent and high. Gas. Too strong for a leaking pipe under the pavement. A huge concentration close at hand. Pendower caught his arm, and he swung round to punch him out of the way.

Something did it for him. The air turned into a fist. Pendower flew backwards. The same force plucked Gideon off his feet: swapped heaven for earth, street for sky, and dropped him and everything neatly into the pit.

Chapter Ten

His brother said, "Gideon, hush."

There was no need. It was a lovely afternoon. Sun beat down strongly on the cliff track at Drift. The hush was over everything, and Gideon was part of it. This was where Lee drew his imagery from when he opened up his mind. This was the borderland: if Gideon just kept walking, he'd find the Mên-an-Tol Stargate, slip through it and be home, and once there he need never come back.

Imperative that he never came back. He fixed his gaze on the church so that he wouldn't slide into the yawning void on his left. Jago Tyack was standing in the churchyard beside Lee's father's grave. He held out one hand, pointing. "It's a corpse path, you know. If you see someone on it, they'll be gone within a year."

That was bollocks, of course. Gideon dealt with bigger local legends than that all the time. He'd grown very fond of Jago, though, after a bumpy start, and he only smiled at him in passing. Lee was on the corpse road, with Tamsyn in his arms. It was only a trail of flattened grass through a meadow. Gideon felt suddenly sick and weak, the skin stinging oddly on his face and hands. He sat down on the coffin-shaped stone to wait.

Elowen stepped out of the hedgerow. She took the baby from Lee's arms. Gideon lurched to his feet. *Don't*, he wanted to shout.

Don't just give her away like that! But Lee hadn't, had he? He'd had his reasons, just as the dog had hers for multiplying herself into four and guarding the cradle, warning him against the masked lamb. Gideon had to trust and believe. The hardest thing he'd ever had to do, against all of his instincts as a copper and a man. His reward was the ability to move. The baby was gone but Lee was at home. Gideon stretched out his limbs and covered the distance between Drift and Dark in a dozen long strides. He ran down Moor Lane once again, and his house exploded, knocking him flat in a rain of masonry and grit.

"Hush, Gid. It's all right."

It fucking wasn't. His brother was kneeling in front of him, trying to wipe his face with a handkerchief. Gideon knocked his arm aside. He made a seismic effort to get up, but someone was holding him tight from behind. He was making a dreadful arse of himself, yelling and fighting like a downed bull. He couldn't seem to stop. "Lee! Oh, God, let me go. Lee's in there. Lee!"

"I'm *not* in there, you moron! Now calm the fuck down and keep still."

Gideon's throat closed. It was scoured and full of dust. He sucked in a truncated gasp and broke into anguished coughing, painful as sandpaper in his gullet, but at least it shut him up. In his own sudden silence, he replayed the last voice he'd heard. Recognised at last the grip around his ribs, the warm body propping his spine. He twisted round as far as he could. Lee tried to stop him then surrendered, submitting to his frantic embrace. "Gideon, sweetheart..."

"What happened? Where were you?" He could barely get the words out for sobs. Lee's response was just as incoherent, and he couldn't give it his attention anyway—was too lost in the living scent of him as he laid his face to Lee's shoulder. He wrapped his arms around Lee's waist, clenched his hands hard enough to leave bruises on beloved skin for a week.

A sound began to penetrate the fizzing rumble in his ears. At first he put it down to the damage done to his eardrums by the blast. A staccato chatter—*da-da-da-da-da*, like a tractor-engine trying to start. Familiar to him from a hundred homecomings—his daughter's first efforts to get out a word that meant him and him alone, because she'd greet her other father with a skull-piercing single-note *eee*! that might or might not one day turn into *Lee*. Both of them got the wild, arm-waving semaphore of joy, but *da-da-da-da-da*....

He jolted upright. Lee aided his indecorous lurch round onto his backside. His mother was standing in the road in front of him, dust blowing around her. She was clean and obviously unhurt, but her face was a mask of shock, and the paramedic propping her up had wrapped a blanket round her anyway. She was holding Tamsyn in her arms.

Gideon got to his feet. He couldn't have done it for any other cause—every muscle in his body complained, and Zeke had to reach in and hoist him from behind. Gideon planted a kiss to the old lady's cheek. "Ma. You brought her home."

"Lee and I did," she said weakly. "Lee and I."

"Can I take her?"

"Yes, my dear. Of course."

It was more like a catch. Tamsyn, having worked out that this bloodstained apparition really was her father, launched herself out to grab him. He seized her: held her little body fast between his hands for a moment, staring into her face. Her machine-gun sounds blended into one huge shriek of delight, and he wrapped her in his arms. "Lee," he managed after a moment. "Where's Pendower? Is anybody hurt?"

"Apart from you, you mean? Pendower took a flying brick to the back of his head. He'll be all right. He's on his way to hospital now."

"That man has no luck."

"I doubt he'll volunteer to investigate weird shit in Dark again any time soon. All our other neighbours were out at work, thank God." Lee grabbed his arm as he swayed. "What do you want?"

"Five minutes with you and our kid. Please."

Lee led him away, parrying protests from Zeke and the ambulance crew. He parted the gathering crowd of their neighbours and friends, guided him up the pavement to a low wall sheltered by rose bushes and a patrol car parked by the kerb. "Sit down."

Clouds were dispersing in Gideon's mind. He subsided onto the wall, still clutching his daughter, who promptly grabbed a fistful of rose petals and shoved them into his face. "You weren't in the flat. You weren't there."

"That's right, Sherlock." Lee sat down beside him. "I had a text from your mum this morning. She said Elowen had contacted her. She was the only one of us Elowen dared speak to."

"My ma can text?"

"Pretty well, though the autocorrect still foxes her a bit."

"When did you get it? This text?"

"It was on my phone when I woke up this morning."

Time rolled back effortlessly inside Gideon's head. He was sitting on the edge of his bed, not this wall opposite the gap where his house had used to be. Lee was checking his mobile—to see what time it was, Gideon had assumed. Then he'd asked Gideon to fetch his meds. "You bloody lied to me."

"Yes, I did," Lee said firmly. "And get this through your thick head—I'd lie to you again, without batting an eyelid, if I had the time over. I didn't know what Elowen wanted and nor did your ma. If she'd just been coming to talk, to mess around with us some more, I didn't want her anywhere near you, breaking your heart again. But she was coming to bring back Tamsyn."

"Christ. Why didn't you *phone* me?"

"I had to be sure." Lee too focussed on the burning ruin across the road, and his voice cracked. "Elowen met us just down the road in Liskeard. And once I had Tamsyn, all I could think about was bringing her home. Having her waiting there for you. We'd just made the turn into the street when—"

"That's just it. You *would* have been at home with her—if we'd done what I wanted, if we'd gone charging over to France and grabbed her back by main force. This is her nap-time. You'd both have been at home."

Lee closed his arms around both of them, completing the sacred circuit of touch. The baby quieted and clutched Gideon by his collar, Lee by his silver chain. The wail of the arriving fire engine faded out, and all Gideon could hear was his lover's breathing and the rush of the wind among the roses. "We weren't home," Lee said, kissing him. "We're here. We're right here."

Typically, it was Darren Prowse who broke the moment. He ducked away from the police officer holding him and darted over the road. From somewhere he'd retrieved Gideon's cap. He came to a panting halt in front of him and thrust it out in a propitiatory gesture. "Here!"

Gideon handed Tamsyn to Lee and reached out to take the cap. "You've missed something, Daz," he said grimly. "The badge is still attached."

"It wasn't me! I never did it. I never—"

His arresting constable caught up with him. "Come back here, you." She grabbed him by the scruff. "Oh, Gideon! Are you all right?"

Gideon smiled. Jenny Spargo seemed to have a knack for witnessing all his worst moments. "Fine, somehow or other. It's all right—let him talk."

Darren promptly fell as silent as a clam. Jenny gave him a shake. "You'd better explain yourself, young man, if Sergeant Frayne is prepared to listen to you."

"I never blew the house up! It were that nutter from the farm." Darren choked with the effort of telling the truth. "I saw him go over your garden wall at the back. He broke a pane in your kitchen door and he went in. So I waited—to see, you know, if..."

"If he came out carrying anything worth blackmailing him for," Gideon supplied. "Do go on."

"He didn't take nothing, as far as I could see. He just ran off and started shouting at the minister in the street. But there was still that broken pane, and I thought..."

"You thought it was a shame to leave a perfectly good house un-robbed, when someone had already broken into it for you."

Darren nodded fervently. "'Zackly." He was clearly relieved to be understood. "Then that old busybody in the upstairs flat opposite yours got her eye on me, so I started pretending to be doing a bit of gardening, like you asked. She must've sat there for nigh on half an hour! Then she finally buggered off, and I went in the same way, and I nearly fucking choked to death. All the hobs on your gas cooker were turned up full. And I heard your crappy old boiler start its ignition, and I thought, if there's a spark..."

"My God, Daz. You tried to stop me going in."

"Well, I thought about it, didn't I? I remembered stuff. Like when you came to our house that time, and you were the only one who believed me about the Beast. And when I lost my gloves in the snow, and how you always look after people around here even if they don't deserve it. Even if that does make you a bloody fool."

Gideon regarded him seriously. Beside him, Lee was trying desperately hard not to laugh. "You probably saved my life," he said. "Having said that, you really are a little shit, Darren Prowse."

***

The big farmhouse kitchen at Drift was utterly peaceful. The back door was propped open, Isolde trotting in and out as the fancy took her. Jago and Mrs Ivey were sunning themselves in matching striped deckchairs on the lawn. Gideon set down the last of the carrier bags from the car. It had taken a week, but he and Lee had finally gathered together the basics for family life. Some things they'd bought, a very few they'd salvaged from the ruins of the flat, and Jago had made room for it all with delighted welcome, proud of his ability to offer a temporary home. He'd thrown the whole farmhouse open to them, but his shellshocked guests had been only too happy to move into Lee's old room, with the bathroom over the corridor and a little dressing room—whose door stood open all the time—for Tamsyn's cot.

Gideon's insurers were still wrangling over the wreckage in Moor Lane. A rebuild wasn't yet off the cards, but a demolition more likely, given the structural damage. Either way, he knew they would move back to Dark. That was his place in the world, guarding and protecting and forgiving. Even if that did make him a bloody fool.

He leaned on the counter top and took in the wholly satisfactory sight of Lee pacing the kitchen with the baby against his shoulder. "How has she been?"

Lee stopped and beamed at him. "She just had the biggest feed of her life. I thought she was never gonna stop. Tell me you've got more of her goop in that bag."

"Cheesy veg, beef-and-liver, giblets in jelly with tripe. A bit preoccupied now, is she?"

"That's why you didn't get your usual rapturous greeting."

"Uh-oh."

"Don't worry. I'll just keep walking and patting. I'm certain the blockage will clear."

"You know what? I think I should record one of these for posterity."

"Hurry up and get your camera running, then. She's about to blow."

Chuckling, Gideon got his phone out and started a new video. He fell into step behind Lee. His daughter watched him gravely over Lee's shoulder. Lee had a towel ready in case of accidents, but she liked her food too much to let go of it easily. It was just the sound effects. She opened her rosy mouth, rode out another couple of Lee's gently jiggling strides, and unleashed a deep, stately burp.

Gideon creased up. "Oh, my God. That is phenomenal."

"The windows rattled, I swear. How does she do it?"

"Takes after her dad, I reckon."

"Oh, charming. That'll be the dad who likes raw red onions with his curry, right?" Relieved of her digestive problems, the baby caught their laughter like a dose of measles and began to crow in her turn, and like them fell suddenly silent when the doorbell rang. Lee, who'd failed to repress a nervous twitch, held her close. "Who's that?"

"It's a bit soon for our dinner guests. I'll go and have a look."

Gideon ran up the kitchen steps. The hall's inner doorway was open. Beyond the stained glass of the porch, he could make out a pale, solemn face. "Deep breath, Mr Tiger. It's Elowen."

"Why is she ringing the bell of her own home?"

"Maybe she doesn't feel like it is anymore. There's a guy with her—not Michel. Jago's going round to let her in."

"Tell me she's carrying a big fat envelope."

"I can't see from here. But the guy's got a briefcase, and he looks like a lawyer. This might be it."

"Oh, Jesus."

Gideon went back to him. "Do you want to see her? Mrs Ivey will look after Tamsyn."

"It probably sounds horrible of me, but—no, I don't want to see her yet. She's my sister, and I'm scared of saying something unforgivable to her. I let your ma handle all the negotiations in Liskeard. I just grabbed Tamsyn out of her carrycot and ran back to the car with her."

Gideon could imagine the scene. He kissed Lee's eyelids and the corners of his mouth. "All right. Why don't you put her down for her nap and go join the others in the sun?"

"Like I'd leave her alone for a second while that child-snatching monster's in the house." Lee said it lightly, but his eyes filled suddenly with shadows, and he leaned his brow on Gideon's shoulder. Tamsyn, mildly crushed between them, emitted a raspberry noise and a sound like a hen settling down on its eggs. "I couldn't go through that again, premonitions or no premonitions. I'd fucking kill anyone who laid another hand on her now."

"I know." Gideon rocked them both. "Let's wait another twenty years or so for some unsuitable lover to come and snatch her away. You're gonna make a lovely laid-back father-in-law, I can tell."

"I might buy a shotgun."

They were still laughing when Jago leaned into the kitchen and tapped lightly on the door. "Elowen's here, gentlemen."

"Yes. Thanks, Jago—I'm on my way."

"She's my niece," Jago added, "and I love her very much."

Gideon wasn't about to argue family bonds. "I know that. Of course."

"But don't you let her take away that little girl again. All right?"

"All right. Lee's gonna take her upstairs for a while. You don't have to worry about anything now."

"I should bloody hope not. In that case, I'll make everyone a cup of tea."

Gideon entered the living room cautiously. Elowen and her companion were already there, looking awkward among the family photos. The lawyer wasn't from Baragwathen's office. The Bodmin fracking scandal was exploding in fantastic slow motion over the town council, local authority, AONB management and planning department. Poor old lawyer Keast's would be the least of the heads to roll. So far he faced only disbarment, and Gideon wasn't keen to press charges against a man already made so desolate by his grab for wealth. This gentleman looked a lot more sleek and successful. He stood up to shake Gideon's hand. "Saul Welkin of Prynne, Welkin and Co, Falmouth. Miss Tyack thought she wouldn't put you and your husband to the inconvenience of coming into town, not when you've both been through so much."

"Thanks," Gideon said uncertainly. "I'm Gideon Tyack-Frayne. Lee's busy with the baby, Elowen—can we manage without him?"

"I'm not going to get to see her, am I?"

Welkin gave her a repressing glance. "Yes, that's no problem. Miss Tyack has signed all the paperwork you requested. We've brought it along for you to look over, if we could all perhaps sit down...?"

The lawyer spread the papers out on the coffee table. Before Gideon could turn the first sheet, Elowen reached out to touch his wrist. "I don't suppose for a moment you want to hear me explain."

Gideon didn't. But he couldn't help noting that she'd lost weight, and had shadows under her eyes to rival Lee's. "Whatever you want to say, I'll listen."

"Good old Gideon. Always so bloody fair. I wonder if my brother realises what a sodding treasure he's got in you."

He sighed. "Would you rather I kicked your arse, Elowen?"

"Almost." She knotted her hands together in a gesture just like Lee's, knucklebones stretching the skin. "Michel and I were arguing before we got out of Cornwall. We argued all the way across the Channel to Carnac. He wouldn't come right out and say it, but I think he was more inclined to take your side and Lee's than mine. So that was great, and then the house he said he'd rented in Auray turned out to be a one-room flat. And Tamsie might have been a baby angel for you two, but for me she turned into a howling demon, and she screamed the place down in that one bloody room for forty eight hours straight."

"She was probably just unsettled, Elowen."

"Oh, right. That's why she started crooning and making that clucking sound of hers the minute—the *minute*—I gave up and started packing her things to bring her home." She held up a hand, although Gideon hadn't been about to interrupt. "I know— women have brought up babies in much worse circumstances than mine. I don't have any excuses, though it didn't help that Michel suddenly found the excavation site a whole lot more interesting than me and his kid and a pile of dirty nappies, and announced he wasn't coming home for a week."

"I'm sorry. That must have been hard."

"Not if I'd loved her." She read Gideon's shift of expression, paled a bit and quickly amended, "You know what I mean. The way a mother—a parent—*should* love a child, where the nappies and the crying and the absentee husband might drive you crazy, but underneath it all there's this... thing, this bond, that makes it all worthwhile. I didn't have that. I didn't even have a proper home for her, and all I can say to excuse myself for taking her away from you was that I had—God, I dunno, some kind of hormone surge at the prospect of leaving her behind. Can you understand?"

"Yes," Gideon said shortly, and turned the pages until he found the crucial clauses, managing not to add, *Just in case you have another one.* "Thank you for signing these. Has Mr Welkin been through them with you properly?"

"Yes. In painful detail. They're belt-and-braces adoption papers, awarding full custody of Tamsyn to my brother and to you."

"Yes. If they seem a bit... watertight, I'm sure you'll understand."

"Oh, Gideon. I know I've been a dick. You don't have to rub my nose in it."

Now she really did sound like Lee. Gideon drew a deep breath and let it go. "I didn't mean to do that," he said kindly, reaching across the table to take her chilly hand. "We both know you're not signing these for your own benefit, or for mine, or even for your brother's. It's for Tamsyn, isn't it? She needs to know where home is. Who her parents are."

Elowen gave a sob. "Will you let me see her at all?"

"What kind of question is that? Did you make things up with Michel?"

"Kind of. We're working on it."

"Did he come through on the fancy hot-shot job?"

She found a watery smile. "I should bloody think so."

"Well, then—in the intervals of your high-flying archaeology career, once Tamsyn notices she hasn't inherited my ugly mug or

Lee's, I hope you'll be around to help explain." He waited a beat, listening to the silent message from upstairs, the pulse of forgiveness behind the pain. "We both do."

Chapter Eleven

"Do you think it does her any harm, to hear us rolling around in here?"

Gideon considered. "Well, for a start, she's sound asleep. But... I dunno. I grew up in a see-no-evil, hear-no-evil household—bedroom doors firmly closed—and all it did for me was to make me even more clueless about relationships than I would have been anyway. No, I don't think it hurts her to hear us loving each other." He shifted onto his back in delicious surrender. "Not like this, anyway. Some nights we're gonna have to give her earplugs and lock her in the coal shed, of course."

Lee gave a moan of anticipation and continued his slow, well-lubed push into Gideon's body. "Oh, God. *Those* nights."

"Can you hang on for the next one?"

"Long as you like. Just not sure I can give you more than three minutes now."

"Oh, that ought to do fine." Gideon stretched out. He held on to the bars of the headboard where Lee had once tied him up, then couldn't resist the muscular ripple of his lover's back and curled up to hold him, cradling him between his thighs. White curtains blew softly into the room, the rhythm of the sweet sea wind all of one piece with his gathering pleasure. "Mm, yes. Deeper, darlin'. Deeper."

"All the way. Oh, I love you, Gid."

Gideon caught his breath. He didn't want his response to come out as a yell. Mrs Ivey and Jago were still enjoying their summer afternoon, and Lee's room overlooked the garden. "Oh, God. I... I love..."

His mobile rang. He'd made the mistake of assigning DI Lawrence her own ringtone, so he'd know which calls he could ignore, and which—this afternoon anyway—he absolutely had to take. "Lee..."

"You're kidding."

"Nope."

"Oh, great. This is married life, is it—picking up phone calls in the middle of a fu-..."

"Bet you a tenner you can't keep it in there and keep it hard while I talk to her."

"Can I move?"

"Not a muscle."

Gideon conducted his half of the conversation in monosyllables. They were less likely to fracture or squeak, and were all that was required of him. He listened, taking deep, silent breaths through his nose while poor Lee remained frozen between his thighs, turning various shades of rose pink and eventually burying his face in the duvet. "Yes, ma'am. Thank you. That's great news." Another agonising pause, DI Lawrence's tinned voice broadcasting innocently across their scene. "Thank you, ma'am. You too. Goodbye." He cut the line and met Lee's bright gaze as he surfaced. "Well *done*."

"I've studied Tantric."

"Really? You never mentioned that before we were married."

"I was keeping it as a surprise. What did she want?"

"You seriously want to wait while I tell you?"

"Why not? Tantric, I'm telling you. Tantric." Lee pushed upright on his arms. "Oh, God."

"I'll keep it brief. The forensics team found a scythe buried in the garden at Carnysen. It's covered with John Bowe's blood—and Dev's prints."

"Oh, good. You didn't arrest the wrong guy."

"No, although I still don't understand how that poor skinny lad managed to slice up his brother like so much sausage meat... I doubt he'll stand trial. He's in Fletcher Ward, under restraint."

"Do you really not understand that, Gid? After all you've seen?"

"No, I... I do. Partway at least. The Beast came, or he believed it did, and..."

Lee shuddered deeply, withdrawing a little way, pulsing back in. "Godsakes. Sausages, restraints, beasts coming... What else?"

This was becoming a game of control. Gideon grinned up at him. "You're quite something, aren't you? No-one's gonna frack on Bodmin Moor."

"Lawrence knows that for sure?"

"She's rounded up all the councillors Keast named like the Clanton gang. Every one of them admitted to bribery and corruption. The sale itself was illegal, and with John and Bligh gone and Dev incapable of making decisions..."

"The land goes to the Crown?"

"Possibly, unless Dev's lawyers can get 'em to hold it in trust for him until he's well. Either way, Mitchell Shale won't get it. The AONB might make a bid to enclose it inside the park."

"You did it. You saved the moor." Pinning him gently down, Lee trailed kisses along his throat and collar bone. Gideon didn't know that he could take so much credit, but if this was how his moment of glory was going to happen, he couldn't argue. "My guardian," Lee continued, adding the lightest sharp-toothed nip to the words. "My good shepherd. What else? Tell me quick, handsome, so I can take us both where we're going."

"She says..." Gideon gasped and swallowed a raw shout. "She says she's pleased about Tamsyn, and I can take some leave to get sorted about the house, and... she hopes we have a good weekend."

"Nice of her."

"I thought so. Where are you gonna take us?"

"Where would you like to go?"

"Where you took me before. The cliffs."

If Gideon sat up, he would see them—the real ones, tumbling in all their sunny glory along the coast of Drift. Lee destroyed the boundaries between the outer and the inner worlds. One day, if Gideon let him, he would disprove the old lie that life and death were separate things. "You saw that so clearly when I showed you," Lee whispered. "You see all kinds of things you're not meant to be able to now, don't you?"

Gideon couldn't tell him. He hadn't even formulated for himself how he was changing. "Even if I do—can you understand that I don't want to? The world I have right here's enough for me. Even... Even if we hadn't got Tamsyn back. It would have been enough for me."

Lee gathered him up. He cupped the back of his skull and pounded into him. He jolted Gideon up with him into the clear blue sky, laid him out and fucked him in harsh-breathing silence until the sun grew red to his wide-open gaze. They hit the barrier together, hard and fast. Gideon saw—one of the things he wasn't meant to—how the world would have been enough for Lee too, even without their daughter: somehow, eventually. Yes.

***

Lee raised his head. He looked as disreputable as he could ever manage, mouth swollen from rough kisses, a piratical touch of five o'clock shadow darkening his jaw. He yawned enormously. "We seem doomed to be interrupted by doorbells."

"Doorbells or demon knocks. At least they waited until we were done this time." Gideon glanced at his watch. "Oops. Overslept. That *isn't* too soon for our dinner guests."

"Don't worry. Jago's been primed to take them in and make them welcome."

"Shit. We'd better get down there fast." Gideon slithered out from under Lee's attempt to nose-dive back onto his shoulder. An unearthly cackle from the nursery told him that Tamsyn was back in the game as well, and as usual finding something about the state of her fingers or toes hilarious. "Come and help me dress our daughter. She's meant to be on parade."

An odd deputation was waiting for them in the hallway. This informal dinner was to celebrate Pendower's release from hospital. Once Ma Frayne had heard about the part he'd played in keeping her son from rushing into the flat at Dark, she hadn't let anyone rest until she'd extracted a promise from Jago to host the event, Gideon and Lee to have their infant present and correct, and Zeke and Eleanor to pick the injured sergeant up from Trelowarren and transport him over to Drift. Tamsyn was overjoyed at the sight of so much company. She yowled in Gideon's arms as he bore her ceremoniously down the stairs, pointed at her grandmother and said something close enough to *gan* to make the old lady dissolve into tears. "There she is!" Ma Frayne cried, poking Pendower in the ribs. "Oh, she's wearing the new dress I bought her. Doesn't she look like an angel?"

Gideon thought she looked like an explosion in a meringue factory, but handed her over smiling. "Yeah. She loves it. How are you, Rufus? It's good to see you on your feet."

"Thank you." Pendower shook his outstretched hand, reached to shake Lee's too and beamed with pleasure when Lee returned him a brief hug. "I'm fine now. So, this is your girl?"

"The creature herself. Tamsyn Elizabeth Tyack-Frayne, named after her grandmother, of course."

"She's a beauty, isn't she?" Pendower gave her a wistful chuck under the chin. "Can I have a little hold of her, Mrs Frayne? I used to think I might have something like this of my own one day."

Tamsyn was used to being handed around like a parcel at social gatherings, and went to him willingly, intrigued by the dressing still taped to his skull. Gideon frowned in concern. "Why not? You're going to be all right, aren't you? It was just a head wound."

"I meant... I thought I knew who I was going to marry. I had it all planned out." He jounced Tamsyn on his hip. "But she died."

His words fell like stones into the convivial atmosphere. Tears had come to his eyes. Gideon and Lee exchanged a glance. "I tell you what," Lee said. "Tamsie needs a breath of air. Why don't you take her down to the gate to see the cliffs? Gid and I will come too, and Jago, could you get drinks for everyone?"

Jago nodded happily. He was living it up in his role as host, and would probably uncork his homebrewed moonshine if left unattended for long. As for Zeke, he had the look of a man who would probably drink it today, exhausted under his contentment at the hard-won reunion of his family. He and Eleanor followed his mother into the living room, and Lee steered Pendower and Gideon outside.

Isolde trotted after them, weaving circles around them thrice. A perfect summer's day was drawing to its close above the cliffs. Pendower came to a halt by the garden gate, turning Tamsyn so that she could watch the setting sun. "The thing is," he said, as much to the child as to anyone else, "that I kept seeing her. Amber, I mean—my girlfriend. After the car crash, I'd look up, and she'd just be standing there smiling at me. It made me very happy, to be honest with you, but of course I'm a police officer, and I can't afford to be having hallucinations. So I went to the doctor, and he put me on some anti-psychotic meds, and—well, they made her disappear. That was for the best, but I missed her a lot." He brushed back a strand of Tamsyn's hair from her eyes. "I think that was why I had a slightly... unbalanced reaction to you, Lee. I'd seen you talk to dead people at your stage shows, just as if they were right there in front of you. So either they were real, or you were a fake, and I wanted to find out which."

Lee had taken up position on the path behind him, as if watching his back. Gideon came to stand beside him, and Lee took a tight, hot-skinned grip on his hand. "Did you come to any conclusions?"

"I know you're not a fake. Other than that, all I've really come to believe is that the world was a smaller, stupider place for me, once I couldn't see Amber anymore."

"Rufus—if you want me to advise you to stop taking your meds, I can't. Has it ever occurred to you that it doesn't really matter whether what you saw was real or not? She was there for you."

"Yes, it occurred. I had plenty of time in hospital, and somehow after working with you and Gideon—awful though most of that was—I found I could think about it without wanting to throw things or cry. I stopped taking my pills about a month ago."

He was watching a patch of sunny turf on the cliff top. After a few seconds he seemed to recollect himself. "Well," he said, "that breeze is turning cold. Shall we go back indoors, Miss Tyack-Frayne?"

Lee and Gideon followed him slowly back up the path. When he was out of earshot, Lee glanced back once over his shoulder to the cliff. His grip on Gideon's intensified. "She's a pretty girl, Amber. She likes the dress he bought her, the one with the tulips on the skirt. She wears it all the time."

"Yes," said Gideon, lacing their fingers together. "I know."

Book VI

Third Solstice

Harper Fox

A FoxTales Publication

Chapter One

Going home for Christmas. A mantra for this time of year, a question, a promise. *Are you going home for Christmas?* Weary office workers, hanging up the phone for the last time. Kids fresh from university, holding down a first London job, lonely in bedsits and remembering once-despised villages and towns: *I'm out of here. Going home for Christmas.*

Heartbreak to the homeless. Salt in the wounds of broken families. Bewildering, drug-like excitement to overstimulated kids, a vortex of tinsel and glitter. If you could feel it all—if you, one ordinary man, could walk the city streets and know about all of it—you'd drown. You'd have to make for higher ground. You'd have to build a wall.

An ordinary man, going home for Christmas. The city streets are quiet to him now. Even the babbling, clattering Tube carriage, quiet as a church. The underground garage where he's left his car resounds with engines and slammed doors only, not the dreams and schemes and thousand daily niggles of drivers and passengers, amplified and bouncing off the concrete. Then the westbound roads.

Silence on the windswept brow of Lance Hill, but it's always quiet here. Not many people know the moortop route to Dark. He stops the car in a layby and gets out.

It's all just a season of lights, isn't it? Lights are marking Bodmin Moor like crystalline snail-trails tonight, villages clustering round their green centre or winding with the path of their river or main road. There's a promise of frost in the air. The ordinary man—a family man now—celebrates Christmas with good heart, but he prefers his solstice, the day made doubly sacred by his daughter's birthday.

He can just see the shimmer of Dark on the horizon. Still half an hour away, but maybe he'll get there in time to help put her to bed. For Lee, journey's end isn't any of the festivals of light. It's Gideon and Tamsyn, now and forever.

Going home for Christmas, Lee?

No. Just going home.

***

Gid and the baby agreed about most things, but electronic toys in bathwater wasn't one of them. Gently he removed the talking bear from the starfishing little hands and laid it on the floor behind him. "There. You can have him back when we're finished."

Tamsyn, too placid to raise a fuss, smacked him in the eye with a fistful of suds instead. Her aim was good. She could sit up unaided now, so he let go of her long enough to grab a flannel. "Ow, you little blighter. What's Lee gonna say when he gets home and finds out I let you go down the plughole?"

She let loose a shriek of laughter at the prospect and slapped the surface of the water with her palms, soaking Gideon again.

"Pug'ole," she said, with eerie distinctness, then added solemnly, "Eee."

"Yes. Lee. He'll be back any minute, and I promised to have you in bed by seven."

"Blighter."

"Oh, shi-... Crikey. Don't you pick up any more bad language from me." His sweet-faced infant had transformed overnight into a word-absorbing sponge, startling Ma Frayne and Ezekiel with a crisply-enunciated *bugger* over the lunch table. Gideon rolled his shirt sleeves higher and went back into the fray. "Right. Let me have a go at that potato crop growing behind your ears."

"Bear."

"Not yet, sweetheart. As soon as you're..."

He sat back on his heels, staring. The toy was in her hands again. Had somebody bought her a second one? The various members of her fan club—Ma, Zeke, Sarah and Lorna Kemp, her great-uncle Jago and Mrs Ivey—often doubled up on gifts in their anxiety to get her the latest thing. She'd have been spoiled rotten but for her own imperturbable good nature and the gentle discipline of her home. "Bear."

Gideon took it from her again. "No. No bear in the bath, Tamsie. Dangerous."

It was just as well the various thugs and villains he came across in the course of his daily duties couldn't exert her charm. Even gentle discipline was hard to apply. Something throbbed at the back of his skull, first warning of a headache or a change in the weather. In the corner of the bathroom, Isolde sat up restlessly and began to growl. "Give me a break, dog," Gideon said, perching the bear firmly on the edge of the sink. "I'm not hurting her. I'm trying to stop her electrocuting herself."

The growl became a whine. To Gideon's alarm, his placid old collie—fat and contented, spending her days now sprawled out and farting beside Tamsyn's cot—lifted her hackles and began to back away. And the toy bear wobbled once on the sink, then sailed straight back into the child's outstretched hand.

Gideon clamped his mouth shut. He didn't want Tamsyn to learn any of the words that would have come out of it at that point. He took a deep breath, shook his head. "What did... What did you just do?"

"*Bear.*"

"Yes, I know." An appeal to her generosity would often succeed where an order failed. "Sweetheart, can I have the bear for a minute?"

She shoved it at him. "Dada."

"Thank you." She was more or less clean, so he scooped her out of the bath and wrapped her in a towel. "Right. Let's put Bear over here on the shelf, and you and I will go and sit on the stool beside Isolde, because..." *Because I'm about to raise my hackles and start whining myself.* "Isolde! Hush, stupid. Everything's all right."

He sat with the baby on his lap and one soothing hand on the dog's head. Tamsyn gazed around until she located the toy on the shelf. She reached out, then suddenly looked up at him for permission with a clarity that pierced his heart. "Bear now?"

She was smart as a fresh coat of paint. Every day she said or did something that revealed to Gideon how the universe was unfolding for her and within her. "Yes," he said unsteadily. "That's a clever girl. There's no water now, so... you can have your bear."

She stretched out her hand. Again Gideon felt the throbbing tug deep in his brain. Isolde tucked her tail between her legs, nosed the bathroom door open and fled, and the bear lifted slowly off the shelf.

Whatever Tamsyn was doing, she wasn't quite strong enough yet to pull it off. Gravity and reality took over when the toy was halfway across the room. She gave a little wail of disappointment and began to wriggle in Gideon's arms. "All right," he said, as calmly as he could with his heart pounding and ice cubes slithering down his spine. "Let's do it the old-fashioned way. Come on."

He scooped the toy off the floor, gave it to Tamsyn and helped her pull the string that would make it talk. This was the bear whose porridge was just right—he had two less contented siblings in the little girl's bedroom—and his high-pitched porridge song was enough to drive a strong man demented. Tonight Gideon barely noticed. He carried Tamsyn through into the living room and stood with her in front of the fire, jouncing her gently, rubbing one end of the towel over her dark curls. There were so many things he had to do. It was quarter to seven, and he had no sense yet of Lee coming home. Lee liked to help bed her down, but she had a set bedtime and both he and Gideon tried to observe it. Once she was asleep, Gideon could tidy the bathroom and get some supper ready, tidy up the trail of devastation he and his daughter had left after a week alone together.

At least this room was ready. Like every other child born in late December, she was doomed to spend her birthdays in the shadow of a Christmas tree, to combination birthday-and-Christmas presents wrapped in reindeer paper. "Sorry, kiddo," he said, turning her so she could see the tinsel and the lights. She didn't seem to mind. She'd stopped tugging at the bear's cord and was beginning to fall asleep, purring in pleasure at the sight of the glimmering tree. Lee and Gideon had put her party back a day so that all the major players could be present. There would scarcely be room for them all in the tiny vacant flat their landlord had loaned them while their own was being rebuilt.

Of course they'd invited Elowen and Michel. God alone knew what she was feeling, the day before her baby's first birthday. Gideon let his mind skid away from the thought. He had plenty of unknowns to be going along with for now. He carried Tamsyn over to the sofa and sat down. Just for a minute, he told himself, just until she dropped off properly and he could put her to bed without the usual three-ring circus of stories, songs and games. He leaned back, cradling her, and her head drooped on his chest like a weary flower. "That was all my imagination, wasn't it?" he asked her, stroking her velvety cheek. "You didn't just start... *levitating* things, did you?"

She wasn't quite out. She blew him a long raspberry, watching him sleepily. God, she was starting to look like Lee—those agate-green eyes, turning pure silver in certain lights. Like her mother, too.

That was a good thing. Elowen was a lovely woman, and that dark-haired, olive-skinned Cornish bloodline ran strong. Gideon was sure that his nightmares would eventually stop, that one day he'd quit triple-checking the window lock on the nursery. Elowen with wings, bird-footed Lilith Elowen, swooping down on the cradle...

He twitched, eliciting a grunt of complaint from the baby. But her solid little weight on him was like a drug, and he'd found his week of solo fatherhood exhausting. Still no sign of Lee on his inner radar. The dog emerged from wherever she'd hidden to avoid the poltergeist activity, and sensing his weakness, seized the chance for a forbidden jump onto the sofa. Well, she was a good guardian now she had a baby of her own to watch, and she would alert him to any trouble or noise. He'd just switch the TV on and catch the news. Just close his eyes for five minutes...

Chapter Two

How long had Lee been sitting there? Gideon sat up, catching his sleeping infant before she could slide off his chest. The so-called watchdog was flat on her back, legs sprawled, hairy paws flickering with dreams. "Lee! Um... Hi, sweetheart. I wasn't... I didn't think you'd be back yet."

"Clearly." Lee's face was bright with amusement. He'd had to sit on the edge of the coffee table for want of room on the sofa. "I got in about five minutes ago. I pulled up a pew to watch you three."

"Sorry." Gideon yawned hugely. "Sorry. I meant to have supper ready."

"I stuck a lasagne into the microwave to defrost. We'll have that."

A huge tide of pleasure swept Gideon, as if he'd been offered champagne cocktails under the stars on a luxury liner. This week was the longest time he and Lee had been apart since their wedding. "Sweetheart," he said, and leaned forward to kiss him, keeping Tamsyn out of the way of crushing or suffocation. "Did the last of the filming go well? How was your journey? How come I didn't know you were nearly home?"

"Fine. Long. You were asleep." Lee returned his embrace with hungry warmth. Tamsyn emerged serenely from sleep at the sound of his voice, and he lifted her onto his knee, smiling. "God almighty, look at her. She's grown while I've been away."

"Not surprised. She's been eating like a tentacled sea-monster. Do you have to go back between now and New Year?"

"Nope, we're all done. Jack and Anna just wanted some talking-head stuff to wrap up the *London Hauntings* series. We're cleared for our festive take-off."

"Wonderful." Gideon had bargained away part of his paternity leave to get this first birthday and Christmas at home with his small family. He rubbed his eyes, trying to focus. Lee's outline was blurred to him, somehow unreal. "Weird that I didn't wake up, though. I normally feel you coming a mile off."

Lee raised a suggestive eyebrow at him, then visibly changed the subject. "Seriously, she's huge. A week's too long to be away at the moment, isn't it? What have I missed?"

"Not much. Some truly horrific nappies."

"Must be all those sailors and galleons she's been eating. What else?" His brow creased. "I *did* miss something, didn't I? Oh, no— not her first step."

"No, no. She's been standing on her own, but she always flops down onto that well-padded backside of hers. Speaking of which, I'd better get her swaddled up before she wrecks this towel."

"Hang on a second. Tell me."

Lee would never just reach in. Gideon had learned to lower barricades inside his mind, to offer silent permission. The soft, delicious pushing was absent tonight. Well, having a mindreader in the family was no substitute for honest conversation, and some things just had to be said. "She's developed a bit of a new party trick. Might be better if she showed you, rather than me trying to explain." He patted Tamsyn's cheek with one fingertip to draw her attention. "Tamsie. Where's your bear?"

She pointed to the floor where the toy had fallen, a clear indication that he should pick it up for her. "You get it," he encouraged. "Get the bear for Lee."

"No."

It was clear and decisive, and made both her parents start to laugh. After *Dada* and *Eee*, her first word had been *no*, and she'd made liberal use of it since. "She's not gonna do it," Gideon said, picking up the bear for her instead. "Here. No more porridge song, though, please."

She cackled and began to pull the string. Lee grasped his head in mock agony. "Would it be cruel of us to cut that off? What were you expecting her to do, anyway?"

"I'm not sure." Gideon rubbed his eyes. "It's been a long week. I was probably hallucinating. Right, you little rug rat—let's get you to bed, so your daddies can have some food and sex the way they occasionally used to before you came along."

Lee grinned and got to his feet, hoisting her ceilingwards. "I remember those golden days. The room looks beautiful, Gid. Who knew a big Cornish plod would have such a talent for decoration?"

"Big *gay* Cornish plod. Comes with the territory."

"In that case, shouldn't I be getting a home-baked quiche for my tea, not microwaved lasagne?"

"Only if you want to home-bake one yourself." Gideon watched the two of them—his husband and his baby—with pride and love warring for place in his heart. He'd never imagined that life would hold such riches for him. "I found a box of ornaments in the parish-house attic. What do you think?"

"Beautiful. Especially the little silver sphere with... Does it have lights in it?"

"No, but it catches the light in the room. That one was my mum's favourite too."

"I can't imagine the pastor approving."

"Oh, he didn't. She used to put a little tree up in her parlour where he wouldn't see it."

"Looks like it's found its proper home now."

Yes, it did. Gideon surveyed the replantable fir he'd strapped to the roof of the police truck to bring home. Nothing but the best for his little girl's Christmas—her solstice, her Yule, Pagan trimmings aplenty. The little sphere rotated gently, as if a breeze had touched it. Sparkles flashed hypnotically from within its wire cage. Something tugged at the back of Gideon's brain. Isolde sat up on the sofa and emitted a faint whine.

"Uh-oh. I think she's gonna do it."

"What?" Lee asked in alarm. "Nappy?"

"No. Look at her hand. Watch that bauble."

"Gid, are you all... Oh. Holy fuck."

The sphere drifted slowly off the branch. Its string caught on the needles, and Tamsyn frowned as if she'd been given a new puzzle and shifted her hand, left and then right. She beamed and gave a yell of delight, and then—because Gideon could have no further doubt of cause and effect, that she was deliberately doing this—she brought the glittering thing to a brief halt in midair, then fired it squarely at Lee.

He caught it on reflex in his free hand. For a few long seconds he stood motionless, cradling the child and the bauble with equal care. Then he turned to Gideon, his colour fading. "Gid, no."

"No what? I know it's freaky, but we've seen weirder stuff than this."

"You don't... Look, she should be in bed. Will you help me put her down?"

"Of course, but—"

"Seriously. Now."

Gideon followed him into the nursery. He shook out the blanket in the cot, grabbed an industrial-strength night-time nappy from the box and set it out on the changing mat. "There you go."

"Ta. Come on, you. Don't give us a hard time tonight."

She didn't. She lay watching Lee with huge eyes while he wrapped her up and manoeuvred her little limbs into a romper, his hands long since grown deft about their task. For once she launched no objection to being laid down in her cot. "Wow," Lee said, flashing Gideon a too-bright smile across the cradle. "What did you do to her? Drugs?"

"No, gin. It's cheaper. I think she knows we need to talk."

Lee switched on the monitor, and they went back down the hallway hand-in-hand. Gideon was painfully glad that all their discussions—even the intense ones—began with this gesture of solidarity, the silent promise to find common ground. "I'm sorry," he said, drawing Lee to sit down beside him on the sofa. "I didn't take that seriously enough, did I?"

"I'm not surprised. It does look like a party trick."

"It's not, though. It's something important, and you're worried."

"Look, we both know that, as apples go, she hasn't fallen far from the tree. She can talk to both of us without opening her mouth, and we can talk to her."

"I don't know about that." Gideon had never fully accepted that his easy rapport with Tamsyn was anything more than good luck. "*You* can."

"C'mon, lover. It's both of us, and that's... great. It's good. I don't want it to be any more, though. I don't want her to be like me."

"Apart from the good looks and intelligence."

"Apart from those things, of course."

"Okay. I get that." Gideon put an arm around him, planted a rough kiss to the side of his brow. "You don't send things flying about the room without touching them, though. Not last time I looked."

"I know. After a long time—and a lot of help from you—I'm starting to get some kind of handle on what I see and what I don't. What I can do and what I can't. Takes me all my time, though, and I'm thirty two. She's twelve months old. I just want her to be... *normal*, Gid, as far as she can."

He sounded dead-beat weary. "She will," Gideon said uneasily. There was more to this even than the considerable amount that met the eye. "We're not exactly shining examples of normality ourselves."

"Yes, but there's a place in the world for our kind of weird these days, even..." They both involuntarily glanced at the TV, still flickering away on mute, where the latest American presidential hopeful was denouncing same-sex marriage before a conference audience of thousands. "Even if it's an insecure one. If she carries on doing things like that, she'll be treated as a freak."

Gideon found the remote under a cushion and switched the TV off. He tried to look into Lee's face, but only the tired profile was presented to him. Gently he pushed at certain inner doors—connection points he'd only recently acknowledged existed between them at all—and found them shut. "A freak?" he echoed. "Slow down a bit, love. She's not gonna turn into Carrie."

The doorbell rang, breaking a strange silence. Gideon had installed the bell as soon as they'd moved in, declaring to Lee that any visitors who couldn't use one—who preferred to announce themselves by bangs, thuds or bestial scratchings—could just bloody well stay outside. "You expecting anyone?" Lee asked, sitting up.

"No."

"Me neither."

"Not carol singers, surely."

"Not in Dark. Although Darren Prowse's Christmas Rapper gang did all right last year."

"Until someone chased 'em off with a shotgun. Shall we ignore it?"

"Ah, better not." Gideon got up, stretching. "'Tis the season of goodwill and all that. Who knows what the storm's blown to our door?"

In fact it was Granny Ragwen. She was such an apparition that for a moment Gideon just stood staring at her. As usual she was top-to-toe in the smartest fashions the Truro outlet shops could provide, but the moorland wind had caught her hair, turning her neat bun into a pewter-grey stream. He scanned the street behind her for any stalkers or night-creatures that might have driven her to seek refuge on his doorstep. Only the wind was haunting Dark tonight, though, piling the last of the sycamore leaves in a dun-coloured tumble against the garden walls. He remembered his manners. "Evening, Granny—er, Mrs Ragwen. Come in out of the cold."

She stepped inside regally. "I smelled something, Constable," she declared, and Gideon shot Lee a look which said more plainly than words that he wished he'd remembered the old girl was mad as a balloon before inviting her in. Lee wiped his expression clear with admirable rapidity and came to meet their guest. "Mrs Ragwen? Don't tell me you've walked all the way down here just to see us."

"No, of course not. I was on my way back from visiting young Dev Bowe, and I smelled something coming from your house." She tipped back her head, inhaling deeply. "Ah, how strong it is! Fair makes your eyes water."

Automatically Gideon looked at Isolde, who'd waddled over to sit at the old lady's feet. "I hope it's not the dog. She's getting to be a bit elderly, and..."

"Nonsense! She's a fine beast, blood of King Arthur's own hounds, as your lad here told you long ago. No, it was magic I smelled, pure and bright. Is it your girl?"

"No," Gideon said, on a kneejerk instinct of protection, then pulled himself together. "Magic? What do you mean?"

"Oh, don't stand there like a pillar of the community, as if you'd never heard the word, or seen the poor few things an ancient creature like myself can do! How *is* Sergeant Pendower? Can I see the child?"

"Rufus is fine. We had dinner with him and his new lady friend a few weeks ago. Er... Tamsyn's in bed. We just got her to sleep, so..."

"I shan't wake her. I just want to breathe in that smell."

"I don't think—"

"Gideon." Lee held out a hand, his tired half-smile like a touch to the shoulder, to the heart. "It's all right."

"Is it?"

"Yes. Really. Come on, Mrs Ragwen—she's just down here."

Gideon watched them go, the dog following after. He'd have to ask Lee why levitation was a bridge too far and night-time visits by a mad old woman who apparently wanted to sniff their daughter was not, but it could wait. Lee's word was good enough. He began to pick up some of the debris he, Isolde and Tamsyn had scattered about the room—jumped like a rookie on his first duty shift at the ping of the microwave.

He needed to get a grip. The sound of Dev Bowe's name had unnerved him, that was all, though he was glad that the old lady had taken it upon herself to continue making visits. There was no-one else, not now. He'd gone along himself a couple of times, but the boy spent his days staring at the wall of a maximum-security cell in Bodmin hospital, everything he'd been—whatever thing had possessed him—wiped clean away.

The baby monitor clicked and rustled. Through it came Tamsyn's waking mewl, then the ear-bursting shriek she reserved for particular friends. That was odd. She'd only met Granny Ragwen a couple of times before. Well, there was no accounting for taste. He was turning away when Granny's voice tugged his attention back.

There she is! I knew it. Can I have a hold?

And Lee, resigned, smiling—*All right. Here, I'll lift her out for you.*

No harm in that, though if the baby woke up properly, Lee could have the hour-long delight of persuading her back to sleep. Shaking his head, Gideon went back to work.

Look at you! What have you been up to, then, my lovely? Making the flowers grow? Turning the postman into a toad? It's about time, then—we'll soon need a new witch at Dark.

She's not a witch, Mrs Ragwen. She's an ordinary little girl.

Well, shame on you, Locryn Tyack! As if I didn't know your family line from back when they were flying stones around for the Kernowek priests! You of all people can't deny her.

I'm not denying her anything. But it's Locryn Tyack-Frayne now, and we're just an ordinary family.

Oh, I see. It's the policeman you're worried about. Well, you're going to have to tell him, boy. The solstice gate swings wide for the Frayne brood—he should know that by now. I can help out, but it's a trade-in. You'll have to make him understand.

Mrs Ragwen—you're a nice lady, and if you're the witch of Dark, you've been a good one. But I don't have a clue what you're talking about now.

Nor did Gideon. Furthermore, he didn't have the right to listen. He couldn't believe he'd been standing here eavesdropping for so long. He strode down the corridor and leaned his shoulder in the nursery doorway. He took in the strange scene: the warm little room painted amber by Tamsyn's night-light, the old woman cradling the baby, who was chuckling and binding the streaming white hair into a cat's-cradle knot. Lee standing apart, arms folded. Granny Ragwen looked up. "He says he doesn't know what I'm talking about," she said hoarsely to Gideon, "because he's been and tried to put up his walls. I don't blame him. I would too, if I'd had to see Dev Bowe with his skin off. But he knows it's not going to work, because—"

"Thanks," Lee interrupted, calmly as if she'd been offering him a recipe. "I tell you what—it's getting a bit late. Can I give you a lift?"

"Throwing me out, are you? All right. The constable can take me, though. Your little car will play havoc with my hips."

Gideon allowed himself a low whistle of admiration. "Lee's right. You *are* a nice lady—sorry, Lee, the baby monitor was on— but you about take the biscuit for cheek. Tamsie, let go of Mrs Ragwen's hair so I can escort her home."

"No, Gid. Let me do it." Lee moved to block his path to the door. He laid a hand to Gideon's chest, an odd anxiety darkening his eyes. "Don't ask just yet. I'll be five minutes—I'll tell you everything when I get back."

Chapter Three

An engine roared in the street outside. The note of it was familiar. Gideon pushed back the living-room curtain in time to see Lee take the corner like a Brands Hatch pro and bring the Escort to a screeching halt by the kerb. Catching his urgency, Gideon ran for the front door, but before he could get there, Lee had darted inside and slammed it behind him. "Oh, Gid. I did something stupid."

They stood facing one another in the hallway. "Did you invite her back for Christmas sherries?"

"No. In London. I saw Siobhan Reeves."

The name was familiar. Gideon cast back to a long-ago conversation in Lee's harbourside flat, when Lee had first begun to tell him the price of his gift. "The hypnotist lady? The one who used to help you—"

"Build walls in my head, yes. I didn't plan to see her. When I'd been in the city for a few days, I realised how... eroded I was, how open. I couldn't shut anything out. I couldn't stop thinking about Dev, and Elowen, and coming into our street that day and seeing our house blown to shreds, and..."

"Did she help?"

"I thought so at the time, but..." He shivered, as if the walls of his home were inadequate too, the door behind him open to the wind. "I'm sorry. I should've told you."

"Only because I'd have gone with you. You know that."

"Yeah, I do, and that's the whole point." Their landlord had installed two rather grand lanterns on either side of tiny hallway. Lee looked like some heraldic night-creature caught between them, their light incandescing in the silver of his hair and eyes. "If you'd been there, I'd have remembered why I can't have the walls anymore."

"Because of... Because of me?"

"You didn't feel me come home, did you?"

"No. And once you were there, it was like I couldn't *see* you properly." Gideon's voice had wavered. He swallowed hard, then ruined it by adding, pathetically, "I still can't."

"I know. They're easier to put up than take down—the walls, I mean. Please help."

Gideon held out his arms. Lee shot into them, his last stride a pure leap for safety. His momentum carried both of them through the bedroom door, and Gideon seized the advantage and half-lifted him over to the bed, going down like a controlled ton of bricks on top. "You want me to take these walls down?"

"Yes. I can't bear it."

"But if you need them—"

"You're my wall. You're my higher ground." Lee seized him powerfully, sending the bedside light flying. The bulb broke and the room plunged into darkness. They froze, waiting tensely, but no frightened cry arose from the next room. "Is she asleep?"

"Sound. I left the monitor in the other room. Do you want me to—"

"Afterwards."

"I'm sorry I listened to you and the old lady. I didn't mean to."

"God knows what you heard. Do you want to talk about it?"

"Afterwards."

***

The phone woke Gideon at eight in the morning. He'd have ignored it, in the first fragile dawn of his shared holiday with his husband, but Lee had set the *Hawaii Five-0* theme as the ringtone for calls from the station. Silently cursing him, Gideon rolled over and grabbed the receiver. "Hello?"

"Morning, Sergeant. I'm sorry—I know you're on leave, but..."

He fell back against the pillows, listening with as much grace as he could muster. Lee appeared in the doorway, jouncing Tamsyn in his arms. Gideon put a hand over his eyes. "Yes, ma'am," he said eventually. "No, it's all right. I understand. Yes, a very merry Christmas to you too."

He hung up. Lee brought the baby over and deposited her in the wreckage of the bedsheets, where she began to crawl around, crowing happily. "Oh, Gid," he said, resignation already shadowing his tone. "All of it?"

"No. No, I got off pretty lightly—just tonight, in Penzance."

"What, for the Montol?"

"Yep. DI Lawrence says half their squad's gone down with some kind of flu, and they're expecting trouble, kids coming in from outside to mess things up." He retrieved his daughter from the edge of the bed. "I'll have to go. I'm sorry, sweetheart. She promised to leave us alone for anything short of a nuclear war after that."

"Is it a uniform job?"

"No. Plainclothes and casual, so I won't be getting too many bricks lobbed at me. She just wants a presence on the streets in case."

"Why don't we come with you, then?" Lee sat down cross-legged on the bed. "It's time she saw her first Montol. We can be part of your cover—the boyfriend and the cute baby."

"Adorable. But did you not hear the part about the lobbed bricks?"

"We'll be fine."

Gideon gave it thought. He could see his lovely man in glorious detail and colour today, and *we'll be fine* wasn't a vague reassurance, not coming from Lee like that. It meant that he probably knew. Gideon loved the revived midwinter festival that roared through the Penzance streets at solstice, but a revival was all it was, not like the bone-ancient Kelyndar Golowan. "I dunno," he said, stifling a yawn. "Things tend to get a little freaky for us around December twenty-first, in case you haven't noticed. I was thinking more TV and pizza than frolics on the promenade."

"I'm not sure me and madam can eat a whole stuffed-crust on our own. But I take your point about the date." Shadows chased across Lee's morning brightness, and he reached across and retrieved the baby in his turn, settling her in his lap. "Part of what you heard Granny Ragwen say last night, right? Part of what we need to talk about."

Afterwards. After a long night of loving so sweet that Gideon scarcely cared about what had gone before. On mornings like this, he wanted to take all their lives' mysteries, roll them up and punt them into the fire he could see glimmering through the open living-room door. Lee must have got up early. The baby was dressed and clean, and to judge by the fragments stuck to Lee's jumper, had enjoyed a hearty breakfast. Lee's walls were down, the only trace of them a glimmer of dust-motes in the air. "I guess so," he said reluctantly. "What did she mean about the solstice gates, do you reckon?"

"The ones that swing wide for your brood?"

"Those ones, yeah."

"Well, leaving aside the possibility that she *is* the all-knowing witch of Dark—she's a nosy old girl, and she probably heard that your dad died a year ago today. And the Island case was in all the papers the year before."

"She couldn't have known about Fisher, though—the time of his death." Gideon pulled a face and hitched up the duvet. "Maybe we *should* all just take cover for the day. I could catch flu just as well as a Penzance copper."

Lee smiled. "Not you, Sergeant."

"Why not?"

"In all the time I've known you, you've never left a colleague in the lurch. You'll be at Montol tonight. Anyway, you ought to be safe, technically speaking—solstice doesn't fall until tomorrow, 4:48 AM."

Gideon surveyed him in amusement. "Checked, did you?"

"Seemed worthwhile."

"Come here, both of you. If I've got to spend the first proper night of my leave out there plodding, I want some serious family time now."

"Is this where we all end up under the duvet like a Christmas ad for one of the more forward-thinking stores?"

"Yeah. So not Trago, obviously." Gideon put out an arm, shivering in pleasure as Lee and the baby scrambled into place. He should have remembered the disadvantages of having that perceptive head pressed to his shoulder: after a minute's contented silence, Lee murmured, "Wow. We *do* worry about the same things."

"Comes with the marriage certificate, I think. What's uppermost?"

"Poltergeist Annie here, for both of us." Lee ruffled the little girl's hair. She had curled up between them and was serenading herself with a tuneless version of the porridge song. "The last time I saw Siobhan was long before I met you, you know. What if Tamsyn doesn't happen to find someone in her life who can protect her, make her decide she doesn't need walls?"

"She'll have us," Gideon said staunchly. "For as long as she needs us, and probably long after."

"You're good as gold, you are. I'm not sure I want her having to make those choices, though—what to conceal about herself, what to risk revealing."

"Everybody has to do that. Look, she scared the bejesus out of me too. But she was on hyperdrive, remember, getting you back after a whole week away. It's like everything else with kids— if *we* don't make a big deal of it..."

"She might not?"

"Worth a try, isn't it? She might never do it again. And, you know, it's normal to have things like Elowen and the explosion rattling around in your head. We had the baby to look after, so we didn't have the chance to react to it all at the time."

"Maybe I've been freaking out quietly about it ever since. I'm sorry, love. I sometimes can't tell the difference between my shadow-side stuff and the things everybody has to cope with." He lifted his face to meet and return Gideon's kiss, ordinary as day. Then all his sunshine changed to silver, the transition smooth and unstoppable. "Your brother's outside," he said flatly. "He's just sitting out there in his car. He's really upset."

"Shit." Gideon winced at himself. There went another pound into the swear jar. Tamsyn wouldn't have to worry about her student debt at this rate. "Seriously?"

"I'm afraid so. Do you want me to go to him?"

"No, no." Reluctantly disentangling, Gideon recalled the last time he'd seen his brother really upset. *Things like Elowen rattling round in your head...* It might be normal, but he reckoned he and his husband were suffering from a good domestic case of PTSD after the events of last August. "I'll sort him out. Probably he's stuck for ideas for a sermon."

"What, so he's come to visit the gays?"

"We're a great inspiration." Gideon avoided Lee's swipe, grabbing a jumper from beside the bed. "I know he's much better now, but we're still his best example of the high road to hell."

"Just go and bring him in. I'll put the kettle on."

Until he saw Ezekiel's hearse-like Volvo parked by the kerb, Gideon hoped that for once Lee had been wrong. A callout for the end of the day was one thing, but he really didn't want to spend the rest of it enmeshed in a family crisis. Trusting that his pyjama bottoms were decent for the street, he pushed his feet into a pair of boots and stamped out to the car. Cautiously he tapped on the window. "Morning. You all right?"

Zeke jumped as if he'd been shot. He stared at his brother through the glass. He was as near to a mess as Gideon had ever seen him—hair rumpled, suit creased, a distinct trace of beard darkening his jaw. He wound down the window. "How did you know I was here?"

"Oh, you know. Same way we know most things around here."

"Lee?"

"No. The window."

"Your curtains are shut."

Gideon sighed. He refrained from observing to Zeke that the Goth-priest look rather suited him, and indicated the open front door. "You look awful. Do you want to come in?"

The kitchen wasn't big enough for Lee to retreat out of earshot once he'd welcomed Zeke and offered a cup of tea, though Gideon could sense him trying. He wondered at the necessity. He couldn't think of anything Zeke might have to say that Lee shouldn't hear.

Yes, he could. Ma Frayne had been the only person to show Elowen any consistent kindness, and the old lady might have contacted Zeke. Involuntarily Gideon glanced at the locked kitchen cupboard where he and Lee kept disinfectants, medicines and copies of vital legal documents, Tamsyn's watertight adoption papers amongst them. Distractedly he sat down at the table with his brother. Lee was settling Tamsyn into her high chair, fastening a bib around her neck for the next round of her morning feeds. "What's up, Zeke? Bit early for a social call, isn't it?"

"Yes, and I'm aware that Lee just got home last night. I just... I need to talk to you. Though I scarcely know how to begin."

Gideon rested his elbows on the table. He laced his fingers together, tightened his grip until it hurt. "Tell you what," he said softly. "Begin by telling me this is nothing to do with Elowen."

Zeke went white. Then, weirdly, he blushed to the hairline. "Lee hears too much," he rasped. "This is my own private matter, and I'm not yet ready to—"

"Wait. *Your* private matter?" Gideon leaned toward him, lowering his voice with an effort that almost choked him. "This is his house. He's practically gone out into the garden so that he doesn't have to hear you. What's going on? What does she want now?"

"Who?"

Gideon's head spun. One of his ears began to sing with the change in blood pressure. "For God's sake. Elowen!"

"Elowen? I don't know. I haven't heard from her in months."

"Then—why did you say this was about her?"

"I didn't!" Zeke swallowed audibly and turned a deeper shade of crimson. "You said it was about Eleanor, and I—"

"Your Eleanor? No."

"Yes, you did."

Gideon drew a deep breath. He had unsuspected reservoirs of fear and hate within him for Elowen Tyack, and he was about to unleash the flood on his brother. It wasn't right or fair, but his nerves were stripped to buzzing copper wire. "Ezekiel—"

Lee set the teapot down on the surface with a bang. "Gideon Tyack-Frayne," he declared. "I love you more than life, but if you say *did not*, I'm divorcing you."

"I wasn't. I—"

"Yeah, you were. And then Zeke was gonna say *did too*, and we were all about to find out what it would've been like in your nursery class if you'd been kids at the same time." He grabbed a couple of mugs out of a cupboard. "Whatever it is, the pair of you put a sock in it until I can pour this tea and get out of your hair. Okay?"

A vibrant silence descended. Tamsyn, briefly ignored, gave a mewling cry and began to wave her hands in the air.

She loved Ezekiel. Part of her delight in him was his solemnity, which she strove on all occasions to crack, pinging the lid on her jack-in-the-box to make him jump, rolling her spring-loaded walker at him from unexpected doorways. Despite this, or maybe because of it, he adored her in his turn. His arrival usually meant playtime, a walk on the moors or a visit to the village park. Instead Lee had carried her away from her friend and imprisoned her. If Gideon had been paying proper attention, he'd have recognised the shift in her gesticulations, the new focus. He'd have listened to the throb in the base of his skull.

Her pompom ball, a fantastical creation knitted for her by Ma Frayne, rose into the air. It had been missing for a couple of days.

Isolde must have taken a fancy to it and carried it off to her basket. Gideon opened his mouth in warning—of what, he had no idea—but it was too late. Tamsyn raised her hand like Andy Murray about to fire a good one over the net.

The ball hit Zeke square on the back of the skull. "Oh—Jesus," Gideon said helplessly, and clapped his hands to his mouth. "Tamsyn!"

It wasn't funny. The situation was horrendous, and Gideon had almost lost track of which of the two women—Elowen or Eleanor—his brother was talking about. Either way, something difficult, painful and sensitive was going down. He couldn't possibly laugh.

But Lee's face was such a picture. His eyes were wide in consternation. And he was about to hurl himself under the bus for his child. "Zeke!" he gasped. "I am... so, so sorry. I meant to throw that for Isolde. I can't think how I missed."

Zeke turned round. He looked more puzzled than anything else. The ball had impacted softly, and he was used to a certain amount of chaos in his brother-in-law's home. "That's quite all right," he said. "By the way, Lee, I didn't mean to imply that you would ever deliberately overhear anything I said, or—or thought. I just..."

He fell silent. On the floor, the pompom ball was twitching like a live thing. Tamsyn's brow rucked as she strove to get a grip on it, showing it what it was meant to do with small upward jerks of her palm. Slowly, gracefully, the ball rose into the air.

This time she delivered it without fuss. Zeke sat open-mouthed as it floated across the room towards him. Any hope that he might not know who was doing this died as his attention fixed on Tamsyn. The ball came to a hovering halt above his lap, and he scrambled out from under it, knocking over his chair. "No. No."

"Zeke, take it easy."

"Your child is doing this. Keep it away from me."

Did he mean the ball or the child? Gideon's sickening doubt immediately transferred itself to Tamsyn. She let the ball drop with a splash into Isolde's water dish. After a moment of blood-chilling silence, she released a desolate wail.

It had been five months since Gideon had seen her really upset. She was too little for the terrible twos he'd been warned about, and the worst he'd expected of those were tantrums in the supermarket—not for every loose item in his kitchen to lift from its moorings, like small boats on an incoming Falmouth tide, and begin a mid-air dance.

Cups, mugs, cookbooks. The toaster, tugging at the end of its cord. There was a wild humour to it, flashing Gideon back to Mickey Mouse as the sorcerer's apprentice in *Fantasia*, but then the knives began to rattle in their block.

He got to his feet. He was an adult, a policeman and a householder, and more important than any of these things, he was husband to his white-faced other half and father to his child. He stepped through the chaos—swept Tamsyn out of her high chair with one arm and caught Lee into the other. "Stop it," he commanded. Who did he expect to obey him? Ezekiel, maybe, to quit staring at the baby as if she'd been a snake. The forces of nature, raw and incomprehensible, to let go of their hold on his home. "Stop it now."

The mugs dropped and shattered. The toaster crashed down on its side, several weeks of unattended crumbs spraying out across the surface. Tamsyn huddled like a woodlouse into his embrace. The static in the air cleared, leaving an ice-blade clarity, frost-bound fields round a church after the bells have stopped. Lee stepped forward into the hush. "Zeke," he said carefully, holding out a hand. "She's only a little girl."

The sugar bowl had disgorged its contents in a widespread cloud. Blindly Zeke brushed the crystals from his jersey. "What... What did I just see?"

"We don't know yet. She's just started doing it. But it isn't anything harmful, and—"

"Not *harmful?*" Zeke held out one shaking finger towards the knife block. "I have seen things—countenanced things—in your company and my brother's, until I've begun to... doubt my own sanity, let alone my faith. I've even tried to help you. But this— this is..."

Gideon handed the baby to Lee. He came to stand squarely in front of his brother, arms folded. "Choose your words carefully."

"You must know what they're going to be." Zeke's voice was a ghost of itself, thin and attenuated with fear. "You know who I am. You know what I do. And this is... devil's work, Gideon. You have a demon in your home."

"A *demon?*"

"Bring the child to my church. I'll do what I can for her."

"An actual *demon*, Ezekiel?"

"You heard me."

"Yes, I did. Get out."

Lee stepped between them. "Don't. He's just scared."

"He's not. He thinks he's got the right to come in here and drag off our child to whatever medieval bloody exorcism he imagines is gonna—what, Zeke? Cast out the devil from her?"

"Not a right. My duty."

"Fine, Matthew Hopkins. Don't let the door bang your arse on the way out."

Chapter Four

The night had made good on its promise of frost. Gideon only realised this when he stood up from the rail and found the cotton of his pyjamas sticking to the wrought iron. His motives for following Zeke outside had been complex. There had been the element of seeing him off the premises, making sure every trace of him was gone. He shivered, rubbing his arms. The village was small this morning, the moor rising silent and vast as the sky beyond the furthermost rooftops. Sunlight on the ice-daubed crests only emphasised their loneliness. When Zeke's tail lights had disappeared around the corner—and good riddance to him— loss had struck Gideon so sharply that he'd had to sit down.

He was freezing his butt to the rail. This was ridiculous. Carefully he detached himself and went inside. Tamsyn was crawling around in her playpen, chortling at things only she could see. The kettle was on again, and his kitchen and his morning were perfectly normal apart from the shattered crockery. Lee was sweeping up. Gideon grabbed a dustpan and brush and went to help him.

They worked in silence until every shard was gone. Gideon hoovered the sugar from around the table, Isolde snuffling at his heels. He set the toaster upright, checked that it was still working, and went to join Lee by the side of the pen. Together they stood and watched their daughter, who seemed to be putting on a display of ordinary babyhood for them, drooling and gnawing on a teething ring. After a moment she grinned and pointed at Gideon, as if assigning him to speak first. "You're a troublemaker, you are," he told her, resting his hands on the top bar of the pen.

"Oh, *she's* a troublemaker?"

Reluctantly Gideon met Lee's gaze. "I didn't mean to throw him out of the house." Lee's eyebrows rose, and he reviewed his words and actions. "Okay. Yes, I did."

"He's lucky he doesn't have the print of your size-ten on his backside."

"I'm sorry. I didn't know what else to do."

"Do you remember, a little while back—when I'd thought it was okay not to get our adoption papers formalised, and you disagreed?"

"Yeah. I remember that."

"And I said afterwards that it was okay for you—nobody else, just you—to put your foot down with me?"

Gideon nodded miserably. He supposed it wasn't okay all the time. That he could go too far, even for Lee. Despite their differences, Lee and Zeke had developed their own strong bond. "You heard what he said."

"Yes. Sometimes you have to be boss. You were defending your family, and I'm grateful."

Not as grateful as Gideon. He took a deep breath, oxygen and relief flaring. He put out an arm and Lee walked into it. "I see," he said, holding him tight. "I can be boss, as long as it's all right with you?"

"Something along those lines."

"Do you see the irony of that?"

"Plainly. What are we going to do, Gid? He called her a demon. And that came from someone who loves her. Who loves *us*."

"He's a twat. He doesn't love anybody."

Lee led him back to the table. Neither of them quite wanted to sit down in the chair Zeke had knocked over in his wrath. Lee perched on the table edge, drawing Gideon to stand between his thighs. "That's not true."

"I know. But he was so terrified, or mind-blown, or whatever it was, that he forgot he loves her, and I was so pissed off with him that I never even found out why he came here in the first place."

"He was worried about something."

"Something to do with Eleanor. I thought he said Elowen and I nearly bloody died." He rubbed his brow against Lee's, feeling the rush and wash of his own fears reflected there, the margins of a storm-racked sea. "It's going to be a problem, isn't it—this new thing of Tamsyn's?"

"Yes. I don't think I'm being a fussy dad if I say that psychokinesis is not gonna help our kid integrate into society. We have to stop her."

"How?"

"In so many ways she's ordinary. And she's just started doing this. Maybe we can stop her in the same way we would if she'd started doing anything else that was..." Lee's voice roughened. "That was wrong."

"You don't think it's wrong at all."

"Nor do you, because she's your baby and you can't believe any harm of her. But she's too little to control it, and even if she ever learns, she'll terrify some people, and others—worst-case scenario—will want her strapped down in a military lab somewhere, being dissected for her weapons potential."

"Fuck's sake, love."

"I said it was worst-case. Stop her, Gideon. Teach her not to, just like you taught her not to pull Isolde's tail or crawl too near the fire. Don't even think about it."

Gideon straightened up. He let Lee go and went to crouch by the playpen. He *had* done those things, hadn't he? They hadn't been hard. He'd never questioned the necessity. The dog had a right to a peaceful life, and obviously his child, who was bright and cooperative, needed to learn not to burn herself. Tamsyn had taken these corrections in good part, as if she'd been able to look into her father's mind and understand his intentions.

And that was a very good point. "Lee," he said softly, not taking his eyes off the baby. "Why don't you ever do the scoldings?"

"Scoldings?" Lee's smile warmed his voice. "Is that what you call them?"

"Don't avoid the question."

"I was wondering when you'd notice. Which one of us gets called *Dada* around here?"

"Well—me, I suppose. But—"

"And she calls me Lee, as if she was my friend or my equal. In some ways that's how she sees herself."

Gideon fought back laughter. "I'd regret asking how she sees me, wouldn't I?"

"No, you wouldn't. She sees you as her dad. And part of that involves discipline." Lee came and stood behind him, laid a hand on his shoulder. "I'll never leave you alone with it, I promise, and things might change as she gets older. For now I'm more like a brother to her. We share too much of a wavelength for her to take me seriously."

"All right. Telling her not to put food up her nose is one thing, though. How am I meant to stop her from levitating the furniture?"

"You know when she's about to do it, don't you?"

"Yes. I feel a kind of tugging in my head."

"Well, your family's as ancient and mixed up in old Cornish magic as mine. You've learned to see things and do things you never thought you could. If she tugs at you, can you... tug back, show her that this isn't right?"

"I don't know. I guess I could try."

He stretched out a hand between the bars of the playpen. Tamsyn gave a gurgle of pleasure and crawled over. She grabbed his thumb in one fist and his little finger in the other. "Dada."

"That's right, sweet pie. Dada needs to tell you something."

Words wouldn't do it. He closed his eyes. Her clutch made it easy, opening up the channels between them he hadn't dared acknowledge yet were there, because all he'd wanted to be was her father, the guy who went out to work and came back, who put a roof over her head and defended her from all the world's ordinary badness. Fresh and bright in her memory he found the scene with Ezekiel. He saw the back of his brother's skull, a lovely target, and there at last was the wondrous lost woollen ball. Disorientation swept him and he grabbed for the bars of the playpen with his free hand. He could lift the ball without touching it. His head throbbed with the knowledge of his power. He was one year old, practically everything he wanted hopelessly out of his reach, but now he could...

"No," he said, right into the centre of her gift. He gathered it all up—the images, the temptation, the results, crushed them into nothing and made them go dark. "Tamsyn, no more. No."

She let go of his hand. He surfaced from her strange waters, gasping. After a moment when he thought he might faint, he met and returned her wide, unblinking stare.

She burst into tears. Gideon jolted back—would have fallen if Lee hadn't caught him. Shock rattled through him. Not his own: the grief of the small entity beginning to separate itself from the world, to individuate and think of itself as Tamsyn, most treasured focus of the giant loving god whose power could be summoned with the smallest smile or cry. "She feels as if I hit her with a thunderbolt," Gideon choked out. "She doesn't understand, any more than if I'd asked her to stop singing, or playing, or—or breathing." A huge sob racked him, but he pushed away from Lee's horrified embrace. "I'm all right. See to her."

Lee scooped her out of the pen. He dropped to his knees beside Gideon, cradling her, handing her into his arms. "I'm sorry. I'm sorry!"

"Not your fault." Gideon swiped a hand over his eyes— reached much more tenderly to brush the tears off Lee's face. Awkwardly he took his husband and his wailing daughter into his arms. "But I tell you what—I'm done with this psychic-parenting lark. If I've got any kind of gift, I don't want it, any more than we want her to have this."

"God forgive me for asking you to do it."

"You just wanted to keep her safe. Oh, don't *you* cry, you daft sod!"

"Why not? Look what I did!"

"What *we* did. Please. I can't cope with all three of us in floods."

***

Calm restored, Lee made all of them a long-delayed breakfast. A post-earthquake hush reigned, pale sunlight finding its way over the flank of the hill and daubing the tiled kitchen walls. Gideon kept Tamsyn on his knee while they ate, gently correcting her aim as she dipped her toast soldiers into her egg. Every so often she would stop, lay down the bread and run her sticky fingers over his face, as if reassuring herself of a well-known landscape. Lee sat opposite, quiet but watchful, the newspaper in front of him no more than a prop. "You two all right over there?"

"Fine. Is that the property section?"

"Um... I'm not sure. Yeah."

"That looks like the old Lowen place on Morgan's Hill. Never thought I'd see that on the market."

"It's part of old man Bowe's estate. Now that John and Bligh are gone, and Dev's not capable of managing the land, they're selling off some of the farm workers' cottages."

Gideon whistled softly. "Some cottage. That's proper old Cornish Georgian, three hundred years old if it's a day. Mellor-quarry granite, the one that goes rose pink in the sun because of the lichen that grows on it."

"Sounds lovely." Lee turned the page, paying attention this time. "Arched windows, two acres of land and an orchard. Standing derelict, looks like."

"Yeah. It's a shame." Gideon squinted at the price tag. "Derelict or not, we'd have to win the lottery. Zeke and I used to walk up there when we were kids, or he'd walk and give me a piggyback. We'd wander around and pretend we were lords of the manor. That was before he got too godly to scrump apples."

"Oh, Gid. Did he text you yet?"

"Nope."

"Do you think you ought to text him?"

"No. Let him steep for a while." Absently Gideon wiped his daughter's face clear of toast crumbs and egg yolk. "Tell you what—maybe we could all use an outing today after all. Still fancy a jaunt to Penzance?"

"I'd love it. She can wear that horrendous set of reindeer horns your ma bought her. She might as well look like the spawn of Satan she is."

"Can the pair of you stay out of trouble?"

"Yeah, we promise. I'll keep her away from the main parades."

"Hoorah! You hear that, Tamsie? You're going to Montol after all."

She threw her hands into the air and beamed. She had no clue what Montol was, but if her dad said it was good, she wanted it. Catching her mood and the outside edge of her power, the butter dish lifted gently into the air—then, just as carefully, went down. She twisted round on Gideon's lap so she could see him, anxiety shadowing her silver-moss gaze.

"It's all right." He kissed the top of her head. "I don't know what we're going to do with you, but it really is all right, sweetheart." He looked up wryly at Lee. "Don't know why I bothered chucking poor Zeke out of the house. She could've picked him up and thrown him herself."

Chapter Five

The dark had come down, and Penzance was glowing like a casket of jewels. Caught between sea and windswept stone pines on the hillcrests, and beyond them the mystical hillfort of Lesingey Round, all the ancient town's lights were held and reflected—dancing off the water in Mount's Bay, carved into sculptures of wild orange cloud overhead. Gideon helped Lee out of the back of the police truck with Tamsyn. Already a pulsating beat was rising from the streets below the police station, though it was barely past six o'clock. The fire dancers had swung their blazing torches and leapt through burning hoops along Chapel Street. Gideon shook his head, listening to a distant band strike up their hypnotic drums. One, two, one-two-three—a song anybody could dance to or play, the same heartbeat you could hear at Padstow or Helstone or Kelyndar, so deep it had soaked right into the stones, the town's bones. "Are you going to be all right on the streets with these nutters?"

"We'll be fine." Lee settled Tamsyn into her sling. "Text me when you're done patrolling, and we'll meet up for the fireworks. I'll bring her majesty back up here if she gets tired before then."

"Good. Go inside and get someone to make you a cuppa if you do." Gideon stole a kiss, one from Lee and one from the enthralled baby, who was already wriggling in time to the music. "Sorry I can't come with you. But let's face it—how else would you get parked in Penzance town tonight?"

"Mm. It's lovely being married to a cop."

"I'd better go in and get briefed. Please take care."

"Don't worry. I somehow feel as if we *should* be here tonight—all three of us."

Gideon winced. "That makes me worry more than anything else. Can't you just go and be insignificant for a change?"

"I'll certainly do my best." Lee backed away, turning Tamsyn so that she could wave goodbye. With the sea behind him and smoke-misted streetlight turning him into a fine-framed silhouette, his chances of insignificance were small. Watching him go was always hard for Gideon, whose imagination—fuelled by the cradle-snatching Lilith/Elowen dreams—now provided him with a dozen fates that could befall his small family each time they were out of his sight. Lee stopped in the gateway to the car park. "Hoi," he called back. "Text your brother. It didn't hurt when he exorcised me, and he only *thinks* he's a god-fearing Methodist minister."

"Oh? What is he really?"

"I don't know. But something much bigger than that."

They were gone, the sea-fret and the veils of light dissolving them. Gideon made his way inside, dismissing his fears with an effort. Good coppers weren't necessarily over-burdened with imagination. Nor was he, except when it came to Lee and his kid.

In the squad room, he found a gathering of the unimaginative best. To his amusement—after all, it served her right—DI Lawrence had been called in too, and was over by the whiteboard, wearily counting heads and giving orders. Jenny Spargo, his saviour from the Bodmin streets, came up smiling to show off her new sergeant's stripes. Jim Ryde was there too. Gideon had doubted the lad's future in the force after the killing of Jake Mandel, and he was still a constable, but there was a serenity about him now, and he returned Gideon's wave with a small salute. All in all there was a festive air in the room, with so many familiar faces from the Truro and Bodmin squads. Gideon let himself be absorbed into the crowd, exchanging greetings, answering questions about Tamsyn with a quick flash of a photo on his mobile. *Yes, she's fine. Yes, she's grown. Yes, she's a year old today. We're having her party tomorrow—come over and see her if you like.*

DI Lawrence cleared her throat. The chatter in the room died down. "Montol," she said tiredly, as if announcing a funeral. "Lovely festival. Lovely expression of community spirit, and I'm sure there's a crying need for it, or we wouldn't have ten thousand people out on the streets of Penzance on a bitter cold night, dressed in long flowing costumes which must on no account be exposed to a naked flame. Which brings me to my next point." She put her hands on her hips. "Fire. Although I must say the new organisers have taken every step to ensure public safety, whenever anyone from our department or the town council raised an objection, that's all we got. *Oh, it's a fire festival, ma'am.* Well, isn't it always? Montol, Golowan, Guldize—nobody's happy around these parts until someone's set something alight. In narrow, crowded streets. So there's your basic remit, ladies and gentlemen. Don't let anyone go up in flames, in their... What are the damn costumes called?"

"Mock posh and tatters, ma'am."

Gideon smiled at the prompt response. He hadn't noticed Sergeant Pendower in the crowd. A few months ago he'd have run a mile to avoid him, but Pendower was a different man these days, and a firm favourite of Tamsyn's. "Thank you, Sergeant," Lawrence said. "Now, if we can—"

"Interesting derivation, ma'am, and socially intriguing, too—a deliberate subversion of elegant dress, perhaps with the intent of sending up a ruling class no Cornishman has ever bent his head to, a feeling that's perhaps more intense than ever today. That, in combination with the choice of a Lord of Misrule, and the intriguing fact that the Yule log selected for the festivities is called a Mock—"

"*Thank* you, Sergeant."

Pendower, unabashed, winked at Gideon over his shoulder. Lawrence waited till the wave of laughter had died down. "Folklore aside," she continued, "tonight's a wild night in Penzance. I doubt we'll be getting the busloads of thugs that were threatened, but keep your eyes peeled for anyone who wants to spoil the fun for everyone else. These aren't our streets, so pay attention to the local officers, my Bodmin and Truro lot. Right! Uniforms, you know your beat. Plainclothes volunteers..." She paused and gave Gideon an apologetic glance for the choice of words. "Especially those who've come in on their kid's first birthday, thank you very much, and just go out and do what you do best."

"What exactly is that, ma'am?" Gideon asked innocently, unable to resist.

Lawrence grinned. "Be yourself. Well, look at him!" she added, when the room broke into laughter again. "Who ever would dare get up to mischief within fifty yards of that?"

***

The Montol was a reconstruction, a rebirth of rites so ancient that their origins were anyone's guess. Their modern expression was just as wild and varied. Gideon entered the tide of people now moving up the herringbone pavement of Causewayhead. The street was lined with shops, some cautiously shuttered, others staying open late to catch the festive trade. A rich tang of woodsmoke and barbecue filled the air, and through this miasma danced, jogged and waltzed a menagerie undreamed of under a summer sun. Mock posh and tatters—the contents of every child's dressing-up box, the vintage rails of the charity shops, long velvet gowns, trousers made of patchwork and lace. Everything beribboned, floating, swaying on the breeze. Faces concealed by elaborate Venetian masks, some in the shape of great beaked birds, some gilded, some polished black. And everywhere that music—one, two, one-two-three, pipes and crowdy-crawn drums...

Gideon should have felt invisible, in his thick winter jacket and jeans. Maybe Lawrence was right, though: when he moved, even slowly and calmly through the edge of the crowd, people looked his way. Just a glance, the tilt of a raven's beak—reassured or nervous, each according to his nature. He was noticed. Before a minute was up, a four-foot monster detached itself from the parade and threw itself in his direction. On reflex he reached to catch. "Lorna," he said, laughing and pushing back her mask. "What are you supposed to be?"

"The Beast, of course, Constable."

"Bloody hell. So you are." What fears had she conquered, to dress up as her own deepest nightmare? She was nine years old now, blooming with untrammelled life. "You look terrifying. Where's your mum?"

"Right here!" Sarah Kemp came running up, barely recognisable under face-paint and pirate's tricorn hat. "Lorna, stop it. Gideon's a sergeant now, and you might be... I dunno, blowing his cover or something. And you nearly made me drop my Sun Resplendent."

She was holding a giant paper lantern in the shape of a solar disk. That was one aspect of Montol everyone could agree on— the return of the light after the shortest day of the year. Someone had gone to a great deal of trouble with the lantern. The sun god's smiling face was hooked up on a wooden frame too wide for one person to handle, and Sarah wasn't bearing it alone. "Ah," she said, noticing Gideon's attention. "You haven't met Wilfred yet, have you? Wilfred, this is Sergeant Frayne, who looks after all of us at Dark. Wilf and I are... going out, I suppose you could say." She blushed beneath her paint. "I hope it doesn't seem odd."

The world spun on. The sun returned from darkness every day. Wilfred stuck out his free hand. Gideon took it, shaking it cordially. "Why on earth would it seem odd?"

"Well, you'd think I'd have had enough of men, what with one thing and another. But I met him online, and he's got two kids of his own, and he's lovely with my brats. So we're giving it a try."

"All right." Now it was Gideon's turn to blush: she'd hardly been asking him for his permission. Then, he'd been a fixed point in her life since her husband had vanished and her brother-in-law had morphed into a child-abducting nutcase. Wilfred could meet a police sergeant's gaze with serene cheerfulness, and something inside Gideon's head—the new thing, the tug and the reach—told him that this was a good man. "I'd better give you your kid back, hadn't I?"

Lorna let go of him reluctantly. "Where's Tamsyn and Mr Tiger?"

"Somewhere up ahead of you, I should think. Are you going to the playing fields for the Midwinter Fire?"

"Yes, we are." Sarah pulled the girl's mask back down so she became once again a surprisingly convincing Bodmin Beast. "We'll look out for them. What's going on up there, do you reckon?"

The crowd was slowing down. Gideon could see leaping flames among the safer bell-shaped paper lanterns. Torch-bearing hadn't been prohibited as such—no point in trying to bottle up that genie—but he'd thought, given the narrow streets and the ever-growing sea of revellers, that people would restrain themselves without need for a ban.

The triumph of hope over experience. Gideon ducked into the mouth of an alley that would leapfrog him past the obstruction. "I'll go and take a look. If there's trouble, get into one of the shops and stay clear, all right? Or ask one of the uniform lads to help you."

Sarah tipped her hat to him, beaming broadly. "Aye aye, Sergeant. *Montol lowen* to you. See you tomorrow at the party."

"Absolutely. Bring Wilfred along with you too."

He set off at a jog along the patched tarmac, accelerating to a sprint as wild cries began to ring from the Tolver Road junction ahead. Maybe DI Lawrence had underestimated the chances of busloads of thugs. That was fine with Gideon. He wanted a happy Montol as much as anyone else, but Zeke and his sister-in-law were ever-present thorns in the back of his mind, and if his duties called him to knock a few heads together, so be it.

No. The chaos was arising from a solitary figure in the middle of the road. His costume was more fantastic still than any of the guise-dancing crowd who'd come to a halt behind him. He had a huge umbrella open over his head and was twirling it around, dancing with enormous, skinny-legged strides. "Who's that?" Gideon asked the nearest intelligent face, with a sinking feeling that he already knew.

"Don't you know? We got one from out of town this year, but never mind. That's the Lord of Misrule."

Gideon had been briefed by his Celtic Revivalist husband during the journey down. The Lord of Misrule was another

Cornish yell of rebellion into the face of authority, a king-for-the-night who would lead processions, cause mischief, dance and generally help create fiery chaos all round. He couldn't think of anyone who would be better or worse, more gifted by nature and dangerous for the part, than...

"Darren," he said, stepping up to the gyrating figure. "You're going to have someone's eye out with that."

For once the wretched boy didn't seem dismayed to see him. He knocked up his great raven mask with one hand and issued a yowl of delight. "It's you! How did you know me?"

"I don't know. Just something in the air."

"They *chose* me, Gideon! Chose me to be Lord of Misrule!"

Gideon couldn't remember when Darren had ever addressed him by his first name. *Constable*, yes, even long after he'd been promoted. *You interfering bastard* a couple of times, and, once, *you stupid bloody plod*. He sounded like an adult when he said *Gideon*. He sounded almost sane. "That's nice," Gideon replied. "And I don't want to piss on your chips, but isn't it done by casting lots?"

"That's right. The Montol beans."

"Then... didn't you just pick the right bean?" A terrible thought struck Gideon. "Tell me you didn't fix the draw."

"No, no." Darren did another twirl, beckoning the semi-legal torchbearers close to him. "Everybody knows you can't be chosen for Lord unless the old gods want you. Prance about, you lazy sods! *Golow ha tewlder!* Call back the sun!"

They were obeying him. The procession must have halted at his command so that he could perform his dance. Gideon supposed there was a place for everyone somewhere in the world. "You'd better get on with misruling, then. Don't let them bottleneck here for too long, and keep those torches away from the kids."

"Er, Gideon?"

He paused on his way back to the alley. "What?"

"I've got a place on a junior apprentice course in Liskeard. Only they need a reference."

"You've got a bloody cheek, mate."

"I know. But you're the only one who ever gave a crap about me, really. Aren't you?"

Again, that strange adult note. Gideon stared at him. "You can give them my name and address," he said after a moment. "Take care, Darren."

"Don't worry, Sergeant. Everyone's becoming what they should be."

"I'm sorry?"

"If those kids are coming from out of town, they'll go to the playing fields."

***

Everyone's becoming what they should be. Distractedly Gideon played the words back in his mind. Maybe they were another Montol cry, like *golow ha tewlder* for *light and dark*. He was more immediately focussed on the fact that Darren Prowse, juvenile delinquent and jailbait, had given him a tip-off. Maybe not a good one—though if the boy wanted that reference, it had better at least be valid—but worth checking out.

The streets ahead of the procession were quiet. Gideon made quick progress, not yet running. He wanted to be an ordinary man for as long as he could. Smiling and apologising, he dodged through a cluster of drinkers outside the Black Weasel pub. Behind him he could hear Darren's parade moving on, the cries arising from it filled with excitement and laughter now. If Lee and the baby were down there, they'd be having a good time. Odd to think of leaving anybody safe in Darren's hands...

The night hadn't finished throwing strange encounters into his path. He bumped up against a squat, solid figure, hard enough to rock him back on his heels. "Oh. Sorry."

"No need. It was my fault. Where's my teaser gone?"

Not squat after all. Gideon looked up through six feet of ragged grey cloak and into the gleaming sockets of a huge horse's skull. "Bloody hell. Is that Cosmic Ray in there?"

"Gideon!" A tiny curtain in the creature's neck flew back. Behind it appeared the rosy, brown-eyed face of Ray Tregear from Kelyndar, wreathed in smiles. "Well, I never. What are you doing here?"

"I could ask you the same. Don't tell me you're the Montol 'Oss."

"Oh, no. They've got their own chap for that. But I carried Old Penglas here so well at our last Golowan, the Penzance organisers asked me to come and dance around a bit for the kiddies. Who knows? They could end up with a two-'Oss festival, like they have at Padstow."

"Maybe they will." Gideon glanced dubiously up at the wicked old head. "You've altered him a bit, haven't you?"

"That I have. I got this shoulder-frame made, see, so that he can sit right on top of my head instead of over it, and I can look out of his neck. I'm not the short-arsed Penglas anymore."

Everyone's becoming what they should be. "Yes, I can see that."

"And because I didn't need his eyes, I put some lovely old glass marbles in 'em. All the better to see you with! And I decided to saw through him just there, and attach a pole I can move up and down like this, so..." The hinged jaw swung in Gideon's direction, snapping ferociously. "So he bites! All the better to eat you with."

"Good grief, Ray." Gideon edged back. "Those are quite some alterations."

"I know. Wouldn't my old man turn in his—well, in his bunk, I suppose, in whatever prison cell he's in? But I thought, sod him. What does he matter?"

"He doesn't matter at all," Gideon agreed. "Is Kitto here tonight?"

"Yes, just inside there. He's meant to be my teaser, dance around in front of Old Penglas, stop me bumping into things. He's got a new boyfriend, though. He's oblivious."

Gideon glanced through the pub's open door. On the edge of the scrum by the bar, an exquisitely beautiful curly-haired lad was talking animatedly to a skinny one in glasses. "He looks well."

"He's fine. They're an odd couple, aren't they? But Kitto doesn't see that. It's like he doesn't see the outsides of people at all. Hoi, Gwylim! Bring Jem out to say hello to Gideon."

"No, leave them. I've got to be getting along."

"Oh, right. On duty, are you? Me too, I suppose." He pulled the little curtain across his face and was instantly lost in the majestic, terrifying frame of Old Penglas. When he spoke again, his voice had altered, cheerful Falmouth burr overlain by a sonorous chant. "See me here, Guardian Frayne—a live man in the old death's head. That's the nature of the solstice door—death in life, and life in death."

"Er... Ray?"

A shift like changing weather. "Yes?"

"Was that you, or Old Penglas?"

"Oh. Did he make a pronouncement? Kitto says I've got to learn to control him, but it's easier said than... Hang on." The great skull whipped round, narrowly missing the top of Gideon's. "Isn't that Jana Ragwen?"

Something black and swift-moving caught Gideon's eye, the tail of a raggedy crow disappearing round the corner into Hob Lane. "What—Granny Ragwen from Dark?"

"Yes, your village witch. Her Madge was in my shop the other day—said she can't let the old girl out on her own anymore."

"She must have slipped Madge's leash. I'll go make sure she's okay."

"Right you are, Sergeant! What would any of us do without you? Say hello to Lee and Tamsyn for me."

The lane was empty when Gideon turned the corner. A single streetlamp was shedding a cone of light onto the pavement. The alley had an air of a vacated stage, the sea-salt breeze still vibrant, as if he'd just missed the performance. There was no sign of the old lady, although that didn't mean she wasn't there. "Mrs Ragwen?" Gideon called. He was beginning to feel foolish. His friends and neighbours had sent him uphill like a pinball in a machine. The houses and shops here had turned their backs to him, tight-drawn curtains shutting him out from the warm indoor world. He could barely hear the music and shouts from the town behind him. He waited, listening to the bump of his own pulse. What had Ray Tregear called him—*Guardian Frayne*?

A shriek pierced the night. In his years as a copper, Gideon had heard almost every variation of pain and terror the human throat could produce. This was new. He began his run towards it without questioning the elation shimmering through the sound. The backyard walls were too high for Granny to have climbed them. She had to be up ahead of him, somewhere in the only building she could possibly have accessed from the street.

A derelict warehouse, once part of Penzance's lively shipbuilding trade. It was poised on the very crest of Gwidder Hill, the town laid out below it in glimmering gridlines and clusters. The glass was long gone from its windows, the remains of its door kicked wide and sagging from a single hinge. Inside it was one huge space, gutted and left empty years ago.

Nowhere for anyone to hide. Gideon paused in the doorway long enough to make sure. He found a torch in one deep jacket pocket and shone the beam around, but only cobwebs and streamers of dust glowed back at him. He was about to retreat and run on when the conviction seized him that he wasn't alone. "Mrs Ragwen," he repeated, quietly this time. "You're in here, aren't you?"

"Why, yes, Constable. How clever of you to know!"

He jerked the torch beam up. His breath caught in his throat and he had to swallow a cry of fear and laughter mixed. "Dear God. How did you get up there?"

She sat poised in the middle of a rafter, fifteen feet off the ground, her heels swinging merrily. Her feet were bare, and from somewhere she'd obtained a full-on Halloween witch's fancy-dress costume, complete with ragged skirts and pointy black hat. "I didn't think I still could," she said, grinning down at him. "Screamed like a vixen with her first dog-fox, I did. And you came running."

"Yes, I did. You're going to be all right."

"I know I am, dear."

"You need to stay very still." Gideon lowered the torch so that it wouldn't dazzle her. "I'm just gonna get my phone out, okay? I can have the fire brigade here in five minutes, and they'll get you down."

She exploded into cackles. "Like a mangy old cat out of a tree! Put your phone away."

"I can't, Mrs Ragwen. You're in danger, and I have to get help for you."

"Don't. I'll lose my balance if you make me laugh much more."

She began to rock on the beam, and Gideon took a few steps towards her. She was little and frail, and maybe he could catch her, or at least break her fall. He'd worry about how an old lady had got into the roofspace from ground level some other time. "Listen to me. Listen. If you've got problems at home, or you're upset about anything else at all, I'll help you sort it out. There's no need for you to—"

"Oh! Oh, stop. You're killing me!"

Literally, any second. He froze, holding his breath. "Please don't."

"All right, all right. Don't look so scared." She stopped her terrifying back-and-forth yaw and settled on the beam as casually as if it had been her armchair at home. "Tell me. Who did you see on your way up here?"

"Why is that important?"

"Never mind. Humour an old lady."

"Well, I... Lots of people. Sarah Kemp and her little girl. Darren Prowse."

"No. Who did you *see*?"

Gideon stood immobile. The warehouse was very quiet, and his heartrate gradually slowed. Was it just yesterday she'd stood by Tamsyn's cradle? *The solstice gate swings wide for the Frayne brood...* He let her question enter his Kernowek marrow, the ancient glitter-spirals of his blood. "I saw," he said quietly at last, "the Beast, the Lord of Misrule, and Old Penglas."

She nodded as if satisfied. "And what did he call you, Constable, that last one? That old death's head?"

"He called me... He called me Guardian Frayne." He must have run up here too fast. The vacant space began to spin around him. He wiped what felt like cobwebs from his eyes. "That's wrong, though. I'm Gideon."

"It isn't wrong. Do you understand, Guardian Frayne, that this world is stranger than anything you could imagine? That there is no *golow ha tewlder*, no light and dark?"

"I'm a policeman. Of course I know that." Every time he arrested one bad bastard or another for some heinous crime, out would come the story. A rotten childhood, a broken home. A lost job, debt, addiction... All the nuances of twilight that brought decent men from daylight into the dark. "That's not what you mean, though, is it?"

"No. Even your preacher brother knows it by now. Think how you've protected them—the little girl, the hooligan, the junkie. You don't mix up the light with goodness, or darkness with the bad. And so the creatures show themselves to you, and so they'll stay near you—you and the Tyack boy, and your child—like beasts on an old-fashioned shield."

Gideon could hear sirens. They brought him to surface, from waters so deep he'd been losing his sense of the shore. "I don't understand."

"I know. But one day you will. Oh, in the meantime I have a message from Dev Bowe for you. He told me last time I visited him in hospital. He wants you to have the Lowen house on Morgan hill."

"Right." It was best to keep a suicide talking, no matter how surreal the topic. "Is he gonna buy us some lottery tickets, then?"

"Oh, there'll be no need for that. Hadn't you better go and see what all those sirens are about?"

"No. I've got to stay and look after you."

"Well, I promise faithfully to sit here until you get back. Go on, Guardian Frayne. Save the day."

Police, fire and ambulance. Gideon knew all their songs. More than one crying out into a Cornish night meant trouble, more than a car prang or childbirth, more than a cat—or an old lady—stuck in a tree. Drawn to their symphony, he took one step and then another towards the empty window frame. The back of the warehouse looked right out over Penzance, all the way to St Michael's Mount in the east.

The town was on fire. "Jesus Christ," Gideon whispered, clambering out through the window. He jumped, and landed hard on the waste ground six feet below. Spinning blue lights were threading the streetlamps and torch flares. They were homing in on Chybucca Square, an open space where the Midwinter Fire procession would stop to watch dance troupes, buy roast chestnuts and sample mulled wine from the stalls. The bank and both buildings flanking it were ablaze, smaller fires breaking out as people backed away in terror, dropping torches in their wake. Out of habit, Gideon scanned the scene for its focal point, the cause of all these effects.

Yes—there on the seaward side of the square, pouring out of the narrow road that led to the bus station. From this distance he couldn't be sure, but it looked as if DI Lawrence's busloads of out-of-town kids had made it to the party after all. They were grabbing torches from the hands of the revellers, chucking the brands into shop doorways and directly into the crowd. And bloody Darren Prowse had sent him off the wrong way.

Then, if he'd stayed in the streets below, he'd never have seen what was going on. The Beast, the Lord of Misrule, and Old Penglas... Higher and higher, each one of them had brought him, and in the wrong direction, but from here he had a bird's-eye view. He pulled out his mobile and dialled the inspector's number. She answered on the first ring, sounding frayed and grim. "They're coming in from the bus station," Gideon told her. "You need to send as many lads as you can down to Chybucca Square, and some of the local boys to block off access from station. From here it looks like they'll need riot gear. I'm on my way down."

Shit, he'd forgotten about Granny Ragwen. He ran back to the window, grabbed the ledge and hoisted himself up far enough to shine his torch inside. He'd be lucky to get any kind of rescue team out here to help her now, but...

His stomach dropped. She was gone. The rafter she'd perched on was vacant but for a huge Penzance seagull, idly preening. Bracing himself to discover her shattered remains, he directed the torch beam to the floor.

Nothing. His precarious grip on the window ledge failed him, and he half-fell back onto the frosty ground. Righting himself, he reflected that many things inside him had changed. He was puzzled by the old girl's disappearance but not dismayed. And even a few months ago, his first reflex would have been a frantic call to Lee. As it was, the signal between them lay deep and undisturbed. Gideon knew his man—at the first sign of trouble, he'd have taken Tamsyn and carried her out of harm's reach. That left Gideon free to do his job and ensure the harm reached no bloody further. The waste ground lay in a broad, tempting sweep all the way back down to Tolver Road. Pocketing his mobile, he began to run.

A shadow crossed his path, once then again and again. At each pass, an eerie cry rang out. Gideon spared an upward glance. There'd been horror-story news reports all that summer of rogue seagulls landing in babies' pushchairs, trying to snatch small dogs off the pavements. Had the gull from the warehouse decided to follow him? He paused for a moment on the brow of the hill, sweeping the beam of his torch into the sky.

A witch on a broomstick strafed him. The seagull's cry resounded from the heavens once more, cracking into wild, ecstatic laughter. The insane vision stayed with him for a fraction of a second, then a cloud passed over the face of the gibbous moon, and she was gone.

Gideon stood motionless, trying to catch his breath. There was a kind of kite or remote-controlled model shaped like a witch on her broom. He'd seen it on YouTube. Tamsyn thought it was the funniest thing she'd ever seen, and Lee had insisted he watch the clip. The model was pretty convincing. People had pointed and shouted, and there'd been a few cries of real fear. Probably that was what he'd just seen. He didn't know who the hell would be buzzing him up on Gwidder Hill at this hour, but...

But he didn't know anything, did he? Not really. His whole night since leaving Lee had been a kind of dream. He'd run from one strange meeting, one mythological encounter, to the next. And these things, these monsters, hadn't even called him by his right name. He was Gideon Frayne, Gideon—not Guardian. His head spun again and he grabbed at a fence post to stay upright. All his certainties were faltering. What if his connection to Lee wasn't quiet at all? What if it was gone?

Fear ate him whole. He tapped up Lee's number from the phone's memory, sweat-damped fingertips barely able to manipulate the screen. Still clinging to the fence post with one hand, he listened to the call ring out and out, and finally click to voicemail.

Chapter Six

He left a message, barely aware of what he was saying. *Get out of the town centre. Take Tamsie back to the police station. I'll be there soon.* Then, after a dry-throated three-second wait—*Lee, for God's sake. Why aren't you answering?*

There was only one way to find that out. Gideon had almost worn out the rubber track on the police-gym treadmill, had jogged over untold miles of Bodmin moorland, in his efforts not just to get back to his usual form after his injury but to surpass that old standard. He'd discovered and accepted his mortality in his Trelowarren hospital bed, but had decided since then that he was going to be the best damn mortal the Cornish police force had ever seen. He'd known that one day he would need to run, without fatigue or pause for breath. To run and run...

He covered the barren ground in less than a minute. Back on Tolver Road, he had to ease his pace: frightened revellers, parents with kids, lanterns and banners trailing, were making their way uphill away from the blaze. He wove a path amongst them, barely aware of how he dodged them or gently put them aside. He had one thought, one goal only.

No. He was a copper as well as a husband and a dad. He rounded the corner into Chybucca Square and saw that his duty lay everywhere, scattered about him in flaring rags. Two fire trucks were parked outside the bank, bringing that blaze under control, but the stiff sea breeze was feeding every torch that had been dropped or thrown. Gideon caught sight of a couple of uniformed constables running from one fire to the next, trying to stamp out the brands and only getting their trousers singed for their pains. "Hoi," he yelled, pulling his ID. "Never mind that. Go into the open shops and get their fire extinguishers. The chippy over there will have a couple."

He waited until they'd run to obey him, then he darted across the flame-lit green. Most of the troublemakers had vanished at the sound of the sirens, but a little group of them—too drunk or high for caution—were still at work, gleefully chucking torches through the broken windows of the photographer's shop and helping themselves to the equipment on display. He waited until he was right in the middle of the shrieking, laughing mob before letting loose his law-enforcement bellow. "Police!" Before they could react, he reached in amongst the bodies and accurately collared the ringleader. He used the lad and his own bulk to corner the gang in the shop doorway. "How do you like it?" he demanded, as one pale face and then another fixed on his. "How do you like being stuck in a burning bloody building?" He shook the kid he was holding like a rat. "Wow, Saul Priddy, is that you? Didn't I arrest you just last year for a spot of B and E in Liskeard? This has got to be parole violation of the century."

The boy went the colour of cottage cheese. "Don't tell! Don't tell, or I'll go down proper."

"You will. Adult jail for you this time, too." Gideon glanced across the square. His two constables were doing a lot better now, and the Penzance citizens were stepping up, passing buckets, washing-up bowls and any other container they could find in a human chain from the fountain. "I *will* tell, you little sod, but if you get your pack of hooligans to help those people over there, I'll tell that too. All right?"

"All right, all right. Just let me—"

Gideon tossed him aside, forgetting him. A figure had appeared behind the shop's glass door, half-wrapped in flames, staggering and pawing at the handle. Gideon grabbed it from the outside and discovered for himself that it was searing hot. The pain shot through him and vanished in adrenaline. "Get back!" he roared, hoping the terrified shopkeeper could hear him. He took three backward strides, braced up and rammed the door with his shoulder.

He tumbled into the shop. The burning man was still on his feet but beginning to shriek in panic. One glance around the flame-lit interior showed Gideon what he wanted: a thick baize cloth in the window, with the remains of the display merchandise still on it amidst the pieces of broken glass. He snatched the cloth free. The shopkeeper was far enough gone to try to fight off his saviour, but Gideon didn't give him the chance: grabbed him, bundled the cloth around him and hoisted him out onto the green.

He knelt beside him, beating out the last of the flames. "You'll be all right," he declared when the shock-blanked stare met his. He had no idea, but he'd learned that convincing a survivor he'd make it was half the battle. "Lie still. I'll get an ambulance for you." By a miracle, a vacant one was pulling up by the kerb. Frantically Gideon waved, and a pair of paramedics scrambled out and came racing across the green. "Burns victim," he said, falling back to give them room. "I don't know how bad." He wrapped his arms around himself. His hand hurt like hell, and there was nothing in all the burnt-out darkness of his mind to tell him what had happened to his husband and his little girl. "I've got to go."

One of the paramedics glanced up, grinning. "Yeah, of course. It's Sergeant Frayne, isn't it, from over in Dark?"

"Er... yes."

"You won't remember me. My team and I picked you up after you got stabbed in Bodmin town. Nice to see you on your feet again. And don't worry about this chap—his burns look superficial."

"Thank God."

"More a case of thank the local bobby, if you ask me. Another thirty seconds and he would've been fried. If you're looking for your other half, by the way, he's down on the quayside. Saw him two minutes ago."

Air rushed into Gideon's lungs, sweet and pure with relief. He couldn't find his voice to thank the medic, who had turned her attentions back to her patient anyway. He turned and stumbled away. If anything further needed doing here tonight, any more fires doused or hoodlums arrested, someone else would have to manage it, at least for now. Gideon would return to the fray and gladly, but not before he'd set eyes on Tamsyn and Lee.

An odd hush had descended on the town. Saul Priddy and his mates had vanished, of course, seeing a charge of manslaughter in their shared futures. The crowd in the square was thinning. Gideon didn't quite get it. He couldn't work out how the promising riot he'd observed from Gwidder Hill had dispersed so fast. Either the Penzance coppers had done a phenomenally good job, or...

Or somebody had ordered up a miracle. He emerged from Quay Street onto the sea front. Battery Road, normally thronged with harbour traffic, was closed off and silent. People were coming from all directions to the open space in front of the Dolphin Tavern. Among them Gideon saw faces he would store away for later identity parades, feral or idle or just plain thick, the very lads who'd been wreaking havoc in the town. His fingers itched to collar them, but he was on his own, and anyway they'd ceased to behave like thugs. They were just walking in silence, some of them with torches still borne aloft, joining the outskirts of the crowd.

The crowd had a centre. Gideon couldn't quite see it, but the people flowing in were moving clockwise around it, each one dropping to a slow, almost stately pace, like a dustcloud around a newly formed star. A couple of the crowdy-crawn drummers were giving them the beat. Round and round they circled, expressions becoming young with wonder as they drew closer to the core, torchlight mingling with moonlight in the clearing sky, boats gleaming on the high-tide waters in the harbour beyond.

Compelling and beautiful, and if Gideon could get enough uniformed muscle down here, easy pickings. Fish in a trawl net. He had no idea what had drawn the little bastards' attention, what was holding it now, and he didn't care. He pulled out his mobile.

Lee met his eyes through the crowd. It was a glimpse only. He was in the inner circle, walking clockwise with the rest, the baby in his arms. Gideon forgot the kids and his potential arrests with perfect totality. That look, brief though it had been, meant *get your arse here right now*. The serenity Gideon had read through their strange link had been a front. Beneath it Lee was terrified, elated, holding back fireworks by a pure effort of will. *Gid, come here!*

He went. He was good at parting crowds without disturbing them. Even out of uniform, when he pushed, people moved. He accepted the circular current, spiralled in through it and joined Lee with a gasp of relief. "There you are. Are you both all right?"

"Fine. Just walk with us, okay? Don't say anything."

"About what?"

Lee made the smallest gesture. "That."

In the centre of the circle, fire was floating in mid-air. Gideon's eyes were sore and stinging with smoke. He blinked and focussed, trying to make sense of what he was seeing. "Keep walking," Lee said softly, an edge of warning in his voice. "They think it's the Candle Dance."

"Doesn't that happen later, with the Montol 'Oss?"

"Yep."

"And... what is it really?"

"It's Tamsyn."

Nobody was looking at her. She was doing nothing to draw attention to herself, sitting crooning in Lee's arms. Only her hands were busy, pushing and shaping the air. She was making a pattern. Gideon recognised it—the Christmas-tree ornament she liked best, the sphere with its array of little lights. Saul Priddy had worked his way to the front row. He gave a faint squawk as his torch went out, the fire lifting from its head and floating to join the others in the sphere. A look of wondering innocence overcame him, a face Gideon doubted even his mother had seen. "I have to nick that lad."

"I know. Not yet."

No. It was very important that Gideon didn't disturb any aspect of this. He noticed that people were pacing in pairs to the beat of the crowdy-crawn drums, so he tucked his arm through Lee's, shivering in pleasure as Lee drew him close. "I see why you weren't answering your phone."

"I knew you'd be worried. I'm sorry. A group of kids were trying to set fire to a boat down here, and she just... took their torches from them and started doing this. And everyone came drifting down to watch."

"Why aren't they freaking out?"

"Don't know. They've seen Derren Brown, I suppose. Maybe they think it's all done with mirrors."

Whatever they thought, they were peaceful. Gideon had never been part of a crowd so united, so surrendered to its central focus. No-one who came here could be harbouring thoughts of destruction, and half Penzance was down on the quayside now, swirling slowly around the sphere of fire. Tamsyn was making it big enough for all of them to see, stealing light after light from the torches and setting them in her display. Her face was rapt, the dark curls escaping from under her woolly hat dancing in the breeze. Lee held her more closely. "What are we going to do with her, Gid?"

His eyes were full of tears. Gideon tightened his grip on his arm. "Everyone's becoming what they should be," he said. "She will, too—whatever she has to be, sweetheart, no matter what you and I think about it."

The pattern was done. The sphere stopped its rotation. All the people gathered round came to a gentle halt as well, and a ripple of laughter and applause rose up, praise for the unseen magician who'd arranged this new Montol delight. Gideon lifted Tamsyn carefully out of Lee's arms. "Give me that heavy kid," he said, smiling. He was father to the child. Whatever she became, he had to guide her. He kissed her, and she gave her usual squawk of delight at the sight of him. "Tamsyn. Put the fire in the water. Can you manage that?"

The words on their own were no good. The places she tugged in his head were tough fibres, strong ropes of love. He could tug back without hurting her. Holding her lambent gaze, he showed her what he wanted—like any father, told her what to do.

The sphere shot into the air. She gave it one last spin for the hell of it, and then effortlessly fired the whole structure off like a meteor shower, far out into the waters of Mount's Bay.

***

Gideon steered his family back towards the car. He met DI Lawrence outside the police station, and paused by her patrol car long enough to get signed off duty for the night. He sidestepped her questions as best he could. She looked dazed, clearly unable to believe how the town she'd been supervising had exploded under her hands, or how eerily it had calmed down afterwards. The fires were out, Saul Priddy and his gang rounded up, the Montol celebrations continuing as if nothing had happened. An officer had been dispatched to the Gwidder Hill to check for any signs of Jana Ragwen, and had reported the warehouse empty. Lawrence thanked Gideon for his services, wished Tamsyn a happy birthday, and motioned to her sergeant to drive her on.

Tamsyn's head was drooping on Gideon's shoulder. Lee rearranged her scarf to keep out the cold night wind, then took off his own and gave it to Gideon. "Well," he said, drawing them both into an embrace. "You'd be sleepy too, if you'd had to stop a riot." He paused, and Gideon felt the indescribable shimmer of contact renewed. "Oh, wait. You did."

"Not really. Just a scuffle or two."

"Bollocks. You came down off the hill, and Chybucca Square was on fire. Kids everywhere chucking torches, and... a burning man. Oh—your poor hand."

Gideon had forgotten. Lee detached his grip on Tamsyn and opened out his palm in the streetlight. They both stared at the mark of the photographer's door handle seared into his skin. "It's nothing. I'm fine."

"It's not. It really hurts."

"Get out of my head, then you won't feel it, will you?"

"Come on. A&E."

"Ah, no. We'll be in there all night while they patch up everyone's bumps and scrapes. Just get me home, and I'll let you play doctor there."

Lee's eyes met his with a promise that no night was too long or weird for mischief. "Really?"

"Yes, you kinky sod." Gideon leaned over their sleeping daughter's head and kissed him. "Man, I was worried about you. Look, she's spark out. Don't suppose we could tuck her into her baby seat and grab a quickie in the—"

"In the police car park?" Lee pushed him back, snorting with laughter. "I tell you what, big man—I'll actually consider it, if you can tell me you've phoned your bloody brother."

"Shit." Gideon put a hand to his mouth. Then he checked that Tamsyn was really asleep, and let rip. "Shit, shit, shit. Fuck. I forgot all about him."

"Do it now. I don't know what's going on, but it's really important. Far more of a big deal than whatever he was upset about before."

Gideon took out his phone. He'd forgotten about Zeke, but Zeke hadn't forgotten him. He'd phoned five times and sent eight texts. Gingerly Gideon opened the most recent. He read it, his mouth going dry. His blood seemed to recede from the surface of his skin. He reached blindly for Lee, who took hold of him anxiously in return, warming him, steadying. "Oh God, Lee. It's Ma."

Chapter Seven

Trelowarren hospital was a maze of mid-century corridors and modern add-on blocks. Gideon knew two routes through it so well that Lee had to grab his arm and redirect him twice, as shock and muscle memory tried to send him first towards the physiotherapy centre and then the maternity wing.

At last they found the lift that would take them to the ICU. Lee pressed the button and they stood in breathless silence, listening to the clunk and grind of cables in the shaft. Gideon brushed a strand of hair back from his daughter's sleeping face. She was blissfully out cold, snoring faintly in her sling around Lee's shoulders. "It's a year ago to the day that we were last here, Lee. To the day."

"I know." The lift doors opened and Lee ushered him inside. "To see this one being born."

"Is this what the old woman meant by the solstice door? One year someone comes in through it, and the next, someone goes..."

His voice cracked. Lee took his hand. "I don't know what she meant, okay? That's why this is so damn frustrating. Another reason why I don't want Tamsyn growing up like me. I didn't feel any of this coming on—just that you should call your brother. I'm sorry."

"It isn't your responsibility to feel things coming on. And if you think about it, if I'd just bloody *listened* to you about calling my brother..."

"Don't."

"I'll be lucky if he ever speaks to me again."

"Zeke's a good guy. He'll understand."

The lift jolted to a stop, depositing them straight into the ICU reception. Ezekiel was waiting, bolt upright, in a chair directly opposite the doors. He got up stiffly and stood glaring at Gideon. "You bastard," he said icily. "Why didn't you answer your phone?"

Gideon was all out of excuses. He spread his hands helplessly. "Because I'm a complete dick."

"He's not," Lee interposed. "He was on duty in Penzance. A riot broke out and he stopped it."

The wintry gaze settled on Lee. "You'd defend him if he turned out to be the damned Beast of Bodmin himself, wouldn't you?"

"Probably, but—"

"Be quiet, both of you. Gideon, our mother had a fall in her room at Roselands. She banged her head, and she hasn't regained consciousness since. She's in intensive care because she won't wake up, and nobody knows why."

"Oh, Zeke." Gideon took a step towards him.

"Stay there, please. I want you to know something. Matthew Hopkins was a sadist and a brute, well paid to hound innocent girls and women to death on trumped-up charges of witchcraft."

"Er... yes." Gideon had no idea why this had come up now. "So..."

"So don't ever call me that again."

He had, hadn't he? Memories of his last conversation with his brother leapt up like lurid flames. "I'm sorry," he said roughly. "Truly I am. But—Zeke, Ma's gonna be okay, isn't she?"

"They don't know. She's having a brain scan now. They say they need her to come round soon, or... or she'll lose too much ground."

A single tear, unlikely as a violet on the wall of a glacier, fell down Ezekiel's face. It splashed onto the front of his anorak, and he and Gideon stared at it as if neither of them could work out where it had come from. Lee gave Gideon a little shove, recalling him to life and humanity. "Bloody hell," he whispered, strode over to his brother and seized him in his arms.

Ezekiel broke into noisy sobs. Clutching him, Gideon conveyed over his shoulder to Lee his absolute astonishment, then helped him back to the row of seats against the far wall. "Zeke, I'm here now. I'm so, so sorry you had all that to deal with on your own."

"I can't lose her!" Ezekiel grabbed the tissue Lee was cautiously holding out, buried his face in it and blew his nose explosively. "I can't, and—nor can you, Gideon. You were estranged from her for so many years, but now you have her back, and she thinks it's the best thing in the world to have a gay son..." He paused for breath, then added, fervently, "Damn you. You're gay, ten years younger than I am, and you *still* gave her grandchild before... before..."

Gideon swallowed down his own rising tide of grief. He tightened his arm around Zeke's waist. "Don't be stupid. You'll give her dozens once you and Eleanor get married, I bet."

Something in the words brought Zeke's tears to a stop. He sat up a little, shivering. Lee took a seat on his other side, his mouth quirking up in an expression Gideon knew well: surmise and amusement, a forbidden smile. "Would you like a hold of Tamsie, Zeke?"

"I would. I should just stop asking myself how you know things, shouldn't I?"

"Maybe. Here you go."

Lee unfastened the harness and handed the sleeping child over wholesale, still tucked into her sling. Zeke took awkward, tender hold of her. "I said some bad things about you, little girl. You won't remember them, and your dads won't remind you... I hope."

"They won't," Lee said firmly. "Will we, Gid?"

Gideon cleared his throat. "If you can get over Matthew Hopkins, I guess we can forget the whole *devil's work* thing. The *demon child*, though—"

"Gideon!" Lee fetched him a cuff behind Zeke's back. But the reprimand lacked conviction, and a moment later he asked, with careful sobriety, "Where's your Eleanor tonight, Zeke? I'd have thought wild horses wouldn't keep her away."

Zeke nodded, settling Tamsyn in his arms. Lee's question had raised painful colour in his cheeks. "Eleanor loves Ma. I haven't told her this has happened. I didn't want to give her a shock, not in..."

A brief silence fell. Gideon broke it, irrepressible laughter shaking his voice. "In her *condition*? Are you *kidding* me?"

"It was why I came to see you this morning. For some unknowable reason, I thought you might be sympathetic."

Gideon bounced to his feet. This was too bloody much, this was, after years of moral high ground and *holier-than-thou*. He strode to the end of the little waiting room and back. Its confines felt too small to contain his reaction: he wanted to run and shout. "Eleanor's *pregnant*?"

"Yes. She only just told me. She hasn't even had a scan. Enjoy yourself, Gideon, but remember what this means to me. I've proved myself a hypocrite to my congregation. I may have to give up my ministry."

His words fell harmlessly as spent arrows, deprived of momentum and meaning. Gideon could scarcely hear him. The entire situation was too beautiful—the ultimate levelling of the mountainous playing field between them, and best of all a perfect excuse not to think about what was happening in the ICU ward beyond the glass doors. He took another turn of the waiting room, stopped and folded his arms. "Wow, Ezekiel. Devil's work indeed."

But a white-coated figure had appeared through the glass. Lee, who could read the tiniest shift in his expression as well as his mind, got up and came to stand beside him. Gideon held out a hand to Zeke: steadied him as he lurched upright with the baby. The three were shoulder-to-shoulder when the glass doors swished apart.

The doctor's name was Pearce. Hers had been the third face Gideon had registered upon emerging from his coma on this very same ICU ward, and she'd become painfully familiar to him during the days and weeks that had followed. He'd wiped out the memory of her afterwards, just as he'd set aside all other recall of his brush with death. Was it better or worse that she was here now? She was tough as nails, but very good at what she did. If anyone could restore his mother to life... "How is she?" he asked, because although Zeke was the eldest and a minister, the nominal head of the family now that their father was gone, he was speechless with terror and grief. "Is there any change?"

"I'm sorry, Sergeant. Her EEG shows a serious reduction in brain activity."

"Is she on life support?"

"Minimal. You'll be aware that she has strict instructions in place."

Gideon was aware. She'd asked him to help her draw up her living will, afraid that her other son would try and put God's will before it. "And her cutoff point's been reached?"

"Yes. If you and your family want to go to the bedside, that's fine. I'll have a cot brought in for the little girl."

Ezekiel twitched. "I don't understand," he rasped. "What are you saying?"

"We're losing her, I'm afraid."

***

Despite everything, Gideon slept. He'd worn himself out with his race through the Montol streets, and once a passing nurse had stopped off to bandage his hand, the cessation of pain had knocked away his last prop. He jolted awake in the small hours, horrified at his dereliction of duty. Lee was crouching in front of the armchair in the warm little ICU room. "Hush, love. It's all right."

"Tamsyn?"

"Asleep in the next room. Zeke's having a nap through there too."

"Ma?"

"No change."

That covered Gideon's list of concerns. No, not quite. He sat up, rubbing his eyes. "Shit. I forgot the dog."

"I phoned Sarah Kemp. She said she'd go and take her back to hers."

Silently blessing good mindful husbands and neighbours with spare door keys, Gideon planted a kiss on Lee's brow. "Thank you. Are you all right?"

"Fine. I've just been sitting by Ma's bed."

"Well, come and sit here for a minute with me." Gideon scrunched over as far as he could in the armchair, held his arms out and grunted in relief as Lee scrambled into place beside him. "That's better. God, I can't believe this is happening."

"Can you talk to me about ordinary stuff for a bit? I'm trying to work something out, and it'll be easier if—"

"If you can hear me droning on in the background?"

"Something like that, yeah."

"Cheeky sod." Gideon racked his brains. "She's got a boyfriend, you know. No, not Ma," he clarified at Lee's astonished glance. "Sarah Kemp. I bumped into her in the procession with Lorna, and she introduced me to her new bloke. Wilfred, I think he's called. Seems like a nice enough chap, and he's got a couple of kids of his own to add to the menagerie. I invited him round to Tamsyn's party tomorrow. If she has one, poor little bugger."

"Oh, she will." Lee settled his head on Gideon's shoulder. "And it *is* tomorrow. Carry on."

"Not bored yet? I also ran into Granny Ragwen, or rather I ran after her. I found her in a warehouse, perched on a rafter. No way she could've got up there on her own. I'd be worried about her if she hadn't zoomed over my head on a broomstick five minutes later."

"Oh, okay."

"You believe me, right?"

"Course I do. Just a normal night on the beat for Sergeant Frayne. More, please."

"I met Darren Prowse. He's got a legitimate job."

"What? Now you *are* pulling my leg."

"Seriously. Wants a reference and everything."

"Wow." Lee took this in quietly, running a hand over Gideon's chest, tracing a thoughtful pattern. "People move on, don't they? They become what they should be, just as you said."

"Actually, Darren said that too."

"They change and they move on, whether we're ready or not. The thing is, Gid—I'm really not sure it's your ma's time to go, and I'm struggling to figure out if I feel that way because it's true, or because I'm not ready to part with her."

Gideon swallowed a hot lump in his throat. "I'm not bloody ready either."

"That's why I hesitated to say it. I didn't want to make you hope."

"Not your responsibility. Let's have a look at her."

They went to take a seat on either side of the bed. Gideon had avoided this place, reserved as it was for mourners and those who watched hopelessly through long nights. If he could have helped the old lady by going out and getting stabbed again, breaking every bone in his body, he'd have gone to do it bravely, but settling here was hard. He suspected a little makeup had crept into Ma Frayne's life since the pastor had died last year, and he was certain she got her hair done once a month because she'd learned to text him a wobbly selfie of the end result, guiltily thrilled with herself. All that was gone now. The nurses had washed her hair after stitching the cut on her brow, and her face was a grey-white mask. "They did it wrong," he said hoarsely, dabbing at her fringe. "Her parting. It's on the wrong side."

"Fix it, then." Lee passed him the comb which the good son Zeke—the dutiful one, who picked up his phone when needed—had remembered to pack and bring in. "You're her good son too. Don't be afraid."

With infinite caution, Gideon plied the comb through the white hair. The tracks he was making reminded him of ploughed fields in the snow, and being with Lee in a lane on the outskirts of Dark two years ago. Zeke had cast a demon from Lee that day. That had been Zeke's view of the situation, anyway. Lee had said, not wholly jokingly, that any demon trapped between two big Frayne lads would vacate the premises out of sheer terror. Gideon hadn't known what to believe. He supposed the point was that the three of them together had made a stand. "Lee. Did you tell me it was tomorrow?"

"Yes, I did." Lee glanced at him from the far side of the bed, his expression kind and penetrating. "After half four in the morning. You slept a long time."

"Just about long enough?"

"Maybe. Here's Zeke."

Ezekiel stumbled through from the side room, rubbing his eyes blearily. "Did somebody call me?"

"Neither of us." Lee sat up, smiling. "How's the demon child?"

"I suppose there's just the outside chance that you and my rotten brother might let me forget that some day. She's still asleep. What I don't understand is how IIIIIIII could have slept so long. I didn't think I'd close my eyes."

"It's okay. Come and sit down with us."

"Lee, you'll think me a coward. I rode with her in the ambulance, and I stayed with her while she was being admitted. I don't want to look at her as she is now."

"Nevertheless."

Lee was holding out his hand. The gesture was affectionate but somehow peremptory, a summons. Gideon was aware of Zeke obeying it, moving to stand at Lee's side. He was losing track a little, starting to drift. His husband's negotiations with his brother were important, but he had no part in them. Still, there they were, the pair of them, arrayed opposite to him on the far side of his mother's bed. Gideon had heard that a triangle was the most stable structure of all. "What time is it now?"

"Twenty to five. It's time."

Zeke shifted nervously. "Time for what?"

"A journey I'd have taken for your brother if I could. He knows that—don't you, Gid?" Gideon looked up in response. He gave a brief, smiling nod, and Lee went on: "He has to find the point in the past where things changed, so they can be different tonight. I can't do that. I don't know Ma Frayne's trackways."

"Her trackways? Is it dangerous?"

"For someone who hasn't seen both sides of the veil. But Gideon has. He's walked there often now, with the Beast and the witch and Old Penglas. And..." He paused, voice roughening to a chuckle. "Darren Prowse, the Lord of Misrule? That's kind of perfect."

"I don't know what you're talking about, but this sounds crazy, Lee. Why can't I do it? I know our mother's trackways, better than Gideon ever could. I'm the oldest. Why—"

"It's not a competition. You have to forgive him for being born. He's forgiven you."

"What?"

"Never mind. Just stay close."

"I can't. I can't watch this."

"You can, Ezekiel. Because he needs you to."

Gideon let their voices fade. He had no need of them anymore, though he remained conscious of their presences, like great trees on the edge of a river. He was five years old, walking home through the village with his mother after school, and he hadn't a care in the world.

Nor had Ma. Gideon knew her thoughts as completely as his own, and she was elated—day in, day out, dawn till dusk—at having another child. A cheerful little boy, so different to his taciturn teenage brother that Ma was sure the pastor's shadow would never consume him. She loved her elder son—of course— but these days he was so hard to reach. And Gideon, sturdy and affectionate, was there, surprising late fruit of a womb beginning the syncopated dance of menopause. Running down the lane now, never so far ahead that she felt he didn't need her. Just bold and independent, testing the boundaries of his world.

Some things could still scare him. The lane ran along the back of Pellar Street, a rough council block much haunted by lads coming home from afternoon sessions at Bodmin college. Normally Ma brought Gideon through earlier, but today Mrs Waite had detained her with gossip in the shop. A cluster of the young thugs were blocking the path ahead, laughing and throwing stones at some unseen target. Gideon had stopped in his tracks and was looking back at her, eyes wide. "Ma! Ma!"

As if she could fix everything. Well, that was her job, as long as he believed she could. She scooped him up, grunting a little at his solid weight. She cleared her throat, settled herself more firmly on her heels. "You boys! What are you doing?"

They swung round to face her. Through a gap in their ranks she glimpsed a huddled figure by the wall. "Is that... Mrs Ragwen, is that you?"

One of the boys gave a shrill laugh. "That's not no *missus*! Show me where her *mister* is, her babby's father. How can she be missus, when she been *Miss* Ragwen all her life?"

Ma sighed. These were valid questions, according to the very church she'd married into. The pastor would ask the same. But everyone who'd grown up in the Bodmin villages knew that, once a woman had passed a certain age or produced a child without the aid of a husband, you stuck a courtesy *Mrs* in front of her maiden name. It saved her face with the postman, and put off predators scanning the electoral roll for single women. No point in trying to explain that to this mob. There were eight of them, the delinquent Bill Prowse among them, and she was here alone with her son. She should just find another way home.

They were losing interest in her anyway, turning around, picking up loose stones and chippings from the gutters again. Mrs Ragwen—Jana, they called her, didn't they?—gave a moan of fear. She wasn't very nice. She never turned up at any of Ma's parish-house coffee mornings, or came to knit hats for African babies with the WI. Still, Ma Frayne's church had taught her some useful things as well as the harsh, bewildering stuff about women and wedlock, and her blood boiled. "Hoi!" she cried, in the voice of her moorland childhood, carrying and fierce. "Let he who is without sin cast the first bloody stone. I bet that doesn't cover any of you little buggers, does it?"

They whipped round in astonishment. She pressed her advantage, clutching Gideon tight and marching straight past them. When she set him down so that she could crouch by Mrs Ragwen's side, to her amusement and fright he folded his arms and faced the lads down, scowling fearfully. "Gideon! Stay behind me."

"No, Ma."

She couldn't let her baby outdo her in courage. "You get out of here," she told the gathered crowd. "I know some of your names—yours, Bill Prowse—and most of the rest of your faces. Go on. Get!"

Bill, always more coward than aggressor, came to her rescue. "She'n the pastor's missus, boys. Be a bad lookout for us if that old crow comes after us, with his long face and his great black bible!"

They scattered, laughing and shoving. When the lane was empty, Ma turned her attention to the woman huddled by the wall, arms still raised to shield her head. "Mrs Ragwen? Are you all right?"

She was little more than a bundle of cloth, patched-together velvets under a long black cloak. "Let me alone."

"Don't be scared. They've gone. I'm Mrs Frayne, the pastor's wife. This is my son, Gideon."

At the mention of the child, Mrs Ragwen threw back the edge of her cloak and risked a look. "Ah. I know both of you. The good wife, and..." She pinched Gideon's cheek, not with affection but as if she was checking his texture and composition. "The little policeman. That's right." She got up stiffly, brushing at her long skirt. "I'm all right. I let the little sods catch me with my robes on, that's all."

"It seems a very dangerous street. Would you like the pastor to find out if there's somewhere nicer you could rent in the village?"

She swept her hair back from her face. "The Ragwens don't move *out* of places, my dear. They name places *after* us—Pellar Street, Cros-an-Wra, hundreds more. We'll be here when the likes of Billy Prowse have passed from the face of the earth." Her voice wobbled. "Still, it ain't very nice to be stoned, is it?"

"Not nice at all," Ma Frayne agreed. She put an arm around the woman's thin shoulders, passed her a dainty handkerchief which she demolished at once with a honking blow of her nose. "Do you want to call the police?"

"No, no. No use in that, not here." She tweaked Gideon's cheek again. "Not yet, anyway. Here, this don't mean I have to start trotting along to your husband's chapel, do it—because his missus came and saved my life?"

"I don't think I quite did that." Ma Frayne smiled. "And as for the chapel—no, I don't think that would do anybody any good, though don't tell the pastor I said so. Here, I've got an idea.

Why don't you dress a bit differently when you go out? Not to... to hide who you are or anything, but just to make your life a little bit easier? And it would be a grand joke on them all, wouldn't it, if the village witch wore Marks and Sparks?"

Gideon looked at her in wonder. How had his mother found out that Granny Ragwen was a witch? The paths of her life—her trackways—were narrow ones. But then, perhaps she'd always known, carving out a route through the world unimaginable to her husband. Mrs Ragwen was nodding, as if she too understood. "Perhaps I will, my dear. Perhaps I will. But remember, we always take on our own guise at the end. And my kind—we pay back our favours. Remember that too."

"I will, but there's really no need—"

"Go on with you." Mrs Ragwen gave Ma a gentle shove. "I've got to go in and see to my Madgie now. And you... It's time for you to go home."

She scuttled off, gathering her cloak around her. Ma Frayne leaned down to kiss her boy. "There. She was a funny person, wasn't she? You were very brave, son, but you're not to try and scare off big groups of lads until you're a grown-up. Let's get you home for your tea."

There was a gate at the end of the alley. Gideon had never seen it before. Nor had his mother—she straightened up and stared at it in wonder.

Gideon would have remembered. He could never have forgotten such a gate. It towered over the cottages around it, and instead of wood or iron, it was made of close-cropped turf. Laughter rose up in him, chasing away his fear. Tiny sheep were grazing on it. Daisies and coltsfoot starred it like galactic dust, and cloud-shadows rippled its sunlit green. "Look, dear," Ma said to him, turning to hold out her hand. "It's the door in the hill."

Yes. Cornwall had no chalk figures cut into her hills, but when Pastor Frayne had been called to a ministerial conference in Brighton, Ma had taken Gideon on a bus to a place called Wilmington. He'd barely been four years old. He'd stood holding her hand while she read out from a guide book some theories about the huge faceless man shining in chalk-cut outline on the side of Windover Hill. Perhaps the two great sticks he was grasping were surveyor's tools, or markers to follow Orion's progress across the winter sky. *I don't think so*, she'd said, closing up the book. *I think it looks like he's holding a door.*

He wasn't faceless now. His mouth was open—smiling—full of stars. His eyes were two bright suns. He grasped either side of the hillside portal, and with a huge, slow power like the shift of a glacier in spring, he began to open the gate.

There was clear sky beyond it, shading to deep-space blue. "Oh, my darling," Ma Frayne said suddenly, dropping to one knee and kissing Gideon. "That's for me. I have to go, and you mustn't follow me. You have to stay here. You've got all your life ahead of you, your beautiful long life. Goodbye."

Gideon tried to howl, but the chalk man turned his star-filled smile upon him, and he knew he had to be good. No, better than good—he had to be big, to reach past all the years of his painful growing-up and become Ma's fine son, the strapping policeman who could change the world. He did it—diving like a dolphin through waves of time, shaking off the waters of childhood. His legs were strong. A bleeding wound in his thigh healed up as he watched, and a deeper scar—the black gash of rage at the loss of his daughter—vanished from his heart. He took one step and then another. Ma was a long way ahead, almost in the shadow of the gate, but he knew he could catch her. Lee Tyack stepped out from the shade of a holly tree, holding an oak-leaf crown like the one he'd had thrust on him in Kelyndar. This was the crown of his manhood, and he stopped, fearless, for Lee to set it in place. He took an unhurried moment to hold his lover's face between his hands, to kiss him five times—brow, eyelids, cheeks, soft welcoming mouth. Then he ran after his mother.

He caught her on the very brink. Granny Ragwen had somehow got there before her and was waiting, arms folded. She was old again and so was Ma. She was wearing a fancy-dress witch costume that didn't look like fancy dress at all. "Told you she wouldn't remember," she said to Gideon. "You'd better explain to her, or she'll want to go through anyway. When they get this far— when they see what's waiting—they usually do."

How on earth could Gideon explain? What could he offer, against the infinite spiralling dark-light beyond the gate? "Ma," he said hopelessly, taking her hand. "I don't want you to leave." That was no good—his own childish wants—but he wasn't looking through the gate anymore. All he could see was a plain white wall, and Lee sitting across from him beside a hospital bed. "Tamsyn Elizabeth needs her grandma," he went on more confidently. "It's just not your time yet, and... I don't think anyone but you can convince poor Zeke it's not the end of the world."

The old lady drew a breath, coughed, and opened her eyes. "What isn't, dear?"

"That he's knocked his girlfriend up out of wedlock."

"*Gideon!*"

He twisted round on the hospital chair. There was his brother, wrath-of-God face much altered by the tears running down it. "Well," Gideon protested weakly. "That's the problem, isn't it? Even if you could forgive yourself, you've still got our dad breathing hellfire down your neck. But he's dead, Zeke, and we've still got Ma. Look—she's awake."

Wide awake, pushing upright on her pillows, ignoring the nurses running to her side. "A baby, Ezekiel? Eleanor?"

Zeke thudded down on the chair next to Gideon's. "Yes, Ma."

"And is the child wanted?"

"Yes." He took a deep, rasping breath. "Oh, yes."

"A cousin for Tamsyn, and another beautiful grandchild I'll live to see?"

"Yes, Ma."

"Then, praise be to the Goddess of increase and life!" She lifted a silencing finger. "I'm sorry, my dear, but it *just* doesn't feel like a God, not where these things are concerned. Listen to me, Ezekiel. I grieve deeply that your father's religion has shadowed you. You've followed in his ways as best you can, but those ways must be changed now. Do you understand? You don't have the right to preach one way of life and live another."

"No, Ma."

"And I have to say something else to you. I neglected you greatly after Gideon's birth, my lovely firstborn son. I left you in your father's hands. Can you ever forgive me?"

Chapter Eight

Gideon didn't wait to hear the answer. He knew what it would be, although poor Zeke was unable to get the word out, going down for the third time with his face pressed to Ma's blanket. Lee had slipped out into the corridor. Gideon followed on instinct, closing the door silently behind him.

"Sweetheart. This way."

He was so tired. He needed Lee's pause in the doorway a few rooms down, his smile and beckoning gesture. Earlier today he'd have tracked him down without the signal, but the inside of his head was silent, filled only with relief and desire. He stumbled into the little office—the kind of bland space where doctors took loved ones to break the worst news—and into Lee's arms. "What just happened?"

"I think you popped one of my ribs."

"Oh." Gideon unclenched his grip the bare minimum to allow Lee to breathe. "Sorry. But what did I do?"

"A spirit journey, some people would call it. You brought her home."

"Okay. That's what it feels like. But... *how?*"

"It's something you can do. I realised that when we lost Tamsie, and I could take you into my visions with me, and you could travel with me and see everything I was seeing."

"I don't think I could do it now. I can't even feel our link, just... the outside of you. Your voice and your hands and the way you smell."

Lee caressed him, holding tight. "You've probably burned it out for now. Maybe even long term. Isn't the outside of me enough?"

Oh, yes. Warm and solidly muscled, rich with the knowledge of how Gideon loved to be touched. "Very much so."

"Sorry about the smell. I've been in this shirt all night."

Gideon shivered with laughter. Lee was drawing him powerfully forward into the one corner of the room that couldn't be seen from the porthole in the door. "What are you up to? We can't do this in here."

"Well, I can't wait to do it anywhere else. And I put up the room-in-use sign."

"Oh, you did, did you?" Gideon pushed him back a little to look at him. Everything he wanted was right here. Soon he would start to think about his daughter again, his brother and his mum, his house and his life and what it meant not to be able to read Lee's mind anymore. Just for this moment, he didn't care. He could see all the lights of solstice in the green eyes raised to his. "Is it shut now—the gateway? Is everyone safe on this side?"

"Everyone who should be." Lee clasped his shoulders, caressing. "You can come off duty now. You can stand down."

"I think I need to. How do you do this, Lee? All the voices, all the visions... You must end up feeling as if you belong to the whole world."

"Sometimes. Until you close the doors. Then you make me feel as if I just belong to you."

Gideon smiled. Lee had done the same for him, and hung out a do-not-disturb sign. For the next five minutes—because that was all it would take—they would belong to one another, forsaking all others. And then they would take up their places, shoulder-to-shoulder, in their candle dance with the world, for as long as they both should live.

***

Tamsyn had her party after all. Like many events in her short life so far, it was strange. Eleanor opened the festivities at eight AM, blowing into the side ward where Ma had been sent to recover, buttoned primly up to the chin and in a storming rage. Gideon and Lee stood aside as she buttonholed Zeke: ripped him off a fiery strip for keeping Ma's illness a secret. The words *our baby's grandmother* got bandied about until not only Zeke but most of the ward staff had become accustomed to the idea of the minister's unplanned child. Then she pulled out of her handbag the musical plush ball she and Zeke had bought for Tamsyn, sat down hard on the edge of Ma Frayne's bed and began to cry.

Ma held her hand. The old lady was nicely dressed in day clothes, and other than the stitches in her brow, looked the picture of health. She had to submit to a day's observation and more tests, then she could go home. It turned out she still had a lot to say on the subject of children and how they found their way into the world. Lee and Tamsyn sat in the corner looking on, a pair of worried referees.

Amused by the family drama swirling around the bed, Gideon went to return a phone call from DI Lawrence. He took his first deep breaths of new-year air on the pavement outside the hospital. A few days would have to elapse before the dawns brightened, but the wheel had turned, palpable in the song of the blackbirds across the misty car park. Lawrence took a while picking up, and Gideon set off unconsciously towards the hidden music. "Morning, ma'am," he said eventually. "How's Penzance this morning?"

"Slightly barbecued, but still there—mostly thanks to you, I gather."

"Not at all. I just helped the locals put out a few fires."

"Well, the owner of Jenkins Photography thinks it was a bit more than that. He's in the burns unit at Trelowarren, if you want to go and enjoy his gratitude in person. I heard about your mum, Sergeant. How is she?"

"She's fine." Gideon sidestepped a scuffling and banging of car doors, determined to let Cornwall look after itself for a few minutes at least. "She woke up a few hours ago, right as rain. Nobody's quite sure what happened."

"I'm so pleased she's all right. I'm sorry to disturb you yet again, but this is a follow-up on an issue from last night. You reported having seen a lady from Dark, a Jana Ragwen, in one of the warehouses up on Gwidder Hill?"

"Yes, ma'am." Gideon considered the truth, then decided he'd do better as a copper if he wasn't strapped down in a psych ward next door to Dev Bowe. "She'd got herself up into the rafters somehow. There must have been a way back down, because when I went back to check on her, she was nowhere to be seen. Have you been in touch with her daughter?"

"That's the strange thing. We sent a constable around there this morning to see if the old lady had made her way home. Madge Ragwen not only refused to report her mother missing, she seemed completely unconcerned about her disappearance. Said it was time—and I quote—for the old bird to fly."

We'll soon need a new witch at Dark. A conversation overheard through a baby monitor, unreal and like an echo from years ago now. Still, Gideon suddenly wanted to be back upstairs with his daughter and Lee. "Will there be an investigation?"

"She's elderly and vulnerable, so the Penzance squad will conduct some enquiries around the places she was last seen there. If I know you, you'll do the same at Dark, whether you're on leave or not."

"Yes, ma'am."

Gideon hung up. He could see his mother's side-ward window from here, and there seemed to be a lot of to-ing and fro-ing, more than could be accounted for by Zeke, Lee and Eleanor. Frightened Ma had taken a turn for the worse, he ran back indoors, dodging the smokers and wheelchairs. He made short work of the four flights of stairs: pounded down the corridor, where an odd silence was emanating from the room despite the extra people. He darted inside, braking sharply at the sight of the strange tableau around his mother's bed.

Eleanor was still in pride of place, her mortification turning to pleasure in the fuss the old lady was making of her. Zeke and Lee had been giving Tamsyn her breakfast, to judge from the state of their sweaters, and Tamsyn was sitting in Zeke's arms, clutching her plush ball. So far so good, but the sheepdog with a helium balloon attached to its collar was harder to explain. Isolde gave a grunt of joy at the sight of him and shot across the room, all her manners forgotten. Gideon absorbed the impact as best he could, ruffling her ears and beginning to laugh at the absurd silver balloon with its *One Today!* message emblazoned in bright pink. "Hello, you. What's all this, then?"

Sarah Kemp stood up from the end of Ma's bed. She had one infant by the hand, and Wilfred, the new boyfriend, had charge of the other. Lorna came romping up after the dog. "Gideon! That's what you're *supposed* to say."

"What is, chick?"

"*What's all this, then.*" She dipped her knees, tugged at imaginary braces. "And this. *Evening, all.*"

She was hilarious. He couldn't work out why no-one else was laughing. Sarah's smile was distinctly watery as she gestured the little girl back to her side. "Ignore her, Gid. She's been watching *Carry On* movies."

"How did you sneak the dog in here?"

"We took our chances and ran in when there was a crowd around the reception desk. It was probably stupid, but..."

That was the ruckus Gideon had heard in the car park. "Of course it wasn't. Thank you."

"Well, I went round to yours this morning to get some food for Isolde, and I saw Tamsie's presents piled up, and I wasn't sure if you and Lee would get home today. And it seemed such a shame if she missed her party, so—"

"You brought it here." Gideon nodded at Wilfred, gestured round the cramped little room made festive by well known faces and the parcels set out on Ma's bed. "That's great. Now, we're all probably gonna get kicked out any second, so I suggest we sit down, grab a cup of coffee, and... What's the matter, Ma? Why are you all looking so worried?"

A figure stirred in the corner. She was so nearly concealed by the door that Gideon hadn't spotted her. "It's me," she said miserably. "They're all worried because I'm here."

Gideon grabbed a breath. "Elowen!"

"Yes. Hi. I would never have come near you all, only Ezekiel texted me that Ma was ill, and Michel and I were on our way to see Uncle Jago for Christmas. And you did invite me to Tamsyn's party, so—"

"Zeke texted you?"

"Why shouldn't I?" Zeke interrupted. "It wasn't a family secret, and if you recall, Gid, Ma was the only one of us who really showed Elowen any compassion, after..."

He faded out, as if realising what kind of wolf he might have invited into the fold. Gideon gave him a look which told him he really wasn't on safe ground with the whole family-secrets thing at all, and turned to his mother, who was propping herself up vigorously on her pillows. "You all right, Ma?"

"Yes, dear. Elowen, it's nice to see you. But I have to say, my compassion will be limited this time, depending on the object of your visit."

From Ma, this was practically a punch in the face. Elowen winced, and it was Gideon's turn to feel an unwanted sympathy. He thought about the chalk figure on the sunny hill, and the gate swinging wide, and the star-filled smile, and the necessity for all things to grow up, move on, become what they should. "I think," he said cautiously, "Elowen's only object is to see that Ma's okay. And maybe to wish Tamsyn happy birthday."

"Oh, it is!" Elowen burst out. "That's all, I swear."

"How are you, Elowen?"

"I'm fine. Job's going brilliantly. Michel and I are going to get married next year. Locryn, won't you even *look* at me?"

Lee had taken Tamsyn back from Zeke. He was standing with his head down, his face buried in the baby's curls. His hold on her was gentle as ever, but his knuckles were white. Gideon knew that his patience and good nature were almost without limit, but he'd refused even to speak about Elowen since last August, and Gideon had feared that the bonds between brother and sister had been severed.

Maybe he'd secretly hoped so. Shame swept over him. He broke paralysis, strode over and took his husband by the hand. "Lee, it's all right."

Lee's hand was cold. He swallowed audibly. "Is it?"

"Yes. I promise. I won't let harm come to you or Tamsyn ever again."

Lee straightened up. A smile like solstice dawn touched his face. He kissed Gideon once: silent, fervent, on the cheek. Tamsyn, who'd shrieked the house down for a whole night and a day the last time her mother had come near her, put out her arms and began to crow. Lee turned to Elowen. "Come and have a hold of her. Look how much she's grown!"

***

"I've just had the strangest call from the estate agent." Ezekiel returned to his seat by Ma's bed, putting away his phone. "I thought they'd be closed for Christmas by now, but apparently not."

Ma looked up from her knitting. She was chafing against her confinement, even though the doctors had promised she could leave before sundown. She'd enjoyed Tamsyn's party—all the more once Michel Duroy had come to pick Elowen up, kissed the baby wistfully and left—but Gideon had had to persuade her that her granddaughter would freeze to death without the knitted jacket she'd been working on. "Not bad news, I hope."

"No. Good news and... weird."

Good news and weird was about as good as it got around a Tyack-Frayne family solstice. Gideon exchanged a glance with Lee, who was entertaining Tamsyn with her new plush ball. It chimed softly if you held it the right way, which was a big improvement on the porridge song. "Everything all right, Zeke?"

"Yes. That young couple who've been dithering over the parish house—they've signed their contract and marched into Kern Estates, wanting to exchange as soon as possible."

"Wow." Gideon had almost forgotten about the sale of his old family home in Dark. There'd been offers, drop-outs and all kinds of drama since Ma had decided to sell the place, all of which he'd left his brother to get on with. "That *is* good news."

Ma laid down her knitting, eyes sparkling. "Yes, it is. Now I can split the proceeds between you two boys, and you can get out of that tiny flat, Gideon. It isn't good for Tamsyn Elizabeth not to have a garden."

"Well—this is something we've been meaning to talk to you and Zeke about." Gideon caught Lee's affirmative nod. "Lee and I are all right, you know. We're both working, or we will be once Tamsyn's in nursery. Zeke's the one who's always helped you and Dad out, especially when he got ill, and we thought it would be fairer if you just—"

"Don't be stupid," Zeke interrupted him, blushing purple. "Or irresponsible, for that matter. You have a daughter."

"I know," Lee said absently. "But you'll have two sons by July." He looked up into the astounded silence that followed. "Oh, God. I'm so sorry."

"Honestly, Lee." Gideon could barely keep back laughter. Zeke had scrambled to sit beside Eleanor, who was turning pink and white by turns and staring at her belly as if she expected a whole football team to spring out of it. "They might have wanted a surprise. What was the weird part of the news, Zeke?"

"It concerns you two," Zeke replied, when he recovered the power of speech, "as these things usually do. Kern Estates are handling the sale of the Bowe Farm houses as well. It seems Dev Bowe had a few hours of clarity yesterday, and called his lawyers in. He's developed a conviction that the old Lowen house on Morgan's hill should belong to you and Lee."

"Seriously? Old Jana Ragwen told me that too."

"Do you remember the place?"

"Sure I do. Lee and I were talking about it the other day. We used to go up there to scrump apples."

"No, you used to make me carry you up there so *you* could scrump them. It's very beautiful, as I recall."

"Yes, with a beautiful price tag. It's very kind of Dev, but—"

"That's just the thing. He's lowered the price to—well, Kern Estates reckon it's pretty much what you and Lee could afford by way of mortgage if you had half the proceeds of the parish-house sale. He must have worked it all out."

Gideon took Tamsyn out of Lee's arms. He jounced her on his hip, imagining her and his husband in the sunlight of the Lowen House orchard. "We couldn't," he said slowly, trying and failing to pick up a signal from Lee that this was an impossible dream. "Dev isn't capable of making that kind of decision, is he?"

"He was capable enough yesterday. His lawyers say he won't sell it to anyone else. And given that he blew up your old house and tried to murder Lee and your daughter, I think you should give him the chance."

Ma began to clap her hands in sheer pleasure. Tamsyn caught the infection of joy and applauded too, dropping her ball for Lee to catch. Gideon hadn't really looked at it until now, and for some reason it captured his attention. The patterns on its velvet weren't random. It was a little globe, beautifully made, the continents delicately marked on blue plush oceans and seas. Typical of Zeke and Eleanor, a gift like this. Never too soon to begin a child's education...

Lee's eyes widened in alarm. The ball had leapt out of his hand. This time Gideon hadn't felt the slightest inner warning or tug. But he didn't need to, did he? All he needed was to watch and listen to the person he loved, like anybody else. "Sorry, everyone," he said, collecting Lee and the baby and the ball into a comprehensive embrace. "Nappy time. You'd better get used to this, Zeke, in time for next July. Come on, Lee—help me get the little blighter changed."

Tamsyn contained herself as far as the hospital corridor. Then, in an alcove, protected on both sides by her wondering parents, she lifted the world into the warm space between them, tipped it correctly on its axis, and set it to spin.

About the Author

Harper Fox is the author of many critically acclaimed M/M Romance novels, including Stonewall Book Award-nominated Scrap Metal and Brothers Of The Wild North Sea, Publishers Weekly Best Book 2013. Her novels and novellas are powerfully sensual, with a dynamic of strongly developed characters finding love and a forever future—after an appropriate degree of turmoil. She loves to show the romance implicit in everyday life, and she writes a sharp action scene too.

To find out more about Harper and see updates on her current writing projects, please visit www.harperfox.net.

Coming soon in paperback
by Harper Fox –

Priddy's Tale
Half Moon Chambers
Wolf Hall